Arivaca Out Yonder

A Novel of the Bar-V-Bar Ranch

Jim Clarke

Dedication

For my children and my grandchildren.

And, for all Clarkes—those who are still with us and those yet to come—that you will get a sense of how our family has evolved through the years. Be true to yourselves and cherish the legacy of who we are.

And, I separately dedicate this book to the memory of all Arivacans who were able to share their own personal life journeys with Phil and Gipsy in Ruby, Arivaca, Tucson and beyond.

To Carol

For two years, you stood by and watched me peck away at this keyboard.

When I first mentioned I wanted to do this, you didn't laugh or roll your eyes. You just said, "Go for it."

Six months later, you said, "Keep it going".

After six more months you said, You have to finish it."

And after six more months, you said, "You finished! Good for you!"

Thank you for your unending encouragement and support through the hours, days, and weeks. Without you, this journey would never have finished.

ACKNOWLEDGEMENTS

I gratefully acknowledge the numerous contributions of the many Arivaca "old timers" who through their stories and memories of the past one hundred years or so of the Arivaca district's history and lore, have helped me to develop this story of Phil and Gipsy's search for "out yonder." They have built into my life the love for this story and made the writing of this book possible.

In particular, I am grateful to Mary Noon Kasualitis, my niece, Krista Westmoreland, Al Ring, my cousin Bonnie Marshall, and my cousin Clarke Cooper.

Mary Noon Kasualitis is well known for her many years of contributing and writing wonderful articles about the vast history of this area, mostly for the very popular *Connection* in Arivaca but also the *Green Valley News*, the *Santa Cruz Valley News* and on occasion, various articles for the *Daily Star* and *Tucson Citizen*. She was very generous with her time and energy, helping me with this. I can't thank her enough. Thank you, Mary

Krista, in the midst of her career as an elementary school teacher, spent endless hours gathering and sorting through much of Phil and Gipsy's ancestry. She made it possible for me to develop real time-lines and to tell tales that, for the most part, actually happened. At the outset she helped me work through my grammar, spelling, and other structural issues. Thank you, Krista

Al Ring, through the sharing of much of the work you and brother Bob and Tallia Pfrimmer Cahoon have done over the years with your historical studies of the mines in southern Arizona and the murders at the Ruby Mercantile store enabled me to reconstruct what likely actually happened in Ruby back in 1920–21. I am sincerely thankful you allowed me to read so much of your wonderful work. Thank you all.

My cousins Bonnie Marshall and Clarke Cooper. Thank you for sending me the letters and articles and pictures your mothers collected over the years. I was able to learn a lot from those letters and clippings.

The Arizona Historical Society and the University of Arizona library provided an enormous amount of information I doubt I could have collected from other sources.

And, so many others: my Aunt Patsy; my Aunt Ginny, Clarke's mother; and my Aunt Nancy, Bonnie's mother for so much memorabilia you shared from your collections. Also, cousin Mike, cousin Scott, and Chris's daughter Lisa, Along with the wonderful article "The Rise and Fall of Ruby" that your mother wrote.

And, thanks to JETLAUNCH Publishing, especially Chris and Debbie. You have been tremendously helpful and encouraging, getting this project to the end.

PREFACE

In the late 1800s and early 1900s the history of southern Arizona is filled with many stories, mostly of ordinary men and women who, while searching for a new life filled with possibilities, took a chance when opportunity beckoned and ultimately ended up creating enduring legacies for those of us who followed.

In 1910, Phil Clarke and Gipsy Harper came together solely by happenstance in the isolated little Mexican village of Arivaca in the Territory of Arizona. Gipsy was just twenty-two years old, and Phil would be the same in just two weeks.

So began a lifetime journey for these two extraordinary people. He, having arrived four years previous, from a childhood on the streets of New York, sought a life as a cowboy "out yonder." She, after a childhood in south Texas and pursuing more education, left home and attended North Texas Teachers College. After unsuccessfully searching for a teaching job in southern California, she arrived to become the schoolteacher in Arivaca.

Although the two came from different backgrounds and brought varied personalities and values to their new relationship, they soon fell in love. They got married, started a family, and purchased the mercantile store in the small mining camp at the base of Montana Peak. As a result of bartering with local squatters and other homesteaders, they grew their cattle herd by trading for goods.

This epic story captures the trials and triumphs of life in the early 1900s. They endured raids by bandits and rebels during the Mexican Revolution, two tragic and vicious massacres at their store, the first world war, a banking career in Tucson, the Great Depression, bankruptcy, the restoration of one of the largest cattle operations in the district, and later, the building of the dam that created Arivaca lake.

Their journey lasted fifty-three years and was fashioned by love, hardship, happiness, poverty and prosperity, success and failure, and triumph and resilience.

This book is sure to be a favorite of historical fiction lovers all across America

Charles R. "Butch" Farabee
Author, Historian, National Park Ranger

CHAPTER 1

I had been feeling kind of low for a couple of days. It was the middle of September 1910; the summer was already coming to an end, and I still hadn't found a school to teach at. My friends and I would go to the beaches and the beautiful orange groves and even go to the San Gabriel Mission and stand under their beautiful grapevines, yet all I could think was, *What will be next for me?*

For the past couple of weeks, I had been thinking about going home to my family. I was missing my mama and papa; my sisters Nannie, Bert, and Minnie; and my brother Bruce, my buddy. I remembered the house down on the creek at Yoakam in southern Texas where I was born in Sweet Home and had spent most of my childhood years. I had left south Texas a few years earlier to go to school and then teach.

That day in September, I was sitting in my room, munching on a roll, wondering if I should go back to Texas to teach. The Los Angeles heat was bearing down on Southern California, my room was overwhelmingly hot, and the heat blurred the edges off of the objects around me, and the room began to spin.

The phone rang, bringing me to attention and jarring my senses. I was vigilant as I snatched up the receiver, hoping the call would bring good news about a teaching opportunity.

"Miss Harper," the lady on the other end said.

"Yes, This is Gipsy Harper."

"This is Miss Hopkins at the Sisk Teachers Agency, and you've been talking to me about finding you a teaching job. Unfortunately, we have been unable to find you anything in the Los Angeles area or in southern California, but an opportunity has come to us, and I thought I would tell you about it to see if you might be interested. I have been contacted by Mr. Noah Bernard from southern Arizona, I believe we may have a school for you. He is looking for a teacher to teach in their little town of Arivaca. I don't know much about the school or the area, but would you like to consider it?"

Without any hesitation, I answered, "Oh, yes, ma'am, but how can I learn more about it?"

Miss Hopkins said, "Come right down to the office. Mr. Bernard will come in to meet you, and you can visit with him and ask him any questions you have. I'll have the paperwork ready for you to sign if you decide you will accept it."

The words "I have a school for you" kept ringing in my ears as I hastily pinned on my hat, grabbed my parasol, and checked my hair to see that the rat wasn't loose. I arranged my best hat over the whole mess and ran down the stairs to catch the streetcar to the office. When I settled in the streetcar, I tried to think things over more thoroughly.

I had very little money. I had no idea how much money I would need to get to Arizona. I knew nothing about Arizona except that it was desert and sweltering. I had just spent the last few months enjoying all of southern California and had made numerous friends. I'd rather have stayed here. But before I could imagine what Arizona would be like, the streetcar arrived at the Sisk Teachers Agency.

Inside her cool office, Miss Hopkins explained to me the details of the teaching contract. "The school is on the Mexico border. You will receive fifty-five dollars a month. You might love it and like the superintendent, Mr. Bernard. He's a nice man, wears a cowboy hat, and owns a cattle ranch and a real automobile. If you look out the window, you can see his machine. See, look right there. You can see his machine next to the curb on the road."

"Wait till you see him!" she beamed. "Mr. Bernard drove all the way here in his machine," Miss Hopkins repeated.

"A machine?" I questioned.

"Yes, the automobile, you just saw it. He's going back on the train tonight but has to have a teacher hired before he returns to Arizona, so his driver is driving it back to Arizona."

Mr. Bernard came in and introduced himself. He was a tall man, maybe 6' 4", and pretty heavy, maybe 245 pounds. He had a friendly smile and a twinkle in his eyes. He wore a light gray suit and a red bow tie, and I took him to be good-natured and easy-going. He came over to meet us, his big Stetson in his hand.

Miss Hopkins introduced us and did most of the talking as though she knew everything about the job. "Miss Harper is just the teacher for Arivaca, Mr. Bernard. She is from Texas and has had numerous experiences while teaching in Texas over the past couple of years. Miss. Harper has interacted with Mexicans throughout her life, having been raised in southern Texas. I believe she will be able to do well in southern Arizona, teaching the young children in your town of Arivaca. She has the personality and grit to do well with the cattle people down there along the border."

I interrupted Miss Hopkins, asking Mr. Bernard, "Were there were many teachers interested in this job and were many men teachers inquiring about it?"

"Nope, Arivaca is a long way from the city. Our school is made mostly of young Mexican children. Years ago, we had a man teacher, but he had the jimmies all the time. He had the notion the bandits or renegades were coming across the line for him. Then there was Ol' Lady Myers, who was stone deaf and half-blind too, so we had to let her go. We also had Mrs. Noon for a very long time. She is a perfect teacher, the kids all like her, but last year she told us she wouldn't want to be teaching after this school year ends."

"I would like you to take the job, Miss Harper," he said impatiently. "We need a teacher now. The school has to start next week, and I must get back to Tucson tonight."

"Miss Harper will like it, I'm sure." Miss Hopkins injected; she glanced at me and made some attempt at an awkward smile. "And, I'm sure you will be delighted with her."

Mr. Noah Bernard sat beside me, patiently awaiting my decision. If I took the job, he would meet me at the train station later that night. The next thing I knew, Miss Hopkins handed me the contract and said, "Please sign here."

My thoughts raced as they both stared at me. Miss Hopkins said he was leaving that night, and that the school must begin soon as it was already the middle of September. Miss Hopkins wouldn't like it if I refused the offer, and she would probably not get me another anytime soon. But Arizona? Really? I had left my home in Texas to be on the Pacific Coast! I wanted to cry. Arizona was nothing but desert, I thought, as I remembered the view from the S. P. train I had seen on the route to California last spring.

I didn't have time to hesitate any further. Mr. Bernard handed me a pen, and I signed, "Gipsy Grace Harper."

Mr. Bernard got up, "I'd better be getting along. The place is Arivaca, A-R-I-V-A-C-A. Think you can find it? You get off at Tucson. We'll both take the train to Tucson, but then you're going to be on your own. Do you think you'll be able to manage?"

"Arivaca," I said. "Yes, I'll remember that." He nodded his head, tipping his Stetson to me, and left.

I located my parasol, and I said goodbye to Miss Hopkins. As we parted ways, she said, "Be sure to call on me if you need anything."

"Thank you; I shall."

The wind was strong when I reached the sidewalk. It turned my parasol inside out and broke a rib. I closed it the best I could, smoothing down the yellow ruffles and looking regretfully at the names written on the sides by my friends. *Summer beaux,* I thought, *were not as lasting as the sweet peas.* The boys at the beach in straw sailors' hats and striped bathing suits were already fading memories, and I could not connect all the names with faces.

Honestly, I couldn't say that I'd regret leaving California. True, the sweet peas were fragrant, the geraniums tall, and the waves of the

Pacific hypnotizing, but the intense flowers only reminded me that I was alone. I was growing weary of my lonely life in Los Angeles.

I lost no time getting to the apartment. I packed hurriedly, crowding the last shoe into the grip. The parasol would not fit, and I had to cast it into the wastebasket. The trunk was packed and locked, but I didn't have time to wait for a transfer.

Again, I pinned my hat more firmly to my hair, picked up the grip, and dashed down the stairs to my landlady, Bertha. "Goodbye. I got me a school," I cried, "in Arizona!"

"Don't say!" She kissed me and told me to write.

She was a pretty woman, and she was from Texas too. Her image lingered with me as I ran for the streetcar. She called after me, "I'll see that you get your trunk. I'll express it when you get settled, so send me your address. And don't bother about the gas bill. You used so little."

How did she know that I hadn't used the gas except for coffee for a week?

Gipsy Harper Clarke

On Seventh and Broadway, we got stuck in a traffic jam. It was Labor Day. Though the stores were closed, everyone seemed to be going somewhere. After half an hour, we began to creep along, stopping again and again until I knew I had missed my train and would not see Mr. Bernard. I started to worry. Where was Arivaca? How would I get there? Would I have enough money? Why didn't Mr. Bernard offer to pay for my train ticket?

When I finally reached the station, I ran to the ticket window and asked for a ticket to Arivaca, Arizona. The clerk tried to look it up in a book without any luck. Then, he started questioning other clerks and came back ten minutes later. "The nearest railway station to the town is Tucson. I'll sell you a ticket there if you like."

As he spoke, I remembered Mr. Bernard's instructions, but in all the confusion, I had completely forgotten to ask if he was going to pay my fare. So, I was stuck at the train station with only a few dollars in my purse, not thinking about where I was going, and had completely forgotten about Tucson. He handed me the ticket, and I threw him two bills, which was a good part of my money, but, fortunately, was enough. Then I quickly hurried out to the tracks.

The porters had taken in the little stools. The train was gathering steam and started to move. I screamed for it to wait. A porter reached out a hand and pulled me aboard. "Your change, lady, your change," a man behind me cried, and I saw that the clerk had followed me. We must have been a sight because everyone was laughing.

The porter rescued the change and asked calmly, "Your reservations, please."

"Reservation? I have none. I just purchased a ticket for a seat to Tucson."

"But you must have a reservation. This train doesn't carry a chair car, but I'll see if I can fix you up with a compartment," he said with a wink.

To my regret, he "fixed me up" all right, taking one more of my precious bills and leaving only a few dollars left in the red Peter Pan bill roll I had attached to my belt.

CHAPTER 2

I don't remember much else about that journey except the heat and the sand. The windows were left wide open for air. Soft, warm sand drifted in on my bed, covering me in little ripples and waves until I looked like a figure at the beach. The heat was beyond anything I could describe. I could not sleep or stay awake. I seemed to be suspended in some purgatory between heaven and earth. I aroused once or twice at the sudden stops and looked out the window. It was a moonlit night, and the space was bluish, unreal like a heavenly vapor, not earthly at all, for there were no trees or water. To me, there could be no landscape without trees or water.

I slept again and dreamt I was a child down on the farm in Sweet Home, Texas. Then the squeal of the steam engine grinding to a halt jarred me from my dreams. As we approached the train station on Congress Road, I began to gather my things and shake the dust off. Tucson was a sleepy little town of about 13,000 citizens. The summer days were smoldering in the monsoon heat. In the afternoons, no one was on the streets except Papago indians, walking with baskets on their heads. Other residents lolled under umbrella trees or in basement living rooms. Many others had not returned from their summer homes along the Pacific Coast or in the mountains up north. I had read of Arizona as a land of adventure and lawlessness; instead, I found it one of peace and silence. I wanted to curl up and sleep in the shade, but first, I had to file for my teaching certificate and find out how to get to Arivaca.

Mr. Pryce, Tucson's superintendent, helped me find Arivaca and showed me how to find the stage station. I have no idea what happened to Mr. Bernard. I didn't see him again after he left the Sisk Teachers Agency. So, I was on my own. "The stage leaves tomorrow morning at six," he said, "The town's 'bout seventy-five miles from here, a good day's trip. When you get to the town, ask for Mr. Phil Clarke. He's the clerk of the school board."

"Will I see Mr. Bernard? He was supposed to come with me on the train from Los Angeles, but I think he must have gone ahead of me."

Mr. Pryce said, "Well, Mr. Bernard will be staying in Tucson. I don't think he's going to be going out to his ranch in Arivaca for some time. You don't need him, though. You can see the stage at La Placita. Just walk down Stone Avenue one block and turn right."

I had only one option for lodgings that night: The Orndorff Hotel, just a short walk to Main Street from the train station. Luckily, I found that they had plenty of single rooms. After paying for the room, I climbed the stairs and collapsed, exhausted from the journey and the heat.

The next morning, I started before daylight. Walking along the sidewalk, I caught a whiff of the smoke and other smells seeping out of the Orndorff Hotel Bar. They were what was left from the festivities that went late into the night that I had so soundly slept through. I stopped for breakfast at a café on West Congress Road.

When I reached La Placita, a Mexican driver named Lupe was hitching four horses to the stagecoach. Apparently, he did not speak English because he ignored my questions. Since I was the only passenger, we left as soon as he tied my grip to the back of the coach. I sat in silence as he completed some chores before leaving Tucson. We stopped at the post office for the mailbags and at Steinfeld's grocery on Main Street for produce boxes. Then we headed west between low adobes backed by the golden dawn. Leaving Main Street, we continued south onto the San Xavier Mission road and followed the Santa Cruz River valley, a dry sand bed bordered by cottonwood trees. Beyond the Papago Indian Reservation, little fields of corn and squash bumped into blue mountain ridges stretching across the horizon. The view of a lavender peak in the far distance dominated the scene.

I fastened my eyes on the road ahead, following its curves and bends. A verse I had written in my childhood came to mind, "Life is like a road, going, going, never any end, a halt here and there, then on again as it turns a bend."

The road kept me curious. I watched civilization recede rapidly. Desert shrubs replaced cornfields as the wild space overwhelmed. I began to understand the word desert. The leafless cacti and bare soil looked lonely and deserted. I could not detect any sign of human life, only the sounds of the stage, the rattling wheels, and the clip-clop of hooves. I shifted my focus again to the lavender peak, now partially hidden by heavy bottom clouds, waiting to let loose. How much time had passed for the thunderheads to build already?

The stage changed teams a total of four times. The only one I remember clearly was at noon when we stopped at Angelita Leon's for lunch. Her adobe house was nestled at the base of low, rolling hills. A narrow verandah, covered with Virginia creepers and honeysuckles, ran the length of the house. In front of it, zinnias bloomed. Angelita, a Mexican, cooked both Mexican and American dishes, and she set the table for each nationality. She gave me stewed chicken while she gave the driver, whom she called Lupe, a plate of beans and chili. (I would have preferred the beans.)

After lunch, I slept in dozes, my head bobbing until the stage hit a bump. Sitting up, I'd stare at the purple peak, which never got any closer. Then, I spotted a row of tall cottonwood trees in the late afternoon. Big trees meant water and maybe a town. When the horses perked up and trotted faster, I knew they were heading for their feeding trough. We passed a whitewashed house with geraniums in the windows, the first house I'd seen since we changed horses and had lunch at the Moiza Ranch. A hen squawked as she fled from the horses. A little girl in long black braids, tied with red ribbons, called to the driver. He threw her a bag and, grabbing it, she went running into the geranium house, her bows flying like red birds.

I stretched my cramped legs, smoothed the wrinkles in my skirt, and pushed the hair off my low forehead. The road widened into a street lined with duplicate whitewashed houses. Hitching posts stood outside each doorway. The big trees I mentioned were farther down the valley. I could see their tops above the houses, and the magnificent purple peak loomed behind the trees.

And yes, it did look more significant now, very much a presence. Two rows of houses and the street that passed between them, that was it for Arivaca.

The little girl with the red bows came out of her building, and I heard people cheering with excitement and enthusiasm. Then, looking out the carriage window, I saw groups of Mexican families, maybe, running toward the stagecoach, and I heard one Mexican man calling, "Hay viene. Hay viene. The stage is here."

Lupe slowed the stagecoach to a halt nearing the front of the store. He quickly began unloading the bags and mail from the coach's top. The Mexican man who was cheering our arrival came and opened the door. I stepped out onto the wheel, expecting to see Mr. Clarke, but all the people were Mexicans. So, I asked one man nearby unloading the packages, "Where can I find Mr. Clarke, the clerk of the school board?" The man, I later learned his name was Pepe, only understood enough English to get the name Clarke, and he told me, "Oh, si, señorita, Felipe. He ees coming; he ees coming, señorita. Se llama Philip Clarke, pero los Mexicanos les dicen Felipe."

Just then, a man riding a big white horse came around the corner at the end of the main road. He was riding at a quick gallop because he was late for the stage. He came to a sliding stop before the stage-coach and dismounted, bringing swirling dust clouds around him. As he approached, he had a serious-looking frown on his face; he was probably angry for being late. But when he looked at me, he stopped in his tracks and stared. I, too, remember our eyes locking, and it was as if time had stopped.

Mr. Clarke stared at me, speechless. Finally, Pepe said, "Señor Felipe, this is the new teacher." He just kept staring, and I smiled awkwardly. Then he smiled back and asked, "Are you the new teacher? So, Nonie Bernard hired you in California to come here and teach the kids?"

"Yes, I am the new teacher. My name is Gipsy Harper. And are you Mr. Clarke?"

"You can call me Phil, and yes, I am clerk of the school board. I'm also the justice of the peace, postmaster, storekeeper, and cowboy," he said, smiling to himself, "Well, are you going to get down here, or are you going on up to Old Glory?"

"If this is Arivaca, this is where I belong." Mr. Clarke reached up and grabbed me around the waist, lifted me off the wheel, and set me to the ground. I must have turned three shades of red; I was so embarrassed but still felt an unexpected charge. I had come on my own, all the way from California, Texas, really, with no one to guide me. Mr. Bernard had gone off ahead of me. I had to manage on my own in Tucson. I felt a welcome relief at having someone to help me climb down onto the ground.

"Thank you, Mr. Clarke. Can you please take me to where I am staying so I can get settled in?"

"I can't take care of you right now. I've got to tend to the mail." Mr. Clarke responded. "Then may I just wait here until you're done?"

"That'll be fine, but I thought Noni Bernard would be coming with you. Why the hell don't he take care of you? He knows I have plenty of other things to do. First, I must go through the mail and get it all sorted."

Mr. Clarke seemed to be a little out of sorts at that moment. I didn't know if he was angry with Mr. Bernard for not coming with me, but I hoped he would help me get situated and get me set up in the schoolhouse. With that, he disappeared around the store corner and left me staring wide-eyed at my surroundings.

A crowd of Mexicans had gathered by the store's door and were waiting for their mail across the street. A significant number lingered in front of a building bearing the Cantina de la Doña Josefa sign. Next door, a young woman sat strumming her guitar and singing in a high-pitched voice. She looked attractive in the fading twilight with black hair and thick braids, her high cheekbones showing Indian blood. Everything and everybody on the street looked strange to me—the burros, the old women, and the cowboys.

I followed the locals into the store building. There was no floor, just hard-packed, moist, black dirt. Across the room stood one long counter that was marked, carved, and stained with age. Shelves covered with every conceivable object ran from floor to ceiling. When my eyes grew accustomed to the darkness, I found a stool and sat down. An old Mexican man rested on a coil of rope; another sat on a stack of tin wash tubs. The post office was located at the far end of the room, separated by a wall of pigeonholes holding the mail.

Gradually, people came in for their mail and supplies. First, Mr. Clarke handed a large mailbag to an older man who strapped the bag to his burro and started into the mountain country. A prospector told me that he would carry it to the Sturges Ranch and other ranches over the western mountains. Then, one by one, the people came up to the window. Mr. Clarke spoke to them in Spanish—a joke or a laugh. They stepped aside, pouring over their catalogs and letters. When it was over, Mr. Clarke came out and began weighing the customers' coffee, sugar, and beans. I waited. When it seemed like they were done, they would think of something else. They paid for each object as they purchased it, and they certainly took their time. When the last person was gone, Mr. Clarke turned to me and said, "Now I'll see about finding you a place to stay. People usually stay at the hotel. I'll show you that." Across the way, the girl was still singing. "What is that song?" I asked him. "Cielito Lindo" It means beautiful heaven.

I walked beside him up the street a half block to a deserted house with four doors opening onto the street. He took out a bunch of keys and tried them all. Then, failing, he went to the next door and tested them there. The lock yielded. Inside, we found a cot with a pad but no bedding.

"I'll get some blankets out of the store," he said, "and lend them to you for the night."

The rest of the room consisted of a washstand, a bowl and pitcher, a dusty bedchamber, and a stool. An offensive odor filled the room, "I'd like to stay with my hosts, if I may," I said meekly. "I have never stayed in a hotel alone."

"You don't have any hosts, but the Mexican children will be your students if that's what you mean," he explained.

"Why can't I stay with them?"

Avoiding the question, he listed other places I could stay, essentially carrying on a conversation with himself. As he talked, I lost interest in finding a bed and began to wonder about him. He looked young for a judge; I would have guessed his age to be close to mine, maybe twenty-one years old. He was much younger than I expected the clerk of the school board to be. He was rather handsome. He had coal-black hair and a ruddy face. He was wearing suspenders and a bow tie with his gray flannel shirt, which was interesting to me. I was so busy studying him that I only caught the end of his speech, "Our last teacher, Mrs. Noon, told us she didn't want to teach after last year. Before her, Mrs. Myers stayed in a room that is at the back of the store. I'll show you that."

"Okay," I agreed.

Back at the store, he unlocked the east end door, and we entered a large chamber with a black cook stove in the corner. He continued, "We ate our meals together here. My room is in there, next to the post office."

"Oh, I can't stay here!"

"Why the hell not?"

"It just wouldn't be proper."

"Well, I don't know what you're going to do. It's Nonie's fault. He should have made plans with me for you to have a place to stay. Doña Josefa keeps a boarding house. I'll take you over and ask her."

We crossed the street to the saloon. Several Mexicans squatted on the ground, standing or leaning against hitching posts. Three were playing musical instruments and singing "La Paloma." Mr. Clarke spoke to a man and went in to get Josefa. When the old lady appeared, Mr. Clarke introduced us in Spanish. They talked at length; he argued against her shrugs and protests until she gave in.

"She'll keep you tonight," he said, "Marta will show you your room. Then, I'm riding up to the ranch for supper. I'll help you get situated tomorrow."

"I'm sorry to have bothered you. Thank you."

He continued, "You haven't bothered me. I'm just upset that Nonie didn't make plans for you." He lifted his hat, smiling, but not at me. "How are you, Felipe?" a woman cried.

"Marta, this is the new schoolteacher," he gestured back at me on his way out the door. "Her name is Gipsy."

Marta, with her guitar, was tall and straight like some Indians, her mouth firm, her skin fair. She wore her hair in a regal roll around her head. I follow her to a room, hoping this third place will be suitable.

"Tonight, we dance," she announced as she led me into a charming room. "This is Independence Day; we have the dance on the sixteenth."

"At home, my family was Baptist, and I've never been allowed to dance. But I'd like to see a dance, especially a Mexican dance."

"All my patrons will be there. There'll be cowboys, Mexican and American alike. Perhaps, Mr. Clarke will return after his supper."

Marta had much to do and excused herself. I took off my hat and waist, washed in the bowl, and put on a dressing gown. I was combing my hair when Marta returned. She set the table for my supper, and another girl brought a coffee pot.

"This is my sister, Lucia, and she is engaged to Felipe." Marta said curtly. Lucia was also tall but very dark and had large, languid eyes.

I found this new detail about Mr. Clarke interesting, but I didn't have time to question the ladies before they quickly left me alone with my dinner. I sat down to test the dishes. I recognized a cake of dry-blood cheese I had once eaten as a child. This one was seasoned with chili instead of garlic. I devoured everything—the dried meat, a bowl of chili, and a plate of tamales. When I finished, Doña Josefa came in with a bottle of wine. Pouring me a glass, she insisted I drink it all and stayed to confirm that I did. The girls came to clear my tray, suppressing giggles as they softly latch the door. Feeling lightheaded, I took my hair down, laying my pompadour beside the window.

Outside, it was already dark, so I decided to rest awhile before the dance began, but first, I peeked into the hall separated from my room by only a curtain in the doorway. A dim hanging lamp barely illuminated the lonely corners. Disillusioned by the mediocrity of the room and the town, I returned to my bed and fell asleep at once.

CHAPTER 3

The next thing I know, Marta is placing a tray of coffee, steaming milk, and sugar beside my bed. A rectangle of sunlight shines through the window. I sit up and look through the now open curtain into the dance hall, where an unusual stillness now hangs over the room.

"Buenos dias," Marta broke the silence. "Did you have a good sleep?"

"What happened? Why didn't you have the dance?"

She laughed. "We danced until four. You never heard the music?"

"But how could you without me hearing? I don't understand."

"You tired, no? Very tired."

Had I been drugged, or was it just the wine and the fatigue that made me sleep so soundly? How could I have failed to hear the noise through the courtyard? I hadn't even undressed. Touching my hair, I noticed the pomp was gone and not on the table. I saw a young American cowboy riding horseback with my pomp around his head through the window. He rode past three times. Then, seeing me, he ducked around the house. Soon after, another boy threw the pomp into the room. Reaching my head out the window to yell, and I saw a row of American cowboys sitting in front of my door, each identical to the next.

Suddenly, the dance didn't matter. I had to get the key to the schoolhouse, see Mr. Clarke about a place to board, and take a walk around the countryside. I drank the strong coffee, took a sponge bath, and dressed in fresh clothing. The curl had returned to my hair, and it set well over the pomp that had, fortunately, not been damaged. I brushed my hair and pinned it on carefully, looking at it from all sides in my hand mirror. I put on my gloves and hesitated a moment before opening the door. The town was quiet. No one stayed in town after the dance except the cowboys. When I entered the store, a boy was restocking the shelves. "May I see, Mr. Clarke?" I ask him.

"Felipe is busy," he says, glancing toward the post office.

The boy soon forgot about me and continued his morning routine. He brought in a sack of beans and poured them into a bin, filled another container with potatoes, and then another with green coffee. Next, he picked rotten onions from a box and threw them into a garbage can. Then he begins to sweep, first sprinkling the dirt floor with water.

"Will you please tell Mr. Clarke I'd like to see him?"

"He knows." He shrugged without looking up.

A tall thin man entered the store. He strolled as though in pain, hesitating with each step. He had a red mustache, red hair, a red face, and blood-streaked blue eyes. "Well, what do you know," he said loudly. "So, you're the new school marm from down yonder in Texas."

"Yes, sir. How did you know I was from Texas?"

"How do I know anything after talking to that Irishman half the night and morning? What do you think of him? Pretty rough, eh? Listen, if he gets too rough with you, just tell your Uncle Beanie. Hey, anybody around this joint? Felipe, where the hell are you? Where're you keeping yourself?" He went into the office.

"I've got work to do," I hear Mr. Clarke from inside.

"Ramon is coming to take her to Doña Anita's. He said he'd be here at nine, but that don't mean anything."

When "Uncle Beanie" came back out, I ventured, "I'd like to get the key to the schoolhouse from Mr. Clarke as soon as possible; I have quite a bit of work to do."

"Mr. Clarke? Who the hell's that? You call that rascal, mister?" he responded with a chuckle.

Through the office window, I heard, "I'll take you to the school-house after work tonight, or you can go tomorrow."

"I'd like to go over today and see what it needs."

"It doesn't need anything. It's still there, all of it that was there before," he said as he continued going through papers, arranging, and rearranging.

"Where can I get the key?"

"I'll get it for you when I show you the school."

Uncle Beanie laughs heartily, his mustache twitching. "You'd think he don't want you to see the school unless he shows it to you himself. You'd never know I've had to straighten that rascal out since he arrived here a few years ago. You think you're going to like it out here, Tex?"

"Yes, sir, I think I will. I only hope that Mr. Clarke will be a little nicer than he's been so far."

"Listen here dear, you call me Uncle Beanie. And don't worry nothing about Philip, I can tell he has a liking to you. You just be patient. He's just strutting around like an ol' rooster, trying to show you just how important he is around here." Uncle Beanie continued.

"Well, look, here comes the king cowboy of this here cow country himself."

A man entered wearing a leather jacket, jeweled spurs, and leather chaps heavily decorated with silver. His eyes were bright and merry, his skin clear brown. He had no mustache like most Mexican cow-boys, but he was very polite and shook hands with me. Beanie told him I was Gipsy Harper, the new schoolteacher. "This is Ramon Ahumada. He is the foreman and head wrangler for the Arivaca Land and Cattle Company. He is the main boss around here, except when that young Irishman is strutting his stuff."

Ramon said a few words, but I couldn't understand what he said because he was talking to Beanie, and it was all in Spanish. "Ramon has been teaching Felipe all he knows about the cattle business for the past couple of years. Ramon is going to take you to Doña Anita's and make arrangements for her to take care of you while you're getting to know people here."

"Thank you so much, Mr. Beanie."

"Uncle Beanie, dear."

"Thank you, Uncle Beanie."

The cowboys were standing beside their horses when Ramon and I went out. They called out to Ramon, and one said something in Spanish that made Ramon and the other cowboys laugh. We walked down the road, crossed an arroyo, and followed the bank up the creek. We passed orchards heavy with ripening grapes, apples, pears, and even quinces. Finally, we hiked up a hill to an adobe house with two front doors. One door had the word "Cantina" painted on the wall in black. A small garden of verbenas grew around the other.

Ramon opened the garden gate and knocked. A girl of about sixteen opened the door. When he introduced her as Nita, she answered in English. She was a beautiful girl, exceedingly white, with drooping black eyes and crow black hair braided around her head. She wore a dressing sacque of flowered mull, a black skirt, and black shoes. We waited in la Sala while she asked her grandmother about boarding me.

La sala, the living room, welcomed us. The clean white walls complemented the red rug. A phonograph stood on one table, a lamp on another table beside the divan. On the wall, a niche displayed a crucifix and candles; a Madonna print hung opposite. Doña Anita was not so hospitable. She argued with Ramon until he excused himself and took her through the curtained doorway. After a long time, he returned, smiling, and said that Doña Anita had agreed to keep me for twenty-five dollars a month. He spoke to me at length, and Nita interpreted for him. "He says he hopes you will like Arivaca. He will send his wife, Virginia, to see you, and he will send you a horse and saddle."

"How nice. Thank you so much. Thank you for everything." I held out my hand.

When Ramon had gone, Nita and I began to get acquainted. And after a while, I decided to ask if Mr. Clarke was engaged. "Nita," I asked, "Earlier, Marta told me that your sister Lucia was going to marry Mr. Clarke. Is this correct?"

"Yes, he is engaged to Lucia, the widow who sings. You heard her? No?"

"Yes, I remember her. She brought me my supper."

I decided no more discussion about Mr. Clarke's relationships. It wasn't any of my business. So, we talked about the dance. "Did you go to the dance?" she asked me.

"No," I said, "I wanted to go, but I fell asleep and missed it. Wasn't that silly of me? Did you go?"

"No, I never go to them. My grandmother will not allow it."

I decided to change the conversation. So, I asked, "Where does Mr. Bernard live?"

Nita explained that he stayed at a little house up at the corrals near headquarters when he came out from Tucson. And the Murrays lived in the main house. She continued to tell me more about Mr. Bernard. She said his first name was Noah, but everybody called him Nonie. He was engaged to a girl in Tucson, and he was rich.

It was his father who started the Arivaca Ranch, Mr. Bernard, Sr. He was a freighter in the seventies and brought goods from Missouri to Tucson. Mi abuelita told me his route crossed the creek here, and he would stop at her house. Later, he started the Arivaca store and got a branding iron. He took in partners, leaving young Noah as manager when he died. There were other children, but all them moved. I was not the most attentive listener; my thoughts wandered rather than trying to follow her thick accented story about the Bernard's.

Changing the subject a second time, I asked, perhaps a bit abruptly, "Are there any American women here?"

"American women? There are not many white women in the area. Many of the women in the area are married to men who own the ranches and are in the cattle business. But one, in particular, you must meet is Mrs. Bailey. You will see; she is charming. She is—how you say—a woman with a past. She left her husband for Hank, who she stole from Marta. That was all right because Marta had too many. Marta thinks she's the queen of Arivaca. What do you think of Marta? Did you see her?"

I thought that was interesting, but I answered, "Yes, I remember her."

Last night I was too tired to think about her, but now that I had the question put to me, I knew there was something significant about Marta. She wasn't what I would call a girl; she was probably in her late twenties or older. But she could imitate the grace of a princess.

"Yes," I told Nita, "She's wonderful."

"Well, she did not get Hank," Nita said.

An old woman looked in and spoke to Nita in Spanish. "Pancha wants to know if you have any washing,"

Nita explained, "Pancha washes for everyone."

I thought I would probably hear the rest of that story at a later time, so I just answered "No, thank you. I will wash my own clothes."

Pancha sat down on the threshold, rolled a tobacco cigarette, and lit it while she looked me over. Her nose had been cut away, leaving her face disfigured. Then, glaring at me, she whispered and laughed with Nita. As she got up to go, she gave an unpleasant grunt and looked at me again over her shoulder.

Nita giggled again. "Please tell me what she said," I asked.

"You won't get mad?"

"No, I won't get mad."

"All right, then," she said, "She doesn't like you because you won't talk to her."

"But, Nita, I can't talk to her because I don't speak Spanish. Will you explain that to her? And tell her I am going to learn as soon as

I can. Maybe you will help me learn, or do you know someone who will?"

Nita says, "Maybe Felipe will teach you. You see, he knows the language very well."

"Well," I said, "We'll have to see. If he is engaged to be married to Lucia, he might not want to help me."

Nita responded, "Then I will try to help you. All the gringo boys around here speak Spanish. When Felipe came here, he spoke very well in three months. Lucia taught him, and he taught her all the gringo songs that he likes to sing and dance."

"Mr. Clarke knows songs?"

"Sure, he learned all the old songs when he lived in New York. Felipe loves to sing and dance to all those songs from his old country, where he comes from. I think it is called Ireland."

CHAPTER 4

Through the course of our friendship, Nita taught me the basics of her language, but while I was learning, she was gossiping. Nita told me about the people in the village and around the area. For example, Old Willie, the drunk, commonly known as "Jesus" by the Americans because of his long shirt that hung to his knees as he wavered about on liquor legs. He earned just enough to buy tequila Saturday nights. When his money was gone, Doña Anita called her helper, Viejo, to drag him out and fasten the bar across the door.

Louisa, the cook, was another old soak who sat in her corner by the earthen stove, smoking her pipe while the beans and coffee simmered. Right before mealtime, she would make up the tortilla dough, patting the tortillas and cooking them fresh. She got her liquor from Viejo, who would smuggle it out to her despite Doña Anita's threat to fire them both.

Then there was Doña Anita herself, a Yaqui Indian, small, shrewd, and stooping. Her bright eyes never overlooked anything that went on around her. She managed simply by keeping silent and negative. She must have been nearly eighty. She had raised Nita, yet I could see no resemblance between the two. She started to tell me about others, but she stopped, then said, "They're coming here."

"Who?" I said.

"Wait," she responded.

She waited awhile after the knock before opening the door. She said they were from the older man's ranch when they came in. They were dressed as cowboys in leather chaps, boots, and spurs. One named Jack was the fair one. He had light gray eyes and a medium build. About twenty-one, I guessed. Then there was Ples. He was the youngest, probably eighteen. He had sharp blue eyes, brown hair, and a rough voice.

Then Nita introduced Johnnie Barnes, probably the oldest of the three, and evidently, the owner was taller than the other two, and quiet. When he spoke, his words and syllables were more exact and correct, as though English was not his native tongue. He lit a cigarette and listened while the others talked. Jack and Ples seated themselves on the divan with Nita. Barnes and I had the chairs near the phonograph.

Doña Anita entered with a round of beer, which Nita and I declined. The boys talked about college and asked about my school experiences, so I explained that I got my annual from the North Texas Teachers College, where I went to school after leaving my home in south Texas.

Jack and Ples perched on the arms of my chair as I turned the pages. "Listen to this," Ples exclaimed, as we came to my photograph, and he read the caption beneath: "To doubt her fairness was to want an eye; to doubt her pureness was to want a heart."

They laughed at the sentiment and my hairdo in the picture. After a while, it became evident that they had enough talk about my school and changed the subject.

"How about a ride this afternoon?" Jack asked.

"I'm sorry, but I have business with Mr. Clarke."

"Mr. Clarke! How does he rank that?" Ples mused.

"Well, he's the clerk of the school and on the school board. And he's the justice of the peace and the postmaster. But, most importantly, he's my boss. So, what should I call him? Judge? Or Mr. Postmaster? Or Superintendent? Or what?" I thought they'd never stop laughing, even Nita.

"What about coming to our ranch tomorrow, you and Nita?" Jack asked. "I'll send over a horse."

"Thank you, that would be nice, but you don't need to get us a horse because Mr. Ramon is getting me a horse and saddle."

"Mister?" They laughed again.

"Then that's settled. We'll be expecting you. I can't promise you much entertainment. The ranch is dull right now. But we can show you around and see a little more of the country. We haven't any company, but you'll meet the new members of the family, Matthew, Mark, Luke, and John, Mary's pups. The cutest pups you've ever seen. We drowned Martha and Mary Magdalene—couldn't afford to keep them. Maybe they'll grow and get us some little bastards."

I blushed, and Nita got up and left the room on some pretense, returning when the conversation turned to safer subjects: the fall roundup and Nonie's engagement.

As the morning advanced, the room grew hot despite its deep dirt walls. Nita handed us each a palmetto fan, and we fanned the flies. "Let's go out and kid old Jesus," someone suggested. And they spent the rest of the afternoon and evening walking around the village and down by the creek before ending up at Doña Anita's cantina.

"I like Jack," I told Nita after they have gone to the bar. "Ples is likable too, despite his profanity, which seems rather childish. I guess all boys that age want to show off."

"And Mr. Barnes, What do you think of him?" Nita questioned.

"Oh nothing," I responded. "But he is very rich."

"You said that about Mr. Bernard."

"And you, Nita, which one have you picked for yourself?"

Her eyelids dropped. "I do not pick anybody anymore." She was sad as she said, "I had a young man. His name was Danny, but he is dead."

"Oh, forgive me. I'm so sorry," I said.

"He was a best friend of Felipe's. He came from New York just before Felipe came here. He and Felipe came from New York to work on a ranch south of here. But Felipe stayed in Texas for a while to look for his brother, Willie.

"After Danny was here for a short time, we fell in love and were to be married, but one day, he was putting medicine on a calf out at the ranch and got bit by a rattlesnake. He got very sick, and he was in much pain. The doctor came from Amado but could not help him. After a couple of days, he died. The whole village was somber for many days. We had a big celebration for his good life with all of his friends here. After lunch, I will take you to his grave at the cemetery." Nita shared.

After lunch, she took me to Danny's grave, as planned. Like the rest of Arivaca, the cemetery blended into the natural environment. Primitive tombstones lay scattered among the rocks and shrubs, and mesquite crosses dated one hundred years back to 1810 and older. Numerous ornaments decorated the graves: dolls, images of saints, broken glass, and paper flowers. Occasional paths crisscrossed, leading to the famous graves. Other graves disappeared into the woods.

I followed Nita up a well-worn path to the tallest shrine. Bright white against the cloudless sky, Danny's monument looked like a miniature Spanish mission. I stood aside while she placed her flowers in the vases and lit a candle. Nita knelt in prayer. I left her alone and wandered toward a nearby abandoned building. This made me wonder if some of Mr. Clarke's behavior was a reflection of sadness over the loss of his best friend. Perhaps one day, he would share his feelings with me.

As I got closer, I realized it was my schoolhouse. My excitement diminished as I circled the dilapidated building. Crumbling plaster hung only around the windows and doors, leaving the mud walls bare. The windowpanes were either broken or filmed with dust. The grounds were overgrown with thick dry weeds.

When Nita started home, I walked a ways with her. I thanked her for sharing her story with me and told her again how sorry I was for her. I have to see Mr. Clarke and arrange about getting the school in order. He promised to open the building for me this afternoon. I'll see you at suppertime. Busy with the Saturday afternoon customers, Mr. Clarke simply nodded toward me and mumbled, "Good evening."

I settled on a cowhide chair and watched as one woman did her weekly shopping. First, she related all the gossip to Mr. Clarke. Then, taking a can of beans off the shelf and turning it over, she carefully read the label and checked the price. Then, paying, she moved on to the next item. Once finished with her list, she tied up her gunny sack and started for the door. "But wait, I forgot my dulces."

By this time, my patience waned.

"I should check my mail." Mr. Clarke shuffled through stacks of letters and catalogs. I thought it would never end.

Finally, I stepped up to the counter and said, "I think I'm next, but before you take me to the schoolhouse, I'd like a pair of shoes, please."

"You wouldn't want the kind we carry."

"Why is that? May I see them anyway?" He motioned me to a stool. I sat down and held out my foot.

"What is this?" he asked, "You unbutton your own shoe. I ain't no shoe salesperson. You try your own. But they won't fit, you watch. Mexican women have little feet, so I ain't got a pair that's over three."

He took down many boxes and placed them on the counter. I made him take down every shoe he had. When we found some that halfway fit, I had him fasten them clear up to the sixteenth button, and he did. "I'll take these."

"Where ya' think you'll wear them? These are for our Mexican trade."

"I'd like these, please," I repeated and took out some bills. "Why don't you charge them and pay when you get your voucher?"

"I'd like to pay now, thank you."

The other customers, tired of waiting, had gone over to the saloon. It was closing time, and Mr. Clarke wrapped the shoebox and told me I might as well leave it until we came back from the school. He locked up, and we went out back. Behind the store, I noticed the church adobe with a silver cross on its gable.

"Were butchering a steer tonight down at the butchering scaffold. I'm going to take you down there cause I betcha you never saw a butchering before."

"My goodness, why should I even want to see a butchering?"

"It's interesting. You'll get to see what people do with all the parts of a beef. Most city folks just think there's a steak and nothing much else. All the other girls and women go because they want to get the best parts. The first one there gets the head, and the next one the heart and liver."

"What do they do with the heads?"

"They put the meat in the tamales, and then there are the brains, see? How did you like the blood cheese last night?" He laughed for the first time.

"Who told you about my supper?"

"I heard. Betcha didn't know what the blood was. Josefa comes to the butchering and catches it in a bucket. She has a contract for the full supply."

"Really?" To change the subject, I said, "Mr. Clarke, have you notified the children that school is opening Monday?"

"When they see the school door open, they'll know. Besides, they already know just from you being around."

He unlocked the door and pushed it open. The school was depressingly empty. About fifteen ink-stained desks were crammed into a corner. A rusty stove sat forlornly beside the teacher's table. Even the blackboard erasers—if there had ever been any—had been carried away. How could I teach without maps, charts, or even a globe?

"Where is the equipment?"

"How do you mean by equipment?"

"I mean desks and blackboards and charts and maps and a globe. Not to mention books and pencils and crayons. Doesn't the territory furnish books, paper, pencils, and all that for a teacher to use?"

"What are you talking about? It pays the teacher. Ain't that enough?"

"Are you telling me that there won't even be books for the children to read? Can the children buy books for themselves?"

"Of course, they ain't buyin' books."

"Perhaps if you order books and put them in the store, some of the more ambitious parents would pay for them."

"Look here, I've got that whole cattle company and every person for twenty miles around telling me what to order for that store; I'm not going to have you telling me to start a bookstore. You know what I had to order last week? Fresh mushrooms and asparagus!"

"Who on earth for?"

"For Mrs. Bailey. And you know how much her husband gets a month?"

"I'm sure I really don't care. And, if you're expecting me to teach these kids anything at all, you and your school board better be getting me some supplies in here as soon as possible. And, Mr. Clarke, if you don't get somebody hired to come in here and wash these windows and get this place cleaned up, I'm going to have to do it myself before I'm going to be able to teach."

"Why do you have to do it? The kids will do it Monday. You just make them do it. I'll send the constable after them if they don't mind you." He looked at his watch. "Guess I'll see how the butchering is coming."

"If you don't mind, I'll go back with you to get my shoes. I'd like to buy some paper and pencils for the school, too, so I can get started."

"All right, but I want to show you some pictures I have first if you want to see them. One is a picture of my gold mine I have down south of here near the border. The pictures came out swell. I'll show you some more another time. Right now, we have to get going."

We walked fast to beat the sunset, "We'll go through the back to get your shoes because if I open the front door, I'll have to let them miners in. Then I'll never get away." He took me through two walled enclosures, a patio, and a stable yard. "Come on over and look at the horse I had Ramon bring over for you."

We stood looking over two horses. He explained, "A sorrel that had been captured from Geronimo, and a dark bay that he had ordered for me. Ramon wanted to send you a fast horse, but I had him bring this one. I've had greenhorns on my hands before, and the Company won't take any chances with these crazy tenderfeet who can't sit on a horse. Do you want to try him out? We call him Flojo, which means lazy."

"No, thank you. I'll wait till he's saddled. But I'm going to have to learn to ride first. Can Ramon send somebody over to help me?"

"What," he said, "You don't ride? Well, now, I reckon I better be the one to teach you because I want to be sure you learn to ride the correct way. Ramon's cowboys will just try to show you how to chase cows. Okay, that's settled. We'll start in a day or so."

He turned toward the office door. On the way, we passed a homemade punching bag. He stopped to show me his skill, punching until his face was purple.

"You wouldn't know it," he said, "but I belonged to the New York Athletic Club when I was a kid. I won a medal in an amateur contest and became the peewee champion."

Since prizefighting was classified along with gambling, horse racing, and card playing in my home, I did not congratulate him. So far, he had failed to impress me much. Although, he was obviously trying.

"I'm really in a hurry. Can we just please get my shoes?"

With one last stroke, he made the bag spin. Then he opened the rear door and took me through his bedroom. He tried to hurry me across the room into the post office, but I couldn't help but look around. His walls were plastered with girls cut out of magazines and calendars. "Do you like the Gibson Girls?" he asked.

"I'm not much interested in them," I said.

In the office, he took down a stack of snapshots. "These are some photos I took in New York the last time I was there."

Gipsy responded, "I haven't time to look at them. I'm sorry. Maybe you can bring them over tomorrow night when we have more time? While we're here, will you get me some chalk and some paper and pencils so I can teach something tomorrow? You do have that sort of stuff here, don't you?"

"I'll look, and I'll send them over Monday. There's something I wanted to ask you. How'd you like to go for a ride with me tomorrow after school? We can ride up to see the Barnes ranch."

"Well, I'm already going with Nita."

"But you two can't go alone. It isn't safe. You need somebody to go with you just in case."

"Just in case what?" I asked.

"Well," he said, "There are always some scoundrels out there on the road between here and there. It's just better to be safe, so I'll take you out there."

The boys and Nita didn't say anything about scoundrels and the like. I think he just wanted to ride along.

He continued, "Nita is a wild rider and not very good, so she'll get you thrown, which will be another worry for me. You're a big responsibility as it is, you know?"

"No, I don't know that," I responded.

"I'll be over at eight in the morning, but I think I will bring one of the buggies instead of using the horses. Besides, Flojo is too slow and lazy. It will be easier and give us a better chance to visit and get to know more about each other. We'll have to go slow because the road is rough and rutted in many places."

"Thank you very much. Now, I really need to go. I'm not going to go to the butchering with you. I sure hope you haven't missed the killing."

"The what?"

"The butchering."

"They'll be waiting for me, see? They don't do the butchering without me being there. Okay, I'll be over at eight in the morning to get you, and we'll make our way to the Barnes ranch."

He let me out the front door just as it was growing dark. I retraced my steps back to Doña Anita's, crossing the arroyo to her house on the hill. Below, many of the residents of the town were at the butchering, but many sat outside their doors, enjoying the evening air.

"Hello," I called from the parlor. Nita appeared with a cold supper of apple pie and cheese. "Mr. Clarke is going with us to the Barnes ranch tomorrow, and we are going to take one of the buggies from the ranch instead of riding horses."

"Well, then, I will not go with you. You go on alone with him."

"But, Nita, I want you to go too. I don't think it's a good idea for me to go on a buggy ride alone with Mr. Clarke."

"It is okay, Gipsy. Felipe goes for rides many times with the señoritas in the district. Do not worry. It makes him think he is protecting you."

"Okay." I said, "Another time, you and I will go on a ride together."

"Si," she responded.

So, I left her. I went to bed early but couldn't sleep. I thought about the school and mostly the ride I was to have. I awoke early the following day to the sounds of chickens clucking, a rooster crowing, and a dog barking in the distance. I dreamed I was a girl on the farm again, but as I drifted out of the dreams, my real life came back to me.

The late September air carried a subtle chill that hinted at the coming change of seasons. The impending first day of school loomed in my mind and threatened to ruin my fresh new day with worries. I did my best to shrug off the uncertainty I felt about classroom discipline, new students who didn't speak English, and limited teaching materials, and I focused instead on Sunday.

CHAPTER 5

*T**oday is a day for new beginnings*, I told myself as I searched for something appropriate to wear on a horse ride. Nita loaned me a divided khaki skirt. It was short for me, striking above my ankles, but my new high-buttoned shoes protected my legs.

Mr. Clarke took some time getting the buggy ready for our trip. He said he had told Ramon not to bring the horses because Flojo is too lazy but to bring a buggy because he wanted us to have time to visit.

When I got up in the buggy, one of the straps that fastened to my skirt beneath the shoe broke. Mr. Clarke had trouble fixing that and making the lightweight khaki hang straight. I hated to think about my skirt flying up in the wind.

We crossed over the creek where the cottonwoods grew and followed the wagon road, sitting side by side. The still morning hung awkwardly between us. We had not spoken many words between us, mostly just casual exchanges. I wondered if now would be a good time to ask questions of this young man sitting next to me. So, I ventured a question and hoped he'd start talking about his early years.

"You were going to show me your snapshots of New York last night. Is that because you're from New York?"

"Well, yes, in a way," he said. I thought maybe he was going to tell me about himself. And at that, he started.

"I left there four years ago in 1906 and came here when I was seventeen."

So that makes him twenty, I thought, *yet he seems much older.* Trying to keep the conversation going, I offered, "Someday, I'm going to live in New York and be an artist. I'm dying to know all about Greenwich Village, the art schools, the publishing houses, and all about all the tall buildings. Please tell me about your life in New York, and what all the tall buildings are like."

"What do you want to know about them? They're just ordinary old buildings. They're very tall and the ugliest in the world. The only way you can see the sky is to look straight up. And you wouldn't want to see the art; it's not very nice. Us boys used to go to the art museum to see the nudes, the statues, see?"

"That's not nice."

"If I was you, I wouldn't want to go to any of them."

"Oh my goodness. I'm sorry! Please excuse me for asking, but I love art and hope to paint someday. And I love to read and sing. Will you tell me about other things? There must be other things and places where friendly people go. Were you born in New York? Did you live all of your years there in the city? Do children live the way writers say they live—on the street, fighting with gangs of bad kids? And are those bad kids called slang names? Mr. Clarke, please tell me your story."

"Well, Gipsy, you sure are asking a lot of questions. I'll try to tell you a little. I wasn't born in New York. I was born in Dublin, Ireland, in 1888. But Pap didn't like what was going on in our home country, and with that trouble, he didn't want to raise us kids there."

I said, "Irish people always say that Ireland is just like heaven. So, why do they leave it and come over here where everything is big cities, deserts, and mountains?"

"What does it matter? Why worry about it?"

"Because I've always wanted to know. Why do people want to come here when your homeland is so beautiful and seems to be so ideal? Didn't you ever think or wonder about that? Was it for money or adventure or was your father just a wanderer and never satisfied in one place? My father's folks were like that. They lived in the covered wagon. Neighbors called their wagon the gipsy wagon. That's how I got my name. 'Another gipsy' they said when I was born, and the name stuck."

"My father wasn't like that," he said angrily. "He came when thousands of other Irish were coming to escape English oppression. On the island, he belonged to a club called Seekers of Freedom. They had meetings and tried to find a way to save themselves from the English. Some favored migration. Uncle Paddy Collins had come to America a few years before. He wrote that over here in the United States, the government let folks alone and let them work at their jobs. Finally, a fellow had a chance to get ahead. He had a livery stable, and he asked Pap to come over and help him. Pap thought about that for a long time, but he wouldn't bring us until he knew for himself, knew if it was going to be safe for us."

"I see. Then he came for freedom from the English government. In the early years, my folks did that, too. Some of them were run out of Scotland during the religious wars because they wouldn't conform, and they went to Holland. Later, they came to America, but that was nearly three hundred years ago. Why did you leave New York and come to Arizona?"

He said, "I wasn't happy in New York. When I was growing up, I didn't like it. I never liked it. It's an awful place to grow up, and I never had a chance."

As we rode, he told me about his childhood. His story sounded familiar, like the new style of literature. Realism, they were beginning to call it.

As soon as I was old enough, I got a job driving the bank wagon for McCreery. I felt like a gentleman in my derby and black suit. I made sixty dollars a month on that job, but all I bought was some good clothes. The rest went to savings, some pool playing, and to help out at home."

Phil working as a wagon driver in New York City

He started to tell me about his days in the pool halls, but I think he thought maybe he shouldn't be telling me about those times. So, after a lengthy pause, seeming to be in some sort of deep thought, he spoke up and said we needed to get on to the ranch.

He switched the horse's rump, and we continued to the ranch. He remained pretty silent for the next thirty minutes, and I wanted to ask him about Danny. Interrupting my thoughts, he said, "We're just about to the ranch. I'll tell you more when we leave."

Though the ranch belonged to Barnes, it occurred to us that it was really Jack's. They bought the homestead from Morales, and when they did, they got a permit from the government to run steers in the forest along the Mexican border. That area had been declared a national forest three or four years before he came out here. It surprised me to hear it was called a forest because there was little timber to speak of.

As we rode along, he began to talk about the number of cattle that could be run over these mountains on these forest grazing permits.

He said, "I wouldn't be surprised if Barnes and the boys aren't running 2,000 to 3,000 head of steers between their permit and across the border and back, and they're running all over the mountains overgrazing these pastures, eroding the soul everywhere they go.

"Where are they?" I asked. "I don't see any."

He continued, "That's because they're scattered all over this open range country, all the way from Tres Bellotas to the San Luis Valley and on over to the Patagonia area. Everybody knows there will be some government intervention pretty soon to control this overgrazing, and not many folks are going to like it when that happens.

"You see, the problem is, if you're going to buy and run cattle on this open range, you better have a brand on your cattle to prove they're yours. Unfortunately, anybody can make a brand. and every Mexican renegade in the district did just that. They steal other people's cattle, put their brand over the old one, then they run all the cattle they can catch and brand. Then, they take them across the border and sell them to another renegade who wound up moving them back near Bear Valley and selling to the Yaqui Indians, who would then bring them back to the Montana camp country and sell them right back to the same ranches that had them in the first place. It won't be long before these open ranges are gone, and the government comes in with laws restricting the sizes of these permits, and everybody will be limited to the size of their herds allowed in the forests of San Luis Valley and beyond."

The boys were perched on top of the fence rails in the corral, talking about the cows and horses. When we finally arrived, we stepped down from the buggy. The cattle started coming in for water as it grew late, and the conversation switched to the steers. We scrambled down and went to the hillside, where the boys showed us a concrete tank they had built under the spring. Around the tank were watering troughs. We climbed up a ladder to the top of the tank and caught drinking water in a can as it seeped from the spring. All of a sudden, Jack said, "Gosh, I'm hungry. How about you folks? Let's go see how John's doing with dinner."

We entered the house through the kitchen door. John, a white-haired, alcohol-bloated figure with a juvenile face, took his hands out of a bowl of ground beef, wiped them, and shook our hands. He spoke in a foreign language I could not recognize. I felt like I was in a foreign land, yet the people I met in Arizona were Americans and had lived most of their lives in America.

"What, hamburgers again?" Jack said. "Gee whiz,"

Ples noted, "The damn beef is always so tough it has to be ground up."

The hamburgers tasted acceptable to me, and after dinner, we sat around the big kitchen table talking. We talked about traveling and speaking in different languages. Barnes had spent most of his childhood in France and had French nurses and governesses. He could speak French, Spanish, and English.

Mr. Clarke jumped in and said, "I can speak five languages."

So, I asked him, "What five languages do you speak?"

He said, "I speak Gaelic, Spanish, and a little of Hebrew, Chinese, and English. I know I have a bit of an Irish accent, but I only speak a little Irish. Back in the old country, there's a saying that 'a little broken Irish is a lot better than clever English.'"

Then they started talking about schools. Ples, the only native Arizonan, had gone through grammar school, and since there was no high school, he attended the University of Arizona in Tucson. That is where he met Jack, who had hired him for a summer job as a cowboy. He quit school and came out to the ranch.

At that time, Barnes said, "Speaking of education, that reminds me, I have a paper I would like you to help me fill out, Miss. Harper." He went to the bedroom and returned with a printed form.

"This questionnaire is sent out to all alumni of certain universities and colleges. It's asks, 'Do you think it's worth it?' That was asking whether we alumni believe it was worth going to college. Dad said that in my one year at Princeton, it cost him over $5,000. I've tried to figure it out, but I can't account for over $4,000."

"That's silly," I said. "I know a girl who went to a teacher's college when I did, and it cost her $88.75. She had an attic room without a fire, and her room and board was $10 per month. She had a tuition scholarship. She never did graduate, though."

"Jesus," Ples said. "You don't believe that yarn do you. Why was she going if she didn't get anything out of it?"

"She got something out of it, all right," I said. "She was always the best dressed at parties, her hair was lovely, and although she had only one party dress, it always looked different because she changed her accessories every time she wore it. She was relatively older than the rest of us. That was why I suppose she was so able to get away with that, but try as I did, I couldn't get my expenses under $125 for the whole nine months I was there."

"Well," Barnes said, "Was it worth it?"

"That's my question," I said. "In a way, it was, but when the English teacher sent my themes to the journal editor for publication, and they were rejected because I wasn't a subscriber to the journal. It made me feel very low. Also, when the class president came to me and said I was ruining the class record by preventing them going 100 percent on subscriptions, I again felt just terrible."

"What did you do about it?" he asked.

"Well, it was either subscribe or quit. I didn't quit, but after that last semester, I left the school and started teaching."

"Well," Barnes said, "I don't think it was worth it. After my previous trip to New York, I was expelled, and the old man sent me out here."

Then he said, "I think anybody's a damn fool if they don't quit a thing if it ain't going the way they want it to go."

"Well," Mr. Clarke chimed in, "There's another way you can make it go the way you want it to go instead of quitting, see?"

"But Gipsy didn't see," Jack said. "She let the editor of that lousy journal throw away her good papers and print those stinking ones from the other subscribers."

"Well, how do you know they stunk?" Ples said.

"Well, they always do!"

"Then why did it matter whether she got a paper published or not? She lost a dollar to the lousy paper and had to quit school because she couldn't pay the lousy subscriptions," he said. "It made her feel awful. She says so herself that she got let down by the fraud of an editor. They're all frauds, and she had to learn it early. Good god, at least she knew it in the school."

Barnes said, "I just realized that Princeton wasn't worth Dad's $4,000. I got kicked out, but Dad brought me to this ranch, and that's a damn lot better."

"I'll bet Felipe here was a teacher's pet and a star pupil," Jack teased. "You can tell by the way he hasn't said a word. Just hasn't had a word to say."

Mr. Clarke said, "I don't remember school. I only went for three years, and I can't remember much about it. I guess I learned to read and write. I have pretty good handwriting, but that's all I can remember. I went to night school for a month when I was about twelve years old. Still, one day the teacher whipped a little bohunk fellow for no big reason, so I told him he had no right to do that. He turned to me and told me to sit down and shut my mouth, and I told him again he has no right to beat up on kids. He came after me, and I just tore into him and knocked him on his butt, and that was the end of school for me. I tell you my pappy wasn't happy with me about that."

About then, I decided I'd had enough of this bantering back and forth, and I got up and said to Mr. Clarke that I was ready to go home. We were late getting away, and when we stepped out of the house, the temperature had dropped significantly. It amazed me how hot it could be in the afternoon and how cool it got after dark.

"Didn't you bring any wraps?" Barnes asked.

I said, "No, just my shawl."

"I'll fix you up," he said. "Come back inside here." He brought out a heavy Navajo rug as big as a bed and draped it over my shoulders until it touched my feet. The one he gave Mr. Clarke was woven in a rattlesnake design with a huge, white pattern down the middle of a black background.

We got in the buggy and started down the road with a full moon showing over the peaks. It was hard to talk as we rode along, but it was nice to think about the day. As we rode off the mountain onto the wagon road along the bottom of the canyon, Mr. Clarke slowed down the buggy.

We came to a stop, and he looked at me and said, "You know those fellows have it pretty soft."

"Well, yes," I said. "I guess it's folks like that who make the outside world think cattle-raising is pretty easy."

"Exactly," he said. "Same for Nonie too. It wasn't that way with Nonie's father. He came by his ranch the hard way. He started with nothing and just started buying a few head of cattle, and then he started a freighting company and later, the store. Gradually, with some partners, as time went on, he created one of the best ranches in Arizona. I'd like to be the manager of that ranch someday just to keep it going strong. But see, Nonie don't spend much time out here anymore, and sometimes, I wonder if he is losing his interest in the ranch."

"Why don't you just get your own place, Mr. Clarke?"

"I sure would like to. I would really like to get a homestead. I know some swell places, but The Company's cattle run on them. I think Mr. Barnes, or even Nonie, might not like it if I told them I would try to get one. And maybe it wouldn't be treating them right if I did. And I think I can't get a branding iron as long as I work for them.

"And I can't get cattle until I get money to buy them anyway. The only other way is to take a partner, and I won't have that. Them back up there at the Barnes' place, they have everything—college education, money, everything. All because of Barnes' father's money. They have what I'll have to work most of my life to get close to.

"And then there's Nonie and his brothers. Nonie is the only one who will live here, and that's only part of the time because he lives in Tucson most of the time, and he's not the ranch-type, anyway. None of them are.

"I just turned twenty-two years old, I've been working by myself for twelve years, and what do I have? I have a mine if the ore turns out as I expect, a good job, and a chance of being the manager of somebody's ranch in another ten years or so."

"Why didn't you tell us it was your birthday? What is the date?"

"I was born September 17. And well, the gang knew it, and Josefa lit candles at the church for my saint."

"Well, Nita and I could have baked you a cake. I'll be sure to remember it after this because it's the day after Mexican Independence Day and the day after I came to Arizona. Then, next year, when I'm off in New York, in my attic studio painting pictures, I'll think of it and send you a card or a letter."

"Imagine you in New York," he said. "You don't belong there."

"Well, lots of people don't belong there, I'm sure. But look at you, all the way out here in southern Arizona, and me too. There are probably some folks who might not think neither of us belongs here."

We rode along silently for a while. Eventually, I said, "Mr. Clarke, I wonder if you'd mind me asking you a question."

"No, go ahead," he said.

"Are you angry?"

He stopped, thought for a minute, then looked at me and said, "No, not angry." He continued, "Do you have to call me Mr. Clarke?"

His question surprised me, but I said, "I call you Mr. Clarke because you're on the school board, and you're the superintendent of the school. But, besides that, I just feel I should. Besides, I can't say what they call you. Felipe, is it? You know my Spanish is not good. At least, not yet."

"My name is Phil, and I would like you to call me Phil. You can get by with it better than you can with that mister stuff." We both laughed at that.

"Where I come from, people are called mister and miss or missus, but I'll try saying Phil. I guess I'll get used to it."

"Phil said, "Now tell me about yourself and how in the world you happen to be here in southern Arizona."

I paused, and as I was beginning to answer him, he said, "First, tell me what your real name is?"

"What?" I said, "My given name is Gipsy."

"I know that," he said. "Isn't it just a nickname, a middle name, or some made-up name?"

"No, it's my birth name, and the only one I have."

"Well then, what is your baptismal name?"

"Well, I wasn't baptized," I said.

He stopped the buggy. "What? Now you know that ain't true! You know you were baptized. Everybody's baptized."

"I haven't," I said, "And what's so shocking about that?"

He said, "I knew Texas was wild, but I didn't know heathens lived there!"

"You don't know what you're talking about. I was raised in a very devout Southern Baptist family, and just because I haven't been baptized, it doesn't mean I'm not a God-fearing Christian. And what do you know about Texas, anyway? Tonight, you talked as though you didn't know Texas was part of the Union. So, I would just like to see what you do know about Texas."

"As a Texan, do you know that Texas is the biggest state in the Union and that there are more cattle in Texas than anyplace else in the country?" he shared. "And, Texas has more varieties of birds and wildflowers, and it produces oil and gas and raises excellent crops of rice and cotton? Do you know all that?"

I was angry then. How dare he talk like he knew so much.

"I know all about Texas," he said. "I lived there for six weeks on that damn ranch above San Antonio I was telling you about, see. It's a dry country, and it don't have any water. Can't run cattle without water and can't raise corn or cotton without water. What else do you want to know?" he asked with a slight chuckle in his voice.

Well, I just couldn't stay mad at him. I think he just wanted me to believe he knew much more about the country than he really did. Plus, I had the most exciting day of my life that day. That evening was so beautiful, and the air was just divine. I couldn't be mad that night, even with Texas being criticized and him calling me a heathen—and my name being laughed at.

After a bit, he said, "Texas can't be all heathens because that's where you came from," with another little smile.

"Really?" I said, "Well, now that's just fine. It's nice of you to say that." So, I decided to continue my story, thinking he would likely interrupt me and change the subject at any moment.

"I was born in Sweet Home on December 28, 1887. My mother and father are Albert and Dora Harper. They were born in south Texas, and so were my grandparents. And as I already told you, I am very proud of my Texas heritage. I have three sisters and a brother we call Buddy. I call him Buddy because he was my best friend when we were growing up, my playmate. And he and I did almost everything together.

"He actually came out to Arizona a few years ago to work in the mines in a town east of here. I think it is called Bisbee. I grew up in a loving and religious family. I was raised with a very severe, stout Southern Baptist upbringing. My parents were strict in raising us, but they were also very loving and caring. My father built the Baptist church near what is called the Pilot Grove Cemetery. It is about three miles from Sweet Home. We would often go there for family picnics when we would go out there to visit the family graves. My mother's parents and my father's grandfather are buried there. The marker on his grave shows he fought in the Mexican-American war at San Jacinto in the 1830s.

"My parents not only held our religious beliefs in very high regard, but they also felt the same about education. Every evening, we would read an educational story and passages from the Bible. I really enjoyed school, and I was an outstanding student. One of the highlights of my growing-up years was the annual Baptist camp at Palacios, a beach city on the coast.

"In 1901, when I was just about thirteen years old, we moved to Bay City, where my father opened and operated a hardware, lumber yard, and grocery store. I always enjoyed music and art, but as I grew older, I began to enjoy writing more and more.

"At some point, I decided I wanted to become a schoolteacher, so after I graduated from high school, I left home to attend a young women's college in northern Texas near San Antonio. I only went to that school for a year because of what I told you earlier this evening about what happened to me there. But I got a teaching certificate, so I moved to a little college in a small rural town near Fredericksburg to teach.

"The town was made up mostly of Dutch and German farmers, and I had a difficult time living up to their expectations. My living conditions were terrible, and the community was poor. The hardest part was that the administration was utterly unsympathetic to the situation. I became homesick for my family and my father's happy, loving spirit, so one night, I sat down and wrote the folks a letter to let them know how I was doing. I wanted to tell them I was beginning to write some short stories and some poetry and that I had had a chance to take some painting classes and have done a couple of small oil paintings, mostly landscapes.

"And, Mr. Clarke, it just dawned on me that when I wrote that letter, it was summer in 1906. I told the folks that I had a holiday and had been invited to Mrs. Morris's ranch near Fredericksburg for a lady's bazaar and dinner supper affair. Perhaps our paths could have crossed back then in Texas.

"Well, I continued to teach in the Fredericksburg area for the next couple of years but decided I wanted to return to school to get my degree. I thought it would help me pursue my interests in writing and painting. I hope that I can go into the hills when I get settled here and continue to paint.

"I attended North Texas Normal school, and I loved Denton. About a year ago, I received my graduate diploma. The girls I had become friends with at school started talking about going out to southern California, having heard how beautiful the beaches and orange groves were and how many handsome young men were out there. Soon after, they left and urged me to come. So earlier this year, I went too. I really enjoyed my short time out there but was unable to get a teaching job, and then one day, Mrs. Hopkins at the Sisk Teaching Agency, called to tell me she had a job in Arizona.

"In September, I met Mr. Bernard, who offered me this job. I didn't much care for this place at first, but the people have been so lovely and friendly. I think I will continue to enjoy it more and more. There is much, much more to my story. If you ever want to hear more, I'll tell you, but you now have an idea of who I am and where I came from."

He didn't stop or interrupt me, so I wasn't sure what he might be thinking.

"Hey now," he said, "Who would ever think we both have lived such exciting lives? So you have made me start thinking, and I have a question. You know I'm really busy with my company job, but if I come over sometime in the evening, maybe you could help me with my arithmetic, my letter writing, and my accounting. I know you're already helping me with my English and the language I use, but I would really like to learn how to write better, do arithmetic better, and do The Company's accounting better. You could start doing your paintings and writing."

I said, "Yes, if you'll let me teach you about Texas, too."

With a smile, he said, "Well, I've already been to Texas."

"You only saw one part of it, and I was born there. I can remember growing up there, just like you grew up in New York. So let's just leave it at that for now. Now, can we go on? I have to get some sleep tonight. Tomorrow is a school day."

We rode until we came to a little stream, and he stopped again to let the horses drink. While we were sitting there, he was silent, and then he said, "Gipsy, I'll call you Gipsy. Before we return to the village and you have to go in, I would like to tell you the rest of my story, if you would like?"

I said, "Yes, of course."

He switched the horse on the rump, we started off to the village of Arivaca, and he continued with his story.

"Pap returned to Ireland to get us in 1892, and we left for America. I remember only a little about coming over on the ship. I was only about three-half years old by then and was barely walking, but I do remember the boat riding up and down on the ocean. It was exciting watching the waves, but then it grew tiresome because Mam constantly made me sit back, making me sit on bundles of luggage with all the other young immigrant children. I began to cry. I wanted to go home, so she quieted me down by telling me Pappy was going to be waiting for us. His hands were going to be full of money, and she would hold her hands together, pretending they were full of silver coins.

"When we arrived in America, we had to go through that place they call Ellis Island, where all immigrants from other countries must stop before they are allowed to enter America. We spent two days on Ellis Island and were checked by doctors. Everybody else put their hands in our mouths and ears and touched us all over, looking inside our luggage to see what we had brought.

We were finally allowed to go across the harbor and into New York City. We got a house close to Uncle Paddy's near the elevator station, police station, and firehouse. When I was a little older, there was a fire at the Campbell Paper Factory, and I had an idea that I wanted to be a fireman when I grew up because I wanted to follow those fire wagons every time there was a fire.

"When I was about seven years old, my older brother Willie and I were sent to the Holy Cross Catholic Church. We became altar boys, and I liked that. I liked to carry the candles while standing by the priest in my robe. I felt different, and it made me feel like I wasn't the same boy who had to fight those big dagos and Polacks and bohunks every day to protect our money when we were selling our newspapers."

I said, "Phil, could you stop there for a minute and explain what you mean? You had to fight those dagos and bohunks while selling newspapers. What do you mean?"

"Well, Gipsy, I didn't like New York. When I was barely seven or eight years old, Willie and I had to sell newspapers morning and night so we could help Mam and Pap with rent and groceries. One night, it was freezing, and I was on one corner near 42nd and Broadway, and Willie was on another corner across the street. I turned around and saw these three big boys coming up the street. They went right toward Willie, and they tore the newspapers right out of Willie's hands and started beating up on him, trying to get his money.

"Well, I dropped my papers, and I ran across the street, and I tore into those 'doity rats,' and I started swinging and kicking. But they kicked and swung back, and pretty soon, I was beaten pretty badly and so was Willie, and they had taken all our nickels and dimes. When we went home, we didn't have newspapers, and we didn't have any money, and Mam was really upset, and when Pap got home, he took us into the other room and sat us down and asked us what had happened.

"I told him about the streets, and how in the evening and in the early morning, there were a lot of bully boys out there, and they were always trying to beat us up and take our money. I apologized and promised to never get beat up again. I told him that I would learn how to fight and take care of myself. I would not let those bully kids come after Willie and me anymore.

"A short time later, Pap came to me one evening and said, 'Philip, I have a friend who has a gymnasium about six blocks away from here, and I talked to him about teaching you how to box so that you can be able to take care of yourself and Willie.'

"I agreed. I wanted to learn as well, and that's how I got into boxing.

"On Saturdays and Sundays, I minded the baby carriage with Lizzie on the stoop while Mam and Pap went to church. Baby Lizzy could pull herself up and out of the carriage, so I had to watch her close until she fell asleep. That gave those bums a chance. Vito DeAngelo was one of them bad ones, and he would call me names and make fun of me. He'd say, 'Look at Mama's boy tending the baby.' I'd yell, 'Go chase yourself, you doity bum.' I'd have to stand and listen to that until Lizzy went to sleep. Then I'd chase after him, catch up to him, and beat the crap out of him, wiping up the street with the little wop. Then I would yell at him and tell him to leave me and my brother alone, or he'd get more of this, and I held up my fists.

I interrupted and said, "Phil, do you have to use that bad language? It's not nice!"

He looked at me with the strangest expression but didn't say anything and continued with his story.

"Most of my childhood was spent fighting, and after I grew up, it seemed like it was the same. The other thing in my life was my job. When I was ten, my folks took me out of school and said I had to find work. My first job was as a cash boy for Daniels & Sons, and I'd walk two miles daily to Daniel's, carrying my lunch. I got $2.25 a week. I never lost a job; when I left one, it was to get a better one. I brought home my pay envelopes and handed them to Mam, and she gave me a nickel and said, 'Look, five sticks of candy. You can get five Big Sticks of candy, and you earned it all by yourself, the smart boy you are.' Well, I bought candy once.

Then I learned more important things, but Mam always said, get yourself some candy. She used the money for a big roast and potatoes and cabbage balls. Mam never thought of money being for anything aside from food or maybe a treat at Coney Island on Mother's Day. Mam loved to cook. She loved to make corned beef and cabbage, and she loved to make Irish Stew. A favorite Irish dish she liked is called colcannon, and it's made with boiled potatoes, cabbage, onions, carrot, and lots of other vegetables. It was one of our favorite meals, and she loved to fix it.

"I hated the picnics we went on to Coney Island because I had to dress up like Willie, and he liked the stiff sailor type of collars. I couldn't stand them. I couldn't do anything fun for fear of spoiling my white linen suit, which I always did. So I always got in trouble with Mam. We took the streetcar home along with the other tourists, and Ma would turn to me in front of everyone and say, 'For shame, Philip, you soiled your pretty white suit, and look at your brother Willie. Look how white he keeps his clothes.'

"Then there were outings with my father to the zoo on Sundays. Once, he took us to the opera house to see *Oliver Twist*. He brought his set of Charles Dickens books to America with him, and he made us read them, or sometimes, he'd read them aloud to us. *Oliver Twist* was our favorite, and it was a great day when we went to see it played at the theater. Near the end, when Bill Sykes crept up behind Oliver with a long knife, just about to stick it to the boy's back, I jumped and yelled, 'Cheez-it, Sykes! Look out, Oliver!' Everyone, even the actors, laughed and looked at me. I never liked going to the theater after that.

"My main hobby was raising homing pigeons. Once, I almost got killed. I crawled out onto the ledge of a fire escape six stories up in the building we were living in, and I crept along the edge, trying to catch a pigeon perched on the far beam. Reaching for him, I slipped and fell halfway to the ground. My pants caught on a clothesline hook, and I just hung there screaming until a woman reached through her window and pulled me in. The clothesline hook had caught not only my clothing but a good chunk of my thigh. I had to have several stitches in my leg.

"As soon as I was old enough, I got a job driving the bank wagon for McCreery's. It made me feel like a gentleman with my derby and black suit on. I made $60 a month on that job, and I saved all of it except I spent some on good clothes. The rest would be for entertainment or to help out at home. By that time, Pap had started his livery business. He had horses and carriages and liveries. When I got a little older, I think about twelve years old, I was able to help him in the livery business. I loved taking care of the horses, brushing them at the end of the day when they were done on the streets for the day. And pretty soon, I became a driver. When I was about fourteen, I was able to get a job working at Macy's dry goods store as a driver on their delivery wagons.

"As I said before, I wasn't born in New York. I was born in Dublin, Ireland, September 1888. My father received a letter from my Uncle Paddy in 1890 asking him to move to New York and help him with his livery business. Livery is the same as our taxi and chauffeur business today. But my father didn't want to move our whole family across the ocean to New York unless he knew for sure that it was safe for us, so he went to New York in 1890 to meet with Uncle Paddy and see what New York was all about. He helped Uncle Paddy for a couple of years and decided that it would be good for him to bring the rest of us to America.

"I was such an ornery kid. I hated getting dressed up all fancy, but the outings weren't all that bad. I remember it was in the summer of 1900, and all of New York was celebrating its centennial, from the 1800s to the new 1900s, and Pap said, 'We all should go out to that island with the giant statue on it.'

"we packed up a nice picnic lunch and took the boat over to Ellis Island. We got off the boat and walked around looking at different things. But I noticed Mam and Pa were being really quiet and not saying much, and once I glanced over, and I think I saw tears in their eyes. So I looked up at Mam and asked, 'Is something wrong?' She shook her head and nodded over to my Pap. He reached down, put his arms around me and Willie's shoulders, and told us why he and Mam felt like they were.

"He said, 'When we first came into this harbor and saw that Liberty Lady, like most people, it gave us a memory that we will carry for the rest of our lives. We came here with nothing but a dream, a dream for a better life for us and you kids. In this country, that Statue of Liberty stands as a powerful reminder of the promise of freedom and the chance to create a better life for your family without the fear of penalty.' After he told us that, we went over to a plaque at the bottom of the great statue, and he told us to read what it said."

"And Gipsy, I can still remember. It said: 'Give me your tired, your poor, your huddled masses, yearning to breathe free …' To see that beautiful lady, lifting high her beacon of liberty, very few can describe the feeling—our tears are our only words."

"I'll never forget those words, and maybe that explains why we came to America and even why, I'm sure, I left New York to go West and make my own life, and maybe, why I'm here in Arivaca.

"Why don't we let these horses rest for a bit?" he suggested, blinking back a twinkle in his eye. "These pesky gnats are making my eyes water."

Yes, I thought to myself, *Those pesky gnats will make your eyes water. And they did mine too.*

The horses appreciated a break under the oak trees in the cool evening air. They seemed content with some green grass to munch on and a clear water creek nearby. The water brought insects, and their tails twitched in the cool evening air. He took one of the saddle blankets out of the buggy and laid it down as a spot for us to sit on while we rested.

"Are you comfortable, Gipsy?"

"Why, yes, this is much more comfortable and warmer. And I think the horses needed a rest."

After a short rest, Phil said, "It's getting a bit cooler, so we should get on down the road."

I said, "But I'm anxious to hear more of your story if you can continue to share it with me. I have always been interested in what life is like in New York. Can you tell me more of your memories?"

With this, I lightly placed my hand on his knee, encouraging him to go on. His blue eyes lit up at this, and he continued talking with new confidence and pride.

"I had been going to the West Christopher Athletic Club for the past couple of years and began to build up my muscles. I started learning how to box better every morning, and I would get up early. I would run around the block numerous times so I could get in better shape. I even went on a diet. It was supposed to make me into a big strong man. I boxed many matches, but my training as a prize fighter ended right after I won the Pee Wee Championship medal. I was so proud of myself and showed it to my father. Still, he said that was the end of that. He thought it would be best if I gave up fighting, but I continued to box occasionally and had an interest in continuing as a boxer and started to save my money so that I could leave New York and go out West on my own.

"My good friend Danny O'Leary and I would go to the pool halls once in a while when we had some free time. And while we were at a pool hall once, we met a man from Arizona named Tim Nolan. He was from Arizona and said he was visiting New York to see family and friends he had known when he lived there. We became friends and played pool together quite a bit.

"One evening, when we were at the pool hall, he said he needed cowboys on his cattle ranch in a little town called Arivaca in southern Arizona. He offered us both jobs if we wanted to come to Arizona. We thought it was strange that he would offer two young guys like us jobs on his ranch. He didn't know us, and he surely had to know we didn't know anything about cowboying. But I think that's when I started thinking about going West and seeing what this cowboy life might be like. Danny was thinking the same, and we began talking more and more about it.

"My parents thought I was talking crazy and wouldn't hear any talk about being a cowboy. So, soon after, Danny and I started making plans to get money saved up so that we could go when we were sure we were ready. I had been saving my money from boxing and my delivery jobs, and some of my friends offered to help me out. So, we saved enough for railroad tickets to San Antonio in just a few short months. I didn't have a lot of money, and didn't think I had enough to get all the way to Arizona, where Mr. Nolan's Ranch was, so I decided I would go to San Antonio.

"My older brother, Willie, had left home just about a year before and had told everybody he was heading for Texas to work in mines, but nobody had heard from him. I thought maybe I could go to San Antonio for a while and try to locate him.

"We told our folks we were going to leave, and we both got lots of resistance. Mam was very sad, and Pap was low, too, but he was really mad. He felt like I was running out on the family. Willie told me the same thing had happened to him when he said he was leaving, but he went anyway, and I decided I would go and try to find him. I'd had enough of the dirty streets of New York and decided it was time for me to strike on my own. I thought Willie might have a job and be able to help me find one if I did.

"In the spring of 1906, Danny and I bought tickets to Texas, and we told our folks we were leaving. Mam was crying, and she asked, 'Where are you going to end up?'

"I thought for a minute, then said, 'Mam, I'm heading out yonder to see what's out there.' And with that, Danny and I headed West.

"The train ride to San Antonio was long and tiresome. We had to sit on boxes in the freight car, and it was not very comfortable. We didn't get to sleep very much. The train was old and a rough ride, but when we got to San Antonio, Danny decided he would go on to

Tucson and find Mr. Nolan and get a job. I decided I would stay in San Antonio until I had saved enough money to go to Tucson and had some time to try to find Willie.

"I met a rancher from up north of San Antonio at the train station and told him I was on my way to Arizona to work on a ranch but was going to stay in San Antonio for a few days to look for my brother. He looked me over for a bit like he wondered if I knew how to cowboy. But I think he thought if I had a job waiting in Arizona, I must be a cowboy. He told me that when I was finished looking for my brother, if I still wanted a job, to come on up. His place was about forty miles northwest of Fredericksburg. His name was Morris, and the ranch's name was the Circle M Morris Ranch. He told me that if I could get to Fredericksburg, I would be able to find his place.

"I spent some time looking for Willie around San Antonio for a few days without much luck, so I decided to go to the ranch and work until I had saved enough money to go to Tucson. When I arrived, I observed that this ranch was not much of a ranch and was not in good working condition. I had to sleep in the hayloft and eat with the Mexican help. He had me doing pretty menial kinds of work, mostly cleaning horse stalls and cleaning up his shop and whatever else he wanted to be done.

"I didn't mind because I was just trying to get enough to move on. But you know, I never did get paid. I worked there for over two months, and he kept telling me he was going to sell some calves, and he would be able to pay me then. I think he never planned to pay me and assumed I would just take off. And that's what happened. I thought about just taking something of his worth about what he owed me but kind of figured that would be stealing, and I'm not a thief, so I just left one morning and never said I was and never looked back.

"I still had some money, so when I got back to San Antonio, I wrote a letter to Mr. Nolan asking if his offer was still good. I also asked him if Danny had arrived, and if he was working for him. I said I was leaving Texas and heading for Tucson and Arivaca and would be there in about a week."

Phil's story made me sad. He had missed out on what growing up for a young boy was all about. He hadn't experienced the country or the woods or heard the birds sing. He hadn't had the opportunity to experience going to school in an old log schoolhouse, like the one I had gone to. He hadn't had a kind old teacher like Miss Betty Matthews to make him want an education. He hadn't had an Aunt Minnie to tell him, "Go to school, and someday, you'll grow up to be a fine gentleman."

And yet, he had lived in New York. He spent all his young years on the streets just trying to help provide a little for his family. He learned to fight early on to keep the bad kids from stealing what few pennies he earned selling newspapers. Even though he had a good, strong family and a good mother and father, the family was large.

From what he had said, there were six children, and though he spent a lot of time on the streets, he had responsibilities helping his father and uncle Paddy run the livery stables and take care of the horses, carriages, and buggies. At one point, he thought about just making a career in boxing. But, like me, he had a very serious and devout religious upbringing, only his was in the Catholic Church, which was probably one of the reasons he chose to leave. Even though his religious upbringing was severe, he obviously wasn't practicing it much now. I just couldn't understand it. Today, with me, I could tell he was a happy-go-lucky young man, full of zest for life and an enthusiasm for what he might be able to accomplish.

I decided I needed to ask him about Danny before we got back to the village, so I said, "Phil, I know about your friend Danny. Will you tell me about him sometime?"

He was silent for some time, and I knew I had gone to a place he didn't want to discuss. Then, he turned to me a bit and just looked very sad. Soon, he said, "He's dead." I felt like I had taken away all the happiness and joy we had that day.

I said, "I'm sorry, I won't ask again." I changed the subject of the conversation as quickly as I could. "What was the name of the Texas ranch you worked on?"

Phil said it was called The Morris Ranch, which was in the spring and summer of 1906, and he was just seventeen years old. *How strange is that?* I thought.

"That's the same time I taught at the Red Rock School in Harper, which is just about forty miles west of the Morris Ranch. As a matter of fact, I went to a holiday bazaar at Mrs. Morris's early in the spring when I was there. Just think, we could have met in Texas. Do you believe in destiny?"

He looked at me and said, "No, I believe in myself—my plans and my ability to carry out what I plan to do. That's what I believe."

"Well, don't you think it's strange that we nearly met there in Central Texas? And then four years have passed, and we finally meet here? All that time, you were growing up in New York, and I wanted to go there to study art? And, then I changed my mind and went to California instead to become a schoolteacher. But as we both know, I didn't stay there. So, I came here when I had never even thought about Arizona and didn't know anything about Arizona, and for sure, I didn't know about this little village called Arivaca. Don't you think that could be destiny?"

Phil said, "No, it wasn't destiny. It's just that Nonie was in Los Angeles, and we needed a teacher here quick, so he hired you, probably because that Sisk Agency couldn't get anybody else to take this job. That's not destiny."

"Okay, okay! Well then, excuse me. I'm just thinking that it's pretty interesting how our journeys have come together."

He was silent then and didn't speak for a long time. Eventually, he turned and looked at me and said, "But it's good you took the job." Then he switched the horse, and the buggy moved along, and we rode slowly until we were back in the little village. I was so sore and stiff when we finally got to the village I could hardly get down from the buggy, but he got down and helped me and asked me if I would come to the store after school tomorrow and if I would please call him Phil.

I said, "All right, Phil, I'll come to the store, and I will call you Phil, but will you also call me by my proper name?"

He didn't answer. He just said I was shivering and wrapped the blanket around me a little tighter. He said, "You'd better be going in."

I responded, "Good night, Phil. I enjoyed this day immensely, but will you tell me the story of the rest of your journey out yonder to Arivaca soon?"

I stood with my hand on the doorknob and watched him get in the buggy, and he turned to me before leaving and said. "Yes, I will, Gipsy!"

When he went down the arroyo and out of sight, I turned the doorknob, but the door was locked. I knocked, but no one answered.

"Nita," I called. "Please let me in." To my repeated knocks and calls, there was no answer. I yelled at the top of my voice until I knew I had disturbed the entire village all the way up to Josefa's. I tried the parlor window; it was fastened. I tried the gate in the wall, but it was also locked. There was no way of climbing the wall, so I went to the saloon at the end of the house and threw rocks on the roof. The roof was made of dirt and made no sound. I sat on the step of the parlor door and wrapped the Navajo blanket around me.

After a long time, I heard the stealthy steps inside, and I jumped up and begged, Doña Anita, please open the door; it's very cold." I heard the bolt turn, and I opened the door and went in. The person went out of the room in darkness. I tiptoed across the parlor, entered my room, and failing to find a match, I undressed in the dark and crawled under the covers as tired as I was from the long ride.

I could not sleep. Was it John's coffee that kept me awake or the wonderful visit I'd had with Mr. Clarke—Phil—today? The trouble at the door was already a passing episode. The day itself receded to the background of my memory. Thinking back to our conversation, all I could imagine was a little boy running through the snow and crying in the streets of New York. Then, I thought about my frozen fingers struggling with the shoe button down on a Texas farm when I was a little girl. Phil had come a long way.

CHAPTER 6

The first day of school was always a jubilant occasion. Though this one threatened to be one of house cleaning and repairing broken desks and chairs, I felt gay nevertheless over the prospect of returning to work after my long vacation. Viejo was washing beer bottles outside my window and humming 'La Golondrina' across the patio. A rectangle of sunlight fell on the far wall. And chickens were clucking all around. It was all fascinating, and I smiled to myself with the excitement of the coming day and another year of work. I had forgotten all about my distress the night before.

This mural is located on the wall of the existing schoolhouse in Arivaca

I wore my dark long-sleeved linen dress and red checked gingham bungalow apron. The bungalow apron buttoned down the back, completely covering the dress's back. I had a boudoir cap to match; a boudoir cap could also make a good dust cap. I had cross-stitched the apron and boudoir cap in a floral pattern copied from a Japanese print from a sack of rags Nita had given me. She also provided me with some washing soap and a broom to clean the place up.

Uncle Beanie had rounded up all the children, and there were sixty-five of them. I rang the bell and wrote the names and ages in my register with the help of Maria, an older girl who spoke some English. Then we went to work. The boys got the water. There was no well; all the village's water was hauled in a barrel on a burro from the creek or a well a mile up the valley. The boys got the water because I didn't know how. I had learned the word "agua," and when I spoke it, off they went.

We scrubbed walls, windows, blackboards, desks, and even the floor. The boys raked the yard and piled the rocks on the arroyo bank. At noon, I sent a note to Phil asking for chalk, paper, and pencils, charging it to myself. The ones he promised had not arrived. I raced home, ate hurriedly, and was back again.

Probably a dozen children had some kind of book, and some had tablets and pencils. I had Maria tell them to ask their parents if they would buy books, and I gave each of them the slip with their requirements after classifying them the best I could.

Many of them were acting like they pretended not to understand, but they'd had a good teacher and so had their parents before them. Mrs. Noon, the most exemplary teacher ever, had taught them. Perhaps some had books at home and refused to bring them.

I wrote the multiplication table and a long list of words for spelling on one sideboard. After those were learned, I covered the board with fabric and had the children recite them. On another board, I printed the reading lesson for the beginners. I passed paper and pencils to all the students, and when the work was finished, I had every pencil collected. Then there was the singing lesson, with which we had a lot of fun. I wrote one verse of "America" on the board, but as few could read it all, they memorized the words from my singing faster than from the board.

That afternoon was mail day, and I sent an order to Tucson for thirty readers—first, second and third—and charged them to myself. I selected the art readers we had used as supplementary readers back home. They were expensive, but I thought the children would enjoy the pictures, and the little stories were real literature. I hoped that many would buy the regular books that were required for the course of study. Also, I ordered crayons and drawing paper for every child.

While I taught one section, the others had recess. Of course, they made a terrific noise, threw rocks at the house, and broke several windows, making it necessary for me to keep them after school until I discovered who did it. All faces were blank, and tongues were tied. Manuelito's eyes were downcast, making me believe he was the culprit. Though I had only circumstantial evidence, I accused Manuelito of breaking the windows and told him he would have to pay for them. I wrote a letter to his father, saying that until Manuelito brought three dollars, he could not return to school.

That night I took it up with Phil when he came over for help with his bookkeeping. His accounts hadn't balanced that month or for many months before that since many people connected with The Company helped themselves to everything. It was no wonder his books didn't balance.

He laughed when I told him about the note that I sent Manuelito's father. The man was a cowboy on The Company ranch, he said, and Manuelito made money hauling water and chopping wood.

"So, why shouldn't he pay for the windows?" I asked.

"Why didn't you just whip him?" Phil responded.

That was my duty, controlling those boys. So, he questioned why I sent them out without anybody watching over them. How could I not expect something like that to happen?

We left the subject and proceeded to my Spanish that he and Nita were teaching me. In my notebook, I had written all the words I had learned, and each day, I added more. Phil made it as difficult as possible, running over a line rapidly to make it hard for me so he could laugh. Nita was very patient.

He asked to have his speech corrected, but he always insisted on saying, "He don't." He told me Uncle Beanie and Uncle Johnnie both said, "He don't," and that cinched it for him. He would no longer change that and wouldn't stop saying that cotton didn't grow in Texas.

Later, as we got further along, he continued to educate himself. He became more and more committed to speaking clearly and using good language with proper grammar. He already had excellent handwriting and would put pretty little swirls in some of his letters. I asked him how he learned that, and he said Mam taught him that. After he dropped out of school, she was trying to continue his education at home when he wasn't working.

Sometimes, he didn't come over, and that's when Nita and I studied her lessons. Because she was in the eighth grade, she preferred doing her schoolwork at home.

On one occasion, Phil was over, and we were working on his handwriting, and the subject of legal issues came up. Suddenly, Phil said, "I should have been a lawyer." I asked him why, and he said, "Cause I understand it. You know that I'm the justice of the peace and the clerk of the court, don't you?"

I said, "Yes, I do. So, why don't you take it up now?"

He looked at me somewhat puzzled and asked, "Now, where do you think I could go to law school around here?"

I said, "Well, you can do it through the mail with what is called a correspondence course."

He said, "Well, can you help me find something?"

I said, "Let's look through some of the advertisements in my Harper's Magazine."

We selected a correspondence school in Chicago for Phil to study law at the LaSalle Extension University. We wrote to them for information. That interested Nita.

"You can learn by mail?" she asked, selecting a bookkeeping course. If she could get a job in Tucson, she could go there and live. Perhaps she could get her grandmother to retire, and they could both go to town.

I ordered some more magazines—Metropolitan, Scribner's, and one on art. The winter promised to be busy, with little time left for painting, embroidering, and crocheting, and even time to do other things I wanted to do. The landscapes and mountain colors were beautiful, so it would be wonderful to go up to the hills and paint some of the stunning scenes.

Nearly every evening, when Phil didn't come to Nita's, I went over to the store. One evening, after Phil finished with the other customers and while he was giving me my mail, he said, "Come out in the yard and watch me spin the bag." He had an idea that I didn't get enough exercise at school with nothing to do but sit and wanted me to learn to punch the bag. It always went wild for me, and I could never get it under control.

"It's so simple," he said, "You teach school. You ought to have enough sense to punch a bag and talk Spanish. I wasn't here a week before I could talk."

I didn't care much for the bag. It grew monotonous watching him show his ability, and when he'd give it a punch that snapped the rope, I was glad because then we could talk. He would sit on a stack of boxes and talk about the ore in his mine, how rich it looked, and how anxious he was for the first shipment. *I must see his mine.*

We sat for a while quietly, and I thought that maybe now would be a good time for him to finish telling me the story of his journey to Arivaca. I asked him if he would like to tell me the rest of his story, and he said, "Sure, now would be a good time."

"I got on the train in San Antonio about midday. It was in the middle of the summer, and it was sweltering. The train pulled out of San Antonio, heading for Tucson. Soon after we departed San Antonio, the conductor came by and asked for tickets, and he assigned me a seat next to a window which was good.

"All the windows on the train were open to let air flow through the train, but it was a long hard trip because it was dusty. All you could hear was the rattle of the wheels on the tracks, and there were no mountains, no hills, just flat West Texas country.

"I wondered how anybody could live in this country. I also wondered how anybody could raise cattle in this flat dry, desolate place. Along the way toward El Paso, we had to stop three times to get water loaded into the boiler on the engine. Each time we stopped, it was an opportunity for me to get off the train and walk around and look at the country.

"At the second stop, we pulled into a little town, and somebody told me the name of the town was Midland. I thought that was interesting, but this guy said it was called Midland because it was about halfway between San Antonio and El Paso. It was just a little town, but it was a good place to get something cold to drink and a little to eat before the train pulled out for El Paso.

"The rest of the journey was very dull and very uncomfortable because it was so hot. Also, there were no pretty trees or mountains to gaze at. It soon began to get dark, and after we pulled into El Paso, we stopped for about two hours.

"At this place, I got off, walked through town, got something else to eat, and started asking people about cattle ranches where a guy could get a job working on a ranch. Many people said that the best place to get jobs on a ranch would be in Arizona. I felt good that I was on my way to Tucson.

"I got back on the train. When it pulled out, it was dark and pretty late, so I could not see any of the scenery, and we chugged along until we passed through Lordsburg and on through Willcox to Benson, Arizona, and pretty soon, at about ten in the morning, we pulled into Tucson.

"I decided to spend a few days in Tucson to get acquainted with some of the people and find opportunities for ranch work. So I got my old cardboard suitcase and was told to go stay at the Old Saint Augustine Hotel, which was at the old plaza off Congress Street and Church.

"The population of Tucson at this time was about 1,300 people, which made it a pretty large city. All the transportation was by horseback or horse-drawn buggies and hacks and buckboards. As I was walking around town and meeting people, I came upon a pawn shop on Myers Street; it turns out this one was owned by a man named Francisco Soto and Oscar Devan. They also owned the stagecoach line, so I learned from them that the stagecoach went south toward the Mexican border three times a week to deliver mail and passengers to various stops along the way.

"While I was visiting with this Mr. Soto, I asked him if he knew a man named Tim Nolan who was supposed to have a ranch somewhere near Tucson. Mr. Soto told me Tim Nolan had a little place about 65 miles south of here, near a little Mexican village named Arivaca. Still, the chances of getting a job with him were probably slim because he was not around much anymore.

"I told him that Mr. Nolan had offered me and my friend, Danny, a job and that I had ridden the train from San Antonio to work for him. Mister Soto suggested I go to Arivaca and look for a Mister Noah Bernard. He was the owner of a huge ranch down in that area, and he would very likely have a job for me.

"I told Mr. Soto that I would like to go to Arivaca. He told me that the stage left at 6:00 a.m. and traveled all the way to the Old Glory Mine at Ruby. He explained that Ruby was a little mining town about 70 miles south of Tucson. I purchased a ticket and planned to be at the stagecoach early the next morning.

"The next morning, we left and drove four miles on the first part of the journey, where he changed mules for horses. It was the first time I had seen the San Xavier Mission, and it was beautiful.

"As we moved along, the ride headed toward Arivaca became more beautiful. We were traveling along the Santa Cruz River Valley, which was covered on both sides with many cottonwood trees and lots of grass. The mountains surrounding the city of Tucson were in bloom with flowers on the cactus, and it was a beautiful ride.

"The next change was at what was known as the Tesilar, just west of Sahuarita, and the rest of the changes were at the halfway junction, which is about halfway between the Kingsley Ranch and Basilio's, east of the river. The next change was at the Moiza Ranch, and the last change was at the Cerro Colorado. There was considerable mining activity going on at the Cerro Colorado. The next stop was Arivaca, and then Oro Blanco, then onto Ruby and the Old Glory Mine. These stops were necessary because most of the trip was on a gallop or a fast trot, a pace we kept to maintain the schedule.

"The stagecoach arrived in Arivaca at about two in the afternoon. It required many changes of horses along the way. Arivaca, the main post office, where all the mail was sorted and put in two separate sacks. One sack would go to Oro Blanco, one would go to the Old Glory Mine, and one would go west to Sasabe to the Los Altos Ranch and south to the Buenos Aires Ranch. The mail was usually carried by Pony Express. The courier was a Mexican Indian named Augustine Duran who homesteaded the Aguanita Ranch north of Sasabe. After delivering mail to Sasabe, he would ride to his ranch, which is not but a few miles from there. He made three round trips a week.

"While I was riding the stage, I met a rancher by the name of George Atkinson, who was on his way to his ranch, which was south along the Santa Cruz Valley to what is known as the Calabasas. We got along fairly well, and as we became better acquainted, we had a considerable conversation on the journey. He asked where I was going and what I was going to do. I told him I was going to hook up with my friend, Danny O'Leary, who had come out from San Antonio a couple of months ago to work for a guy named Tim Nolan, and maybe I could get a job with him, too. Or a Noah Bernard as Mr. Bernard was considered at that time to be the largest ranch owner in the area.

"George Atkinson left me at the junction; he had to change to another stage for the rest of his trip to the Calabasas. Before his departure, he handed me a $10 gold piece, which really surprised me. He said, 'If you don't get on with Noni Bernard, you come to Calabasas 61 Ranch, and I'll give you a job of some kind.'

"When I arrived in Arivaca, I wasn't very impressed when we pulled up in front of the post office. All I could think of as I stepped off the stage was that it was just a little old Mexican village. All I could see were six or seven ancient adobe dwellings with scattered pieces of plaster on their walls, and going down the middle of this little village was just a simple dusty road.

"After throwing the mail sacks through the windows, Lupe drove off to change horses and left me standing there alone with my big cardboard suitcase. It seemed like the only people there were thirty or forty Mexicans who were sitting in front of the old store staring at me, having a good time jabbering in Spanish and laughing at the newly arrived little Irish tenderfoot. There were buckboards, buggies, pack burros, and horses tied up to the hitching post, probably all from outline mining camps and ranches that had come to town to pick up their mail and supplies from the store.

Arivaca store

"I tried to talk to some of these Mexicans, but they couldn't understand me, and I couldn't understand them. After the stage left, I went over to the store and introduced myself to the storekeeper, whose name was Les Farrell. He was also the postmaster.

"I told him that I came out to get a job on a ranch working for a man by the name of Tim Nolan and to meet up with my friend, Danny O'Leary. I told Mr. Farrell that this man Soto in Tucson, who owns the stagecoach line, told me that he thought Mr. Nolan had gone back to New York and that his ranch wasn't operating anymore.

"I remember how disappointed I was when he told me that Mr. Bernard would probably not be out for more than a month or so and that the ranch was only using Mexicans to work, anyway. I didn't know what I was going to do; it looked to me that he was the only white man living at Arivaca at the time.

"He asked all about me and why I came away out there way off the beaten path in southern Arizona. Maybe he suspected that I might be a bad guy, and I was hiding out from the law or something. I explained to him that I wasn't hiding from the law and that I had not done anything bad, but that my friend and I had come from New York to go West and work on a cattle ranch of Nolan's. I continued to explain that I had stayed in San Antonio to look for my brother, and Danny came out here to work for Mr. Nolan, whom we had met in New York a while back.

"I asked if he could tell me where Mr. Nolan's place was and if he knew if Danny was working for him. He responded that he didn't have good news for me.

"'Your friend came out here all right and went to work for Nolan, but a short time ago, Danny was doctoring sick calves up toward Bartolo Mountain and got bit by a rattlesnake. He got ill and passed away before we could get him to Tucson to a hospital. Danny was a really nice young man, and everybody in the area liked him a lot. He had made many friends around, and during the short time he had been here, he got sweet on a young señorita named Nita. She lives over there at Doña Josefa's place,' he said, pointing across the road to what looked like a tavern or bar. 'When we brought him back from Tucson, we buried him out back here in the cemetery. And then the folks from all around had a big celebration for him.

"'Nolan knew of you but said he didn't know how to get ahold of you. I'm really sorry for your loss. Also, Nolan's place wasn't doing so well, and a short while back, he shut his place down and told some folks he was going back to New York. I haven't heard any more of him since.

"This news stunned me. I didn't know what to do. Danny was my best friend, and we had so many plans of things we were going to do together. I never cried much in my life. As I stood there trying to understand all of this, I couldn't hold back the tears falling from my eyes.

"I asked him where I could find this Nita girl. I wanted to learn as much as possible about what happened after Danny got out here. He pointed the place out, but while I was planning to find her, Mr. Farrell suggested I come with him to the store and have something cool to drink and just sit for a while. So, I went to the store and just thought about Danny. I knew I needed to send something to his mam and pap and let them know what happened.

"Soon, another rancher from out in the country came in, and his name was Bill Earl. While visiting for quite some time, he told me how sorry he was about my friend, and he told me I could come stay with him at his place until I could get settled somewhere. So I got on his buckboard and went to his ranch, which was about two miles south of Arivaca.

"While I was at his ranch, I got acquainted with a doctor, JH Ball. His farm was just south of the Earl Ranch. He was highly educated, spoke several languages, and stressed the necessity of learning Spanish if I intended to stay in this country. He told me about the surrounding countryside, the mines, and the ranches, including where they were located and who owned them.

"I worked for him during the hay harvest time, running the baler and hauling the baled hay to the barn. The rest of the hands were Mexicans, so I quickly learned to speak Spanish. While working for Dr. Ball, I noticed how beautiful the surrounding country was. It was covered with a heavy growth of grama grass, and in the mountains, there was a dense growth of oak trees, and it seemed like there was running water everywhere. I began to think this would be pretty nice country to stay at for a while.

"When the harvest was over, I went back to Arivaca to see Bernard, but he had not been out. Farrell wasn't sure when he would be coming, but he said he had some odd jobs that I could do if I wanted to wait around for him. I took this opportunity to work and earn some money. I put a new floor in the schoolhouse, fixed the shingles on the old hotel, and did other handyman work for him at the store. While there, I got paid $2 a day which was 50¢ more a day than I earned working for Dr. Ball.

"At the time, there was a ton of mining activity in the area. The Cerro Colorado was working a lot of men. The Yellow Jacket, down near Oro Blanco, was working a lot too. And the Consolidated

Arizona cotton and wheat mill, just below Dr. Ball's farm, was about to hire more men.

"Besides these mines, there was a lot of prospecting going on in all the camps around the Oro Blanco district. A good-sized store at Oro Blanco was run by a Charles Schulz, who was also interested in mining. There was the Warsaw, the Old Glory, and the Austerlitz Mine, owned by Dr. Adolphus Noon.

"While I was working at the store, Mr. Farrell helped me become a decent rider, and when I wasn't working on odd jobs for him, he would loan me his horse and saddle and tell me to go look around the country and visit some of the ranches. I could speak a bit of Spanish by now, so I visited as many of the ranches as I could. I rode as far as I could in as many days as I could. I went east to the Tumacacori and the Atascosa Mountains and south, beyond the busy little mining town called Montana Camp. I even went down through what is known as California Gulch to the border and even a little way into Mexico. I went west along the border to the Tres Bellotas Ranch and back farther west into the southern part of the Altar Valley near Sasabe. Finally, back past the Las Jarillas Ranch and then back to Arivaca.

"One day, Mr. Farrell asked me how I was liking this Arivaca country. I told him I was really enjoying it but wondered where all these different people came from and what made them come here. He asked me if I meant all them Mexicans, Europeans, Chinese, Italians, and such? And I said yes and asked if he knew. He told me to sit, and he'd tell me all he knew.

"He told me this country had been occupied for hundreds of years, going clear back to the mid-1700s. In those days, it was mostly the Hohokam's, and later, the Papago's came in along with the Yaquis and Opatan Indians from Mexico. Pretty soon, the Spaniards began moving north from Mexico, and created what became known as the Arabic Land Grant. Arabic, meaning small water or little water.

"In the mid-1800s, the early day mining operations began to spring up all over the district. The Germans sent engineers over to open the Cerro Colorado just north of here, and two Germans came shortly after and sank a shaft at what is called the Austerlitz Mine, just south of here. Soon after, Italians and Chinese began to arrive, and numerous other mines began to open up, including that big operation down at the base of Montana Peak called the Montana Camp. At about the same time, the Old Glory, south of the camp, and the Yellow Jacket, southwest of Oro Blanco, began operations. And from that time, for many years, more and more mines have continued to open and prosper. It was about this time, maybe thirty or forty years ago, that many of the prominent cattle and mining people we have around here began to arrive in the area.

"In 1879, Dr. Adolphus Noon and his son, Alonzo, arrived looking for a place to relocate from the Midwest, having originally come from England. He wanted to find a warmer and drier climate for his family. He had been told of the southern Arizona country and ended up at Oro Blanco.

"In early 1880, he had located a homestead north of town and planned to prove up on it as required while growing his cattle herd. Later, in 1881, he built an adobe house and office. Soon after, he brought his wife Emma and the rest of the family from San Francisco. He recorded his own brand, the ND. Two of the boys, Alonzo and Arthur, took right to cattle ranching and spent a good part of their younger years among the Mexican cowboys, learning how to rope, ride, and do many other jobs involved in the cattle business, such as blacksmithing, making lariats, and doing leather work.

"Eventually, these two boys acquired their own homesteads and started their own herds. Alonzo recorded his own brand, and, Arthur, the Quarter Circle Running N. After many years in the area, Dr. and Mrs. Noon moved to Nogales in 1898 and left the Oro Blanco Ranch to Alonzo and Arthur. But Arthur was becoming more interested in mining and soon left for Mexico, where he worked mines at Nacozari and Chilpancingo.

"In 1903, Alonzo passed away, and Arthur returned from Mexico, continuing to prospect. He returned to the ranch in Oro Blanco and continued to operate it with the help of the Mexican cowboys that Alonzo had used for years.

"An exciting part of this story, Gipsy, is what happened next for Arthur. In late 1906, Martha Clayton arrived from California to teach school in the little schoolhouse in Oro Blanco. When she and Arthur met, there was almost an immediate connection between them, and just about a year later, they married. It wasn't but a few years later, she became the teacher here in Arivaca, and except for a short interruption, when Mrs. Myer was here, she was the teacher until you came. I'll be happy when we have a chance for you to meet the Noons.

"About 1882, a Spaniard by the name of Augustine Ortiz applied for the title to the Grant. It conveyed ownership by the Spanish Government, but in later years, it became a problem for future owners to prove the legality of the title. Around 1886, the Ortiz family sold the Grant to the Sonoran Mining and Exploration Company, with whom Charles Poston, supposedly known as the father of Arizona, was associated.

"After many years of sporadic work and dwindling interest, the Arabic Grant was sold to what was called the Arivaca Cattle Company. The Company soon faced problems, proving the legality of the grant to the US Government some years past. The Company did not have the original deed issued to Augustine Ortiz. Still, it did have other papers of legal value registered in the Mexican book of records, which is known to be highly respected by the US Government.

"The biggest issue in the case to prove the legality was to verify the location of the boundaries. During the hearings, the government retained the services of a surveyor named Ysidro Bonillas. He was retained to establish the location of the original Arabic boundary point.

"It was from this point the remaining boundaries were laid out. From older residents of the Arivaca Valley, he established where these boundaries were and were able to verify them through testimony by numerous witnesses, including Charles Poston and many other long-time residents of the area. And the decision to validate the legality of the boundaries was passed down. Shortly after that, the Arivaca Land and Cattle Company was created.

"It was about this time that the Arivaca Valley was opening more to homesteading, and The Company's principals began obtaining as many parcels of the cienega bottomland homesteads as they could. A successful protest of a desert land entry by one of the principals then allowed opportunities for others to open up a few 160-acre parcels along with other homestead applications.

"Arthur and Martha quickly filed on a parcel on a pretty hillside just south of town. Then, just a year or so later, he built a small farmhouse and barn and began to prove up the parcels as required.

"When Arthur returned from Mexico the last time, the National Forests were being established in southern Arizona. The forests were being sectioned across the country to protect these publicly owned lands into the future. The boundaries were drawn mostly around the mountains, the assumption being made that these lands would be least disturbed by population growth. The little town of Oro Blanco and Dr. Noon's original homestead were excluded, as did anyone else's land that had been homesteaded.

"I sat there for some time thinking about this historical story that Mr. Farrell had told me. I didn't really understand what he meant by these homestead applications, so I asked him to explain what they were and why somebody would want to have one.

"He said, 'Sure, son, I'll do the best I can because, knowing how anxious you are to better yourself as you get older, I think it will be good for you to understand as much as you can about what they are and how it works to apply for one.'

"He explained that in 1862, Congress created what we now know as the Homestead Act of 1862. It was designed to grant up to 160 acres of surveyed government-owned land to any adult citizen. The requirements were that the claimant or applicant had to improve on the land by cultivating it and building a residence on it, and he must live on the property continuously for five years. You would have to pay a fee of $18—$10 to make a claim or application and a $2 commission for the agent then an additional $6 after five years as a final payment to get the deed to the property. I think there is an option that you could pay $1.25 per acre after six months of residence and obtain the title to the deed early. An important thing to know is that, early on, the General Land Office, which oversaw these application processes, was greatly undermanned, so many people have been able to acquire numerous homesteads through various loopholes in the requirements.

"I began to wonder how I could acquire one of these homesteads. I had no job or extra money, but I was determined right then and there that one day I would, and before I left Mr. Farrell that day, I told him so. As I was getting up to go to the ranch Mr. Farrell said, 'Phil, I know you don't have a steady job yet, but I think I know of a small parcel with a dried-up mine on it down yonder near the Montana Camp. An old Mexican squatter owns it, but he can't prove it up as is required, and he might sell it real cheap.' I told him how I sure would like to get a shot at that, and I'd appreciate him trying to get more information if he could.

"He told me that he would investigate it, and if he found anything out, he'd let me know. He also told me that he'd try to help me buy it when I got a steady job. I told him that I'd be in touch and thanked him for his offer to help.

"Next, I visited the Bernard Ranch, hoping to meet Mr. Bernard finally. He had not come out from Tucson, but I got acquainted with the foreman there, a man by the name of Ramon Ahumada. He was standing next to his beautiful horse. His tack was inlaid with silver. His headstall or bridle, saddle, and spurs were all inlaid with silver. It was so pretty, and all the horses on the ranch were first-class cattle horses, having been raised to work cattle in the rugged desert country of this area.

"While visiting with Ramon, I learned that Arivaca Ranch, as it was called then, was considered one of the largest and most successful in this area. He told me this whole country was wide open to cattle grazing; the only fences were those around the various homesteads that were owned by multiple ranchers. It was the days of the open ranges, and all cattle owners used their own brands to identify their cattle during the mass roundups that usually took place twice each year.

"I began to wonder how a fella like me might be able to get one of these homesteads. I thought that if I had one of them, I might be able to get some cows or steers of my own and turn them out on this open range like all the rest of the ranchers were doing. I thought, *One day!*

"Alan Bernard was a nephew of Mr. Noah Bernard, Sr. and a cousin of young Nonie who lived at Arivaca Ranch. He had a wife and two little children about two and three years old at that time, so while I was getting acquainted, I still had no steady job because Mr. Noah Bernard had not shown up. Ramon did not want to hire me until he talked to Mr. Bernard or Nonie.

"I began to debate on several occasions on whether I should just forget this dream and go on to Los Angeles and take up boxing again. I also thought about going over to the Calabasas in the Santa Cruz Valley to see George Atkinson. But everyone kept telling me that when Mr. Bernard or Nonie came out, they would hire me and give me steady work. I was really beginning to like this country and didn't want to leave, so I decided to stay around.

"Finally, I heard that Nonie was coming down from Tucson, so I went to the ranch to try to meet him. Ramon introduced me to him, so I had a chance to ask him if he would put me to work and give me a job on the ranch. He thought for a minute, and then he looked at Ramon, and then he looked back at me. He said he'd leave it up to Ramon. Ramon told Noni that he would like to have me helping and that he would teach me how to become a wrangler.

"At that time, Nonie was homesteading over on the cienega. He was beginning to build a small two-room shack and barn so that he could establish residence over there in order to comply with the homestead requirements that were in place at that time. He suggested that if I could help him build his little house, I could come over there and live with him on the cienega.

"While we were making his small home, he paid me $1.50 a day with room and board, which was very good for those days. Then he gave me a steady job as a wrangler, working with Ramon. Most of my job was to keep the saddle horses within their own remudas and to keep the bell mares together with their remudas of mares.

"All of a sudden, I had a full-time job and was getting paid good wages, and it looked like I was going to be able to stay on at The Company for a long time. But I kept thinking about Mr. Farrell's offer from a while back and decided to go talk to him. Maybe the Mexican might still want to sell his little parcel to me.

"While helping Nonie with the building, Mr. Bernard did come down from Tucson, but only one time because he was ailing. I was never able to meet him, and I later heard that he had passed away not too much later, but I did get acquainted with two of the other Bernard's, Ned and Bill.

"The first roundup was to begin in mid-September, and Ramon told me that he wanted me to be on this roundup with them. This was an exciting time for me because I had been working with Ramon and other cowboys all summer, being taught how to break and train young horses, to really learn what working cattle and horses was all about. Working cattle through a roundup and branding was exciting to me, and I was really looking forward to it. I promised Ramon I would do a good job and not let him down.

"Just before the roundup began, I got a chance to go into the village and talk to Mr. Farrell again. I guess the timing was right because he said he had just found out the Mexican had to get out before he lost his parcel back to the government and would take $50 for the whole thing. I told Mr. Farrell I had saved about $20. If he still would help me get it with a $30 loan, I would pay him back with my first voucher from The Company. He said okay, and he had the deal put together for me within two days. He said he would have the title and deed for me when I came to town the next time. And, Gipsy, that's how I acquired my little parcel and my mine.

"The roundups in this area were made up of many of the various ranches in this part of the country. Some of the larger ranches in the area, in addition to the Arivaca Land and Cattle Company, were the Noon's places around Oro Blanco and over near the south end of the Baca Float, between Nogales and Patagonia, the John Bogan outfit, the

Empire, located on the east side of the Santa Rita Mountains, and the Kane's and the Rail X, also over near Patagonia, the Amado Brothers at Amado, the Canoa near Kingsley's, the Box Canyon near Tubac, and farther south, the Calabasas of George Atkinson. Moving west toward Three Points is the Robles and the Anvil, owned by Manuel King. South of the King Ranch is the Las Oso which covers all the wide-open range, from the Kings down through the Altar Valley to Sasabe and the Mexican border.

"Ramon was always the roundup boss for the whole territory. He would break his crews down into groups of four or five wagons with supplies, and as many as twenty to thirty cowboys, along with each of their own four or more horses, called remudas. He'd send them off to work on the various areas of the coming Vuelta.

"The remudas were taken care of by one of the wranglers, usually one of the youngest and least experienced of the cowboys. His job was to see that the horses were watered and grazed and kept them from straying away from the herd. He also gathered them when the cowboys needed to make a change in his mount, usually each morning before the start of that day's drive. This would be the job I was given responsibility for on my first roundup. The wrangler usually trailed with the chuck wagons and helped haul wood and do other chores as needed. The chuck wagons carried everything that was needed on the trail—food, bedrolls, medicines, and almost all other necessary supplies.

"Most of the cattle people would gather all their cattle and move them to a central location in their area and then sort them by brands. Once each outfit cattle were separated from the others, they would then separate cows from calves, then brand the calves with the same brand as their mother cow, and cut the bull calves into steers.

"Once this was done, each outfit would sort out the cows, steers, and heifers they wanted to send to market and return the rest to pasture. When all the sorting's were done, all the cattle would then be in one herd and ready to move on to Tucson to market, a trip that could take as much as ten to twenty days.

"The roundup would start at the KX Ranch, about twelve miles north of Arivaca and involve many of the more extensive ranches throughout the entire Arivaca district. All these ranchers would gather the cattle in their areas. Whether they had their brands or not didn't matter because, during the roundup, the cattle would be sorted and put into their owners' own herds.

"The roundup would move east toward Amado, and they would be gathered there while the rest of the roundup moved north along the Santa Cruz River toward the San Xavier Mission, south of Tucson. From there, the groups of forty to fifty vaqueros, or cowboys, would move to the Altar Valley west of Tucson to an area that was known as Three Points. Then it would turn south toward Sasabe, driving along both sides of the Altar Valley, with the magnificent spire of Baboquivari Peak looming over the entire valley from the west and the Sierritas and San Luis Mountains on the east toward Fresnel and then end up at the southern end of the Altar Valley near Sasabe. Then move east again to Tres Bellota's, California Gulch, south of Montana camp to Bear Valley, and north through Bartolo Canyon and Chimney Canyon, along the mountainous Apache Gap in the Atascosa Mountains, and finally ending up back in the Amado area. This would have been a distance of approximately one hundred miles, and it took nearly six weeks to make this journey, sometimes moving as many as 5,000 head of cattle.

"Most of these vaqueros, or cowboys, sprang from the long history of working for longhorn herds across the Texas plains clear back to the mid-1880s. They were used to spending days on end living in their saddles. Life was hard, often dull, and sometimes dangerous. The daily grind of twelve to fifteen hours in the saddle, nursing sick or injured cattle, eating the same meals over and over, and sleeping on the ground in a bedroll in all kinds of weather. It was a life they loved.

"A cowboy's closest companions were often their horses and the cattle they were working. But it was a life of freedom for them. They didn't ask for much and didn't expect much, and they loved the life, especially when the roundup time arrived.

"Gipsy, before I go on, I want to tell you a story about a boxing match that took place during the roundup just outside of Sasabe. It was relatively late in the afternoon when the last of about twelve hundred steers were passed up to this side of the border and were put into the herd in a wide draw for the night. This was just east of the Sasabe store where we were camped. There were at least thirty or forty vaqueros, mostly all Mexicans, sitting around a large bright campfire, some playing cards, others singing to the music of a guitar, others just shooting the breeze of stories of earlier days.

"A man by the name of Trifilio owned the store in Sasabe, and he had a son named Tony, who had a reputation as a tough guy and was known as a boxer. He came to the camp and started harassing a young Mexican cowboy by the name of Queiroz. He was bragging about how tough he was and what a great boxer he was. I think he was about half-drunk, and he started talking trashy, saying that he could whip him and any of these other guys sitting around here. The young kid pushed back, but Tony got madder and madder, and pretty soon, he sent Trifilio to the store to get gloves. He came back with the gloves, and all the other activities around the fire stopped so everyone could see what was going to happen.

"All the cowboys and customs officials who were there gathered in a large circle. With a full moon and a large campfire, it was quite a sight to see these two go at one another. Tony probably weighed about 190 pounds, and Queiroz was a little smaller, maybe only about 165 pounds. He was no match for Tony, who actually did know something about boxing. After about five minutes of hammering and beating on Queiroz, Queiroz quit, so Tony started acting real cocky. By then, lots of the cowboys were beginning to get mad at Tony.

"One of them, by the name of Figueroa, who lived at his ranch near the BOB, challenged Tony to try the same thing with him. But the same thing happened to Figueroa that happened to Queiroz. So, this Tony was just running around acting like he was the cock of the walk, cursing and calling cowboys names, and challenging everybody to see if anybody else would like to try him out to take him on. I couldn't figure out why Ramon or the custom inspector guy didn't put a stop to it.

"Walter Bailey, then the customs inspector and later sheriff of Pima County, smiled at Ramon and said, 'Hey Tony, how about you try that little Irish gringo, over there?' pointing to me. I only weighed about 145 pounds at that time. Tony looked at me, laughed, and said, 'Sure. He won't last half as long as the others did, but it will be fun to smack him around a little.'

"I looked at Bailey and Ramon and wondered what they were thinking. But I said, 'Okay, but we don't need them gloves.' I said that because in all my experience in New York, and I figured I could take care of this big guy without too much trouble. I said, 'We'll just go as long as you can last and that ain't going to be very long.'

"Nobody knew that I was just steaming mad about all of this, having watched this big half-drunk bully beat up on two good cowboy friends of mine. And almost all the thirty cowboys around the fire laughed, thinking I was being a smart aleck. They thought I was crazy, and I wouldn't last even one round with the guy. None of them knew of the experience I had on the streets of New York fighting all those dagos and bohunks almost every day.

"Bailey was the timekeeper, and when he called time, Tony rushed at me, like a big bull, swinging both hands with his head down, and instead of standing there as the Mexicans did, I just stepped aside. He went head-on into the crowd, and the Mexicans in the circle began to laugh. That just made Tony madder. He got up and rushed at me again. I just stepped aside a little and let him have a quick little right on the side of his head. He crashed into the crowd on the other side.

"A little blood started coming out of his ear. The next time, he came at me straight up, and he was furious. His face was red, and he was sweating like an old bull. He came right at me, I feigned with a left cross, and then I hit him with a right-right on the button, and down he went. Then he had blood coming out of his nose, too.

"My adrenaline was really flowing, and when he got right back up, I pushed his head back with a stiff left jab and caught him right on the point of the jaw with my right and landed a full swing with my left to his gut. He bent over, and I came up with a big right-hand solid hook and caught him right on the side of the jaw, and then as he was falling back, I let him have two really quick left pops to the other side of his face, and he went down and out. He never touched me and as he lay there on the ground, out cold, blood all over his face, the Mexicans in the circle all begin to cheer for the little gringo, Felipe. They started cheering, 'Felipe! Felipe!' and from that time on, I had a reputation for being a pretty tough guy.

"The story of the fight at Sasabe spread all over the district real fast, and soon I had a real respect and liking from the cowboys and people all over the district. From that day on, Gipsy, I had help from cowboys and the village folks with whatever I needed. Cowboys began in earnest to help me with my Spanish and learning horses and cattle.

"One day, I was at the ranch helping Ramon with some horses, and Walter Bailey showed up to talk to Ramon about some stray steers that had come across down by Tres Bellotas. I had been wanting to ask both of them about why they didn't do something to stop that Tony guy from beating up on our cowboys that night in Sasabe. This chance meeting with both of them together gave me an opportunity to ask them at the same time. They smiled at each other, and Walter said to me, 'Philip Ramon and I thought you might have a good chance against him, and if you could beat him, it would be really good for how people would think about you.'

"I said that I didn't think that was a good idea and asked what if he had beaten me up badly. Ramon said that would have been okay because he was much bigger than me and just for me to fight him in front of the cowboys would help me to earn their respect.

"I kind of thought that was a lousy trick for them to pull, and I told them that and said we shouldn't do that again. Both of them just nodded at me but didn't say anything. And I guess it turned out okay. After the roundup was over and before we turned the calves back out onto their ranges, we did branding and cut the little bullies into steers. Ramon had me helping with that and then said he wanted me to go with them when they took the herds back to their pastures."

Gipsy interrupted saying, "Excuse me, Phil, when you talk about taking the cattle back to their pastures, I'm confused. Aren't their pastures just right there next to the headquarters places?"

"Well, Gipsy, no. A few years ago, about 1906, I think, the Government was establishing the National Forests in southern Arizona, and lines were drawn around the mountains in certain areas. Anyone who had homesteaded in the area could have their land excluded from the forest. So, any ranchers who had historically run cattle on that land when it was still all open range were able to obtain grazing permits on that land. This land was referred to as Forest Reserves, and folks who own homesteads are able to obtain grazing permits for numbers of acres determined by different sizes of their homesteads.

"So, The Company has many homesteads scattered around the district and as a result, they have many acres of pastures all over. Some of those cattle might go north, some may go west, but not many of The Company's cattle go east and south since much of that land has been homesteaded by other ranchers.

"As we were moving these cattle, Ramon said he was going to keep me around the headquarters and get me started learning more. I had become a pretty good rider and roper. He wanted me to learn skills of making lariats (ropes) and leatherwork so that I could repair saddles. He wanted me to learn blacksmithing to make horseshoes and also how to shoe a horse. This way, when my horses threw shoes in the mountains, I could re-shoe them and keep going.

"Most importantly, though, he wanted to teach me how to train the young, green horses. But he didn't mean to break the young horses, he wanted me to train them. He talked about learning a horse and understanding them, knowing what they're thinking, their personalities and what will make your horse your friend. I knew that I would really like that. And he said we'd start when we got back and just about everything I'd learn from this, I would learn from the horse.

"My job would be to go out into these pastures where the various remudas (like herds) of horses were and wrangle them up and bring them into headquarters where we could separate out the colts to be broke and trained to be future cow horses. And this is when my real training was getting started.

"And let me tell you, those other cowboys there were really getting their laughs, having a great time watching the little Irish gringo learn how to bronc break a new colt. I was having a hard time staying up on most of them. They were all pretty wild and snarky. After all, they had not had much exposure to people, and fear was a big part of what was happening with them. Ramon tried to help keep me in the saddle a couple of times, mostly with not good results. But eventually, I began to get the hang of it and became one of the better bronc busters.

"One day, we were getting ready to start again, and Ramon asked me to get a white albino out of the corral. We were going to start with him. He already had the halter on him, so I latched on the lead rope and brought him out. I asked Ramon why he called him albino. He said because he has pink eyes. I later learned that most cowboys don't care much for albinos because they tend to be skittish and undependable. I think I was on and off that white horse eight to nine times that morning, but finally, he settled down and began to respond to me in good ways. And I didn't think that horse had those tendencies. He had settled down really well and was paying attention to me with his ears up and pointed toward me like he was waiting for what was next.

"We stopped for lunch, frijoles and tortillas as always, and while sitting there, Ramon told me tue es muy bien vaquero (I was a very good cowboy) pero más bueno hombre (but more, a good man). He said he told Nonie that they wanted to make Felipe more a part of The Company. Nonie suggested they give me that albino white I'd been working with, and he had some jobs I could take over in town. So, that's how I became part of The Company.

"Over the following days and weeks, I was making more and more progress with El Payaso, the clown. I gave him that name because he had those pink eyes, black spots, and speckles on his face and forehead. And I thought it made him look like a clown. Later I began to think he might have some appaloosa blood in him.

Phil on Payaso

"Ramon worked tirelessly with the horses and me. He kept telling me he thought I was a natural with them. I learned about different headstalls or bridles and bits and how horses respond differently to different kinds. Some take to a bridle with a curbed bit, others work better with a snaffle with a curb (a strap) under the chin, and some do better with a hackamore (a headstall without a bit in the mouth). He taught me how to use the reins to guide the direction and how to use knees and spurs for direction. We learned cutting (the act of separating cows or calves from the herd) and spinning and sliding, and on and on the training went.

"Within a few months, Payaso and I became an excellent team, and Payaso turned out to be one of our better cow horses on the ranch. About halfway through all this training and work, Ramon brought out an old saddle from the tack barn and said, 'Felipe, you remember what I taught you about stitching?' I said yes, and he said 'Okay, you can have this old saddle, but you have to get it fixed up.'

"Oh man, Gipsy, I thought it was Christmas time. My own saddle! It was rough and needed lots of work, but I didn't care. I worked on that thing every chance I got and eventually got it looking like new and one of the best of the bunch. And Gipsy, you might have noticed a little piece of silver on each side of Payaso's headstall. A Christmas back, Ramon gave that to me.

"Eventually, Nonie pulled me off the ranch except for roundup and branding times and put me here in town to take care of company business. Mr. Farrell had moved on, and somebody was needed here. So, eventually, I became the official postmaster, justice of the peace, clerk of the school, and the boss of the mercantile and everything else that needs to be bossed in this little town.

"Pretty soon, Mrs. Noon stepped down as the schoolteacher, then Mrs. Myer didn't last long. And Nonie told me to get busy and get us a teacher here before school starts in September. But he also said he was going to California on Company business and would check out one or two of those teacher agencies and see if they might have anybody.

"Not too long ago, as you know, one day in September, I was working at the ranch, and it was a stagecoach day. When the stagecoach has a passenger, it's part of my job to greet them. As you remember, I was late when it arrived, and when I came around the corner at that quick gallop on Payaso, I brought with me a big cloud of dust. I sure am sorry about that. But then I heard Pepe yelling that the new schoolteacher was here. Well, that made me angry at first because Nonie had told me to hire a teacher. I hadn't been told that Nonie had hired one. I was angry, but when I saw you step out, I just couldn't believe my eyes. You were the prettiest gal I had ever seen. I am so glad you came to Arivaca."

CHAPTER 7

Back at Nita's, I got my mail, and there was a letter from my sister. I was sure it was a reply to the one I sent her when I first arrived here. In that letter, I had told her that life here in Arivaca required numerous adjustments for me. I'm in a man's world with very few white women to talk to and was not getting acquainted with many people other than Mexicans, who speak little or no English. I always loved to read, but I didn't have access to anything more than a few magazines and what few catalogs I brought with me. I had told her about my sorry conditions and about this roughneck, arrogant, and seemingly cocky school clerk named Philip Clarke I had to work with, and how sorry I was to be here.

Dear Gipsy,

For pity's sake, girl, what did you go to that God-forsaken, rough, uncivilized old Arizona for? Sixty-five miles from a railroad! Isn't it the toughest thing you have ever seen?

How did you hear of it? How long is your contract? How much does it pay? Is it cold? How far do you walk? In fact, write everything, where you board, where you eat, etc. And be sure to tell me more about this school clerk you are working for.

Love,
Little Sister

PS. I miss you!

Dear Little Sister,

Thank you for your last letter. I'm sorry I made it sound so bad here, but at that time, I was very depressed over the whole situation. And I was really considering going back to California, and I even was thinking of going back home. But my situation here continues to change every day. And thank goodness, I think it's for the better.

Things continue to be interesting with Mr. Clarke, the school clerk. He is a young Irishman who runs the post office and just about everything else here in town. He has a healthy ego, to say the least! He seems to flirt with me sometimes when we are together though I don't know why. When I first arrived, I was told that he was engaged to be married to a Mexican girl named Lucia. So, I don't know.

He came here from New York about four years ago but was born in Ireland. In New York, he learned how to box to protect himself and his brother, Willie, from bad kids on the streets. He has a big old punching bag hanging in a tree out behind the store, and for some reason, he insists on teaching me to punch the bag and takes much of his time to regale his stories to me whenever he finds a spare moment.

I have to admit that he is a rather handsome man, about my age, and I seem to be enjoying his company more and more as time moves on. He has taken me on several buggy rides around the district, and he insists on introducing me to people all over this country that he calls "His Out Yonder."

Nothing more to report for now. But I'll write again when anything else develops around here. We had beans for supper tonight and green apple pie. The mountains are magnificent and of so many colors. And really, the whole country is green and beautiful. I believe I am beginning to like it here more and more.

Love to you all,
Gipsy

I was down by the creek washing when the Baileys called. The washing place was under the cottonwoods near the crossing where the road went to Las Jarillas. I had persuaded Nita to go with me, but she only took a pair of stockings to wash.

She posed for me, sitting on a rock dipping the black stockings up and down in the stream, her laughing face turned to me as I snapped the picture. Then I gave her the camera and had her photograph me on my knees beside the wash women as we rubbed the clothes on the rocks, a huge pile of clothes on the bank for a background in the picture. She took another of me, hanging my shirt waists on mesquite branches to dry. For a more intimate view that my young sisters could hide in their room and laugh over, I posed beside a tree that was draped with my ruffled drawers, corset covers, and knit vests.

Absorbed in directing Nita, I failed to notice the boys from the Barnes ranch until they crossed the creek. I looked up and saw Jack, Barnes, and Ples riding past. I blushed furiously, and Nita giggled; even the women on their knees smiled. At first, I wanted to run, but remembering the hair rat that Ples had taken and fearing they might do the same to my private apparel, I stood my ground. Fortunately, Ernestine, the little neighbor girl, came running down to tell us that the Baileys had arrived and were waiting up the hill. As we hurried up the hill, the boys rode on to the store.

Mrs. Bailey had a complexion of cream and strawberries. Her figure was on the plumpish side, emphasized by the riding skirt of corduroy. Her features were delicate under the brim of the cowboy hat. Though she wore a starched shirtwaist with linen collar and tie, the stiffness did not detract from her daintiness. Deep dimples appeared on her cheeks as she spoke to me, holding out a cool soft hand. A diamond stud sparkled in her waist front, and as she toyed with her skirt, other diamonds flashed from her fingers. Her eyes were very blue, surrounded by twinkles. The smile on her lips was permanent, but the rose petal complexion came and went as she laughed, fascinating even to me. No wonder all the men adored her. At Nita's request, she removed her hat, and then I saw that the most beautiful thing about her was her hair, which was bright yellow and heaped high on her head in row upon row of curls.

People called him Hank, but Walter was very large, probably six-foot-six, with wide, weather-beaten features. His voice was kind, and his eyes gentle. He wore government clothes of khaki, perhaps because he was the customs agent for the district.

He and Nita had much to say to each other, and of course, it was in Spanish. As Mrs. Bailey and I talked in English, Doña Anita came in, shook hands with them, and offered them beer, which Hank accepted.

"We want you and Nita to come to dinner tomorrow," Mrs. Bailey said sweetly.

Thanking her, we accompanied them to the hitching post, and they got into their buggy and departed.

"Goodbye," they called simultaneously as they rode down the hill.

Early afternoon of the next day, we were getting ready for our evening at the Bailey's. I dressed in Nita's riding skirt again. Unfortunately, the one I had ordered from the Broadway Department Store in Los Angeles had not come. Nita gave me a handkerchief to tie up my hair. She braided hers in two long braids, tied them at the ends, and left them flying.

We walked down to the corral behind the store. We found the gate unlocked and went in to get my horse and saddle, but the saddle shed was locked. Nita showed me how to climb through a window while she held it open. During the process, Phil yelled from the patio, "You girls, get out of that barn!" I slid to the ground, tearing my stockings.

As he approached, I tried to ignore Nita's hysterical giggle and maintain my dignity. "I'm sorry," I apologized, "I was merely getting my saddle; Mr. and Mrs. Bailey invited Nita and me over to dinner."

"Tonight?" He said, "You can't go off by yourself without a chaperone. Go back to Nita's; I'll be by for you shortly."

On the way up the path, Nita laughed and laughed, "What's so funny?" I ask.

"Nada," she said, still laughing.

"What are you thinking, Nita?"

She responded, "I think you are liking Felipe more and more."

I said, "I don't like him any more now than before, Nita, but he is being nice to me and helping me around the school more."

"Well," she asked, "Why do you let him go with us to the Bailey's?"

"It didn't seem like I had much choice in it; do you think?"

She said, "I think Felipe is beginning to think you should be his girl. If I were you, I would have said that I was going with another man," she giggled again and said, "I think it would make Felipe very jealous."

"But then I couldn't have had the horse," I reasoned. But I'm sure Nita noticed the redness in my cheeks.

"The other boys have horses. You could have used it one of them. I'm not going, so please tell Mrs. Bailey I have a headache."

Annoyed, I responded. "You're going,"

Nita said, "Not with you and your novio."

"Don't be ridiculous! Felipe is the judge and my school superintendent, and I am an American girl he thinks he has to take care of." She merely shrugged and, against all my persuasions, remained adamantly opposed.

Then she said, "You are a white girl, and I think he is becoming sweet on you and wants to be with you all the time."

"But, Nita," I said, "You and Marta both told me he is engaged to be married to Lucia! Is that not the truth?"

Nita laughed again. Doña just told us to tell you that so you would not be interested in Felipe. Think nothing of it.

Phil arrived shortly after with the horses and whistled at us to hurry up. When I came out alone, he asked where Nita was. I had to explain to him that she didn't want to come since it would just be her with him and me and that she wouldn't be comfortable. He just said, "Well, we have to go because I have to check on a pump that's irrigating some land a couple of miles down the valley."

It felt like I ended up sitting on a rock forever, just watching him check the water and the pump. As a result, we didn't arrive at the Bailey's until dusk. Hank and Mrs. Bailey greeted us, and when

I said hello to them, Mrs. Bailey said, "Please call me Elizabeth." I said I would, but Phil called her Liz. I don't think she thought too much of that, and the first thing she said to him was, "Philip, what are you doing here? We invited the girls to come out so we could have a girl talk."

Phil didn't hesitate a minute. "I didn't want them riding out here all alone. Besides, I had some work to do back up the valley a ways. Are we ready to eat?" He asked, without hesitation or an apology for being late.

Elizabeth just sighed and said, "Yes, it's ready."

We sat down to a lovely dinner of fried chicken, potatoes, and homemade rolls. After dinner, we visited. Soon, Elizabeth said, "Phil, you've been keeping pretty close attention to Gipsy here. You're not letting your company duties lag, are you?"

Without hesitating, Phil said, "Liz, no, and what I'm doing is none of your business. Besides, Gipsy is helping me with my accounting and reading and writing."

"Okay," Liz said, "Have you taught her all your Irish songs and dances yet?"

"Well, no. One of the reasons I wanted to come out here tonight is because you and Hank have that phonograph record player, and I want to show Gipsy some of the dances I taught you and Hank."

"Well," Liz said, "Let's get it going."

So, Hank got the player going, and right away, Phil jumped up and said, "Liz, get that "Whiskey in the Jar" record going or "The Wild Rover" or how about that "Molly Malone?" Come on, Gipsy, let me show you the Irish jig."

I said, "Wait a minute, Phil, I don't dance. I've never learned any dances."

"Well, shucks," he said and turned to Liz and said, "Come on girl, let's get that jig going." He grabbed her arm, swung her around and around, knocking over a side table, and whirled into the dining room where they had more space.

Pretty soon, the record ended, and Phil turned back the needle and said to me, "Gipsy, will you let me show you the Irish circle waltz." I tried to resist, but he swooped me up in his arms and said, "This is slow, Gipsy; it will be a good one for you to learn how much fun Irish music and dancing can be."

We slowly moved around the room while Liz and Hank smiled and soon joined us. I was nervous but soon got the gist of what Phil was doing, and as we moved around, I became more relaxed and was soon enjoying myself immensely.

Later, as the evening moved along and with some delicious cake that Liz had baked, we sat and visited about Phil's Irish heritage. He was so proud of his past and seemed to especially enjoy talking about his love for music and dance. He talked about the dances he likes—of course, the jig—but also the reel, the horn pipe, the Irish step dance, and many others.

After a bit of silence, he began to sing Irish jig. Pretty soon, Liz and Hank were singing along, and I couldn't help myself. Before long, I was even humming along with them. Later, he said, "I'll sing you one of my favorites, Gipsy," and he moved right into the melody of "Danny Boy."

He paused for just an instant, and I believe I detected a little moisture in his eyes, and he soon ended the song. But he quickly rushed over to the player and started another record. He came over and took my hand and said, "I think you'll like this one." And pretty soon, I was drifting along to "Over the Waves" with him.

Ten o'clock struck. I got up and said, "You know, I'm a working woman, and I must get to bed early." I reached for my coat, and Phil looked at me questioningly. I said, "It's getting late."

He laughed and said, "It's never late till midnight, and after that, it's early."

So, we thanked the Bailey's, gathered up Payaso and Flojo, and started for the village.

As we slowly rode our way up the valley, I felt invigorated. I had really enjoyed the evening, and I was enjoying the moon. It was full now, and the myriad of bright shining stars lighted our way, making the rugged horizon of the Baboquivari almost visible. The night was cool, but in such a refreshing way. I couldn't help but think of how much of Phil I had not let myself come to know. I had only seen stubbornness and arrogance, and with others, I had only seen demanding sternness, harshness, and impatience, but tonight, I learned he was compassionate, caring, and enjoyed being with people—and that he had a lively sense of humor and obviously loved music.

Soon we came to a gate, and he had to get down and open it. As Flojo walked through, he noticed something amiss with my saddle. After he closed the gate, he came over to check and noticed the cinch was loose. As he tightened it, he looked at the stirrups and said he had set them too long, and they needed to be shortened. I said that must explain why my legs hurt.

We continued in quiet conversation. It was easy to visit since Flojo was barely moving along. I thought surely he must be walking along in his sleep. I told Phil that I enjoyed watching him have such a good time that night and thanked him for teaching me how to do the dances. I also told him how much I enjoyed the Irish music.

He responded, "Well, I like to dance and sing, see? But all Irish folks are like that. Irish are about dancing and singing, just like we are about everything else. We're just good. We have rhythm in our bones."

"Oh my gosh," I said. "You Irish are just so wonderful! And so full of yourselves. When the time comes, you will probably sprout wings and fly up to heaven."

He looked shyly at me, and then we both laughed at that.

We rode along quietly for a while until I broke the silence and said to Phil, "I want to get a different horse. Flojo is too slow. He's gentle and easy to ride, but if you continue to take me on rides with you, I would like a horse with a little more life in him. Do you think there is something else at the ranch that Ramon will let me ride?"

"Listen here, girl," he said. "Don't you worry about Ramon. I'll get you a different horse. A nice horse that will keep up with Payaso here."

"Thank you," I said.

When we got to town, instead of going straight ahead to Nita's, he turned in toward the corrals. "I'll just put the horses up, and then we can walk over," he explained.

As I waited, I noticed the stars were bright out still, and the moon was full. It was late, but I had such a wonderful day I wasn't sure I was ready for it to end. When Phil came back, I wondered if he too may have come under the spell of the evening and seemed to have softened as we strolled along toward Nita's. Finally, at Nita's gate, he lingered as though he had something to say. I didn't know if I expected a "goodnight" or not, but instead, he awkwardly bent over to me and kissed me lightly on my lips. Then, he stood straight, smiled, and simply said, "Goodnight, Gipsy."

I went inside, and Nita was there standing and giggling like she did when something is funny to her. I looked at her, startled a bit because I knew my cheeks were flushed and that I was flustered by what had just happened. I asked Nita what she was laughing at.

She continued to giggle and said, "I see Felipe. He kiss you. Is he going to marry you?"

"Nita," I said, "I don't know. Good night. I'm going to bed."

And I did, but I couldn't sleep. What did that kiss mean? I couldn't understand. Yes, Phil had been showing more and more interest in me and what I was doing lately. And he had taught me to ride and had taken me on many trips to the country to visit his friends around the district. *What did it mean? How did it make me feel? Do I have romantic thoughts and feelings for this smart-aleck Irishman that maybe I don't know I have? Is the story of a romance with the Mexican girl Lucia just a lark, as Nita said?* I had so many questions! But when I finally rolled over and fell asleep, I dreamed of many pleasant places I had gone to and experienced with Phil in the past month and a half.

CHAPTER 8

As the days came and went, Phil continued to be a large part of my life. It seemed as though time was flying by. It was early October, and the large round-up was nearing completion over in Santa Cruz. Phil has only been a small part of that this year, but he has been out to the camps numerous times, taking supplies and mail on each trip when he can. Before the round-up started, Ramon had him start three young two-year-old colts, so they decided he should stay back and continue with the colts, only coming out to bring supplies.

He is as busy as ever with Company business, running the post office, and, most importantly, being the justice of the peace and judge over all legal issues. He continues to be stern, demanding, and, sometimes, harsh with the locals and visitors to the village. He has always been strict about enforcing the truancy laws or any laws. He takes all these positions he has very seriously. In fact, just recently, he appointed Nita's cousin, Felix, to be a truant officer. And his duties are to come to the school each morning and get a list of the absentees from me, go check on each one of them. and find out why they were absent or get them rounded up and back to school.

But, with me, he shows a new tenderness and interest in my teaching and my desire to paint, read, and write. And just a week or so ago, he brought me a new horse from the ranch. He had returned Flojo and brought a beautiful sorrel mare for me. He said she was a five-year-old quarter horse, and we were going to call her Molly. I asked him where that name came from, and he said, "She reminds me of the Irish song, "Molly Malone," that we danced to the last time we were at the Bailey's. She has that same spirit that I feel when I do that jig. She has a great spirit, but I think you and she will get along just great. But, for now, I feel better if you don't take her out without me along." *Ah ha,* I thought. *Without me along.*

For some time, he had been planning to take me out to see his mine near Ruby at the Montana Camp, and after school today, he said one of his friends, Billie Marteney, and his wife, wanted us to come by for a visit sometime so they can get to know me better. His place was about four miles up the east end of the cienega and about halfway up to Ruby, and he was thinking we could go to the mine and be back to their place for a bit. I said that sounded like a fun day.

"Okay," he said, "We'll get Payaso and your mare Molly out early and get on up there and see what kind of a big pile of silver I have."

Sunday, I was up before daybreak, excitedly anticipating the day's trip. Phil came with the horses, and we were on our way by sunup. As we rode up the trail and along the stage line road to Ruby, we passed the Noon ranch at Oro Blanco. Next to the size of the Company ranch, the Noon's is likely close to it.

The elder Dr. Noon had acquired several homesteads out here in the Oro Blanco area, and two of his sons, Arthur and Alonzo, took to the cattle business from the time they were youngsters. As I understood it, Arthur took care of the place west of the stage road toward the Fraguita mountains over that way, and Alonzo handled the operation to the east over toward Chimney Canyon. Phil said he had seen Arthur in the village a week or so ago, and he asked him to bring me by sometime soon. Phil said he told him that he would but didn't think we would have time today.

As we continued on, he told me about his claim. "You know a little about it already," he said. "The Mexican I bought it from, Luis Morales, had staked a claim to it sometime back and planned to file a homestead on the parcel with it. But he couldn't complete the filing, so I was able to get it at a good price with the help of Mr. Farrell, who ran the store at that time. So, I'm out very little. I only have about $50 in it so far, but I had to leave Luis a little share until we get our first load out since he has been doing all the digging so far. Since I haven't been out for some time, we'll just have to see what he's gotten done."

We left the main road and struck off across a dry arroyo and headed up into the oak-covered foothills.

"I expect I'll get it all back when I make the first shipment. If it shows up well, I may sell it, or I might just keep on working on it. But any way you look at it, I'll surely make a few thousand, a good nest egg for a married man, you just watch. And you'll be so happy! When The Company finds out that I'm making good money with the mine, they'll be afraid I might plan to leave and go out on my own. And, when they do, I'm going to make them come up with a sizable raise, maybe $10 a month. Then I'll be making $75 a month, plenty enough to be able to get married."

What was all this talk about marriage? I didn't understand. He just took the joy of the day away. I wanted to ask him to tell me what he was talking about, but maybe for fear he would tell me he had plans with Lucia or someone I didn't know about, I decided to change the subject and try to make the best of the rest of the day.

I saw a strange-looking bird run across the trail in front and asked, "What kind of bird is that, Phil?"

"Why that's a roadrunner. Why are you changing the subject?"

I responded, "Can we just get on up to your mine and get back home? I'm not feeling very well right now."

He looked at me strangely but said nothing.

After riding along for another few miles, we came around the bottom of a hill, and I looked up and saw what certainly had to be the prettiest mountain peak I had seen since arriving in Arivaca. Not nearly as awesome as Baboquivari in the Altar Valley, but undoubtedly as beautiful. Phil noticed I was struck by the site and stopped the horses and said, "Isn't Montana Peak a sight to behold?"

I just stared.

"So, this is the great Montana Peak that so many folks talk about?" I said, and my spirits began to pick up a bit. Phil went on to tell me that right around the corner was the mining camp. I'd heard people talk about the Montana camp. There were numerous homes, a couple of mills, and a lovely little lake used to provide water to the mills. At the base of the hill across from the mill was the shaft of his mine.

We rounded the hill and came to a tunnel on the side of a wash. He said, "Here it is!"

There was quite a dump of ore. We got off of the horses, and he said to follow him. We went into the tunnel maybe forty or fifty feet. It was fairly dark that far back, but Phil struck some matches and pointed out the yellow spots and shiny streaks on the rocky sides. His reaction was exciting. He said, "That is really rich. It should mill out at a very good percentage of minerals. I just hope it's silver or zinc. Probably not much chance any of it is gold."

He spent quite a bit of time picking over the dump and explaining to me, as best he could, what all the spots meant.

Soon after, we mounted up and rode back toward the village. As we rode along, his enthusiasm increased. I'm sure pleased with what we have there. It won't surprise me if there isn't a couple a thousand dollars, a good nest egg for a man just starting out. Along the way, he continued talking about his finances and his plans for the future.

"You know," he said, "It's just like Pap used to tell us kids; this America is a great place for a person to get a start on his own. Costs are pretty low now, and opportunities for homesteads around here are still good. Why, I would think, when we get that first shipment sold, I should be able to start looking for one. I think we'll go back down Chimney Canyon, where it comes into the upper end of the cienega, along with where Bartolo canyon and cedar creek all come together. There is a pretty little meadow down there at those headwaters.

"When the summer monsoons come down, water comes rushing out of these mountains like you can't believe. And that's how the valley down below and the village gets the water we have. Billie Marteney's place is down near there. Maybe we'll drop by and see him one day, but we don't have time today. I want to show you a place down there that would be a good place to have a home and a headquarters for a little cattle operation."

I said, "Phil, I don't want to see a place that you want. I just want to go back to the village. You took me to your mine today, and I've enjoyed the day, but now I'm tired and want to get back."

"But Gipsy, I want to show you this place because I have something important that I want to ask you."

"Well, I can't imagine what is important that you want to ask me?"

"Of course, you do, Gipsy. Just guess."

"I'm not in the mood for guessing games," I said.

An important question, I thought, as we rode down the trail and into the pretty little meadow. *What could he be talking about? Another mine to buy, a homestead, another job? (Was he going to move away?) Or was he going to tell me he was going to get married?* My stomach churned at the thought.

Soon, we came to a beautiful little grove of cottonwood trees with a little trickle of water running through the meadow. It was the end of the rainy season, and the monsoon waters had passed through some time ago. We stopped, and he said, "Why don't we rest the horses for a while?" We got down, and he put one of the saddle blankets down so we would have something comfortable to sit on while he asked me his important question.

When he knew I was comfortable, he reached into his coat pocket and removed a piece of paper that looked like a letter. He said, "I have a letter here I received from your Pap the other day. I want to read it to you."

"What in the world is my daddy writing to you for?" I said.

"Just listen, and you'll understand."

It was addressed to:
Mr. P. M. Clarke
Arivaca, Arizona

My Dear Sir,

Your highly appreciated letter has been received. Your request is a hard one to grant, but Gipsy is of age, and I suppose you are too, so you have mine and my wife's consent. We think Gipsy will make you a good wife and hope you will be true to her and be a good husband to her. May the blessings of the all-wise God be with you both all through a long life and make you both happy and prosperous.

I am glad you wrote to me and hope you will write often. Please come and see us soon. God bless you and Gipsy.

Yours truly,

A. C. Harper

He looked at me with this big smile on his face and asked, "What do you think? About you and me getting married?"

I just stared at him. I was startled. I was puzzled and unbelieving.

"What's the matter, Gipsy?" he asked.

"Wh–what are you saying? What are you asking me?"

"I'm asking you to marry me. I don't have much money yet, but if the mine comes through, we will have a nice little nest egg to get started. In a few years, I know we can have our own ranch, maybe right here in this meadow. Would you like that?"

"I don't know," I stalled. I tried adjusting to the fact that he had just proposed to me. That he had asked permission from my father without ever saying anything to me. It just didn't make any sense.

"I know this is kind of sudden," he said as he interrupted my thoughts. "We've only known each other for a couple of months, but out here, that can be considered a long time or enough time. And right now, you know me as well as you'll ever know me. So, will you marry me?"

"Phil, you have never told me that you love me and never asked me if I love you! Knowing the depth of love between two people has to come first. Marriage can't come until that is surely in place."

"Gipsy, from the day I rode up to the stagecoach, and you came out onto the wheel, I knew there would be love for us, and when our eyes met, I knew you felt the same. I'm sorry, Gipsy, I've just never been one to show my affection very well outwardly, and maybe the same goes for you because you have never told me you loved me either. But, Gipsy, I do love you, and I will be a good husband to you, and when we have children, I will be a good father to them. And I know you love me, and I hope you will say yes to me."

"But why did you write to my father? They barely know that we even know each other!"

"Because my pap told me many times when I was young and growing up that when I met the girl I wanted to marry, I needed to ask her father for his permission. Gipsy, I just wanted to be sure your mama and papa would say yes before I asked you."

"Well, Phil, I do love you, and yes, I want to be your wife."

He took me in his arms, hugged me close, then kissed me like I had not been kissed before.

The sun was setting as we started back to the village. The moon began rising over the eastern mountain tops, and the stars were sparkling in the darkening sky. It was a beautiful night, cool and fresh and mystic. Its magic and charm swept over me. I thought, *It is November 12th, 1910. I'll be a married woman to a wonderful man in a wild, beautiful, and mysterious country, "Out Yonder!"*

We planned the wedding for December 28, at a time when the school would be closed for the holidays, and it would also be on my birthday. Our lives could hardly be moving forward with any normalcy.

To my great surprise, word of our pending marriage spread rapidly throughout the entire district. We heard from the Kane's and Gardner's from clear over in the Patagonia area. The Boices from the Empire in the Sonoita Valley, and the Kings up in the north end of the Altar Valley. And, of course, Nonie and the rest of the gang from Tucson. And I just couldn't believe the excitement from throughout the village. Doña Josefa, Anita, Marta, and even Lucia, along with my good friend, Nita, scurried around daily, making plans for a grand celebration and fiesta.

Soon, I became overwhelmed with so many things that needed doing. But, of course, the first thing I did was write home to all the sisters and Mama and Papa. Soon, I was deluged with letters of congratulations and excitement.

Unfortunately, since the date was set during the holidays, it looked like none of the family would be able to attend, so I asked my big sister to send my books and pictures. Within two weeks, boxes began to arrive on the stage. There was everything I had ever collected—my old magazines, letters, my paintings, stories, and poems I had written. Everything. Six or seven of us spent half the night unpacking them in the little room behind the office where we would make our home.

One day, soon after we started making plans, Phil stopped helping with the unpacking and went into the office to sort through the mail, cancel the outgoing letters and packages, and get the mail bags ready for Lupe in the morning. I was placing books and trinkets on a shelf when he came rushing into the room with sure anger on his face and a letter in his hand. He stopped in front of me and stared before asking, "What is this letter you've written to Billie Pryce?"

"Phil, I told you a week ago I was going to resign if you and the school board didn't get this school cleaned up and get the supplies that I have been asking for two months. And furthermore, you have ignored my request to get that stove operating. I can't teach these kids in a room that's freezing. So this letter is to advise Mr. Pryce that I am planning to leave after the holidays in order to give him or you or Nonie sufficient time to find a replacement."

He tore the letter in half and threw it on the floor. Then, as he turned to leave, he said, "You can't quit. It's impossible to find a teacher this time of year. Forget about that idea." But before he left, I calmly said, "Phil, I mean this, and I will send another letter to Dr. Ball, the other member of the board, and I'll hand-deliver a copy to Mr. Pryce when he comes out for Thanksgiving."

I was hanging pictures a little later when he came in again. He was a bit sullen but calm and said, "Gipsy, you have to teach! We are going to need the money you earn."

"Phil," I said, "I love teaching these kids, but I'm not going to do it any longer under these conditions. Besides, you said we are going to have a nice nest egg when the ore sells. And, you know, I had all my painting and photography materials sent to me so I can start doing photography again."

He said, "Gipsy, I'll talk to the board, but please don't send those letters."

I couldn't believe he actually said please, so I said, "Okay, we'll see."

He smiled a little and turned and left.

The next afternoon he sent word that the stove was installed and that he had managed to find enough pipe to complete the installation. When I arrived at the school the following day, there was a nice fire in the stove with a pile of wood beside it.

The next day the stage brought windowpanes, materials to repair the siding, and paints of different colors. We all pitched in, washed and polished windows, and put up bright print curtains from the material he had found in the store. And the next day, the stage arrived with books, chalk, pencils, crayons, and all the other supplies I had been asking for. It was all so exciting.

On the top of the blackboard, I drew a border of turkey gobblers for Thanksgiving. In a vase on my desk, I placed a bouquet of cattails that I had gathered at the creek. The village was full of excitement. The kids were laughing and playing like I hadn't seen from them before. It was a joyous time, especially with Thanksgiving and Christmas coming just around the corner. And, best of all, Phil was the happiest and most excited I had seen him since the evening he had proposed.

CHAPTER 9

We were so busy with Thanksgiving just around the corner. It was only about ten days away, and Christmas was soon after. And we were amidst all the hustle and bustle of our wedding plans.

A day or so later, Phil came into the school to tell me our plans to have Thanksgiving at the store wouldn't work out. There were going to be too many people, and we didn't have room. He thought we should take the Baileys up on their invitation. Hank had said that almost everybody who was coming to town to our place would surely be coming go to their place. I agreed. We had so much going on. It would be better to go there.

The plan for Thanksgiving quickly changed from our little place in the store to the Bailey's, and all our friends would also be going there. There was much excitement from everybody with preparations for the festive day coming in just a week. I prepared my special potatoes and baked my special, very popular bread loaves. I told Phil that we couldn't ride the horses with all this food to take. He said not to worry. He had made arrangements with the ranch for us to use one of the buggies with a pair of the trotters. We could make better time with them, and the ride would be much smoother.

Thanksgiving day arrived, and we headed for the Bailey's. It was a beautiful fall day. The sun was out, the sky was bright, and we were just as happy as we could be. Jack and Ples and even Uncle Beanie were there. And Dr. Ball and his nephew Andrew were there as well. Later, even Johnnie Barnes came out for a while.

All told, it was a great day. We had a wonderful dinner, and after a dessert of pumpkin pie and other sweets, Hank got up and suggested a toast to our recent engagement with a glass of wine. Everybody got up and cheered with excitement, and of course, we got the phonograph going.

Phil and Liz started it off with Phil's jigs and the other Irish dances, the hornpipe, and the slip jig. After slowing things down a bit, he got me up, and we got into the Ceili (pronounced, Kay-lee), which is a traditional Irish dance that resembles the famous fox trot that many locals do when dancing. After many of the folks got into the dance festivities, Phil taught us the circle waltz. He said it is one of the most popular slow dances in Ireland and resembles the waltz Americans often dance to.

Soon the day and evening wound down, and the guests began to leave. We, too, said good night and got started back to town.

Soon, we were all back to our daily routines. I was back to school with the kids and Phil with his ongoing responsibilities with the town and the ranch. I, however, was quickly turning my attention more toward preparations for our wedding and establishing a home and life with Phil.

I sent home for additional things needed to create a nice home. I asked my sister Nannie to shop for some nice household items, like linens from stores in Houston and materials I could make curtains with, and to send some of Mama's nice dishes and silverware if she would let me have them.

One day in early December, Phil came to my room to tell me Nonie and the gang would be coming out in the next few days for what they called their annual ranch meeting. He said what it really amounted to was Nonie coming out to strut around the ranch and village and be important for a few days. But he said he would bring Mary Neal, his fiancée, with him because he wanted her to meet me, and he had heard of our plans.

In a few days, Nonie arrived in his machine, the same one I had seen him in when he came to hire me at the teacher's agency in Los

Angeles just three months earlier. Not only did Nonie and Mary Neal come out, but right behind him was another machine carrying Mr. Pryce, the superintendent of the school board. There were also some young people who I later learned were students from the university and friends of Mary's.

Phil brought them to the school to see how things were going with the new teacher. Mr. Bernard, as I knew him, said hello to me and asked how things were. I was a bit embarrassed since I had not seen or talked to him since the day when I was hired. But I said that things were going fine. He asked about the students and how that was working out. I told him we were doing fine.

We had about sixty-five kids in class almost every day, and they were learning English. I was learning Spanish, and we seemed to be getting along well. They were learning to sing many songs, mainly from memorizing the verses from the art readers I had ordered to help them, and they're also learning to recite the alphabet and do the arithmetic numbers. I asked if he would like to hear them sing one or two of their songs. Mary said she would, and Nonie agreed. So, we sang a couple of songs that they were the most comfortable with, and Nonie and Mary seemed to enjoy it. After singing, I suggested we have a recess, so the kids were excused for a time. Then, with excellent behavior, the children formed their lines and marched out. And was I relieved!

The group then came up to me to visit. Nonie commented that he was very impressed, and Mary asked, "How in the world do you do it? I think it's wonderful to think what you have accomplished when they don't speak hardly a word of English!"

I thanked her, and Nonie agreed with her.

Before leaving, Nonie mentioned he was aware that Phil and I were to be married and that he understood it would take place in Tucson at the end of December. I acknowledged that was correct. He said, "Excellent. We will plan a festive reception in your honor."

I blushed a little and tried to tell him we didn't want that. I simply said we would be coming home shortly after, and he responded, "Nonsense, we will arrange for a wonderful time. And congratulations,

Gipsy. You have done a wonderful job here, and we are so glad how things are working out."

Shortly after they left, Mr. Pryce came in and asked if he might be able to speak with me for a short time. I said, "Of course."

We sat down in the small student chairs. He said he wanted to discuss how things have progressed. I merely nodded my head, not knowing where he might be going with this. He continued, "I'm sorry it took us so long to get your school restocked with supplies and the materials you have been requesting since you arrived.

"To explain a little, Philip has been hounding me since you arrived, but I've just had to keep telling him we didn't have those things budgeted for this school for this year. And, just recently, he told me—in no uncertain terms, I might add—that we better get this school what you need.

"Gipsy, we are pleased with what you have been able to do, and now with the supplies you asked for, we hope you will continue to teach for us. The board has authorized me to offer you $10 more each month for you to do that."

I was a bit flustered by that, since just a week before, I had told Phil I was resigning. I smiled at Mr. Pryce, thanked him, and told him briefly how I enjoyed working with these kids. He said, "Congratulations to you and Philip," and got up to leave. He turned back then said, "I hope to see you in Tucson."

Over the next couple of weeks, we continued planning and preparing for the wedding. The 28th would be on a Wednesday, Christmas on Sunday, and we decided we would go to Tucson on Monday the 26th and return right after the service since the entire village was making plans for a festival of sorts for us. And, of course, Phil didn't want to miss a festival.

But, first, we had Christmas ahead of us, and it was coming up fast. So, I suggested to Phil we take a buggy and go up in the hills near the mine and cut a tree for our soon-to-be home. He thought that would be a good idea.

A few days later, we took off for the Ruby area. We went up to the mine and saw what looked like a good-sized pile of new diggings ready to go to the mill. I asked Phil if he had any response to the first load he had sent out. He said he hadn't but should know by the time we get back from Tucson.

We looked around the hillsides for a while until we found a perfect tree. It might have been more oak than evergreen, but we didn't care. It was our first tree, and it was perfect for us.

When we got back, we set it up in what would become our front room, the nearest room connecting our home to the office and store in front. I had collected ribbons from the store and flowers from down at the creek, making little decorations for our tree. And the folks from Doña's cantina across the street sent Nita over with more Mexican decorations.

When we were done, we had the little place all fixed up and ready for a merry Christmas. Christmas came and went so fast, but we did have time to go out to the Jarrillas' and eat with the boys and Barnes. One evening, Doña Josepha invited us to the saloon for a genuine Mexican fiesta. We had tamales and enchiladas and Chile con carne, along with fresh, homemade menudo and tortillas. I came to love a Mexican soup called albondigas, which was meatballs with rice and potatoes combined with cilantro and mint sprigs, a specialty that Doña made especially for us, she told Phil and giggled her silly laugh. Over the years, it became a favorite of the whole family and expected by all.

Sunday, Christmas Day, was an exciting time. Nita had been helping me knit and crochet a sweater for Phil, and he was very excited when I gave it to him as he was not expecting anything.

A few days before Christmas, Phil and Luis had gone up to the mine. They were to check on getting a pile of ore shipped that we had seen lying on the ground outside the tunnel. He also went up there to check on an old miners' cabin that had been deserted with stuff left behind. When he arrived back at the village that evening, he had one of the buggies and one of the boys from across the street at the door with him to help unload my Christmas gift. In they came with this antique buffet chest and bookcase thing.

He set it down and said, "Gipsy, open it up."

I opened one of the doors to a group of bookshelves full of old books of knowledge.

He said, "Gip, these are encyclopedias. You can use them in school to help the kids, and you can use them for you, too, because you like to read as much as you do."

"These books are a hundred years old, Phil, but I'll use them in the school, anyway. The kids won't know. Thank you for thinking of something for me."

Next, he came over and hugged me and gave me a little kiss, and said "Merry Christmas, Gip."

I said, "Is that what it's going to be now? Gip?"

"Only so you know I love you."

The next day, the 26th, we were ready for the trip to town. School was out for the next week, and Phil had arranged to have the store covered for a couple of days with The Company. Pedro was to bring a buggy with the trotters to take us to the train at Amado, which we would ride into Tucson.

We drove to the junction at the Kingsley's ranch near Amado and stopped at the halfway station to have breakfast at Señora Angelita's. She served us an excellent breakfast of machaca and huevos with tortillas with plenty of hot coffee. It was just what we needed after riding in the buggy facing into the freezing wind all the way from Arivaca.

After breakfast, Pedro drove us to the railroad, about a mile down the road. There was no station, but the train slowed and stopped when he saw us waiting. After only about a two-hour ride, we arrived In Tucson. How exciting! The town was very different from when I saw it in September. The streets were all decorated for the holidays. There were people everywhere, walking, riding horseback, driving buggies, and even a few machines driving around stirring up dust everywhere.

As we stepped down from the train, Phil took my arm to walk us to our hotel, but about then, Nonie and Mary drove up in the machine and said, "Jump in. We'll take you to your hotel."

He had made arrangements for us to stay at the new Santa Rita Hotel. The Santa Rita was recognized as the fanciest and most upscale in town, even more so than the older Pioneer Hotel around the corner and down the street near Congress Street.

We checked in and went to our room. Even though it was just mid-day, I was exhausted, and I believe Phil saw that because he said, "I have some company business to discuss with Nonie and Harry. Harry is the Company secretary. Why don't you stay here and try to get some rest? In a little while, I'll be back, and we can go down the street to do some of the shopping we have planned to do while we're here. And after that, I'll take you to a nice dinner and the show we planned to see."

I thanked him for the thought and took great advantage of that, for I ended up falling fast asleep for more than two hours.

About mid-afternoon, Phil arrived back and suggested we go to Steinfeld's department store. If we could find some furniture we like, we might be able to get it out on that day's freight. We found some nice chairs and a fine sofa and made our purchase.

The next order of business was exciting. We were going to find a lovely dress for my wedding gown. We left Steinfeld's and went to Kitt's dress shop. After looking at many styles and colors, I chose a beautiful pale blue satin dress with a corsage of lilies of the valley.

The last order of business for the day would be to go to the courthouse and get our license. After we secured the license, we walked down the street back to the hotel, where we changed into some evening clothes to go out to dinner. We enjoyed a treat for both of us for dinner and ate at a very nice Chinese restaurant on Congress and 6th Street.

Afterward, we went to see "Mrs. Wiggs of the cabbage patch." Phil laughed and laughed, especially when Mary Robinson blew her nose on her apron. I was more interested in the audience and what the women were wearing. I was amazed how styles seemed to change so much in the short time I had been away from city folks. Pompadours seemed to be going out of fashion, and lower necklines coming in. I seemed to be the only woman with a high-neck-lined dress on. But it was a happy time, and Phil surely didn't notice those kinds of things anyway, so I didn't mind so much.

The next day was to be somewhat quiet for us. Just a few last-minute items to take care of. Additionally, the boys from the Jarrillas and some of the people from the Company office had planned a luncheon for us at the Old Pueblo Club as a little pre-wedding festivity. It was very lovely.

Phil knew I wanted to go to the university campus to see what it looked like. He said he had told Mary of my interest and that she would come to the hotel to pick me up. I said that would be very nice, but asked if he'd be coming along. He said he couldn't because he had some business to take care of.

Mary and I had a great time that afternoon. We drove the machine out to the campus, parked, and walked around the big building they called "Old Main." What a beautiful building, almost out there in the middle of the desert, it seemed, even though it was only about five miles from downtown.

That night, we had dinner in the hotel restaurant and were joined by Nonie, Mary, and a few folks from the village who had come to town for our wedding. The evening was over early for me since the wedding was to take place early in the morning. For Phil, his night went a bit later, visiting and drinking with all the folks who had come.

Hank and Liz came to the hotel for us around 8:00, and we all rode together toward the church, although it was more of a cathedral. We were going to be married in the chapel of the Saint Augustine Cathedral, a Catholic church.

I turned to Phil and said, "We never discussed getting married in a Catholic church. You know, I'm not Catholic, I'm a devout Southern Baptist, and our beliefs are sometimes quite different, especially about raising children."

"I know," he said, "And Gipsy, I wanted to talk about this, but I just don't think it will be a serious issue for us."

"Well," I said, "as long as you know that I will not raise our children as Catholics."

"I know, I know Gipsy. I don't expect to, but this priest will ask you if you are, and you need to say yes, or he won't marry us. Can you do that?"

"Phil, I will do that, but we will not raise our children in the Catholic church."

I heard Phil sighed in relief, and I had to chuckle to myself.

"Well, then," he said, "I guess we're all set for the wedding. Drive on to the cathedral, Hank, and let's get this marriage started with a bang. When we get there, I'll go see the priest and let him know we have discussed this."

Except for Phil, we all went into the chapel and waited. We sat in that little chapel for some time before the Father and Phil came in from an inner room. I hardly recognized Phil. He was wearing a beautiful dark suit with a stiff white collar and a bright blue satin bow tie, the same color as my dress. He had a bright smile, though I could tell he was quite nervous. And the same applied to Hank, Phil's best man, and Jack and Ples, his attendants. They all looked like they had never been to a wedding before. They had very melancholy looks on their faces without smiles.

I looked at Liz as we walked to the altar, and she had a sweet and pleasant smile on her face. When we arrived, and I stood beside Phil, he winked at me and smiled. I tried to smile back, but as I stood there next to him and the priest opened his book, everything around me blurred, and my legs shook like I had never seen before.

As the priest read the words of the ceremony and asked questions, I couldn't seem to hear him; my lips just moved like I had no control over them. In an instant, it seemed, I heard Phil say, "I do," and the Father asked me, "Gipsy Harper, do you take this man, Philip Clarke, to be your wedded husband for better or worse till death do you part?" And, my lips said, "I do!"

Then I heard the priest ask Hank if he had the ring. Hank reached into his jacket pocket and handed a gold band to Phil. The priest instructed Phil to place it on my finger. When he took my finger, I looked down and saw the most beautiful gold band I had ever seen. Now I knew what his important business was yesterday. He placed the ring on my finger, and the priest said, "You can now kiss the bride."

He kissed me and said, "Hello, Mrs. Clarke."

Outside, we got into Bailey's car, avoiding another one the boys had decorated with tin cans and ribbons, and headed back to the hotel. The Company had planned to have a little brunch for all who had come from town and from the district. It seemed like hundreds were there but there were probably only twenty or so. All in all, it was a very merry time.

Shortly after noon, we went to the train station. We had planned to return to the village that day, right after the service. On our way, I noticed the crowds were joyous and merry. A festive air hung over the town, gorgeous in Christmas tinsel, lights, and other decorations. The train left Tucson at about 1:00.

As we rolled along, beside the Santa Cruz River, past the San Xavier Mission, and toward Amado, the day was a blur. It was just a happy time for us, and as we neared Amado, Phil started talking about all the plans he had in his mind. It was an excitement I enjoyed in him throughout all the years together. Pedro was right on time and waiting with the buggy and trotters.

We arrived at the village near dusk, and when the town would usually be settling down for the night, it was abuzz with excitement. Quickly, I remembered that Nita had said there was going to be a festival when we returned, but I had completely forgotten.

I asked Phil if he knew something was in the air or if he remembered people saying there would be some kind of greeting when we returned. He said, "Well, yes, Gip. It's kind of a surprise for us, but I knew what they were up to before we left. I thought I would just let it still be a surprise for you on your birthday. Let's get our grip inside our new home and help all these people get this party started."

We had a marvelous evening. The mariachis were playing, everyone was dancing and eating massive amounts of different kinds of food, and all of our friends were there, from all over the district. I didn't know how all the company folks, the Jarrillas boys, and our other friends got back to the village before us until Uncle Beanie told me that Nonie had gathered up a couple of auto machines for them so they all could be back in time. They had left Tucson right after the service.

By the time midnight finally rolled around, I was so tired I told Phil I had to go to bed. I asked if he was coming with me, but he said, "You go on ahead and get yourself all situated and comfortable, and I'll be along soon."

I laid in bed waiting for him, but after a couple of hours listening to the mariachis and all the hoo-ha from the cantina, I fell asleep. I didn't hear Phil come in, but at 5:00 the following day, he was up and getting breakfast. I struggled up and tried to get myself as presentable as possible because I heard other voices coming from the kitchen.

When I got to the kitchen, Phil had breakfast ready for us and a half a dozen cowboys from The Company. He had to get the store opened so he could get these cowboys' tobacco and supplies before they headed up to the upper range.

CHAPTER 10

As the days passed, our lives continued much like they were before we got married. We had pretty much gotten our home organized and established as we wanted it. Phil, of course, continued his jobs as storekeeper, postmaster, school superintendent, justice of the peace, and all the other jobs taking care of the village's needs.

I continued to teach, as I had assured Phil and Mr. Pryce I would. I also had opportunities to get my paints, books, and photography materials out. It wasn't long before I was getting Molly out on my own and going into the hills with my colors. Often, I would find a spot to sit and paint a little scene.

Phil and I began to have more opportunities to spend time with our circle of friends from all around the land. I enjoy it so much that our friends were a mix of the Anglo folks and Mexicans from the village and the many ranches around.

I sometimes think back to the days when I was much younger and imagined that when I got married, it would be almost solely and simply from the standpoint of love, and everything else would naturally be perfect. But, as time has passed, I am learning that marriage is likely the most complicated partnership on earth.

Most interesting for me is that Phil had definite plans for a successful life for us. He is very driven and determined to succeed. He expects me to be his partner in this journey. Success to him is money, and the way to attain that is through hard work, sacrifice, and education, mainly through experience. To that end, he was relentless in his drive.

He soon learned my role in this partnership would be limited. I was driven, too, with goals and interests of my own. The more he drove, the more I learned about my own drive and determination. Later, I realized that if I had not married him, I probably never would have known it. In the beginning, meeting his expectations and matching his drive were difficult, and at times, I was tired from the effort. But the discovery was good for me and for us and likely defined what our relationship would become.

As the days moved on, Phil became more committed to his education. He continued his correspondence law courses through the LaSalle Law School and was soon moving into more advanced classes.

One day, an old friend from Tucson brought him a set of law books he had found for sale at the University. He began taking more advanced courses, and as he received his exam results, he wasn't surprised that nearly every one of them were perfect scores. As I read through his exam results, I was always amazed at the accuracy of his answers. It was as though he had personally experienced each of the scenarios presented on each exam.

It was interesting that nights when he needed to work on his class studies, and he was working on an exam or writing a paper on some subject, he wanted me beside him to help him with his spelling, or his numbers when he was doing accounting work. And this was very flattering to me until I found out that while he was working on a project and I was sitting next to him reading a book or magazine, I was actually annoying him when turning pages or otherwise interrupting his concentration.

I enjoyed sitting next to him and helping him, but when he was alone, I would sit and read and often hum songs I enjoyed. Once, when he expressed his irritation, I got up to leave, and he said, "Where are you going"? When I said I was going to go to bed, he said, "Well, won't you wait for me?" So, I waited, believing that I really was making myself helpful to him.

One evening, we were reading, and he got up and went through some shelves and came to a book with a poetry collection. "Oh, look here. Here's that poem you told me about." And he read the poem.

That seemed to be the beginning of us seriously reading together. Phil liked poems. He always said he liked the rhythm of how a verse tells its story. So some evenings when he was in a particularly good frame of mind, he'd read for an hour or so and then get up and move into the office and read a bit more before starting on his law books.

One of Phil's ideas of success was to have a good home with plenty to eat and lots of friends to enjoy it with us. So our dining room became an extension of the post office, which already was a gathering place for all who came to the store.

When we started having invitational dinners, it called for much preparation. We began by having one with the Jarrillas boys. Beanie took it upon himself to help me with the cooking and see to it that the table was set correctly. Almost helpless with his stiff leg and cane, he hobbled about doing everything with one hand. He liked to wear my big old, checked apron and mimic me. My big sister, Bert, had made the apron full in hopes I would get pregnant. Though I had been married only two months, Beanie protruded his skinny little body as he strutted about pretending that I was.

Phil was anxious about our first company dinner and wanted it to be successful. We had to have everything from soup to ice cream and everything in between. He had Pedro bring up ice from a water trough to pack around the ice cream freezer he had borrowed from the Baileys. We were turning it when Barnes, Jack, and Ples arrived from the ranch, and they took the turning off of our hands.

It turned out to be a wonderful evening. The dinner included a huge roast that I had fixed with my special mashed potatoes and homemade baked bread that everybody in the district thought was the best they'd ever had. After dinner, we had dessert with the ice cream and a sweet potato pie I had made. It was deliciously spiced with cloves, lemon peel, and everything nice.

Phil took a bite and said, "Well, this is just great, but what is it?"

I answered, "This is sweet potato pie," and Phil said, "Well, where on earth did you ever hear of it?"

I said, "In one of those magazines that I get."

He responded that he had never had sweet potato pie in his life, but it was delicious.

After dinner, we cleaned up the kitchen. Most of the folks stayed around for a while and visited and laughed and talked about how good the dinner was. Phil asked all the boys to take a look around the room so he could show them my paintings, even though they were just kind of elementary imitations of simple landscapes and still lifes.

"Betcha didn't know my wife could paint, did ya? Just look at that. You wouldn't believe she did it, would you?"

"Please, Phil," I'd whisper.

One of them asked, "Where's that scene?"

"Well," I said, "That's up at the top of the hill going toward Tucson. I went up there one day, sat down overlooking that stock water tank, looked over at that beautiful view of Baboquivari Peak, and decided to paint it. You recognize it now?"

"Yes," they all said, "That's beautiful."

I said, "Thanks. It's one of my first paintings."

However, later in life, it would become one of the more favorites of all the ones I did.

After a bit, Beanie whispered in my ear, "Phil sure is proud of you, and he said people all over know he is."

It was interesting that every time we had company after that, he went through the same procedure of showing them all of my pictures and paintings. It was so amazing to me.

One day, Nita and I took a walk down to the creek. She stopped and said, "Gipsy, isn't this country so pretty? We have all these beautiful cottonwood trees, and the creek is always so peaceful. I love coming down here."

And in an instant, a thought came to me. "Nita," I said, "Why don't you just sit here a little? I'm going to run back to the school and get my picture-shooting camera and get some pictures of this."

Soon, I was back, and I had the camera set up. I took some pictures of Nita by the creek under the trees. And later, when we were back in the village, I took snaps of people scurrying up and down the street and old Viejo asleep next to the barrel.

It turned out that taking pictures of the village and all the people was a big treat to everybody because when I began the developing process, all the Doña's household and saloon wanted to watch. They would come around and squat to watch this marvel of a picture appearing on the glass when I took it from the liquid.

Some days later, toward the end of March, Phil was in the post office doing his daily chore of sorting and distributing the mail to the folks with the crowd milling around waiting for theirs, as they usually did. Phil had been expecting the results from the mill, with the results of the ore shipment he had sent some weeks before. All the mail had been distributed, and the crowd in the post office was gone. When the customers in the store were taken care of; Phil returned to the office and sat on the edge of the desk.

"Did you get what you were looking for?" I asked. He got a little smile on his face, not a big, happy smile, and he seemed a little subdued. He looked at me and said, "Ah, yes, Gip. We got the results back, and we made a little money on that first shipment."

"Well, isn't that wonderful," I responded.

He agreed and explained to me what it meant. He said, "As you know, I thought we would make a couple a thousand dollars maybe and get our little nest egg started, but it didn't do that well. However, we did make a few hundred dollars, and I'm able to pay Luis and get my investment back. And if we put it away for later, I'm sure it won't be long before we'll be able to get our own place. But I think maybe I should sell it and give up mining. What do you think?"

"Well, I don't know anything about mining, but there are a lot of people around here mining and making it work."

He said, "Yes, but mining is a big gamble, and a lot of those folks don't survive, and I don't want to risk what we have now and hurt our chance for our own place."

I said, "Phil. It's okay. We don't have to make it all in one shipment. Maybe after a couple more, we'll be able to have enough."

"Yeah, okay," he said, "I'll tell Luis to keep digging!"

"You're through with the kids and school for today, ain't you? What ya say? Shall we take a little buggy ride out toward Dr. Balls' place."

"Okay," I said.

As we rode along, Phil was more subdued than when he told me about the mine, and I thought that maybe he really wanted to sell it more than he said.

"Phil, you really are not yourself right now. Do you want to sell the mine?"

"No, Gipsy!"

He pulled the buggy over under a cottonwood tree and stopped. "Gipsy, I got a letter from my mam today. My pap was killed in a wreck back on the fourth. Said there had been some ongoing trouble between the livery companies and the new auto taxi companies about who has rights of way on the streets nowadays. And Pap and others have been putting up a fuss over these taxi drivers scaring up the horses and causing problems on the streets. She says on that day, a taxi driver swerved to miss another hack and ran into Pap's horses, and his carriage flipped and fell on him, killing him right there. Even had to put the horses down. He didn't have any passengers then, so that was good."

That was such a shock. Phil hadn't seen his family for years, but I knew he loved his pap a great deal, and I knew he felt just as I would if it had been my daddy.

"Phil, I'm so sorry! What can we do?"

He was quiet for some time, then he turned to me and gave me a big hug and said, "I don't believe there's anything that can be done. It's near April, and that was nearly a month ago. I'll send my mam a letter and thank her for letting us know."

We sat there for some time without saying much. My mood had warped into sadness, but the brightness caught my eye as I looked to the west. I said, "Phil, look. There's a bright glow on our magnificent Baboquivari Peak. Things will be okay. Do you think you want to go to New York?"

"No," he said, "I have you here, and Mam has all the family there. We have to get ourselves a ranch!" With that, he turned the buggy, and back to the village we went.

As we drove back to town, he seemed to perk up a bit, as though he had just experienced a revelation of some sort. He talked again about his hopes and plans and dreams for us, as he has said so many times before, "This is a land with great opportunity, and as I've said before, we work hard and get smarter, so we can go far here. The mountains are beautiful, the air is fresh, and the grasses across the hills can't be matched when it rains.

"There are mines and cattle in this country. Mining is the quickest way to make it, but it's risky. The cattle business is the surest way, and I like it much better. I know we both want to live here, so this is where we'll make our money. We'll get us a homestead real soon. We both have good jobs, and we make good salaries. If we save up to $10 a month, why in less than two years, we can get our own place and buy a few cows."

A few days later, we were in the office, and he got out maps, showed me the forest reservation, and pointed out springs and streams, mountain ranges, and mining camps all over the district. He showed me where the state lands lay and where the patented lands were, and lands available for homesteading are. Then we sat, and he started drawing designs for a branding iron, and we talked about possible names for our ranch.

"So many opportunities around here," he said again as he smiled. And I, too, smiled. It was so exciting to think that one day we might achieve the goals he had planned.

He was glad when Sundays came because he could close the store, get on his horse, and ride away. If he stayed home, someone, usually one of the Company people, would always knock on the door and ask him to open the store so they could get a can of tobacco or some matches or some other trivial little thing.

So, he'd get on his horse and ride as far as he could go. Sometimes, he took me, but often, he went alone so he could ride faster and farther and seek a place where we might be able to homestead.

Once, he found a possible location. He returned and said, "You never saw such land. It's rolling hills with waving grass and a dam full of water that some mining company just left. It even has a shack built for somebody to live in. In two years, we ought to have enough money saved to move up there and buy a few cows."

I was enthusiastic. If there was water, we could raise vegetables, corn, and beans and have a lovely garden, and we could have a milk cow and chickens and eggs. We'd get along just fine until our cows calved.

We talked about it for days and days. Two years seemed like a long time to wait, so he said, "Well, why don't we try it next year? We could move up there in the summer, and in the winter, you could come down here and teach the school and stay at the hotel and then go up on weekends. It's a pretty tough trail up to it from here, but then we expected some hardships, and it's only about five miles up toward Ruby."

"Well," I said, "It wouldn't be such a good idea if I should happen to have a baby. He looked at me kind of funny, but said that in that case, we'd have to think of something else. He could take Pedro up there to watch the place on weekends, so he could come down here and be with me.

"Well, Phil, hold on to your hat because I believe I'm pregnant," I said.

"Oh my gosh," he said. And he jumped up and down and laughed and hooped and hollered. "This is so exciting, Gipsy. Tell me more! When? Are you sure?"

"Okay, Phil, settled down. I believe it should be due about the middle of November."

We talked, and we figured, and we dreamed. He was so excited we almost stopped talking about the land.

One day, Jack came in on mail day and said, "Guess what? I'm homesteading the Tanque Verde range. I'm putting that young rodeo cowboy and his wife from over near the Atascosas in that little shack to live there and prove up on it. Then I'm going to move them out in a year or so or buy them out. Do you think that's a smart thing to do?"

Phil and I stared at him in disbelief. We couldn't speak. That was our spot. That's the piece of land that we were going to homestead.

I said to Phil, "What are we going to do? That's our land."

And he said, "That's right, but we didn't claim it. And, shoot, why didn't we think of doing that same thing? I don't know about Jack. It'll cost a lot of money to prove up on that land, and getting the title and buying it from that cowboy is a way I don't like. Jack thinks he's pretty smart, but that cowboy's going to outsmart him. Anyway, Gipsy, he's got that tied up, and I'm not going to jump on his claim or squat on his land. I'll look for something else, and when we find it, we'll get it the right way."

CHAPTER 11

Occasionally, the ranch had barbeques and dances to celebrate various events the Company had accomplished. On one occasion in mid-April, there was a dance at the hotel, Doña Anita's salon, a barbeque, and a horse race the next day out at the corrals. Company people came from town and locals from all around. There were lots of festivities all night with lots of drinking and drunk cowboys.

Phil attended but mostly because he thinks he has to because it's his job to control what happens. I was fatigued and wanted to stay home, but Phil wanted me to go with him. We got home late, and I lay on the bed and went to sleep without changing.

The next day the barbeque and horse races were to be held out at the corrals, so we closed the store for the occasion. Jack came by to get us in his car. Uncle Johnnie and Ples had gone on out earlier with the racehorses. We had not mentioned to Jack anything about the land deal he was trying to put together for the homestead. Phil just felt that Jack had found that spot and claimed it before us, so there could be no hard feelings on our part.

Phil spent the morning looking at the horses as people were getting ready for the races. Then, Petrocinia invited me to sit with her on the spring seat of her buggy. There I had a good view of the races and the other events with ongoing chatter from Petrocinia.

Phil participated in many events and actually won the bronc riding. He was having a great day and was enjoying himself. I had determined a few days before that I was likely pregnant but wanted to wait until the Company events had passed to confirm with him so as not to affect Phil having a good time at the events. Not that I didn't want him to know, but I was nervous that he would tell the entire country.

I saw Hank and asked if Liz was coming, but he said she had a headache and wasn't coming. I had a headache, too, but probably for different reasons. When the events were over, it was time for the barbeque. Long lines went through the servings of food. There was beef, of course, cooked all night in a pit, plus beans, tortillas, and so much more.

When the barbeque ended, many of the Mexicans were drunk with the beer the company had provided. That night they ended up in the saloon. Phil and I went home and tried to get some sleep. I had hoped to tell him tonight, but there was so much going on outside that I decided not to.

The festivities moved out into the street with shrieking like coyotes and yelling. Pretty soon, there were gunshots, and Phil got up, swearing, "I'm going to clean up this damn town if it's the last thing I do. You just watch!" He dressed and went out.

I didn't hear a sound across the street for more than two hours. The lights went out, and all was quiet. Phil came in, yanked off his boots, and lay down without undressing. "I put six of them in jail," he said. "The rest of them left town."

But the lawlessness didn't end. The following day the prisoners had escaped and were gone. Hank and some Indian trackers took off after them and trailed them toward the border. They found them in an arroyo, arrested them again, and brought them back, where Phil tried them immediately and convicted them. Shortly after their trial, he sent them to Tucson, where they were placed in jail for a minimum of four months.

Saturday night dances and drunkenness continued. The mines were working, and miners had plenty of money. When payday came around, Josepha usually stayed open all night. The ongoing shrieking and yelling were very annoying and infuriated Phil.

One night, a long-time troublemaker from the mine, Martinez, decided to openly defy Phil and came out into the street, shooting his two six-shooters into the air. Phil got dressed, and I asked what he was going to do, and he said he was going to go put a stop to that troublemaker. I asked where his guns were. He responded that they were at the post office, but he was going to get them.

When he left for the post office, I followed him and tried to calm him down, but he said that enough was enough. "I'm going to put a stop to that guy," he said sternly.

About then, Martinez came to the post office, and right outside the door, he fired two shots into the air before coming inside, raging at Phil. Phil looked at me and told me to get down behind the counter. And, in an instant, he jumped over the counter, quickly approached Martinez and cracked him on the side of the head with his pistol. He went down in a heap and lay there for a bit as Phil stood over him. I stood up and watched, spellbound, as Martinez started to come around.

As he got up, sputtering some inarticulate threats to Phil, Phil grabbed him and started for the door. As they went out, Martinez turned and tried to run. He got about ten feet away, turned back to Phil, and pulled one of his pistols up as if to shoot at Phil. Immediately, Phil lifted his own pistol and fired. Martinez went down and lay on the ground, moaning in agony.

Soon, everybody was out of the saloon, standing spellbound. Quickly, Beanie and Ricardo were there. When Ricardo asked if he was dead. Phil responded, "No, he's not dead. I shot him in the leg to put him down before he got me. Let's get him out of here and have his leg checked so we can get him to Tucson in the morning."

It turned out he not only had a sizable lump on his head and a pretty good bullet wound in his thigh, but he also had a broken leg. About a month later, Martinez went to trial in Tucson and was sent to the penitentiary in Florence for attempted murder.

Surprisingly, things settled down quickly after that. Josepha cooperated well. She kept the peace at the saloon and started closing the cantina before the drunks got out of hand. Fortunately, she had a great influence on the Mexican trade from down around the border, and we had no trouble to speak of after the incident with Martinez The town became what Phil had sworn to make it—a quiet, little village.

But all the men began to carry guns, and all of us slept with guns under our pillows. Soon after, Phil came to me with a couple of pistols and said, "Come on with me." We went out back, up the hills aways, and he said "We're going to teach you how to use these things."

For days on end, we went up that hill to shoot. It wasn't long before I could raise those pistols with either hand and knock those cans off that fence post from about twenty feet and seldom miss.

After all the teaching and practicing with the pistols, one day, Phil took one of the .30-30 Winchesters and one of the shotguns and said, "Now we need to get you just as capable with these long guns as you are now with the six-shooters." So we spent day after day for weeks with the rifle and shotgun. I think Phil was a little jealous because he thought I was getting better than him with those guns. But he soon became very comfortable with me using them, and later, he told me how good it made him feel to know I could handle those weapons.

I was happy and content with how my pregnancy was progressing and continued looking forward to the birth. The main thing I missed was water. In south Texas, water is everywhere, and it rains more than any south Texan wants it to, but it's far better than the arid desert. True, there is Arivaca Creek that runs with a bit of water most all year, but all around the store and our home is nothing but bare dirt. The buildings are adobe, a mud-colored soil that is gathered from the bottom of the cienega and mixed with water and grass to make building blocks. The building's floor is the same color and texture as the walls, and has to be swept over and over to it as free of dust as possible.

We never allowed a drop of water to go to waste and tried to use every bit for some use or another. Twice a week, Pedro would haul two or three barrels of water from the creek for baths and clean-up, and two or three times a week, Phil and I would go up to the Company well in the buggy and fill large canvas bags of fresh groundwater to use for drinking and cooking. To take a bath required a great deal of organizing and planning. Pedro would have to heat up a large barrel on the stove, haul it to the tub, and pour it in.

One evening after I had my bath, Beanie arrived to help Phil carry out the used water to give to the hogs to slop in. Without fail, he would tease me and ask, "Where'd all that dirt come from? You sure must have been dirty, Gipsy."

I'd snap back at him and say, "That's the way the creek water is. It's never clean."

Scarcity of water and moisture is always at the forefront of daily activity in the village. It seldom rains throughout the year, but in June, July, and August, the monsoons usually start. But this year, it was different. We passed through June and July, and it didn't rain. But then July turned to August, and the rains came. It rained for days and days. Arivaca Creek started building to a flood stage clear back up into Bartolo Canyon and Cedar Creek Canyon, and as it roared down through the cienega, it was a torrent by the time it reached the village.

For many, it was a difficult time, for much damage frequently resulted from these floods. But for me, it was glorious. I ran to the edge of the rushing water and just watched it flow. I just wanted to jump in the current and let it toss me around as it roared downstream toward the Altar valley. I thought, *Oh water, oh water,* as an old poet had written in one of my poetry books, "My soul has been set free and released." It was exciting. For days after, I could walk out to the edge of the village, look out to the Altar valley, and watch some of the most beautiful and colorful sunsets over mountains.

On Sunday, Phil wanted to take me buggy riding to show me the green hills. As we rode out toward the Las Guijas Mountains, he said, "It sure is greening up. Just look over there," he continued, waving the whip toward the hills. "It's going to be an excellent season for the cattle folks."

I put my hands over my eyes to shade them from the glare and said, "Where is the green?" I couldn't see a bit of green. So, he stopped the horses and pointed. "See that fine growth of new grama grass?" And, finally, I saw them, tiny little sprouts of green.

"You watch; these little sprouts will grow up to be lush grass, as much as two feet tall, all over this country. Going to be a great year," he said again.

The Company seemed to be involved in legal issues all the time, mostly over land problems with other homesteaders and landowners, and Phil was expected to be the Company's counsel. This responsibility occasionally resulted in losing friendships he had built over the years, but despite the strains on his relationships, he liked the trials immensely. He said they taught him more about the law. He liked to listen to the arguments from both sides, and he liked to win, even when the Company was wrong. He would come back from these court proceedings always more inspired, and he would go back to his law books to study even more.

Phil actually held several trials in the little village courtroom himself. Mostly, they were minor issues such as drunkenness, disturbing the peace, and other minor violations. But one that stands out was the one against his old friend and mentor, Dr. Ball. The old doctor had been his first employer back in 1906 when he gave him a job pitching hay and running his baler. Over the years, he had become a good friend, having loaned us his phonograph and records, and he was also on my school board. But he was also a very stubborn man. He was born in Alsace-Lorraine and educated in Germany. He later took up medicine and moved to New York before ending up here in Arivaca.

The issue was that his farm was down the creek and below the Company's farm. As such, the Company farm got water coming down from above first. The doctor believed the water should be shared equally by all the farms on the creek, but the Company didn't agree.

One morning, Pedro came running to the store calling for Phil. He said the doctor was making trouble for the Company. He was trying to take water out of the creek and breaking the irrigation ditches.

Phil told him to tell the Company irrigator to fix the trenches. They did, but this behavior continued for many days until the Company filed a complaint, and Phil had to arrest the good doctor, listen to his profanity and dealing with his anger.

He said, "If I'm wrong, put me in jail! If I'm right, put the Company in jail."

Phil said, "All right, I will," and he bound him over to Tucson for trial. In the end, Phil represented the Company to the doctor's anger, but a compromise was negotiated for the mutual benefit of both parties. The Company was happy, but maybe more importantly, Phil retained the doctor's friendship and respect.

It seemed that these types of developments in the village only served to increase the respect and admiration Phil was developing throughout the district, though not always. However, overall, he was being recognized as a very tough, smart, excellent businessman and very fair in his dealings with both the Anglo and Mexican communities in the cattle country and the little villages.

CHAPTER 12

Aside from the rains and monsoon season, most of our attention was focused on the coming birth of our baby. When he wasn't busy with his daily job duties, he worked diligently on his studies. I've often thought about how wonderful it could have been if Phil had the opportunity to attend the University.

While Phil stayed busy, I sewed baby clothes from material from some of the good clothes I had sent from home. I soon realized I was making petticoats, baby dresses, and corset covers with lovely little trimmings. Why did my mind think we were expecting a little girl? Quickly, I began to sew little pants and shirts for an infant boy. I ordered a book on crocheting, hooks, and threads and learned to make little booties and sweaters, stitch by stitch.

When I ordered the book on crocheting, I also took a big leap and ordered a sewing machine, and the day of its expected arrival was an excellent occasion for me. Freight days were always special in the village; when the device was being unloaded, Liz was the first to spot it in the crate. "Look at this," she said to anybody listening. "A sewing machine! Who in the world is it for?"

"It's for me, Liz. Think of the clothes I can make for the baby."

I quickly asked Pedro to take it inside. The first things I started making were shirts and pants for Phil. My gosh. He thought I had gone to town and bought him a new wardrobe.

As the summer and the heat slowly began to drift into fall, the lingering heat was difficult for all. On many occasions, the gals, Liz and Mary Neal, would stop by for visits. On one occasion, Mary said, "Doesn't this weather make life dull and boring?"

I responded, "I don't think it's dull or boring; I keep pretty busy."

"Well, you paint and sew and do other things."

"Yes," I said, "But I get tired of that sometimes. Once, I thought maybe I could write since I don't get new novels anymore. Perhaps I could have fun writing stories about different things. Then, I could entertain myself when I re-read them."

Liz laughed, "Imagine you writing! What on earth would you write about?"

I thought for a minute, then said, "Liz, I could write about you."

She was shocked. "What do you know about me?" She seemed almost afraid that I might know things about her past.

"Well," I said, "I know you love Hank, and I know you love to bake bread and everybody around loves it when you bake. There are lots of other things about you I could write about."

Her face drew back into a slight smile, and she said, "You'd better not."

We all laughed at that.

It was mid-September and still quite hot in the evening, and we usually went to the backyard to sit and visit for a while before making down the little bed in the yard where we slept in the summer when it was too stifling inside, and the summer rains didn't drive us in. Tomorrow would be the sixteenth, and the day after would be Phil's twenty-third birthday. I had been here a whole year.

I remembered that it had been this time last year that I had told Phil I would be in New York by this time and would be sure to send him a card. I had to smile at myself. As I lay next to Phil, I thought the following year for us would be very different from the past one—more different from any in my life—for we would be bringing a baby into this world of ours. Except for the yipping of the coyotes over near the Guijas, the night was very still, and I just laid there and stared at the stars before falling into a peaceful, satisfying sleep.

Since the baby was expected in early November, I decided not to teach the first semester. Phil had written to Mr. Pryce telling him to put a list out for a replacement teacher. He specified that she must be middle-aged and able to take care of herself. We had planned to put her into the vacant room at the far end of the hotel, and she must not be worried about bandits. We soon heard from Mr. Pryce. He had a substitute he would send out to start the school year on Monday and who would teach until I could take over again.

By far, the most important event of the year was the pending birth of the baby. Of course, pregnancy and bearing children were not commonly discussed outside one's family. However, in this country, it was perfectly okay for the cowboys to talk about breeding cattle and horses at any time and in any kind of company, mixed sexes or not. And they often used some of the crudest and primitive words and language one can imagine.

The future event seemed to be kept hush-hush in my presence, but I knew plenty of chatter was going on around the area. One day, Mary Neal came by and asked when I was going to town. I said, "What do you mean, going to town? I'm not going to town."

Another time, Liz asked us to come over for dinner but clarified first by saying, "That is if you haven't gone to town by then."

As I grew larger and larger, they all began to get more uncomfortable, just knowing I was surely going to drop this baby right on the floor, right in front of them. I could hardly keep from laughing at the thought.

A week before the time, Phil spoke to Dr. Ball to be sure he would be ready. The doctor. checked his bag for Phil and confirmed that he was ready. I had asked Nina if she would ask her sister Maria if she could stay with me. Maria came by on her way home from the store to discuss what her duties were going to be. We covered all that I could think of, and I asked her to come over on the 4th, the day before the baby was due. It would give her a chance to get situated herself.

Sunday morning, she came over, and Liz, seeing her, came running over, thinking the time had arrived. She ended up sitting here all day, leaving only at dinner time. She assured me she would be close by when the time came.

At about 10:00, we were getting ready for bed when a severe pain struck me. Phil jumped, and with great excitement, ran out, saddled Payaso, and rode down to get the doctor. He showed up an hour later in his buggy.

As he came in, he was having another asthma attack and was struggling to breathe. But nothing happened for the next couple of hours, and he and Phil visited. Phil told him about a little piece of land in south Texas near Bay City that my folks were helping us purchase. My sister had told us about it, and she said it would be an excellent farm to grow rice and onions on. They argued and argued about every subject that came up, as they always did.

Early in the morning of the fifth, my pains became more frequent and severe, but only after a couple of hours of labor our first little boy was born, and was he ever big—over twelve pounds!

Soon, with Dr. Ball's and Maria's help, the baby was cleaned up, as was I, and order was restored in our tiny home. Phil was filled with pride and excitement. As we sat, each of us exchanging turns holding the little guy, we looked at each other and said, almost simultaneously, "A boy!"

"What shall we name him?" I asked.

We discussed different ideas. I thought for sure he would want to name him Phil Jr. or maybe Matthew after his father. But I wanted his name to include a name from my family. Phil said, "I would like Philip, but not a Jr."

"Well, I said, what about a name from my family for a middle name?"

We sat for a while, and soon, he looked up and smiled and said, "Let's make his middle name after you!"

"Gipsy?" I asked.

I couldn't imagine, but I felt so proud and happy. Philip Gipsy Clarke, it was to be!

The previous day, the village had been quiet all day long, but once the word was out and everybody knew we were okay, people started showing up within an hour. I was lying in bed when people started coming in, and Phil, as always, was center stage. I could hear him in the dining room, using a very unusual low voice, pontificating on what he considered the wonder of our baby. "You should see him!" I heard him say. "He came out with his hands clenched in little fists, just like he was ready to get in the ring."

Mrs. Barnes, Uncle Johnnie's wife, came in first and gave me a kiss and smiled, then she turned to the clothes basket sitting on the floor near the stove and examined the bundle. Liz and Mary Neal followed, stopping at the foot of the bed.

Liz asked, "However did you do it?"

And Mary said, "Tell us about it."

"Well," I said, "A stork didn't bring him, and the old doctor didn't have him hiding in his satchel."

They laughed and after they both had looked at him, they left.

A little later, I heard Beanie's cane thumping on the kitchen floor, more loudly than usual, as he crossed to the door. "Where's that prizefighter?" he yelled. He put his head in the door and hesitated to enter.

Finally, he came in and stood at the foot of the bed. His red-colored mustache drooped over the corners of his mouth, and his red-streaked eyes glared. He took off his hat and stood there staring. "I'll be goddamned," he muttered. In a moment, he regained his humorous self and shouted, "So, we've got another Irishman, eh? Does he have red hair?"

"No," I said, "He's bald!"

"Well, let's have a look at him."

Maria held him up and said, "He sure is a whopper."

"I got a ten for him." He began digging around in his pockets and pulled out a one-dollar bill. "Here," he said, "Buy him something," he said. "Where's that ten? Oh hell, go buy him a set of boxing gloves."

Next to enter were Jack and his fiancé, Julie. They visited for a bit and then got ready to leave. As they turned to go, Jack laid a twenty-dollar bill on the bed and said, "Here's a starter for the little rascal's first bank account."

In obedience to instructions in the journal, I stayed in bed for two weeks. Then Maria went home, and I was able to begin bathing and taking care of little Philip myself. One day, a few weeks later, I heard footsteps, "May I come in?" Nita called from the dining room and entered at the same time. "I brought the camera and have it set for the indoors. I want to take a picture of little Felipito." Thus, our first photograph was taken.

Thanksgiving was soon upon us, and I was trying to decide what to do. Hank and Liz asked us to come over, but Philip was just six weeks old, so I decided to stay in and have chicken and beans. But Ramon and Virginia had already sent us a gobbler dressed out and ready to cook.

Thursday came, and I wasn't feeling good. Phil said, "Don't get up; I'll take care of dinner."

About that time, I saw Beanie coming over from the office. "What are you doing up?" He asked. "You get back to bed and watch what kind of Thanksgiving dinner ol' Beanie can turn out. You hear me; get back to bed," he roared. It was hard to lay there in bed for long, so I got up and dressed by twelve o'clock and told Beanie I was fine.

We took another photograph of the baby that afternoon. In one image, I held him; in another, Phil had him on his knee. Then he put him up on Payaso and stood on the other side of him to make it look like Philip was in the saddle by himself. "He's sure going to be a good cowboy. Look how he handles the reins," he said.

"I thought he was going to be a boxer." I replied.

After that, we took the buggy out for a ride, going up the road to where we went the day Phil proposed to me a year ago. And that night, I wrote about the baby's first outing in my journal.

About the middle of December, I told Phil I was ready to go back to teaching. I had written Mr. Pryce to tell him and received a nice letter from him that greatly encouraged me. Because he and the board had shown such appreciation previously, I was eager to get back.

As expected, Phil complained. "What's your hurry?" he asked.

"Mr. Pryce wants me back and let me know they haven't been all that impressed with the substitute he sent out. And I've found a girl to take care of Philip. He sleeps in his buggy all day anyway, and she can easily wheel him to the school for his nursing and changes."

He didn't argue much because we both knew we could surely use the money to continue our savings plans.

The Christmas season was an exciting time again. It would be Philip's first Christmas, and the second for us as a married couple. We went to the mountains again and picked another beautiful tree. This year, we went farther up into the hills to where the evergreens were and found a beautiful blue spruce. We took it home and had a joyous time putting the decorations on it. Little Philip just wiggled around, squealing and giggling at all the activity.

It was a wonderful time and a godsend for me. It allowed me to catch up with many of the projects I had postponed since last fall before the baby came. The Baileys and Beanie came over for dinner, but the rest of the gang had gone to Tucson.

After dinner, Liz and I listened to the men talk about Mexico and the political troubles brewing down there, and the effects the storm clouds of a revolution might bring to our district. But I wasn't really interested in that now; I had thoughts of my own.

I was disappointed that we had not received any gifts from home. *Surely,* I thought. *It was the stage, and tomorrow there would be something.* But there wasn't, and when my birthday and our anniversary passed without any acknowledgment, I felt really low and depressed.

I wrote my sisters a mean letter, accusing them of forgetting about my family and me. Bert said they thought I would be busy with the baby and wouldn't want to hear bad news during the holidays. But, she said, you need to know now, Papa is very sick. During the holidays, he came down with colic, which turned into pneumonia. He was in the hospital and not doing very well. She said that she would write as soon as we know something firm.

I ran to the store where Phil was working and told him Papa was very sick. He gave me a big hug and asked me for all the information I had, which wasn't much at that time. I asked him if he thought I should plan to catch the train and go down there. His suggestion was that we should wait until I hear again from Bert or Minnie.

Her letter was dated January 10, and I received it on the 15th. I waited anxiously for days for another note, but on January 25th, we received a wire that Papa had passed the previous day. I cried and cried. I had lost my dear sweet Papa without seeing him for nearly two years and without him meeting Phil or seeing my little Philly.

I quickly wrote back to Mama to tell her and the sisters that Phil and I discussed going down right away, but we concluded his funeral and interment would be over by the time we could get down to Bay City. We talked for days and finally decided to wait until summer.

We updated them about our plans to purchase that little piece of land in Bay City on contract. We decided to go visit in June. School would be out, and we would have a chance to look the land over. We originally thought that my parents might want to move out there, and we could build something on it or maybe, just put a fence around it, but now, we just wanted to see if it might be a good investment. It's doubtful we would live there since we were trying to get in a position to get our cattle ranch started. We asked them to continue to write often and keep us informed.

For Valentine's Day, I received an adorable candy set from all them, and it made me think of a candy heart I had hidden in a shoebox years before. It had the words "To My Sweetheart" from our Aunt Minnie. "Study hard, work hard, and always love your family, and you will grow up to be a fine, happy woman."

As always, life moves on. Little Philly was growing like a weed and beginning to crawl and get into things, but he continued to be the happiest baby we could hope for. Phil had decided to quit smoking when the baby was born and was trying very hard, but he was cranky and nervous and hard to get along with much of the time. Sometimes, I think I would just prefer he keep smoking and get back to being his happy-go-lucky self again.

He had to go to Tucson to be a witness in a case involving the Company again. I wasn't happy to have him gone again, but I think it would help him to unwind a little.

My clothes situation hadn't changed much since Philly was born. I was back to wearing the navy skirts and white waist shirts I had worn before I got pregnant. Those and the old gray suit and sailor dress that my sister Bert had made for me were all the winter clothes

I had. So I asked Phil if he would get me some yards of the nice materials Nita had gotten from Tucson, and I showed him a sample of what I wanted.

He scoffed laughingly and said, "My sweet, Gip, I'll get you some of the finest dresses and materials in Tucson; you just watch!"

He thought he would be gone for a few days, so he had Beanie come stay with me. I told him I wanted Nita to, but he said I have to have someone who could shoot and protect both us and the store. Tension had been increasing along the border recently between cattle people and Mexican renegades, and he wasn't sure that we wouldn't have some troubles in the village.

A week went by, and he hadn't come home. He had never been away so long, and I was having a hard time being in the place without him, even if he had been cranky lately. Being alone did not help my spirits any, but it did help me understand how difficult our life would be without him.

The stage arrived a few days later, and Phil jumped out carrying his little bag and a large box he didn't have when he left. He was through the door before I could get to it. Phil dropped the bags, gave me a big hug and kiss, and said, "I sure have missed you, sweet girl!"

And, sure enough, he had been smoking again. But I didn't care! He opened the box and said, "Let's look and see what I found for you." He opened a bag and took out a large roll of the same material I had shown him the sample, then he tore open a bag with many pieces in it. There were dresses and blouses and some gingham riding britches. I could see him looking at me, watching my face.

"I got that material at Jacome's, just like you asked me to, but I went to Kitts for the clothes. Old George sold it all to me himself."

This was wonderful. Now, I could get started sewing new clothes before our trip to Texas. The dresses were perfect and gave me a real nice wardrobe of summer and fall. I could also sew up some new shirts for Phil and make some nice little things for Philly, too. Just getting those yards of materials and the dresses lifted my spirits. I started humming my old songs as I moved around, getting my paints and old books out again.

Sitting down one evening and talking about how things were working out, we started to put our plans to travel together. We decided that the first part of June would be a good time to go. I planned to spend two to three months with my family, but Phil thought he shouldn't be gone more than three to four weeks.

CHAPTER 13

As we moved into March and early April, Company people showed up nearly every week. They have been planning to build a new store and post office since last fall and finally started on it a couple of months ago. However, it seemed that since starting, Phil had been busy with them all the time. It was obvious to me and many others that Nonie and the Company people expected Phil to oversee many parts of the construction, in addition to everything else they expected of him already, but he was always willing to please them.

I sometimes had to remind myself how strongly Phil felt about loyalty and commitment. It made me wonder if he thought that if he continued to do what they asked, when we were ready to get our own place, they wouldn't give us too much trouble over it. I worried, though, because I knew if they pushed too far, he would come back at them one day.

When we got into about mid-May, Phil said that Uncle Johnnie recently indicated that they might not be able to be without him here in June. The building wasn't progressing along as they had expected, and there were doubts he would be able to get away then. But we decided I would go with Philly anyway, and he could come soon after.

Early on the morning of June 2, Pedro came with the trotters. Phil told him that he would take us down to Amado so Pedro could take my horse, Molly, back to the ranch. So we loaded our grips and headed for the train.

Fortunately, Philly wasn't nursing anymore, so I was able to feed him baby food along the way. We arrived in Tucson mid-morning and quickly transferred to a train heading for El Paso, where we disembarked and went to our hotel for the night. Early next morning, we were on our way to San Antonio, where we changed again to our train to Houston.

After a long and hot ride, we arrived and were met by Mama and all my sisters: Nannie, Alberta (Bert), and Minnie. Nannie had married her high school sweetheart, Tom Howard, in 1906 and lived in Houston now, where Tom ran a large construction company. It was exhilarating seeing them all for the first time since I had left for California in 1910. Though it was a happy reunion, it was also sad without dear Papa there.

We loaded up in two autos for the journey out to Bay City and my homecoming after so many years away. Mama and my sisters kept us very busy most of the first couple of weeks we were there.

First, there were the trips out to many of our old places. One day, we went over to Sweet Home, where I was born, and visited the old homestead. Later on the same trip, we went down to Yoakam a little farther south so I could see the old house that I remember as the house down on the creek. That was where we lived for a short time before moving back up to Sweet Home, where I lived most of my childhood. We drove by the two old original churches at Sweet Home later. There were two churches then, a Baptist and a Methodist.

Papa had built the old Baptist church out at the Pilot Grove Cemetery about three miles from Sweet Home, and we drove out there to have another memorable family picnic. Just like old times, we spread blankets and ate on the ground.

After a fun time, we went over to the cemetery to visit the graves of my maternal grandparents, James and Nancy Conner (Mama's maiden name is Dora Conner). We also visited my grandfather's grave on Papa's side, Philip Harper. I remember there being a marker on his grave signifying that he had fought in the battle of San Jacinto back approximately in the mid-1830s.

Surprisingly, on the way back, Philly was sucking on my finger, and I noticed something hard. After further inspection, we noticed that he had a new tooth coming in. I could hardly wait to let Phil know.

Back in 1901, when I was about thirteen, we moved to Bay City, and Mama still lived in the same place. Before Papa died, Phil and I had discussed building a tiny home for them out on the twenty-three acres we purchased outside of town. But, when Phil got down here, we would decide whether to do that or not.

My family was very religious and still devout Southern Baptist. They still went down to the beach at Palacios every summer for the Baptist summer church outing and meetings. That would be happening later while Phil was there, so we were planning to attend as well when he arrived.

This was the first time we had been separated for any length, and I had begun to miss Phil more daily. The good thing was that he was a voracious writer, and I received lovely, long letters from him every couple of days. They always include many references to his love for Philly and me.

He always started his letters with "My dearest girl" or "My dear Gip." In one, he said, "I received your lovely letter today and was just tickled to death to hear that Phil has another tooth." He went on to say, "As I told you in my last letter, I can't live without you. I meant every word of it. Since you left, I miss you more and more and the same for Philly."

He also told me that the State passed a law that said a relative of anyone on the school board can't teach unless they get consent from the entire board, which meant he had to go down and convince old Dr. Ball to sign his support, so I could continue to teach next year. But he went on to say that he was waiting to hear from John Barnes as to when he might be able to leave. They kept telling him he's too busy, and they didn't know when he'd be able to get away. So, he was "working late tonight and tomorrow, posting the books and getting all the reports ready, so just as soon as I hear from Johnnie, I'll be ready to go. And, when I get the word, I won't have anything to do because I'll have my grip packed, and I'll be on my way, to the ones who are dearest and sweetest and beloved to me, my dear little Gip and Philly!"

When I started getting letters from him, I thought how silly all the mushiness and showing of compassion was, but then I thought about how passionate he is about everything he does, whether it's with the Company and their business or his friendships or with strangers. He puts himself into everything completely.

A week later, I received his next letter dated July 3. He still had not heard from Johnnie. The Oro Blanco people were having a dance and a 4th of July celebration that night and the next.

"I thought about going, but I have much to do before Saturday because that is the day I plan to be leaving. And, honey, when I leave, I'm going to tell them I'm going to stay for two months, whether they like it or not! So, I'll be seeing you and the folks real soon.

"When I get there, we'll get a hold of the real estate people your papa was working with, get a buggy, and go out to the property. I am sure we can get long-term rent on the place without needing to put a home on it. But we'll see how that will work out.

"Well, dearest, it's getting kind of late, and I still have some of my law studies to do before I go to bed, so I'll close with fondest of love to you and Philly.

Yours till the end,
XXX, this is for Philly
Phil
XXX, this is for you

A few days later, he sent word he would be leaving on the 8th. So, I was expecting him in only a couple of days.

Phil arrived on the 10th, and we began two months of what would be remembered as one of the many beautiful vacations we would have. Of course, the first thing when we met his train was to meet all the family. Right from the beginning, everybody loved Phil. I was so happy to see him and have his arms around Philly and me.

He had been most anxious to get a hold of the Texas-Gulf Land Co., which held the mortgage on our twenty-three acres out at Wadsworth in Matagorda county. Since we had not seen it yet, we were anxious to see what we could do with it.

In a matter of a couple of days, he had arranged for Mr. Montgomery, the secretary of the company, to pick us up in Bay City and take us out there.

In early August, we went out with Mr. Montgomery and looked it over. We concluded that it was a very good piece of property and could be farmed for rice, onions, or even cotton. The good news was that we could lease it long-term and wouldn't have to build a home on it. But the best news was that Mr. Montgomery advised us that there were mineral rights with that land that included very high possibilities for gas and oil production and that production could start in just a few years.

We discussed finding a long-term lessee while retaining the mineral rights. He said that would not be a problem. We took numerous pictures of our first investment together.

As we were getting ready to return, Phil stopped and said to Mr. Montgomery, "I've just had a thought about this plan. You say it can grow a good crop of rice or onions, is that right?"

"Yes."

"Well," Phil said, "Let's try to do something like this. We could use cash a little sooner with a lease agreement, which would start generating cash flow for us. You see, we have plans to acquire a small ranch and start us a little herd of cattle when we get back home, so let's see if we can get a local rice farmer to lease the place for five years, but after the first year, we'll convert the agreement to a share crop plan.

"We'll furnish the land at no cost to him, and he plants the rice crop and takes care of it, and after harvest, we split the profit. I understand that rice is a big cash crop, and the future market is very strong. I think doing that will provide us with cash short-term that we need sooner than later, and sharecropping will enhance the return on our investment much better than doing annual leases. Do you think you can put that together for us, Mr. Montgomery?"

He said, "I believe I can and think I know just the right grower to do it. I'll get in touch with him and let you know before you head back."

As we were heading back toward Bay City, we passed numerous ranches, some larger than others, but all running very nice-looking cattle. Phil was particularly intrigued by the brands on their left hip.

Mr. Montgomery asked, "Do you know anything about the brand that all these cattle are branded with?"

"It's interesting," Phil replied, "because it's just a letter with a couple of bars on each side. In our country, most brands are configured with people's initials in circles or with various designs of different images. I don't remember seeing anything like this before."

"Well," Mr. Montgomery said, "Phil, those actually are my family's cattle, and my mother came up with that brand back in about 1902 when my daddy started in the cattle business. He wanted something simple and easy to apply. My mother came up with the idea of just using the letter V.

"My dad asked her how she came up with it, so she told him of a story she had read about a baby born back in Virginia many years ago to an English family named Dare. They named her Virginia because she was supposedly the first white child born in Virginia. Shortly after her birth, she, her parents, and all the colonists disappeared, never to be heard of again. Whether that's true or not probably doesn't matter, but according to my mama, this child became a prominent figure in American myth and folklore. And this is the important part: Over these many hundreds of years, she has become a symbol of innocence and purity to many southern Americans, representing new beginnings, promise, and hope as well as adventureand bravery in a new land. And her legacy also symbolizes mystery because of her mysterious fate.

"So, Mama said to my daddy that they should use that V as their brand. We were just starting out in the cattle business, and this

Virginia Dare person represented everything about us. So, we did! We added the bars on each side of the V to signify our past on the left and our future on the right. And today, the Bar-V-Bar represents one of the most extensive cattle operations in Texas."

I think both Phil and I were awestruck by that story, and after a moment of thought, Phil simply said, "Well, Mr. Montgomery, that's really a good story. Someday maybe we could visit more about your family and ranch. See, both Gipsy and I started in Texas before meeting in Arizona. She taught school outside of Fredericksburg for a while, and I worked on a ranch north of San Antonio for a few months."

After finalizing plans for the land as we wanted with Mr. Montgomery and Bill Bower, our new tenant and sharecropper, we said our goodbyes and thanked Mr. Montgomery for all of his help.

We spent the next month or so with family and many of my old friends from my school days. But probably the most enjoyable part were our trips down to Palacios at the beach. We had great times down there; Phil played with Philly in the Gulf and on the sandy beaches.

It was a sad time when the time came for us to leave and return home to Arivaca. The fall elections were approaching, and Phil had been getting more involved with the political activities beginning to go on up there, and he wanted to be home before the campaigning got going.

In early September, we boarded our train in Houston and said our goodbyes, but not until after assuring everybody we would be back soon and often.

CHAPTER 14

We arrived back in Arivaca by September 10, and the gang began to show up right away—Hank and Liz, and of course, Beanie. Everybody was happy to see us and have us back. We spent the better part of the first evening passing Philly around so everybody could jostle him and toss him in the air. Then, of course, we had to tell them about the trip.

I wanted to tell everyone about my family and our trips to the beach at Palacios, and Phil wanted to tell all about our farm. It made him incredibly proud to brag that he was a big-time rice farmer in Texas. He leaned over to Beanie later on and said, "Beanie, you can call me Tex from now on."

Everybody was excited about the farm, and the evening was much fun. Soon the gang left, and we put Philly down and went to bed. I could tell Phil had something on his mind, so I asked him if anything was wrong.

He rolled over and said that Hank and Beanie had said Johnnie had been in a bad mood and had been since Phil left. I guess Murphy had been taking care of the store and post office since Phil has been gone. They said they didn't give him permission to leave when he did and that there was too much going on with them needing him to look after the building project and needing the store looked after. I guess Johnnie knew we were to arrive home about now, and he planned to be down to talk to him.

"Well, Phil," I said, "You're good at discussing things when people get angry so just be yourself when he comes down."

The next day, Phil went to the store expecting to see Murphy there taking care of things. But Murphy wasn't there. He walked in and was greeted by a young cowboy. Phil said, "I'm Phil Clarke. Where is Murphy?"

The young cowboy said Murphy had to leave the previous week, and he would be gone for a couple of weeks. It was something about election campaigns starting up soon, and the Company wanted him in Tucson for a time, and Mr. Barnes asked if he would fill in until he got back.

"So, who are you?" Phil asked.

"My name is Dink Daley," he said. "My wife, Annalee, and I have been working on a little homestead near Jalisco Ridge for Jack Baxter. Guy says he runs a ranch for Mr. Barnes down at Las Jarrillas. Says he just got himself this homestead and wants me to build a little house on it for him and says we can stay there and run a few cows on it.

"We just came over from New Mexico. I have been bronc riding on the rodeo circuit for a while over there, but the wife and I heard we could get ourselves a place of our own out here, so we come over. We've been camping out for the past couple of months, and since I had a little experience from working in a store back in Missouri a while back, Mr. Barnes asked me to take care of this place for a time.

"I reckon since your back now, you'll be taking over this place again, so I'll be going back to Jack's place. Do you want to take over now, or do you want me to stick around for a bit?"

Phil said, "Dink, why don't you just stay on till Uncle Johnnie gets back. I suspect he'll be coming along about any time."

He left Dink to take care of the store and went back over to the house. He thought Gip would like to know what was going on, and she probably needed some help with getting the place back in order. He told her that the young cowboy that they had seen at the company rodeo was working at the store. Johnnie put him in there because Murphy had to go to Tucson for the company—something about elections coming up.

Phil said, "I kind of like this young fella, Gip. He seems like a pretty determined sort of guy. I didn't want to say anything about that homestead was the one you and I were going to apply on. He has a wife; I think he said her name is Annalee. It might be a gal you might want to meet sometime."

Gipsy said, "Okay, but what do you think Johnnie's plans are?"

Phil replied, "I don't know, but he'll be around soon enough. I'm sure he and the Company people had something to do with Jack getting that ranch. Be best be a little careful what we talk about around those folks until we know for sure about Uncle Johnnie."

Gipsy agreed and thought that would be a good idea.

Johnnie came down the next morning. Phil was in the store with Dink, hearing what he had to tell him about happenings since he'd been gone. About the only thing he knew about was the elections coming up. It seemed the whole district was talking about that.

The store had been busy, but he hadn't seen much of our gang. Guess they were just staying away while Phil and Gipsy were gone. Johnnie came in and came up to Phil, put his arms around him and gave him a big hug, and said, "Philip, my boy. Good to have you back. Hope you had a great trip. Are Gipsy and Philly doing good? We sure have missed you around here, but lucky for us, we found this young cowboy out at Jack's new place. Been filling in for Murphy and doing a fine job. Are you ready to go back to work? Got lots of projects for you."

The next day Dink went back to Jack's ranch, and Phil went back to his duties.

CHAPTER 15

PHIL

We had been gone nearly two months, and everything looked different—the village, the people, even the country. Of course, nothing had changed. It was probably just a normal thought when someone left home for a long time. I wondered if Gipsy had those thoughts and feelings when she arrived in south Texas in June.

Life in the village was soon back to normal for us. September quickly moved into October, and that's when the noticeable change began. The new buildings were nearing completion with numerous additions and changes to the old. All of that was good and will be good for our growing business. Maybe that explains why Johnnie is warm and friendly again. Or maybe Hank and Beanie just read him wrong. But there is a change in the air. So many important decisions will be made that might not affect a little village like ours here in Arivaca, but surely could and would in the future. I decided I needed to be active in all of this.

I had not paid too much attention to politics during my first years here, but it seemed that ever since I've been studying business and law courses, I have developed more of an interest in what it all means. I sure have learned the difference between a Republican and a Democrat in the last year or so. There is no doubt about what side I fall on.

It seems the Democrats want to have the government involved in every part of our lives. It makes me remember, so clearly, what

Pap said when we went out to that Statue of Liberty and what Uncle Paddy told Pap when he wanted him to bring us to America. "A land where a man can work and earn a living and keep what he earns." The Democrats believe we all should work and give part of it to people we don't even know just so they can provide us with what they think is best for us. I often wonder, *Are we not smart enough to figure that out on our own?*

I look around at all the people I have met in the six years I have been here and see the ones who have had their good life provided by someone else's hard work and those who work long, hard hours day after day to get ahead in this land of the free. And I think about people like Hank, Ples, Doña Josepha, Anita, and me, and even that new cowboy, Dink, and his wife.

I'm pretty sure things are going to be different this coming year and in years to come. This year we are electing a new president, and Arizona is going to become a state. Are we going to prohibit alcohol and tell people they can't drink? Are we going to allow women the right to vote? So many things that will affect all of us in the future will be decided with this election.

I spent a good part of October working for the Republican Party, and surprisingly, I was asked to be the chairman of the local Arivaca District Chapter. I didn't know anything about being a chairman but decided that, since I felt strongly about these issues we were going to vote on, I should talk to people and discuss what I think is good for us and what I think isn't.

Hank and Liz Bailey are Republican, as are Murphy, Uncle Beanie, and most cattle people and miners. Still, most of the Company folks lean toward the liberal-Democratic side, including Uncle Johnnie Barnes and, surprisingly, my sweetheart, Gipsy.

No sooner had I started putting up a campaign poster for the Republican candidates around the village when Johnnie started putting up pictures and posters of Democratic friends of his. And also, he was running for county treasurer as well. There are maybe two to three hundred eligible voters around the district, not a large number, but fair considering how far and wide the district spread.

In addition to the suffrage issue, prohibition, and pending statehood, it was a presidential election year, and most people in the village gathered to argue over the vices and virtues of the two candidates. The Democratic candidate was Governor Woodrow Wilson, and our Republican candidate was the incumbent, William Howard Taft. Also, of interest, even though not many local folks were aware of it, but former President Theodore Roosevelt ran under the banner of the new progressive or Bull Moose party.

We opened our house up to every Republican candidate we could get to come down to our little town. Gipsy fried chicken almost every night until they were all gone, and then she started on the old hens for stews.

Gipsy was not too tuned into the issue, but she later talked about how enlightening the whole affair was. She leaned toward the liberal views but observed and listened to us argue and debate. Of course, the newspapers kept us somewhat informed on all the issues. Once, she was particularly interested in a proposed bill for an appropriation to subsidize books and all supplies for schools, remembering how difficult it had been for her to get supplies for the school here when she arrived.

GIPSY

As head of the Republican Party, Phil took it upon himself to arrange a series of speeches and gatherings around the district. The most important one would be at Doña Josepha's the night before the election. The main candidate scheduled to speak would be Walter Johnson, the Republican running for sheriff of Santa Cruz county.

Phil had planned for this gathering the night before the election to get as many voters and votes in from the outlying areas around the district. He had posted billboards advertising the affair in all the mining camps and ranches and up and down all the back roads he could. Free drinks were to be offered, a band from Mexico was coming to play, and a few local singers would also contribute their talents for the occasion's success. And, of course, who would introduce the speaker, but the master of ceremonies, Phil Clarke, himself.

At first, it was very exciting, having all this company around, men coming and going, and Phil moving around introducing people to each other and the different candidates. It wouldn't have surprised me in the least if the president himself showed up.

The night of the affair, Phil was in a nervous twit, having trouble picking the right tie for his new suit and getting it tied just right. Finally, after thirty minutes of watching this, I offered to tie it for him. He said his hair had been cut short that day so the premature gray above his ears wouldn't show. I tried to convince him that the gray gave him distinction and set him apart from many of the other young men around.

He had been working on his speech for the past month. He wanted it to be perfect—so perfect one would have thought he was the candidate. As he was getting ready to leave, he asked what I thought of it. With a little chuckle, I told him it was so good it might convert everyone there except for a cute little southern Democrat.

"So, do you think it's okay?" he asked.

"It's good," I said. "Every word of it."

As he and Beanie left, he called back and said, "I shouldn't be late."

I reminded him to be safe, and Beanie turned back and said, "I'll keep an eye on him."

"Okay, but who'll look after you?" I replied.

"Listen, Tex, I've been through so many other elections; I'll manage."

The next day was exciting. Phil was up early and as chipper as could be. He said his speech went over great, and Walter's speech was so good he'd bet everybody votes for the Republican tickets.

I sat on the stoop and watched men of all kinds and many nationalities. I saw Englishmen, Germans, Frenchmen, mining men, cowboys, Mexicans, and Indians. They left their women home, of course, since women couldn't vote and weren't supposed to be near the polls, but our local ladies came in and out, and we had a great time watching all the excitement.

After the polls closed, the votes still had to be counted, and, of course, we wouldn't know the final count until the stage came the next day. But soon, the local votes were counted, and I saw Beanie and Phil on their way to the house. I knew what had happened. They looked like two whipped dogs.

When they came in, I said, "What's the matter, boys? Did the Democrats win?"

Beanie's reply was unprintable. I just chuckled until I realized how upset they were.

So, when they had settled down, I asked how the women's suffrage vote went and what about prohibition? Beanie shouted unmentionables and said, "What's so damned funny, anyway?"

I responded, "You two! You shouldn't feel so defeated just yet; Arivaca is just a drop in the bucket. Wait until tomorrow when the stage arrives. The state and national returns might be different."

The stage arrived early the next day with the news everybody was waiting for. The post office was crowded as we were all anxious to hear the results. The whole territory and the nation went Democrat. The local news was that Johnnie was elected treasurer.

The vote regarding women's suffrage was carried out nationally, so moving forward, women would be able to participate in the elections and, I think, even be able to run for office. Beanie was cursing, and Phil was tight jawed as he went about his duties, sorting the mail and getting it ready to go back to Tucson.

Beanie said, "I can just see Phoebe going about town canvassing for votes and carrying a flag at the head of a parade of some kind."

And Phil likely thought that his good, Republican votes would be offset by his "fool wife's" Democrat votes.

The election was a great triumph in many ways. I read all about it in the paper before I went to bed. I was not so in favor of prohibition and was very happy to see the vote that carried in favor of women's suffrage. The main thing I was interested in was that the proposed bill for the appropriation of funding for books and supplies for public schools passed. As teachers, we would now be assured that books and supplies would be furnished for our children.

In the presidential election, Woodrow Wilson soundly defeated former President Roosevelt and the unpopular William Taft in the general election, winning 42 percent, with Roosevelt receiving only 27 percent. As a result, Wilson became the first Democrat elected president since 1892.

Although defeated by a small majority, the fight for prohibition was to be carried into the legislature. But many counties already had local options, and we would probably start seeing alcohol consumption prohibited in many areas. For example, Doña Josefa and Doña Anita were closing their saloons soon. In place of the sign "La Cantina de la Josefa," the words "Maria's Boarding House" were painted on the wall the saloon.

The Army relocated a troop of cavalry from over at Fort Huachuca to help curtail increasing renegade activity along the border, and they set up tents. They were building barracks to accommodate their stay here. Their presence introduced a new element foreign to Arivaca: government control. Even though they were coming to help protect us, it was still under their control. Our freedoms were going to slowly disappear.

Nonie and his friends and family seldom came out anymore. Instead, they opted to spend most of their time in Tucson and only occasionally came out for Company business or some weekend parties. As a result, a sense of uneasiness moved through town. I felt my feet slipping from under me. The Doñas were leaving, and my best friend Nita was going with them to be where she could work and take care of her grandmother.

CHAPTER 16

Thanksgiving snuck up on all of us very quickly. We had just finished the elections, school was back in session, and Phil was back at his many jobs.

We had Thanksgiving with the Bailey's again, but it wasn't nearly as festive this year as in the past. We all seemed to be feeling down a bit, primarily because of the many changes we all saw coming. But Hank got the player out, and we danced a bit, sang some songs, and managed to make it a happy gathering.

Mid-December was upon us before we knew it, and we were planning for a happy and festive holiday season. The only bad thing was that Nita and the Doñas were leaving for Tucson in the next few days. I dreaded telling Nita goodbye, but I wouldn't let it be a farewell at all.

I wrapped Philly in the cloak Nita had made for him and walked over to see her before they left. She saw me coming and came out to meet me. She took Philly in her arms and fussed over him. "Ah, mi Felipe. You are so sweet. What a big boy you are becoming."

She told me about her trip to Tucson, that she had rented a house on Corral Street near the cathedral where her grandmother could attend mass. She had gotten a job for herself as a bookkeeper for a wholesale grocery company. She was so proud of herself. She had accomplished so much since we started doing correspondence classes together.

Soon, it was time for them to leave, and we grew somber at the thought. I said, "I can just see you sitting at a big desk at your excellent bookkeeping job. I can just see you meeting a lovely, handsome young man, getting married, and starting a family."

"Oh no," she said. "I want to do good with my job and make so much money that Mama Grande will never have to work again."

She walked a short distance with me, and as she turned to go back, I said, "I'll see you in Tucson. You know, I will be going there often."

At dinner that night, I didn't feel like eating.

"Phil," I said, propping my elbows on the table and resting my chin in my hands, "It seems like everybody is leaving. They all have new homes out here but are still leaving. I feel like we're in a rut. We've been married for almost two years now. And I remember we talked about having our own place within two years."

"We will yet, Gip. Actually, I have something just about arranged, but I need to talk it over with Uncle Johnnie just as soon as he comes out."

I asked, "Why do you always have to ask him before doing anything?"

"Mainly, to get his advice. You know, he says I'm just like a son to him, and besides, I work for him, and I owe him the respect to talk things over with him."

"Well, Phil, what is it that you've got arranged?"

"Do you remember where we went buggy riding the day I proposed?"

I nodded.

"Well, one of Ramon's cowboys came the other day and told me about a place right near there. It's just east of that meadow and up on the far side of Bartolo Canyon near Billie Marteney's place. It's not too far from the road and near enough to Arivaca for you to still teach school and for me to keep working at the store."

"Well, how wonderful, Phil. That's so exciting! But why do you have to talk to Johnnie about that?"

"Well, Gip, because I work for the company, and I think I have to get permission to use a brand. And you know, you have to have a brand to run cattle."

"So," I said, "I think that's foolish. Do you think they control all the cattle land and brands in the district?"

"Well, no," he said. "But they want everybody to think they do. So we'll just have to see how it goes when we see him."

On Sunday, we got the buggy and drove up to look at the location. We loved it and picked out a spot for the house and a spot where we could build a little dirt dam to hold some of the water that came out of the mountains during monsoon season.

The land was used by the Company, but it was on the open range, and we would have to fence it. We figured we had saved enough to fence it and put ten to twelve cows on it. We'd buy them already bred so that next year, we'd have income from the calves and be able to add a few more bred cows from our savings. And we already had the two horses, Payaso and Molly, so we didn't have to worry about that part. And we thought we'd be able to pick up a buggy from one of the ranches.

The next day, Phil told Beanie he had something important to talk to Johnnie about and asked when he'd be down again? Beanie said he expected him that day, so Phil said he'd go over that evening to see him if he was still here.

That night, we went together to the hotel, and Phil told Johnnie we wanted to talk to him. His eyes arched, and he looked quizzically at us and said, "Well, sit and talk." So, we told him and the whole gang all about our interest in the land and what our plans were for it.

I thought he was going to go through the roof. He jumped out of his chair and literally hollered, "That's our range, and our cattle are on it! There's no way you're going to go out there and get that piece!"

"But," Phil said, "It's land that's available for a homestead, and all of you with the company have used all your homestead rights. And, you know, Johnnie, somebody will get it, so why wouldn't you want us to have it? You know, we've worked for you for the past six years, and we intend to continue here. Wouldn't you rather have us on it than some outside stranger?"

"Goddammit!" the old man exploded. "So that's what you wanted to talk about? Do you two want to go out and squat on our land?

After all, we have done for you! I've treated you like a son for all these years, gave you a job when you first showed up, and a place to live! My God, man, what more do you want?"

"We want a place of our own, where we can run a few head of cows and make a start for ourselves. We would put up fencing to keep our ten to twelve cows off what you call your pasture, when in fact, it's all still open range."

"By God, it might be open range, but it's *our* open range! And there are plenty of dammed branding irons around this district already. I'm going to put a stop to anybody putting any more of them out here!"

Phil couldn't believe me. I stood up, looked Johnnie square in the eyes, and roared, "Phil, I've heard enough! These are all stories he's telling us; this is nonsense. Let's go home!"

I'm not sure he heard me. His face had turned bright red, and I knew he was about to blow his top too. Murphy puffed on his pipe, but Beanie sat still, staring straight ahead, looking at nothing, in disbelief.

I banged the door as hard as I could as I went out. Phil followed a minute later, and halfway across the road, he caught up to me.

"Phil, you should resign from this dammed company. You know, the school isn't part of this damned company, and we can live okay on my salary."

We went home and talked into the night. After we both had cooled down sufficiently and were thinking rationally again, we decided not to pursue the subject until Christmas was over. The holidays were only a week away. We had made plans to have a merry Christmas, with a lovely tree from up in the hills, along with our friends from the gang and around the area.

It would be Philly's first Christmas, or at least his first that he would remember. Last year, he only got a little rattle and a tin cup. The rattle was all chewed up now, and the tin cup was full of dents and scratches from him banging it on the tray of his highchair. But, this year, we had ordered scores of toys from the Sears catalog. It seemed everything in it was suitable for one-year-old boys—balls, trains, blocks, books, and even dolls for boys. We had much fun ordering all that stuff but were anxious as we waited for the stage to arrive with the box. When it finally came, we sneaked it into the storeroom to hide. *Oh my,* I thought, *Christmas day is going to be glorious.*

We had not heard anything back from Johnnie or the Company after our meeting with him the previous week, and we were wondering what, if anything, was being discussed within the Company. But as we agreed, we would not even talk about it until after the holidays.

The day before Christmas, a messenger from the Old Glory mine came for Phil. It seemed that old man Quitter had died, and one of Phil's jobs was to attend the body and funeral, as well as making contact with any relatives.

"Please hurry back," I said.

"I'll be back by early afternoon," he replied.

He actually got back before I expected him. I made gingerbread boys, fancy little cookies for the tree, and stockings in the kitchen. I had also made an apple pie for supper on Christmas, but Phil took a wedge of pie and said, "Wow, this is one of your best!"

"Thank you," I said in an exaggerated tone.

Philly came in with his hands outstretched for a bite. "Ain't it good," Phil said, handing him a little piece.

"Please, Phil. It isn't 'ain't!'"

"I'm sorry, Gip, I don't always remember!"

"Well, how was your trip?"

"Well, the old man didn't leave a letter or any reference to relations or anything, so I just told those folks to bury him and make a marker. And guess what? I have another secret. It's your Christmas present, and you'll never guess what it is."

"Oh my," I said. "A Christmas present for me?"

"I know you'll be pleased. Just wait till you see it. It belonged to old Quitter, but he has no heirs, at least none I could find. So, listen, I've got to find Pedro and send him up with a pack burro to get it and bring it down."

It was dark when Phil came back from the store. We had ham and potato salad and white cake for supper, saving our appetites for Christmas dinner.

While I finished trimming the tree, Phil kept going out to the corral to see if Pedro was back yet. But Pedro didn't get back until the next day, and by then, all was ready for Santa Claus, all but lighting the candles.

Pedro came to the back door that morning, and Phil and he struggled with a large bundle. Finally, Phil told me to go to the bedroom so it would be a secret.

Soon, he said, "You can come out now."

In front of the tree was another old bookcase. It was filled with more old encyclopedias. I opened my mouth to say something but the only thing I could say was, "How did you know I wanted more encyclopedias? Thank you for being so thoughtful."

He said he knew they were old, but everything in them was true, and if it was true once, it was always true. "Truth and facts don't change," he said.

I wanted to say things change, and knowledge changes, but I kept that thought to myself. But I said, "This makes me feel bad that I have such a small gift for you."

He looked at me, paused for an instant, and said, "I've got you and Philly; that's all I want or need!"

Before the gang showed up for dinner, I picked up a volume I had laid on the table and turned the pages. Soon, I came to a section about art. I began to read. That part was accurate and would always be true. I determined that night I would sit down with that volume and learn what I could about "the truths and facts" of the history of art.

Later in the morning, the gang showed up for dinner. "Merry Christmas," they all said as they came in. Then, Beanie said they had news.

"Well, let's hear it," Phil said.

Beanie said, "A couple of days ago, Ples and I and a couple of other cowboys from the ranch went up to the Yellow Jacket and over to the Warsaw to check on some of their claims and rode back up through California Gulch to the Montana Camp store.

"At one camp, a mining man had been killed, and there was no trace of the murderer or murderers. At the Casa Piedra (the rock house) just across the border down the Gulch, there was a band of renegades, revolutionists they were calling themselves, camped out. There had been many reports from folks down in that country raiding the herds on the north side and butchering the cattle on the other side. Over in Bear Valley to the east, smugglers had been caught taking guns and ammunition into Mexico for the revolutionaries.

"When we got up to Montana Camp and went to the mercantile to get some supplies and say hello to Julius Andrews, we found out that Jake, as he goes by, wants to sell the store. He says his age and that rheumatism bothers him so much he wants to move to Tucson and take it easy and be closer to the doctors."

Phil's eyes brightened, and he said, "As far as I know, Jakes done a pretty good job with that place. Been running that place for a long time, maybe sixteen years."

"From what we've heard for the past couple of months," Beanie continued, "Montana's going to start working on a much bigger scale, and there's going to be a bunch more miners coming in to work it. So, I'll betcha someone will come in and snatch that place up real quick."

"Does he have somebody ready to buy it?" Phil asked.

"Well, I'd be guessing not because he asked us to pass the word around the district as we travel around. I wonder if maybe he's just getting a little nervous about those Mexican raiders moving around down there. A guy needs to be pretty careful about going into that country nowadays. It's not like it used to be, especially since the Mexicans have that revolution getting hotter and hotter all the time."

After dinner and the gang had left, Phil said, "We need to go down there and talk to Jake. You heard what Beanie said. That might be our opportunity, Gip. I know Jake has done really well down there, and you know, our little mine is just around the corner of the hill from the store. What do you say? We could get up early and get down there and back before anyone around here knows what we're up to."

"Okay," Gipsy said, "but it's Christmas. Mr. Andrews might not even be around."

"Hell, Gip, he lives right there in the back of the store. If it's a good thing, we shouldn't wait. If we like what we see and what he says, we can take an option on it and get a hold on it until we can figure everything out."

"Aren't you worried about the Mexicans and it being so far away, and how much wilder it is down there in the mountains?"

"Well, there might be a slight risk, but I believe we can take care of ourselves, and hell, Gip, it's just what we want and more. It's open range all the way down to the border with nothing but squatters camped on it. We can trade a can of beans for one of those places and get a few cows and get our own branding iron right away. Of course, there ain't a school down there now, but with the mines on the upswing again, we could open one up in the store, and you could be teaching again. And, of course, Gipsy, there's the store. If we work that store really hard, we can keep buying more and more cattle and keep picking up more places from those squatters down south."

When we arrived, it was still fairly early. Jake was there, and he was happy to see us.

"Merry Christmas to you and Gipsy. What brings you two down here today, Phil?"

"Well," Phil said, "I'll get right to the point. Some of the cowboys came through here recently and heard you might be interested in moving to town. We heard about that just yesterday and figured we might be interested in talking to you about it. We decided to come down today, even though it's Christmas, so we could do something in case we both have some interest in that idea before the Company people get wind of it and want to stop us."

"Well, Phil, I want to get out of here. Rheumatism is getting worse, and the wife is a little nervous about the Mexicans."

"So," Phil said, "Jake if you know what you want and we think it's something we can handle, I'd like to take an option on it to get you to hold it for us until we can look everything over and get our papers in order. Is that okay with you?"

Jake said, "Sure, Phil. So here's the deal: I want $3,700 for the whole place, including the store with inventory, the separate house, and other associated buildings and structures. If you give me a thousand up front, I'll carry the remaining $2,700 for two years."

Phil turned to me and said, "I got a hundred dollars out of our savings just in case. Why don't we get an option from him to hold it until we can decide for sure."

I agreed and turned to Jake and asked, "Does that work for you?"

He said, "It sure does. And Lillie and I will help you with this all we can."

We took a quick look around and asked a few questions, and before we left, we told Jake this was what we wanted to do. We would come back out in the next day or so and get all the details worked out if that worked for him.

He agreed. We thanked him and got in the buggy. As we left, he wished us Merry Christmas and said he would see us again soon.

When we were on our way down the road back toward Arivaca, I asked Phil what he knew about Julius and this Montana Camp we might be moving to.

He said, "Gip, I'll tell you what I know, but first, why don't we swing around the hill up ahead and check on our mine. Maybe Luis is getting more ore out."

I said okay, so we headed over to the mine. Gipsy said, "Just look at that. Why that pile there is twice as large as Luis has ever pulled out."

"My gosh, Gip, I need to get Luis to load this up and get it down to the mill. No telling what we might have here."

We left the mine behind and moved on down the road, both of us light-hearted with excitement. "Why, if that pile of ore produces twice what the first load did, there's no telling what we might be able to do with that store."

As we rolled along toward the village, I got back to Gipsy's question about Julius.

"Julius and his wife Lillie came down to the camp in about 1897 to take over the store Louis Zeckendorf owned since he took ownership of the mine and the entire camp in the mid-1880s. Zeckendorf held the mine and the whole camp for several years and had a couple of other people running the store up until about 1895. But they didn't do well, and Louis had enough of the store business. He was occupied with numerous other business interests throughout the territory and decided to sell the store.

"He had heard of Julius from one of his partners, J. Corbett, so he asked Corbett to contact Julius and see if he would take it off his hands. Corbett contacted Julius and told him about the opportunity. Julius said he was interested and asked what Zuckendorf wanted. Corbett told him to pay him $900, and he'd transfer the title to him for the store and the land. Julius and Lillie took over the store in 1897, and they have been running it ever since."

CHAPTER 17

PHIL

The next day, instead of going into the store immediately, I decided to go see my friend Billie Marteney at his place near Bertolo Canyon. Billie had been building a nice cattle operation over in that area for some years and had been a good friend for a long time. Of all the people I knew around the district, Billie was one I felt good talking to about different things. I thought I would tell him about the store opportunity and hear his thoughts.

When I pulled into his place, I found him out at the round pen with a couple of yearling colts that I figured he was just starting. "Hey Billie, Merry Christmas! How are you and Della doing?" I greeted him.

After visiting for a little while, I got right to the point and told him what we were thinking of doing and asked for his thoughts on the matter.

"Well, Phil, good for you and Gipsy. First, I know Julius and Lillie pretty well; they seem honest and upright. They have done really well there for, I think, maybe sixteen years. They treat people right, and they get pretty much all the business from around the district. In about 1908 or 1909, The Montana and all the rest of the mines around took a significant upswing, and many people started moving in. Most miners wanted to profit from the new ore findings, but new businesses and buildings also came with them.

"In fact, about 1910, there were enough new people coming that he started getting pressure set up a post office. The old post office in

Oro Blanco had closed down years ago when the mines slowed down so much, and, as you know, folks from around here have had to go all the way to Arivaca for their mail. It wasn't long before he applied to the Government to establish a post office down there. About a year ago, they granted his request, and so he exercised his prerogative as postmaster and decided to give the town a name.

"He wanted something different from Montana Camp. To him, Montana Camp was the ,ines. So, Julius agreed on the name Ruby, which just happens to be Lillie's maiden name, and Julius thought that would be just as good a name as any. For the past year, it's officially been called Ruby, even though most people still call it The Camp. And, of course, he got appointed postmaster.

"He and Lillie have run one of the few successful businesses down there, and I think they've made decent money from the very beginning. You know, their customers come from all over. They have homesteaders, miners from all around, and all the locals.

"Many of these people had to travel long distances in their wagons or on horseback for their supplies, either to Oro Blanco a few miles north or to the Montana, so Julius became the one who had everything they needed from food and clothing to ammunition and guns to mining equipment and all other goods required to run a home, ranch, or even a little mine.

"Of course, the downside for the Andrews was that having all this high-quality inventory created temptations for the raiders. More than one or two times, they were targets of bandidos and the Yaqui Indians from across the border, but nothing serious ever came about it.

"You know, the Yaqui made a run on Nogales on the Mexican side not too long ago and probably would have overrun entirely it had the Army and inhabitants of Nogales on this side not come to their aid. But all that did was cause them to start moving west along the border over this way. Nothing serious has happened yet.

"The Army was supposed to patrol along the border, but you never know what they could do to help if there's a bit of skirmish. You want to be careful. Just a thought, Can Gipsy handle a gun?"

"Oh my gosh, Billie. You wouldn't believe it. We started working her with the guns about a year ago, and right now, she can handle the pistols with both hands as well as anybody, and she can hit a can on a fence post with the Winchester from 150 yards, eight out of ten shots. I feel pretty comfortable about that right now."

"Wow, that's great," he said. "Good for you for thinking about getting her taught on them. And Phil, I think that place could be an excellent opportunity for you. If Julius wants to leave because of the Indians and rebels, you might be able to get a reasonable price on it."

"Actually," Phil said, "I think that's part of the reason. But I think mostly it's his health and their age. He says they want to move to Tucson to be closer to everything. And he quoted us a price that I think is fair, especially since we will be getting all the inventory and the buildings."

"Well, good for you. And another thought is, I think it can be a good opportunity for you to get started in the cattle business too. There are many Mexican squatters below the camp in the California Gulch toward the border, and I don't think it would take much for you to pick up a couple of those places and put a few cows on them. And, if you do, be sure to apply for some of these grazing permits from the Forest Service. If you can get hooked up with the Forest, you'll be able to really increase the number of cows or steers you can run. And, say, I'm guessing you don't have a brand yet, do you?"

"No," I said. "Nonie and Johnnie give me a lot of trouble whenever I talk to them about me getting a place. You know, they always say that it's their land, and they won't let any new brands get registered,"

"Well, Phil, that's bullshit! They don't control these homesteads around here or who can get a brand or not. When you get something you think you want to apply for, I'll help you with that process."

"Thanks, Billie, I've already done that application process for a few other people around here, but I'll still let you know when I'm ready."

"Good," he said. "I don't want them to stand in your way. By the way, have you got something in mind you want to try to get?"

"No, not yet. Gip and I'll probably sit down and work on something after we get settled with Julius."

"Okay," he said. "Oh, by the way. Have you met that new fella over the hill there working on Jack Baxter's new homestead? I believe he said his name was Dink. Real nice young guy, kind of like you, Phil. Says he's from Texas. Been riding rodeo for a while over in New Mexico, but he and his wife, Annalee, want to settle down, and like you, get a place to get started."

I said, "Yeah, I met him in the store when we got back from Texas last summer. Nonie or Johnnie pulled Murphy out of the store to take care of some election business in Tucson and hired this Dink fella. Says it was because he has some experience running a store. But that's all I know about him. Except he said they've been camping out and getting odd jobs around and that he was going to work for Jack on his new place and build a house for him and Julie when they get married. I'm kind of thinking Jack's just got him out there so he can be legal getting that piece homesteaded."

Billie said, "Seems like a hard-working guy, though. Hope it works out for him. Well, let me know how it goes with you and Julius."

"Okay, thanks, Billie. By the way, how's Della doing? Be sure to say hello. I need to get Gipsy out here soon. She's always saying she wants to take a ride out here."

"She's doing good. I'll tell her you asked."

The next couple of days were hectic for both of us. The school was still out, so Gip was able to stay home with Philly and care for him. I was just as busy as ever. Didn't seem to matter that it was the Christmas holidays. People still want their mail, groceries, and other supplies, so I didn't have much time to think about returning to Ruby. But I knew we had to keep going on with it. Jake and Lille expect us back down there in a couple of days, and we needed to get down there and get the paperwork started. But, also, we need to get into the store and house and check his inventory and the situation in the living area.

So, one evening, a few days after Christmas, Gipsy and I sat down and discussed how we should best handle the transaction. The first thing we knew we had to do was be sure of what our finances looked like. So, we pulled our little safe out to tally up all of Gipsy's vouchers and what else we had been saving for the past couple of years. We totaled up the vouchers and cash and came up with $945.

She looked at me, and I looked at her. She had this terrible look on her face and said, "What are we going to do?"

I said, "Gipsy, you'll have to sell all those chickens out there to the new store clerk to make up for the shortage." I smiled at her and chuckled.

"What are you laughing about? We are not going to be able to make this work. Phil, we'll be stuck here for the rest of our lives."

I said, "Gipsy, look here," as I reached back in the cupboard where we kept the safe and pulled out a second one. I opened it up and said, "Gipsy, you remember that first load of ore we sent to the mill?"

"Yes, but you said you only made a couple of hundred dollars. That won't help very much."

"Well, Gipsy, just add another zero to that couple of hundred dollars. I told you I had been saving and that we would be okay one day when we had the right spot. Luis has been pulling a couple of piles out of that tunnel every couple of weeks, and it just keeps adding up. Why this deal of Jake's is going to be great for us. We've got enough here to pay him in full if we want to or enough to increase the inventory in that store, so we'll have anything anybody needs. And, if we have to, we can fix up the house in the back a little and make it real nice for us. What do you think?"

"Oh, Phil, this is terrific news, but why didn't you tell me?"

"I didn't want your heart broken when the Company kept telling us we couldn't get a place. But now, we can say to them what we're going to do. We need to get on down to Jake's and get everything checked out. Do you think you can go down tomorrow?"

"Sure, let's go. I'll tell Maria to watch Philly for us."

The following day, we were on our way on the two horses so we could make good time. Shortly after 9:00, we arrived at the store, and Jake and Lillie welcomed us. We told them we wanted to come sooner, but I was just too busy at the store and didn't want people excited about what we were doing.

"Jake, if we can, we would like to check everything out and look it all over, if that's all right with you two."

"Sure," he said, and Lillie nodded.

We spent a good part of the day there. I reviewed the inventory, and Gipsy checked out the house area. Then we looked around the property at some other buildings that I didn't even know were there, and then Jake took me back up against the hill and showed me this tunnel. He said, "It's about sixty feet deep. Tried to get some ore out of it, but it didn't produce enough to make it worth the effort, but it's perfect for storing perishables and other staples these folks want."

After we all had finished, and Gip and I felt good about everything, I told Jake I could put an agreement and a contract together for us if he wanted. He does legal business with a lawyer named Noon over in Nogales. He was one of Alonzo's boys or a nephew or something, but he was a good man, and Jake had known him for a long time. So, if it was all the same to us, Jake would have him put the paperwork together for us, and he was sure we could get this closed up quickly. We agreed but wanted to review how we were going to do all this.

I said, "You've got $100 option money to hold, but now we can call that earnest money, okay?" Jake agreed.

"Okay then, when we close, we will give you the balance of $1,000. And then you are going to carry back the balance of $2,700 for two years, is that right?"

"That's the way I agree with it," Phil said.

"Okay, we need to get squared away with the company, and Gip needs to get a teacher lined up for the school. Then we could be ready to move down here when we get that all taken care of."

Jake and Lillie looked at each other and nodded, then Jake said, "We just need some time to go to Tucson and get our place lined up down there. Then we should only need a few weeks to get our stuff hauled out. And, Phil, as far as we're concerned, if we're all ready to make this change before Noon can get the paperwork ready, I'd be okay with you coming on down early. When we do that, I'd want you to pay the down payment balance."

I said, "Jake, that's very generous of you."

"Well, Phil, I've known you a long time and Gipsy since she's been here, and I'm comfortable doing that."

We wished them a happy New Year and thanked them for this deal.

We headed back down the road to Arivaca, both of us as excited as we could be. We began to discuss how we thought everybody would take it. We hoped they all would be excited for us. We talked about what each of us had looked at. Gipsy said the living part of the building was pretty nice. Lillie has decorated it and fixed it up real nice. She had burlap on the ceilings and lace curtains on the windows. They had put wood down for the floor, and she had put rugs down throughout. So it was pretty nice and much larger than what we had now. Gipsy looked at me and smiled and slyly said, "Room for more children."

"Well," I said, smiling back, "That's good."

She asked, "What about the inventory and buildings?"

"The buildings are old and in pretty rough shape, but they're built with adobes and lumber, so they'll be okay. The stock is excellent, almost like what I have built up the Company store to be in town. But we have room to expand and bring lots of new things in. I've got a few ideas of some things we can do that I haven't been able to do in town.

"There are a couple of outbuildings that would make a good barn, and I can build some corrals easily." And then I told her about the tunnel. She thought a minute, then said that could serve lots of purposes, especially if we need a safe place to hide sometime. I looked at her and said, "I hadn't thought about that, but you're sure right. And there's a place for chickens and a cow, and Gip, they have a garden spot." Then I said, "Did you see the view? The place sits on that hill and overlooks that pretty little lake below that majestic Montana Peak. It's almost as pretty as the Baboquivari, just not nearly as big."

Overall, it was a great day; we just had to get back and get things moving at the village.

It was so nice that the deal was completed except for the closing. Our hope was that Mr. Noon would get that part ready quickly because I think Gipsy and I could be ready to move in just a couple of weeks.

It didn't take two days for the news to circulate throughout the village and around the district. Most everyone was surprised, thinking that we would just be the storekeeper and the schoolteacher for the rest of our lives. Beanie and the gang seemed surprised too. Beanie later said that he saw a gleam in my eye when he told me about old Jake.

Uncle Johnnie was another story. He wasn't pleased and couldn't be happy for us. His only thought was we would be getting a place and start interfering with the Company's pastures. Little did he know that I already had plans to start picking up some of the squatter places down in the Gulch.

Right away, he said Nonie was coming down to talk to me and I asked him for what. He said that he just wanted to talk things over and maybe I'd want to keep working for the Company. I don't know why he would like to think that. He told me he thought we just wanted to move in on his land.

I looked at Uncle Johnnie and said, "Why do you think that, Johnnie? I've always been honest, loyal, and committed to you."

He said, "I know you have Phil, but I also know what you want for your life."

"But that doesn't mean you have to think I would be a threat to the Company. I've always just wanted a little place for a couple of cows and a place for Gipsy to have a garden. But you didn't want to let me do that. So, now we're going to run the store in Ruby, and Julius and Lillie can retire in Tucson."

He gave me a scornful look but was silent.

CHAPTER 18

About a week later, Nonie showed up in his big machine, along with Mary Neal and the rest of his entourage, and sure enough, before even going out to the ranch, he came to the store to talk to me. I was stunned when he presented himself pleasantly, friendly, and with a smile on his face. The first thing he said was, "I'm happy for you, Phil. I know you both will do well up there, and we probably will be neighbors someday." I didn't know how to react because that idea had not come into my mind, so I simply said, "If that does happen, I'll look forward to it."

"About the town here, Phil, I've got somewhat of a challenge. I need to find a storekeeper, a postmaster, a clerk, a justice of the peace, a school superintendent, and many other things.

"I was thinking of sending Murphy back down here, but I need him in the office in Tucson. Do you have any suggestions? And what about the schoolteacher?"

I wasn't ready for that question, and I just looked at him for a minute. Pretty soon, he said, "Come on, Phil, you've been here a long time. Over the years, I would think you might have come across people who might work out."

So, I thought harder. And it didn't take me long.

"Nonie, I think you might have your solution right here."

"What do you mean?" He asked.

I said, "That young fella you had working here when I went to Texas. Dink Daley is his name. He must have worked out okay for you. I think he covered for Murphy when you pulled him back to Tucson. He's got experience, and he's here now. Maybe you never met him, but he's working on a house out at Jack's place while Jack tries to qualify for the homestead. And I understand his wife, Annalee, was a schoolteacher in Texas before she met Dink. I don't know her, but what little I know of this Dink fella, I think both of them would be pretty good here. Plus, this Dink has been a rodeo cowboy, too, so he might be able to help Ramon out some, too."

"Damn, Phil, that's swell. I wonder why I didn't think of that."

I thought *Probably because you or Johnnie never come around.*

"Okay," he said, "I'm going to get somebody to go out there and talk to them."

We got word from Julius early in May that Noon had the papers ready, so we could get the closing done. The store and buildings were to serve as security on the note in the event of our default, but we would own the inventory so that merchandise sales could be applied to it. We already had most of our stuff ready to go, but Julius and Lillie didn't get their place in Tucson lined up as soon as he thought they would. Finally, on May 16, 1913, we closed on the mercantile in Ruby.

The day before, we left all the Mexicans still in the village, and our friends from the gang came by to help us load up wagons and beg for whatever we might be leaving behind. We had made plans for Hank and Liz to come up with us to help unpack, along with Beanie and Ples, but first, Beanie had to take a run at me over the big stove the Company had given us way back when. He thought we should give that to him. He said, "You won't be able to get it in that place, and if you do, you won't have any place to put it. It's so big."

"We'll just have to make room," I said.

And then Pancha came over and asked to be sure to send all the washing down on the stage for her to do. She was always concerned that I was in clean clothes.

Phil and Hank got away early the following day. Beanie and Ples would come along later, and Liz would ride with Philly and me in a new machine the stage line had purchased to replace the stages running back and forth to Tucson. It was a cold day, so we were glad we weren't riding in one of the old open stages. And, as

we were leaving, I found out that Ramon was also sending a couple
of cowboys down to help.

Gipsy

When we arrived at the front, I looked up, and Phil was standing at
the door with a big, beaming smile. When we were stopped, Philly
saw him in the doorway and screamed, "Papa, Papa," so I put him
down, and he ran up the steps into his papa's arms as best he could.
They had unloaded almost everything by then, and best of all, he
had the big stove in, and he had built a big fire, and the place was
toasty warm. Of course, we had a lot to do before we were all settled
in, but we were here for now and for the next couple of days.

It wasn't long before our new neighbors began to come around.
There were miners and their families, numerous Mexican families,
and some cowboys from neighboring ranches. We knew this would
be a special home and an experience we would never forget.

In just a few days, Phil had his big new sign up above the front
door, and we were in the store business again.

SIGN; PM CLARKE
MERCANTILE

PHIL

Within a week, one evening, we were just finishing supper, and Phil looked at me and said, "Gipsy, we're going to need a brand and an iron real soon. When I visited Billie Marteney a while back, he told me we should get figured out what we want because, one day, before we know it, one of those squatters will come in and want to trade us some beef for supplies. And if we're going to turn them out, we better have them branded. What do you think?"

I said, "We could do a letter, like C or maybe a PC or PG or something that would identify our cattle as ours."

"But now, I remember Ramon telling me, Felipe, your brand, it needs to be simple, not like so many we have around here with all the corners and sharp curves, like the NB and the sideways RX. He said that is too many hot spots on the iron. So I asked him what he meant. He said that when you put a stamp brand like that in the fire, the iron doesn't get hot the same every place, and sometimes you burn the skin too much in one place and don't get enough heat in the other. He said to make it very simple so you can go fast and easy. Lots of cowboys just use a running iron. I remember when he told me that, I asked what it was. And he showed me. It's just an iron with a curl in the end. That way, you can just roll the iron, and it can make a straight line like a bar."

Gipsy jumped up and said, "Phil, I have an idea."

And I looked at her, and I said, "So do I."

She sat back down, and I asked her what she was thinking. She said, "Do you remember what Mr. Montgomery told us about their brand in Texas and how they came up with the idea of the Bar-V-Bar symbol? It was something about a child born hundreds of years ago named Virginia Dare."

"Gipsy, I wasn't paying that much attention, so remind me."

"When we got back from Texas, I sat down one night with those encyclopedias you gave me and looked up what I could find about her. He told us about the mysterious baby born hundreds of years ago. Her name was Virginia Dare, and she became a folklore, mysterious myth. And it was because she symbolized innocence, purity, new beginnings, promise, and hope. But, also, adventure and bravery.

"Mr. Montgomery told us his mother picked the V because of Virginia Dare—because she felt that they were just starting their journey and that the V would give them promise and hope."

Gip continued, "That's us! We are just beginning too. We have high hopes and promises for our new beginnings. It's an idea. What do you think?"

I said, "Gipsy, I think it's precisely who we are. A bar on the left represents the past, and a bar on the right represents our future. The V is in the middle, for what Virginia Dare symbolizes. It's destiny, Gip."

CHAPTER 19

One morning, after they had been in the store for a few weeks, Phil went to the front door of their little store and new home and looked to the southeast and watched as the sun of the new day crept over the horizon of the Oro Blanco Mountains. He set his cup of coffee down and went to get Gipsy.

"Gipsy," he said, "Come here and look at this magnificent view. Look at the sun coming up over the mountains and the sight of it shining on Montana Peak. Why, it's just like a majestic sentinel, of sorts, guarding the priceless treasures of all these mines down here in this little valley. And look at how its rays shine on the little lakes down below our place here."

"It's beautiful Phil," she said. "I think we are going to like it here and do very well."

Soon, they had the store back open and were ready for business again. Phil thought, *Thank goodness, Julius and Lillie will be coming back down for a few days to help us get organized and acquainted with as many of the customers as we can. The store, also serving as the post office, is surely going to help us get off to a good start. We purchased a good-sized inventory from Julius, so we're going to be okay with our initial investment until Luis gets that next load of rocks down to the mill. That's when we will be able to really start bringing new and different types of products in.*

Customers were coming and going, some for goods and supplies but many to pick up their mail and meet the new keepers of the store. It wasn't long before these miners and settlers from around the district and even many of those squatters from down in the gulch were asking Phil if he would do some trading for goods. Phil told Gipsy, "As soon as we get some cash built up, we're going to start trading with some of these folks."

Montana Peak

Phil and Gipsy, along with the Andrews' help, soon had the business growing much faster than they had anticipated. Partly, probably because Phil had ordered two pool tables for customers to enjoy playing on while making purchases and visiting. Another promotional idea he had was to offer folks free drinks, mostly tea or lemonade or cold water, but also, a shot or two of whiskey for the men when they came to the store. He thought that the longer they were in the store, the more they would be inclined to spend.

The idea seemed to be working well, especially after Luis had reported that the returns of the last load of rocks turned out very well. Phil was soon increasing and expanding inventories into products folks had never seen before, and he told Gipsy, "We're going to have anything our customers need or want, and if we don't have it, we'll find out where we can get it and bring it in."

Soon they were providing clothing of all kinds, foodstuffs the folks couldn't grow, and hardware and other kitchen cookware they needed. They had boots and sandals to shirts and dresses to hats and spurs and tack for the cowboys that included halters and lariats, and even saddles. He said, "Gipsy, we're going to sell, barter, and trade for anything we can resell for a profit. Even cattle!"

And, sure enough, one day, not long after they opened for business, an old Mexican settler from down in the Gulch a couple of miles came in and asked Phil if he could talk to him. So, he and Phil went outside, and the old Mexican said he needed supplies but didn't have money.

Phil said, "Well what do you want to do?"

The old man said, "I have a couple of steers and some heifers I will sell you. I don't have enough grass to feed them, so it is better that I have supplies for my family and sell the animals."

Phil said, "I don't want to buy them, but I will trade you for some supplies."

After determining what the old man wanted, I made him an offer of a good amount of goods that we had and ended up with three young heifers and two yearling steers. I asked if he had branded them. The old guy said no, and I decided not to ask where they came from. I told the old man to bring them up, and we would put them in the corral out back.

As soon as the guy left, I asked one of the miners who was in the store if he could find a blacksmith around to make me an iron. Soon, I had a three-foot-long half inch round rod with a J curve on the bottom made for me. I showed Gipsy the iron and asked her if she knew what it was. She said no, and I said, "Gip, we're in the cattle business now. This is our first branding iron."

"But Phil," she said, "We don't have that brand registered yet."

"Yeah, I know. So, tomorrow, first thing, I need to go down to Arivaca and have that Dink fella get this thing registered because that Mexican, Jose Perez is his name, is bringing some young cattle up from down in the gulch that I just traded for. We'll put them in the corral out back until I get them branded, then I'll turn them out on the range.

"That'll make Uncle Johnnie jump up and down all right." I said with a little chuckle.

"By the way, why don't we see if Lillie can watch Philly for us and you can come with me. Would give us a good chance to see some friends, and I've been thinking for a while, we might like to meet Dink's wife, Annalee. Last I heard, Nonie had contacted Pryce in Tucson about putting her on as the schoolteacher to replace you. If he did, she should be there, and we could meet her. You never know, she might be wanting to talk to you, anyway. Might need some ideas about how you did things. And you can meet this Dink fella as well."

Gip said, "Oh, yes. That would be fun. It's been weeks since we left. I can spend some time with Liz, and I guess you will want to see Hank and see what he's been up to."

Lillie was happy to accommodate us and said she and Philly would have a big time. We assured her we would be back by supper time, but we left her food and clothes for Philly just in case.

Early the next morning, we hitched Molly to the wagon and headed for town. We thought it would be a good idea to take the wagon in case we ended up with things to bring back. I pulled up in front of the store and we got down and headed to the door. As we approached the front, Dink came out, and when he saw me, he stopped and, for just a second, smiled and stuck out his hand. "Phil," he said, "It's just great to see you. I've got lots of things to talk to you about. Are you going to be here for a while?"

I said, "Well Dink, yes. I've got some business with you, anyway. By the way, Dink, this is my wife, Gipsy. I know you've heard lots about her. We never heard whether Nonie got Annalee hired on as the teacher or not, but if he did and she's around, Gipsy would like to meet her, and so would I."

Dink, still smiling, said. "Yes, she is teaching and has mentioned many times that she really wants to meet the famous Señora Clarke. I don't think school has started yet, but I know she's there already. Do you want to just go on around and see her?"

"Sure," Gipsy said. "That would be perfect."

"So, Phil, come on over to the store with me. I haven't opened up yet, so we can have some time to visit. I really appreciate you putting in a word for me with Nonie. And Annalee really likes the teaching job. She taught for a few years back in Texas before I swept her off her feet and moved her to New Mexico, but she's gettin back into the swing of things pretty quickly."

"Well, that's really great. I'm glad this is working out for both of you. I know you're out at the Tanque Verde helping Jack with his place. How's that working out with you having this job here in the village too?"

"Well," Dink said, "We actually are living here in the house you and Gipsy lived in, and I go out to Jack's every chance I get. I don't know for sure what Jack's going to do with that place. He doesn't come around much, and you know that he got engaged a while back, and it seems that his gal Julie doesn't care for it way out there. So, when he gets married, and she doesn't want to move out there, he might be interested in letting me take it over."

I paused for just a second, unsure how I wanted to respond, but eventually I said, "Dink, just keep doing what you're doing. If the opportunity comes up, you can deal with it then. Might be a good idea to keep to yourself about wanting to get some land around here. Uncle Johnnie doesn't take well to folks coming into this country and trying to pick up a spread. He thinks all this country belongs to the Company.

"By the way, have you met Billie Marteney yet? His place is not too far from Jack's. He's a good friend of mine and a real decent fella. If you get a chance, it would be a good idea to get to know him. But, for now, I have business with you.

"Dink, I bought a couple of steers the other day, and I need to put a brand on them. So, Gip and I sat down the other night and came up with a design, and I want you to take care of the paperwork to get it registered."

"Well, Phil, I haven't done that before, but I'm guessing you have."

"I have," I said, "And I'll help you with it."

After a few minutes, he had it all figured out, and the paperwork was on its way to Tucson, where in just a few days he should have a registration back for us.

"Well," I said, "How about we go over to the school so I can meet Mrs. Dink?"

"Sure thing, Phil. Annalee would surely like to meet you too."

We walked around to the school and met Gipsy and Annalee, who were just a jabbering away about all kinds of things, but it sounded to me like they were not talking much about school. But that told me that they were surely hitting it off well. Gipsy introduced me to Annalee. I shook her hand and told her I was happy to meet her. She told Dink that Gip had given her lots of new ideas that might make her job much easier. She said she was having a little trouble with the language issue but so many of the kids were now speaking decent English, so she was getting along okay.

I asked how they liked it out near the Jalisco, and she said she liked it better here in the village. There were the locals who liked to come visit, even though there weren't too many still around. We visited for a short time longer before getting ready to leave. She and Gip made plans to see each other as often as they could, and Gip even invited her to come out to Ruby if she ever got a chance.

We told them we were going over to see Hank and Liz, and I asked if they had met the Baileys. They both said they had but had not had much cause to visit. But Annalee said, "That old uncle Beanie sure is the character!" She continued, "He comes around almost every day and just hangs around, talking nonstop, mostly about you two. He told me he sure does miss the two of you here, but also said he was glad that we're here."

We said were very glad for that and then told them goodbye for now.

We headed over to the Bailey's, and both Hank and Liz were there and happy to see us. We all got into lengthy chatter about everything that had been happening to all of us since left.

As time drifted along, Gip and Liz went out toward the kitchen, and Hank and I hung out on the patio. I told him about business and how it was going. He said he had heard that we were doing pretty well, and I told him we were. I didn't want to get too much into my bartering part of the business right then. I figured I should keep a lot of that activity to myself for a while, even though Hank was probably my best friend. But I did tell him I had bought a couple of head of cattle from an old settler down in the gulch and was applying for a brand so I could get them out on the range.

"Well," he said, "By golly Phil, you're going to be a cattleman after all. Good for you. By the way, did you hear about ol' Jasper Scrivener down at the Oro Blanco store?"

"No, what?" I asked.

"Well, just a couple of days ago, somebody went in and shot him several times. Folks are saying he killed him right off and then robbed him of about $1,400. Buck Jones, Billie Marteney's cowboy, arrived shortly after and told the sheriff's deputies he saw a single rider heading off to the south toward the border. It's really a shame. I guess Jasper was in the store alone and had no warning. Buck said he thinks the guy shot him through the window, and Jasper probably didn't even know it was happening. It was probably a renegade Mexican, and he was likely back across the border within a couple of hours."

I replied, "Damn, Hank, this isn't good news. If one coyote Mex can come across the line and go to the Oro Blanco store, he can damn sure come to Ruby and try the same. I'm thinking it's time I get the firearms out and get the place covered. Good thing we taught Gipsy how to handle those guns."

"Yeah," Hank said. "It seems that since about 1910 when that damn revolution started down there, the entire country along the border is became more and more dangerous. Seems that there are legitimate rebels fighting for the overthrow of the government, but there are lots of renegades pretending to be rebels for the cause, and they're creating many incidents of robbery, kidnapping Americans for ransom, destroying property, and even murder, as with Jasper. Why, I even read just a week or so ago where that murderous bastard, Pancho Villa had crossed into New Mexico and raided Columbus, kidnapped some American kids, and stole about a hundred head of cattle. I guess the government is beginning to move cavalry units along the border over there to help protect those folks."

We talked a bit more about the border situation but soon we both were ready to change the focus on the conversation to other things. I asked if he was getting to know Dink and Annalee yet. He said they had met them, but they both come and go quite a bit back and forth to Jack's little place out there.

"Annalee seems to like her job here at the school, and Dink, he just seems to be a very busy guy. I know he wants a place of his own, just like you, but I know he wants to rodeo more, too. I'm not really sure he's too happy out there working on that place for Jack. The tough part for him is Jack hardly ever comes around to help him out. I think Billie helps him out once in a while."

"Well," I said, "They seem to be pretty good folks. I hope things work out for them."

I rounded up Gip after a while, and we headed back up the road to Ruby. I suggested we stop by Marteney's and say hello. When we pulled in, Billie was with Buck out in the barn, so Gip went into see Della.

I told Billie about my little herd and that we went to Arivaca today to file for our brand. Billie got a big smile on his face as he asked, "Well, what did you come up with for your brand?"

I told him the whole story Gipsy had told me about the mysterious Virginia Dare and how that led to the Bar-V-Bar. "But, actually, Billie," I continued, "We chose that mainly because of what you told me about keeping it simple."

"I really like it, Phil."

"I should get the registration back in a couple of days and then I can brand these couple of head I've got coming up from Perez in the gulch."

"What are you going to do with them after you brand them?"

I said, "I'm going to turn them out in the gulch for now. I'm hoping this guy might have some forest permit available. If he does, I'll try to buy up a few more."

"Good for you," Billie said. "When you get them up to your little corral, I'll send Buck and Slim up to help you get em branded and back out. How's that?"

"Swell," I said, "And thanks!"

We were getting ready to go, and I thought to mention, "Billie, maybe we should keep an eye on what's goin on over at that piece of Jack's. We spent some time with Dink and Annalee today and Hank and Liz. I'm kinda thinking it might not be too long before Jack's going to want out of that deal, and I wonder if Dink might want it. Or, even if Dink might just go back to the rodeo in New Mexico. It'd be good to try to keep the Company off it, don't you think?"

"I sure do," Billie said.

We continued our journey back to the store, and the ride gave Gip and me a chance to talk about the things we learned today. Me, especially. I wanted to talk about the killing of Jasper right up the road at his Oro Blanco store.

"Yeah," she said. "Liz told me about that. Do we need to be afraid Phil? Or scared?"

I said, "Gip, we need to be careful. There's a whole bunch of Mexicans down there who know better than to make trouble with ol' Felipe. And that's good for us, but I think we need to get the guns out and put them around the place where we can get to them quickly. Do you still feel good about how you can handle all of them?"

She said, "Yes I do. Why don't we just get them out real soon and work with them for a while."

I said, "That's a good idea, for both of us."

We arrived back about mid-afternoon, and everybody was happy about that. And, who did Philly come running to first? Why, his papa of course! Lillie said their day went very well. Philly was good, and they had lots of fun, but she was glad we were back. Julius said they were busy in the store, and he was kept busy most of the day.

After we had been back for an hour or so, Julius asked me if we had heard about what had happened to Jasper. I told him we had and that we were going to set up precautions tomorrow to protect ourselves. "I'm going to get the guns out, and we're going to go out back and practice a bit and get back to being comfortable using them. Fortunately, a year or so ago, Ramon and I took Gip out and got her real capable with them, so I believe we'll be okay. Now, about you and Lillie. I think you two should think about heading for Tucson as soon as you want to."

"We'll talk it over tonight, Phil, and decide. We just don't want to go off and leave you two too soon."

"Well, thanks, Julius, but don't let that keep you from going."

CHAPTER 20

Julius and Lillie decided they should get to Tucson, so after helping us be sure we were ready to be on our own, they left a couple of days later. We knew the country along the border between Mexico and the United States had been dangerous for years, but since the revolution had begun in Mexico around 1910, there had been an increasing number of incidents. We recognized the threat of violence was very real. The tragedy with Jasper reminded those of us living and working near the border about the potential for activity from bandits and revolutionary rebels.

The next day, we went out behind the store and up the hill toward the tunnel and set up some targets. For the next week or so, we went up there every day to shoot and shoot some more. We took pistols up there and the rifles and a couple of shotguns. And when we weren't shooting, we were placing them around the store and the living area in spots where we knew we could get to them quickly. Eventually, we had guns in every corner of the place, it seemed. I had not worn my pistol much in Arivaca, but I felt with the circumstances being what they were now, it would be best that I be armed most all the time.

It wasn't long before Perez showed up with our cattle, so we put them in the corral out back to hold them there until our brand approval came through. After a week or so, Dink sent word that he had received the certificate back and all was good for us to use the Bar-V-Bar. Phil got a hold of Billie to see if he could use Buck and Slim to come up and help brand.

Normally, if these were new calves, Phil could likely be able to brand them himself, but these were yearlings and older and would take some muscle to get them down and held while placing the brand.

A couple of days later, Billie showed up with Buck and Slim. Phil said, "What'd you come up, Billie?"

"Well, we're not too busy right now, so I thought I'd come along and see what these animals look like and see how things are going with you guys and help if you need me."

We built a little fire, and since right now, we only had one iron, we knew it was going to take longer than it usually would because the iron would have to be reheated after each brand was placed. But, after we were all done, Billie had to razz me a little and said, "These things are so skinny that if the wind comes up it'll blow them away. You need to get some fat on them pretty quick."

I said, "I know Billie, so I'm going to put them on that little pasture up on the hill for a while. I took a Forest permit on that little pasture up above the store on the hillside and was able to get Louis Zuckenberg, the current owner of the mines, to lease a little strip of Montana property down to the lake. By getting that deal, we can fence off a little lane to the water and then be able to put these calves up on the pasture. I didn't really think it would be much of a problem with him since he recently hired me to be the keeper, or actually, the watchman, of the mine properties when the mines are closed. Once we get that fence up, I'll turn them out. In the meantime, I'm just going to let them run up there and try to keep them gathered every day."

Billie asked, "Why don't you just let them run, then they can get to the water when they need it?"

I said, "Billie, that's Montana property, and I damn sure don't want to get on the wrong with Zeckendorf."

"Yeah," Billie agreed. "You don't need any squabble with him for sure. But Felipe, my friend, there's something a fella needs to know if he's going to make it in this here cattle business.

"A long time ago, when I was just getting started myself, Bartolo Caviglia told me a story of an old guy back in his homeland of Italy. The old guy raised oxen to pull carts and wagons. The old man told him, 'Bartolo, if you're going to raise these cattle to be good strong animals, you must understand that you are their master, and the eye of the master is what fattens the ox.'

"Felipe, if you are going to own cattle, you must keep an eye on them. You have to make sure they always have enough feed and water, and you have to know when they are hurt or sick so you can doctor them.

"Felipe, you are the master, and these skinny little steers you just stole in Mexico are your oxen. When you put your brand on them, you must keep your eyes on them, take care of them, and make them into big, fat steers so when you sell them this fall, you will make mucho dinero."

"I will surely remember this story, Billie. Thanks for telling it to me."

GIPSY

There was no school in the Montana Camp when we arrived to take over the store, so I spent most of my time during that first year of 1913 helping Phil with the store. We continued to get more business from the prospectors and small miners from around the district. Interestingly, we recently started getting more Mexicans from south of the border coming up with their sacks and boxes of corn and potatoes and squash and all the other items they grow to trade for goods and other things they couldn't grow or buy down south. We got more into trading and bartering for merchandise that we carried in stock. It was like we were developing a reputation for being easy traders to do business with.

Our trading business with miners was a bit more interesting because suddenly they were coming to us with gold and silver dust and nuggets they had dug from their little mines. It was difficult for them to take their small ounces of ore to the mill. It was easier to use it to purchase necessary items from us, instead.

It also worked out well for us. Phil stuck it all in the tunnel until he had collected enough to melt down into bricks. When he had a couple of bricks, he would ship them to the US Mint in San Francisco. This was very profitable for us and enabled Phil to make more deals for cattle from the settlers down south in the gulch.

I wrote to Minnie quite often. She liked to keep up with all we were doing, and in one of my recent letters, I told her about the murder of Jasper down at Oro Blanco and how we put all the guns out around the place in case we had some trouble. Mostly, though, I told her, I stayed pretty busy with Philip. He was growing up so fast, and it was hard to keep up with him.

In one letter, I wrote:
Just recently, I looked out for him, and he and his little dog were on their way down to the lake. And, somewhere along the way, he had decided he didn't need his pants on anymore. There he is, just waddling along toward the lake, naked as a jaybird, just he and the pooch, having a great time. After I rounded him up and located his pants, we went back to the house, and it was time for his nap.

I told her I've been able to get my paints out again, and I've been sewing, and I even pulled out the camera and developing supplies. I was excited. I really missed the kids and teaching, but I also knew this break from that daily responsibility was good for me, and for Phil and me too. We spent much more time together than before, and he really was happier. He's his own man, and that's what he's wanted all his life.

Our first summer was quickly coming to an end. We had been fortunate not to have experienced any violence even though there had been incidents all along the border. It seemed that as the revolution in Mexico continued to intensify, more people against the government were rebelling and, unfortunately, there were numerous bandits and renegades masquerading as rebels, believing they could raid and pillage at will along the border.

Close to the border, we were forced to take extra care. Perhaps it had been quieter because of the monsoon season. The rains came, and when they did, the water collected up here in the mountains and became an enormous force as it rushed down the creeks into washes, and eventually reached the deep canyons farther down toward Arivaca and on out into the Altar Valley. Phil often commented about how if only there was a way to capture all this water every year, ranchers and farmers down below could have all the water they needed. And so would the villages.

I was able to get a small garden started this summer. Phil had some mine helpers come up and level out a plot out in back, near where water trickles down the creek just about nonstop all year. I was able to grow some corn, squash, peppers, melons, tomatoes, and some lettuce. On top of that, Phil traded for a fairly young cow. It was good for us that she had recently lost her calf so we could have fresh milk. Having that tunnel behind the house gave us a place to store and preserve, if only for a while, much of what we had traded for or I had grown, and it enabled us to have additional food to sell.

Since business had been growing at a good rate, it required us to place more frequent orders for inventory. As a result, with the trading of all these perishables from the locals, it enabled us to send more products to Tucson on the freight wagons to sell to the wholesalers. This gave us the opportunity to realize much more revenue than we expected in the beginning.

As the year moved along, it seemed that bartering became a very significant part of what we did. Phil continued to look for opportunities to acquire more trade goods, especially cattle and fresh dug ore from the small miners around. What we didn't expect in the beginning was that there were many homestead parcels down in the gulch where many of the settlers and squatters couldn't make the prove-ups required by the homestead laws. When he heard about this, Phil actively looked for those people when they came to the store and managed to acquire a couple of small parcels. And, as a bonus, many of these parcels were eligible for Forest grazing permits. With the ability to have more land to run his cattle on with the permits, he became more aggressive in acquiring more cattle.

CHAPTER 21

The holidays of 1913 came so quickly we hardly noticed them. We did have some special get-togethers with the Baileys and Marteneys and were even able, on one trip, to stop and have supper with Ramon and Virginia. We were fortunate to have them as good friends.

While there, Phil and Ramon went out to the corrals. Virginia said she was making a new recipe of sopapillas when we arrived and asked if I want to come in the kitchen and help her finish. Sopapillas are a wonderful dessert that are a mixture of a bread and a pastry and are very good after a meal of enchiladas, tamales, and frijoles. Phil and Ramon came back in a bit, and we got ready to leave. Both of them had fun playing with Philly. Ramon always chuckled when he realized Philly spoke more Spanish than English.

On the way back to Ruby, Phil shared some of the conversation that he and Ramon had out at the corral. Ramon wanted to let Phil know that it was common knowledge now around the district that we were beginning to build a herd of cattle. He wanted Phil to know that he could ask him for help anytime he needed it. If Phil needed help branding or cutting, he would come down or send a couple of cowboys down to help. Since we were building a herd, he said Phil should plan on being involved in the roundup next spring. He said they very likely would be coming through this area on their way over to Bear Valley and George Atkinson's at the Calabasas before heading north through the Santa Cruz to Tucson.

As we moved on into 1914, the store continued to be busy. I kept busy trying to keep up with the business of the store, and Philip and his little schnauzer mixed breed dog. Between that dog and playing with all the little Mexican kids nearby, he was a handful. Phil and I had been talking about starting a school here, thinking it would be a good idea for Philly, but it would also the miners and small ranchers a place for their kids to get more formal schooling than they were getting from home. Phil said he would send word down to Mr. Sykes in Tucson and see what needed to be done to get started.

The Ruby post office was in the store, and after we had owned it for a few months, Phil was appointed postmaster. We got our mail from Tucson three times a week when the stage came on its regular runs, and like most little country stores, we were the gathering place on these days. And there were a lot of visiting and exchanging of news from all over the district.

Recently, most of the chatter was about what happened down at Oro Blanco and the murder of Jasper and also about the revolution down in Mexico. It hadn't been long since Villa had crossed over into New Mexico, and we began hearing that President Wilson had sent General Pershing across the line to try to capture Villa and his bunch of scoundrels. Most folks living or mining or ranching along the border were becoming more nervous with each new incident.

We learned from many friendly Mexicans who came up that there were all sorts of small bands being organized in Sonora under the pretense of being rebels supporting the revolution, but in fact, were nothing but coyote renegades and bandits, just like Villa and Carranza. We would hear from these same friendlies about many of these groups making raids on the small ranches and villages below the line, how they would take anything they wanted, including horses and cattle. They would brag about how the Villistos had murdered American soldiers in some of these skirmishes and how they might begin coming across the border. It seemed that there was a bit of caution on the part of these bandits about coming across the border. It seemed that we had been developing a reputation of toughness. Regardless, Phil fully understood that the threat of violence from these people was very real, so we continued to be very cautious and careful.

I thought my sister Minnie was planning to come out and visit us that year, but she hadn't said if she was, so in my last letter to her, I told her about how our year was going. I told her I had gotten my painting supplies out and had been painting landscapes, mostly around the camp here and over toward Oro Blanco. Phil didn't want me going down into the gulch because of the rebel activity. I had painted some really nice pictures of the mountains, especially one of Montana Peak, the big mountain that overlooked the whole valley.

We had a couple of young men staying in the camp for the last couple of months—Hugo Bergman and Lucas Nilsson. They lived in Wisconsin and said they owned a hotel on Lake Superior but closed it down for the summer so they could travel out West. They ended up here because an old classmate of mine at North Texas State went back to Wisconsin and somehow told them about me, "living out there, nowhere near civilization."

So, they decided they needed to come here on their trip, and it's been a joy having them. We rented them our little house out back and told them they could camp here for a while, and that was three months ago. They built furniture out of wood they got from the oak trees up on the hill, and they brought numerous Navajo rugs they bought up north on their way out here. They hung material over the windows and closets and made the place cozy. We gave them a little stove to cook with and give them a little heat when it was cold. They had their daily cup of tea every night at about ten and played cards and read almost every night.. They were of Scandinavian descent, and Phil took a liking to both and enjoyed listening to them tell their family stories in their accented English.

It wasn't long after that Phil sent word to Mr. Pryce, and we got a letter from him. He said the district would like to have a small school in Ruby and had anticipated that I would be the teacher when that time came, but they had not budgeted for one for the current year. However, he believed the district would redirect some funding to help us get a school up and started, even though it would likely be only moderately funded for the first year. He continued with questions such as how long I anticipated I would teach, what would my expectations be for compensation, what materials and other supplies would I want to get started, and so on. Phil and I discussed it for several days.

We knew a formal school here would be a true value to our little village, especially for all the kids living out on the ranches and around the numerous small mines. But we also wondered what it would be like for Philly to be in a true school environment. After all, he spoke more Spanish than he did English, and he was the only white child in the village.

Since it was late spring, it only made sense to start in the fall. Plus, we had to consider what me not helping and being available in the store would mean for the business. We would have to hire someone to work the store when Phil was gone, and he was gone more frequently, maintaining our ever increasing inventory requirements and im needing to spend more time down in the Gulch checking on the cattle. And, as our herd continued to grow, we might need to hire a cowboy to help.

We knew the value of getting a school started far outweighed this growing little village not having one, so we responded to Sykes and asked him to plan a trip down to visit with us so we could finalize plans and discuss my pay. Would I be paid the same $100 per month Annalee was being paid in Arivaca, or would he do like he did when I arrived there? We would see.

To our surprise, we heard back from Mr. Pryce within a week. He said he planned to come down with one of the superintendents as soon as school was out in Tucson, which would be in just a couple of weeks.

Phil was gone for about three days the following week. He went over into the Patagonia area to see some of the Kane and Gardner family. They had a sizable cattle and horse operation, and Phil wanted to look at some horses they had for sale. He bought four really nice quarter horse geldings. He was thinking that, as our herd grew, we'd need some good ranch stock to work this rugged country when he was out checking for sickness or injuries. But they were mainly when he was out keeping track of where our cattle were and that they hadn't been hustled off across the line.

When he got back, he told me he had stopped at George Atkinson's Calabasas Ranch, which was about five miles west of Nogales. "When I got there," he said, "George came out to meet me, gave me a big hug, and said he was sure glad to see me again. You'll remember Gip, George is the man I met on the stagecoach on my first trip to Arivaca back in '06. He asked me to come on in for a while to catch up on events.

"After visiting for a while, another guy about my age came over from the corrals, and George said he wanted me to meet somebody. 'Phil,' he said, 'This is a good friend of mine, Bud Parker. Bud has a ranch a ways up north along the Santa Cruz near Amado.'

"We shook hands, and Bud said, 'You know, Phil, I know of you, and actually, I believe we met back a couple of years ago. The fall roundup was just getting started and Ramon had hired you on to help out. Is that right?'

"'Yeah,' I said. 'Ramon had been teaching me how to cowboy, and thought if I went along, I might learn quite a bit more. And, boy did I ever. That was the darndest experience I ever had. And lucky for me, Ramon has been one of my best friends since that time. I just keep learning more and more from him all the time.'

"'Yeah," Bud said, "I remember you were pretty green, but you sure did have a lotta spunk. And, you know Phil, you coming through here today is lucky for me."

"Why's that?" I asked.

"Well, story has it that since you bought the mercantile at the Montana Camp—or I guess it's Ruby now—you've started building up a little herd of cattle and really been doing good for yourself. Is that so?"

"Well, Bud, we've been working pretty hard at it, and we've been pretty fortunate. Seems quite a few folks, both Mexicans and anglos settled or squatted on a bunch of land down in California Gulch and are having trouble either proving up their homesteads or making it work profitably if they just squatted. So, they still need supplies and

I just happen to have supplies they need. But they can't always pay so, often we just make trades."

"So," Bud asked, "How's it working out?"

I didn't want to be too specific, so I just told him we had picked up a few head, mostly old scrawny Mexican steers and a few old cows. He just looked at me with a twinkle in his eyes and said, "I'd heard around that once you got loose of Nonie and Johnnie and that bunch at the company, you'd likely do pretty well for yourself. And I've been looking for a reason to come over your way and meet up with you again, so I'm glad we got to visit today. If you ever need anything I have, you can surely help yourself to it, or if you need any help with anything, you can sure just let me know. Good luck moving on."

GIPSY

It's always lonesome here when he goes away for more than a day or so, but Mac is the district ranger for the Forest and is staying here for a while in the little room out back. Philly is talking so much now we play and chit-chat and sing songs together, so he's fun and good company.

Plus, the schoolteacher from Oro Blanco came up Sunday on horses with her friend Josie. They stayed for supper, and she and I talked, and when they left, she said she would be back on Friday and stay until the next Monday. She and I will cook lots of good food, and we'll go climb Montana Peak and get the horses out and ride around the country during the day. At night, we'll all go play cards with the boys from Wisconsin. So, it's not really too bad. I just like it better when he is here.

Mr. Pryce came down in early June accompanied by William Mansfield the president of the Tucson school board, as well as the president of the Mansfield department stores in Tucson. Mr. Mansfield said he has heard so many good things of what we have accomplished in Arivaca and Oro Blanco over the past four years he wanted to come down and meet us. Mostly though, we believed it was really just a good reason to get out of town for a day or so, and while down here, he could go by the Company and visit his friends at the ranch.

Overall, it was a productive visit. We showed them a little corner in the back of the store that we would wall off and have room to set up chairs and tables for the kids to work at. They agreed to have the district supply adequate materials and supplies, enough for the ten to fifteen kids I expected would attend in the beginning. They wouldn't commit to similar compensation as the Arivaca school, but we felt that what they offered was reasonable enough for us to at least get the school up and running.

I am to make a list of all we want for start-up, and we agreed to have the school ready for fall. In the meantime, the district would help with making folks in the area aware that we would be starting school here in September.

I was excited. I have missed the kids and the results we accomplished in Arivaca and was hopeful we could do similar things here.

Fall came quickly, maybe more so than we had expected. We had the school started, and to our surprise, we had fourteen kids in class on the first day—twelve Mexicans from the village, one white boy from one of the mines nearby, and of course, our Philip. Even though he was only three years old, we would have him on a miniature kindergarten program, mostly crayons and playground and naps. It was all working out.

I think one of the best benefits was that, while I was teaching the kids to speak English, I was also teaching Philip the same. It seemed that since he had been able to get around on his own and play with the other kids, Spanish had almost become all he understood and spoke. The other night, Phil looked at me and said, "We've got to teach this boy how to speak English."

"I know Phil. When I'm working with the Mexican kids, I'll work with him, too." I smiled and said, "Phil, wouldn't it be something if our boy grew up and didn't speak English?" We both had a good laugh at that.

With fall comes late round-up time, and we knew the herds would be coming through in late October or early November, so Phil would have his hands full. We needed help in the store, and he needed help rounding up our small herd of approximately eighty-two head, the last count we did, before the large herd from around the whole district came through.

One morning, we were discussing this situation, and Phil told of a couple of ideas he had.

"You know those two brothers, the Frasers who have been working their little mine down the road a ways?"

"Yes, what are you thinking?"

He said, "They come into the store quite often, and one day, John and I were visiting, and he mentioned that he and his brother had operated a store back east for a while before they came out to this country. So, I'm wondering if we should see if they might want to help us out a little.

"You're busy with school now, and you're looking after Philly too, so you won't be able to spend much time working in the store. And I need to get busy gathering our herd. I'm thinking about pulling Luis out of the mine for a while and having him help me gather. If we can get all of that done, we should be okay as far as help is concerned."

I said, "That sounds like a good idea."

He said, "I'll go down to the mine today and talk to the Frasers."

"You know I hate it when you're gone for long periods. Even though we have a steady flow of customers coming and going in the store and Mac is around and the Wisconsin boys are in back, it's not the same as when you're here with your non-stop chatter with everybody that comes in. Just imagine the difference. Going from all of that to practically nothing but people I hardly know coming in for a can of beans and then they're gone. But I'll be okay," I said wistfully

Soon the Fraser brothers were in the store with me when I wasn't teaching, and when I was teaching, they were always close by, so it turned out to be not so bad. Phil got Luis out of the mine and on one of the new horses, and they were gone south down to the Gulch gathering the cattle. If all goes well with that, I think they will be back up to the corrals in a few days. Just before he left, he got word from Billie that the main round-up had started about three weeks ago and was now over near the top of the Altar valley. He expects it to be coming through here in another week or so.

It was about four days later when Phil and Luis arrived back at the corrals. I was so glad to see them, but Phil wasn't happy. He said, "It has been a rough bunch of days. I've been running cattle all over these mountains, trying to find all them, and we've only brought back sixty-seven head. I'm missing fifteen head, and they are mostly good cows with calves. We'll work what we have here and get them sorted out and ready for when Ramon and the bunch come through in a week or so. But, as soon as we're done, I'm going back and find the rest, even if I have to go below the line."

Phil was here for just a couple of days. It was always so joyful when he returned from traveling. We caught up with things, and he got a chance to play with Philly and his dog. He spent one whole day in the store with the Fraser's. They talked about inventories and re-orders and customers and store business in general. The store business has continued to grow since we made the changes, so that was a relief for both of us.

Soon, he had to go. He said, "I should only be gone for a couple of days. If they haven't been rustled off to Mexico, I think I'll be able to find them pretty quick."

He packed up his grip and enough beans and coffee for him and Luis for about four days, gave me a big hug and kiss, saddled up, and away they went.

CHAPTER 22

PHIL

Luis and I rode about three miles down the gulch that afternoon. We had separated as soon as we had left the Montana, and each took up opposite sides of the mountains. We switched back and forth across hoping to pick up some sign that the strays were trying to find their way back to the herd. We were not having any luck by the time the sun was falling behind the hills above the Old Glory, so we found a little cluster of oak trees in a sandy wash bed, settled the horses for the night then heated up some beans and tortillas and coffee and settled down for the night.

I've always enjoyed the solitude of the dark nights in this country. On nights like this when the stars come out sparkling bright and soon after, the first full moon of the fall will come up over the eastern horizon. It is hard not to love being in this beautiful country.

I laid there, enjoying the quiet and finally fell into a fitful slumber. I was startled by some noises, so I sat up and listened carefully. Soon, the sounds I had heard stopped, and the night turned quiet once again. As I laid back down and drifted off into my fitful sleep, I decided the sounds must have been a small herd of deer.

As the morning dawn was creeping over the eastern mountains, we were on our way, again, moving south down the gulch toward the border. Within a mile or so, we came upon cattle and horse tracks that were heading south. Luis, being a decent tracker over the years, suggested that there were about four horses and maybe fifteen head of cattle.

I felt very confident they were my cattle. I yelled at Luis, "Son mi ganados." (Those are my cattle.) And Luis agreed. "Vamanos!" (Let's go.) I said.

We began a fairly rapid gallop down through the wash but tried to stay slow enough so as to not lose the tracks. This went on for over an hour, and we stopped for a little breather and to give our horses a little blow.

I turned to Luis and mentioned the noise I heard last night. He said, "Si, I hear it also, Felipe, and I think it was your cows."

"Yeah," I said, "We should have gotten up then. I won't make that mistake again. We might be four or five hours behind by now."

"Si, señor," he said, "But right now, we are on the line. Over there, you can see the Casa Piedra."

"I know, Luis, but I'm going on to find my cows. You going to come with me?"

"Si, Felipe. I am going with you."

We rode on south, deeper into Mexico than I had any business going, but I wanted my cattle back. By about noon, we were approaching the little village of Cumaral when I spotted my little herd. They were being pushed into a little holding pen by four rough-looking Mexican cowboys where, to my surprise, there were maybe twenty more head being held.

As we approached, one turned toward us, drew his pistol, and fired two shots. Both shots went wild, and both Luis and I drew ours and fired back. One of the bandits fell out of his saddle and hit the ground, laying still.

Soon, another screamed and fell off the back side of his horse. He jumped up, threw his gun to the ground, and hollered to us, "No mas! No mas!"

We stopped our shooting. As we approached, it appeared that the one down was likely dead, and the one screaming was hit in the shoulder.

I quickly made sure the remaining two had dropped their weapons as well, and asked one, "Who is the patron?"

"Soy (I am)," he said.

I was still in my saddle, pointing my gun at him, calling him every bad name in Spanish I could think of. My attempts to scare the daylights out of all them appeared to be working. I knew they were just lousy bandits and had dared to come across the line to steal beef, either for themselves or to sell to some other renegades, so I decided to push it a little further and asked him his name. "Como se llama usted?"

"Ramiro."

"Me llamo Felipe. Soy el dueño de la tienda a la montana, entiendes? You understand?" I said.

"Si," he said.

"You see la Marca on my cattle? The Bar-V-Bar?"

"Si," he said.

"Okay, if you come over the line again, and you see these cattle, you don't take them! Entiendes? Do you understand me?

"Si, Si, Señor Felipe! Bien."

I said, "You take these two banditos to the village."

He and his partner gathered up the two shot bandits and moved over to the shade of a cluster of mesquite trees, probably to rest a bit and collect themselves before beginning the half a mile or so trek to the little village.

While Luis and I gathered up our fifteen head, I stopped and said, "Luis, let's get those other twenty out of the corral and take these two horses and head north." Luis smiled at me and said, "Ah, si, Señor Felipe."

We quickly had my fifteen along with twenty unbranded steers and two saddled horses with Winchesters in the scabbards and were on our way north. Moving as rapidly as we could, we were able to cross back over the line within a couple of hours. We hadn't gone more than a mile or so up the gulch when we were met by Billie and his two cowboys, Buck and Slim.

"Well, what are you guys doing down here?" Billie said. "I went to the Montana to see you, and Gipsy told me what you were doing. I knew if you got to the border without finding your cattle, you wouldn't stop there. So, I hurried back to the ranch to get these two and come after you, but it looks like you and Luis did okay on your own. But, say, Gipsy said you were going after fifteen head you had lost. Looks more like thirty-five here, and two horses I've never seen you with."

"Uh," I said, "Billie, when we were on our way back, these twenty steers just wanted to come along with us. And I don't know where the horses came from."

"Damn, Philip, you scare me. Hell, pretty soon you're going to have the whole bunch of banditos on their way up here to get you."

I responded, "Nah, Billie. I told that patron guy, Ramiro, not to come up here anymore."

Billie just shook his head and smiled.

"Are you going to help us move these animals back up to the corrals?" I asked.

"Yeah, Phil," he said. "I suppose you're going to want to put that Bar-V-Bar brand on them too, aren't you?"

"Come to think of it, Billie, you're right. Would you consider helping me with that?"

"Well, sure. When do you think you're going need us?"

"Well, round-up is going to be here soon, so I sure want to have them done by then. How about tomorrow? We can get it done, and I can turn them out on my little pasture up the mountain. By the way, do you know where the round-up is now?"

"Yeah," he said. "Over near Sasabe, heading for the Fraguitas in a day or so. Should be coming through here in a couple of days. Ramon told me to tell you if I see you, he wants to stop somewhere near the Montana for a couple of days. You have an idea where we should lay them over?"

"Yeah," I said. "I've got a couple of ideas, but I think the best place would be right down below my corrals here where that nice little pond is at the head of the Gulch. It's pretty good sized with lots of shade and water. Good spots for the chuck and blankets, too.

"Billie, this is going to be great. I'll be able to see a bunch of my old friends from around the district. You know, I haven't been around much in the past few years."

"Yeah," he said, "And I hear your good friend Tony is on the crew this year. You treat him good when you see him."

"I will. Will you and the boys be coming through, too?"

"Yeah, we'll be here and then head over to the Santa Cruz with them. Don't know how far north I'll go, but the boys will travel on to Tucson."

"Good, by the way, Billie, why don't you take these two horses down to your place with you. You've got room and maybe more use for them than I do."

"Sure," he said. "Might be better to get them away from your place, anyway."

"Yeah. Also, what do you think about me giving those rifles to Buck and Slim? You know, they have given me a lot of help along the way, and I'd like them to have them if it's okay with you."

"You know, I don't know where those guns came from, and if you want to give them to the guys, you just do that."

"Okay," I said. "When we get back to my place, I'll give them to them."

We arrived at the corrals late that afternoon, and I told Billie to take the guys and go home. I said to come back in the morning, and we'd get the job done pretty quickly. He agreed.

"Hey, Buck and Slim, you two guys have been a big help to me lots of times, so how about you guys take these Winchesters with you? And the scabbards too. I bet if you clean them up real good, they'll make damn good rifles for you."

Buck spoke up and said, "Damn Phil, I've got me a Winchester, but it's about ready for the heap, so thanks very much."

Slim gave his thanks, also, and with big smiles, they all headed back down toward Billie's at Oro Blanco. I yelled after them, "See you in the morning."

The Marteney group arrived back at the camp early next morning, and we proceeded to brand my calves and the rest of the herd we had brought back north with us the previous day. When we were done, Billie asked what I was going to do with them.

I thought for a minute and said, "I think I'm going to just keep them all here in the corrals until the big herd comes in, then I'll put all of them except my cows in the herd. And send them to Tucson with the rest. The cows will go back in the mountains and hook up with the bulls, so we'll have a little calf crop next year."

"Good idea," Billie said. "Well, the boys and I are heading over toward Tres Bellotas. The herd should be somewhere between here and there by now. So, we'll see you again in a couple of days."

It was nearing the middle part of October when the herd arrived. Luis and I had gone down the road toward Oro Blanc to meet up with it and had a bunch of howdies with old friends. For the last couple of miles, I rode along with Ramon, and we talked about happenings at the company and around the district since I had last seen him about a year ago.

He said, "Nonie spends most of his time in Tucson now, and Johnnie has so many other interests around the country that we don't see much of him either."

"So," I said, "Does that mean you're taking care of ranch business, mostly?"

He said, "Yeah, I am."

"Well, Ramon, what the hell? You pretty much have all along, anyway. What do you see of Dink? Is he still working out at Jack's?"

"Yeah, he is, Phil. As a matter of fact, he'll be along here soon. I heard he took a couple of days away from the store so he could come along with us for a ways."

"Is he working out okay for you? Helping at the ranch any?"

"Yeah, he's a pretty good hand, Phil."

"Well, that's good to hear. I'll have a little visit when I see him."

A couple of days later, the round-up arrived and began to settle in for a few days. Normally, Ramon didn't stop the herd until it had reached the next ranch. Then they would stop while that rancher's herd was sorted, and his steers were mixed into the main herd, and his calves and cows were turned back out onto the range. But it was a pretty long drive over the mountains from Sasabe and Tres Bellotas through Ruby and Bear Valley to Atkinson's Calabasas ranch.

When everybody had arrived, I began looking for some old friends. Lo and behold, up from behind me snuck Uncle Beanie and Ples. Beanie jabbed me in the ribs, and I nearly jumped out of my boots. He spun me around and gave me a big hug and started his non-stop chatter.

Pretty soon, who should come up to me other than Tony Arros from Sasabe, the guy I beat in a boxing match so many years ago. My first thought was that we were going to have some trouble, but he just said, "Felipe, Como esta?" I told him that I was good and asked if he was now cowboying for somebody.

"Si," he said, "I work for Señor Manuel King at the Anvil ranch, up north near the Robles at Three Points."

I said, "Good for you, Tony. Do you still box?"

He replied, "Only sometimes when I go south to Saric or Altar on the other side. I don't fight with the cowboys no more. These hombres are my friends."

I said, "Good, Tony. Am I one of your friends, too?"

"Oh si, si, Felipe. Maybe someday you need some help with the banditos, you let me know. I will come and help you."

I looked at him, a little surprised, but thought to myself, *You never know, Phil. This Tony might be able to come in handy someday.*

We had decided the best place to put all those steers, probably about 2,500 of them and about 50 cowboys, most of them young Mexicans, would be down at the head of the Gulch. There was plenty of room, and it was mostly flat. It was a good holding place for the cattle, and the cowboys could bed down close to them.

Each round-up required three or four chuckwagons along to haul supplies and all the cowboys' bedding, which consisted of a roll and two pieces of canvas, and, of course, the food. The wagons followed along with the herd, and when it stopped at night, the first thing out was the cooking utensils and the beans. Most meals on the drive were usually just a big pot of beans, tortillas, hot black coffee, and some chocolate.

One day, Phil approached Ramon and told him to get one of those beef he had brought back from Mexico and make a little fiesta for the boys. An event like this was always a big treat for cowboys who spend eighty percent of their days in their saddle. After their evening meal, they gather around the fire and sing Mexican songs and play Mexican card games and smoke their hand-rolled cigarros. When it came time for sleep, they all put their rolls right on the ground with one canvas under and one over the top, and there they slept, even when it rained.

They ended up staying about four days, and it rained two of those days, and it was very cold. We were in the mountain in Ruby, so at that time of year, it got cold. In addition to all the cowboys, there were about a dozen ranch owners there. They all didn't stay with the round-up the whole trip. Some just came for a few days and went on back to their places while the herd moved on. But you can be sure that when the herd reached Tucson and the selling started, most all them would be there, including Nonie and Johnnie, I would guess.

I left with the herd when they headed over the mountains to the Calabasas. I was only going to be gone for about three days, but Ramon asked me to ride along with them at least until we got to the Santa Cruz and the Baca Float country.

One day, just he and I were riding along visiting and brought up a surprise conversation. He said, "I saw you talking to Tony back at the Ruby camp. Everything okay?"

I said, "Yeah, for me it is."

Ramon said, "Good. Tony is turning out to be a good man, and Manuel thinks a lot of him, but I think someday Tony is going to want to come back to this country."

"Maybe someday, I'll need a good cowboy."

"That's good, Felipe."

He continued, "A couple of weeks ago, one of my cowboys was over at Sasabe chasing some steers we lost, and he was in the cantina one night, and a Mex kid came up to him and asked if he knew you. My cowboy, Carlos, said he did. Well, this kid told him that a couple of weeks ago a gringo from north up the Gulch chased four men across the line. Said they had stolen some of his cattle. Says he and his Mexican cowboy caught up to them near Cumaral, and they had a gunfight. He told Carlos that the gringo shot two of the banditos, killed one, and stole their cattle and two horses. He said the gringo told the bandito to look at the brand on his cattle. The Bar-V-Bar. He told the bandito when you see this marca, you don't touch them because he will be back down here and there will be more muerto (death). Carlos said the kid told him that the bandito was really scared of this gringo malo (bad white man). So, Felipe, who es this gringo malo?"

I just looked at Ramon and said, "No se!" (I don't know.)

"Bien," Ramon said.

"Vamanos." (Let's go.)

So, word had spread across the southern border about our encounter. I guess that meant we would have to be even more careful.

I rode with the herd for another four or five days and finally told Ramon I needed to get back to the store and the rest of my cattle, but I'd try to come down to Tucson when the sale took place. We said goodbye, and I headed home.

I got back to Ruby after being gone for nearly a week, and Gip was so happy to see me, as I was her. Gipsy never liked it when I was gone overnight. I didn't really blame her. With the violence going on around the district, I could understand why she would be scared. Unfortunately, with the way our life was, it was hard for me to avoid being gone. We had cattle scattered around the Gulch that needed to be checked on, and we had to keep up with the store inventory. Our responsibilities made it difficult to stay home all the time, but that was why we asked the Frasiers to come and stay as often as we can.

My first night home, we sat and talked about many things that were happening in the district and with our businesses. We talked about the Pownott Mining Company. They had come in a year or so ago and had taken a lease on the mine from Zeckendorf. They had brought an engineer here to further develop the mines, and they did extensive exploratory work. On his recommendation, they invested in dropping the first deep shaft here. And when done, they had a shaft approximately four hundred feet deep.

The company milled thousands of pounds of ore, mostly focusing on gold and silver and not pursuing what was actually the most abundant ore here, lead and zinc. Because of those efforts, the venture soon failed.

I said, "Gip, I recently learned that when they shut down, they abandoned the claim they had taken on the Excelsior mine right up behind us here. That's the same claim that owns that little easement down to the lake that Zeckendorf granted to us a couple of years ago.

"I believe it would be a good idea for us to file on that claim as soon as we can. That would essentially connect us to our little mine over the hill. And even though Pownott didn't even work it while they were here, I think there's good ore in there. Possibly even gold and silver."

As we continued to visit, Gip brought up the business of the store. She said, "You know, Phil, business just keeps growing, and with you continuing to pick up more and more parcels down in the gulch, we can start thinking about expanding it."

I said, "Gip, I've been thinking, when we get that claim filed on the Excelsior, we should go up there on that hill in front of the mine and build a complete new place. You know, this place we're in right now is nothing but a shack. We don't have any room to expand, and our living area is terrible. I think we can afford a nice building, large enough to enlarge the store and the area where you're teaching, and best of all, we can make our living area a real nice home for us."

We discussed those ideas at length and determined we would get the claim in place as soon as we could and then start on the new building by spring.

CHAPTER 23

The year came to an end so soon we hardly realized it was already Christmas time. Fortunately, we had ordered lots of holiday items to have on hand and that really made our Christmas season more successful. Despite being very busy, we had a great holiday season again. Little Philip received lots of toys and clothes from family and friends from all over. The Baileys came up for a visit, and we saw Billie and Della one day too.

I was also able to pick up two more patents down below just before Christmas. An American settler by the name of Carson came in one day and said he had to go back east and would let his parcels sell for not much. I worked out a partial trade for goods for his two places and some cash for what he said was twenty-six head of cattle, including twelve cows that were bred and the rest calves. The best part was he had eligibility for a large Forest permit. Next spring, we'll see about activating that permit and finding some more cattle to put on it.

It had been what seemed to be a long and cold winter, but we were so busy we didn't even realize it when one morning, we got up, and we had ten inches of snow. That was a fun time for the little kids. Parents made little sleds out of old wood and used tin from the mines, and they all had fun in the snow for a couple of days.

When the Pownott company closed last year, we were concerned that our business would slow down, but most of the few hundred folks living here stayed, and soon after the new year arrived, the Goldfield Consolidated Mine Exploration Company took an option on the entire Montana Mines. Their plan was to bring a George Wingfield down from Nevada where they had operated very successful operations for many years. This Wingfield fellow was placed in charge of operations, and his job was to explore what the possibilities for the mines would be so that within a year or so they would come in and start full mining operations. As a result, many people who had worked for Pownott were able to get jobs.

On January 1, the Excelsior mine claim was transferred to us, and we began to put our plans in place to build the new store. We picked a really nice spot on top of a little hill, just a couple a hundred feet above where we are now. It isn't so steep that it will be difficult to get leveled out. Plus, there will be room for the stage to get turned around and for folks to park their wagons and buggies, and later, automobiles when they become more in use around here.

I went down to the mine office and was able to hire some men to come up and start leveling the spot where we would build. They got started within a couple of days. Gipsy and I had spent a bit of time in the past couple of weeks drawing up some plans for what we would like to have. The building is going to be more than three times larger than the little shack we are operating out of now, about 32 feet by 63 feet, roughly 2,000 square feet. We'll make the store and post office in the front, and they'll occupy about 32 feet by 40 feet, or about 1,200 square feet, and our living quarters will be in the back, about 900 square feet. We're going to build it with adobe and wood framing. When the workers showed up, I helped them lay it out and stake the corners. Within a couple of days, they were busy moving dirt and leveling the pad.

In mid-March, I made a trip over into Bear Valley to check on some cattle. While riding through there, I encountered some Yaquis on foot, coming off the side of a hill. I don't know if they were coming or going from the border. They seemed to be a little timid of me. They were friendly but almost acted like I was going to hurt them. Because I speak fluent Spanish and have a pretty good handle on what the Yaqui dialect is like, I was able to communicate with them.

After talking for some time, mainly about the situation across the line and how the revolution was affecting them on both sides,

I felt like I could befriend these people. I could tell they were poor and hungry. I asked them where they were going. One of them said they were going north, up toward Peña Blanca where they have people and live when they aren't in Mexico. I said, "You come over the mountains to Ruby and work for me for one month, and I'll give you food and some beef. Okay?"

"Oh, si, si, Señor Felipe," they replied.

I asked the fella who seemed to be the leader of the group how he knew my name. "Oh, señor, we know!" My first thought was, *Uh oh. Word of the skirmish Luis and I had last fall has even spread to the Yaquis.* But my instincts told me these people were okay and wouldn't give me any trouble.

"Okay," I said, "And what is your name?" I asked, mostly in Spanish.

"Mi llamo es Tomas," he said.

After a little more conversation I told him to come over within a week and bring plenty of men. He asked what the work was going to be, and I told him we were going to make adobes.

"Oh, si, señor. We know how make los adobes."

"Muy bien," I said.

Ten days later, the whole bunch of them arrived. There must have been close to twenty people of all ages. Gipsy looked at me and asked, "What in the world are we going to do with all of them?"

"I'll be damned if I know Gip, but I think we'll set them up down where we had the herd last fall. It's as good a place to camp as any."

As soon as we got them situated, I sat with Tomas and some others and went over how we would do this. I said, "You have half of your people to gather up scrap lumber from down there at the old mines, bring it up here, and we'll start making molds for the mud. You get the women and rest of the bunch and go down the road a ways where the grass is tallest and chop it off and start bringing it back here. Comprende?"

"Si," he said.

"When we get plenty of grass, you bring dirt from that pile over there that those miners piled up from their excavating the spot. Then, amigo, we make adobes!"

"Muy bien, Felipe," he said.

We were amazed. They went to work like a hive of bees, and within a week, we had piles and pile of adobes stacked up and drying. During all of this time, we talked about laying these things, and Tomas said they knew how, and they wanted to put up the walls.

"Sure," I said. "Let's get started."

I had talked to Dink a while back and asked him if he would help me build. He was able to get away from the mercantile in Arivaca for a short time, and he said Jack's little house project had stopped for some reason, so he had some time.

Right away, we had inside walls going up, and I expected us to be done before the summer was over.

The Ruby Mercantile

GIPSY

Summer arrived, and one evening, Phil and I were sitting on the porch talking. I had just finished the school year about a week earlier. said,

"Phil, it's good to have the school year over. I really enjoy teaching these kids, you know, but I've been a little tired lately, and I just want to rest for a while."

He said, "Well, that's just good, Gip. You deserve it. But are you feeling okay?"

I said, "Phil, I'm okay, but you might want to hold on to your hat. I think I'm pregnant again!"

"Wow!" was all he could say. "Do you know when?"

"Well," I said, "I believe I'm about three months along, so I would think we should be expecting in December."

"Well, you just take it easy through the summer."

"I will, and I think I need to tell Mr. Pryce that we should start looking for a replacement. I won't tell him I'm not going to continue, but I want him to know that I need to be in the store more. Besides, our agreement with him and Nonie was to get a school started here. We've done that, and I think I've done a good job of it."

"Well, you sure have, and I know everybody around appreciated it. You just take it easy now. The Frasers and I will get along fine."

The store was completed by early September, and we were happy we were able to have just about everything we had wanted. Mainly, water! Phil was able to get some help from one of the engineers at the mine to design a system to draw water from a creek in the gulch and pump it up to a holding tank on the hill. From there, we could open a valve and draw water down to the store and living quarters and have running water.

We were ready to start moving everything. To our surprise, we had people come from all over. Even as far away as Nogales and Amado and, of course, Arivaca. There were newspaper people who wanted us to tell our story. I said, "Phil, we don't have a story to tell! This is just our business. This is how we make our living." But it didn't matter.

Days later, there were stories about the new store in Ruby. And for sure, it helped our business. We've always had customers from all over the district, but after the news stories, we had people coming all the way from Nogales and even Sasabe. They told us it was because we give free drinks and, sometimes, whiskey to some people. And we have the pool tables for people to play on while here.

But, Phil says, not so. It's because of what we have here. You know, we stock everything anybody needs. With all this additional space, we've brought in clothes and farming tools and feed for all animals. We even have salt blocks and oats and barley. We have chicken feed and pig feed. We also have housewares like cooking stoves and heating stoves. Phil predicts that when Goldfield gets up and going soon, there will be many more people coming here to work and live, and our store will be crazy.

PHIL

The cattle continued to require more of my time. It is a good thing, for sure. In the last year, I have acquired, if not all, then nearly all the deeds between here and the border. Many people had jumped on the opportunity to homestead but couldn't satisfy the improvement requirements and had no choice but to sell out. Good for us, but not for many of them. And then, of course, there were many people who just squatted on a piece, thinking it would just be theirs.

As soon as I bought or traded for one of these, I immediately filed an application with the Forest for grazing rights, so as of now, I have the rights to most of the permits in what is now known as the Coronado National Forest. Unfortunately, I don't have enough cattle to fill these permits. As the store continues to grow and the two mines keep putting out their little piles of ore, I believe we will be able to continue buying more.

GIPSY

When I was carrying Philip, I really didn't have any difficulties, but since October and into November, I have been having more and more difficulties. Either this baby is very large, or it's turned, or it's just going to be a cranky one. But as we go closer to December and

I continued to get bigger and bigger, I told Phil that I don't think we should plan on having it here like we did Philip. I thought we should start looking for a place for me to be when it's time.

He agreed and is planning to get a hold of Doctor Ball. He's getting way up there in age, but he sure knows what he's doing. Within a week, the old doctor drove up, not in his old buggy, but in a nice, nearly new automobile.

"Wow," Phil said to him, "This is a surprise. And a good one, too."

The doc got out and said, "I've come to check on my little lady. I hear she might be having some troubles with this new one I hear is coming."

"That's right," Phil said. "Why don't you come in and visit with us for a bit."

He replied, "I think I would just like to talk to Gipsy first."

"Sure," he said.

After Doctor Ball and I visited for about an hour or so, he said. "Let's go find Phil." We went back into the store area and sat down with Phil. Dr. Ball told us he couldn't determine if I was having any serious issues, but he acknowledged that I was having difficulty. He believed that I might be as near as one to two weeks away and recommended I go to Tucson fairly soon.

I said, "Well, where would we go? We know people there but not people to go stay with."

"That's okay," he said. "There is what is known as a maternity center near St. Mary's hospital called Sister Sarah's Maternity Home. It is an extension of St. Mary's maternity care and is very reputable. If you like, I will make arrangements for you."

I looked at Phil, and he quickly said, "Sure, whatever you think, Doc. When do you think we should go?"

"I would go soon, and I will send notification to Sister Sarah's when I return home. But if anything happens before you hear from me, call Dink. The Company keeps an automobile in Arivaca, now, just for emergencies, and if need be, Dink or somebody will take you to Tucson."

Early next morning, Billie and Della showed up in their buggy. Billie jumped down and met me at the door. "Gipsy," he asked, "What can we do?"

Phil said, "Billie. Get Della and get in here, and we'll tell what's going on."

After sharing the story of our conversation with Dr. Ball, Della said, "You know we have a little place in Tucson we use when we go there on occasion, so why don't you and Philip and I go down so you can be ready. We can stay at our place until it's time to go to the center."

"Sure," Phil said. "When the time comes, you can phone out to Dink, and I'll be right down. And I'll look out for Philip while you're at the center."

Within a day, we were ready to go, and we took the buggy down to Arivaca. Billie had made arrangements for us to ride to town in the Company car. So, after a long and miserable twelve-mile ride in the buggy, we were able to go on to Tucson in relative comfort.

I was at Marteney's place in Tucson for only three days when the time arrived. We hurried over to Sister Sarah's, sent word down to Phil, and soon after, I was close to delivering. Phil arrived just shortly before the baby came, so he was able to be with me during the final couple of hours.

When the baby arrived on December 3rd, it was a girl, and she was a pretty little girl, a plump little thing with a little speck of red hair. She was healthy as could be. Phil was by the bed, holding my hand when he asked, "Well, Gip, what are going to name this one?"

"Phil, I've been hoping it would be a little girl, and I've been thinking that if it was, I want to name her Virginia Dare"

Phil was startled for a minute before he asked how and why I came up with that name.

"Well, Phil, your memory is short. We created our brand, the Bar-V-Bar, because of the inspiration we got from those folks in Texas, and I love that story. And even though Virginia Dare was born hundreds of years ago in Virginia, she became mystical over the years, and she symbolizes all the many things I want for this little girl. You remember? Hope and promise and determination. My hope is that she will be adventuresome, like I have been, and brave and strong like you."

And so, Virginia Dare it was to be. But almost from day one, she was just Ginny. I have always thought, *How strange we go to such lengths to create beautiful names for our children and then almost immediately start calling them by a nickname.*

We were soon back to the Mercantile. With the two kids now, one nursing and trying to keep up with a rambunctious four-year-old, I had my hands full. Phil was gone much of the time. He continued to take advantage of every opportunity to buy or trade for more cattle and acquire more parcels of land through the Gulch. It wasn't too long ago that he told me he was pretty sure we now owned about every deed from here down to the border. He said that if we don't, he's going to find and buy whatever is left so that our cows and steers with the Bar-V-Bar are the only cattle still running in the gulch. And when he's not overseeing the cattle operation, it seems that he's on buying trips for the store.

One day, Phil came in and said, "You know Gip, conditions along the border aren't improving any, and I'm really uncomfortable when I have to be gone. Thank goodness we have the Frasers around most of the time, but they still want to work their mine as much as they can, so I don't think we can count on them to be around all the time."

"I know, Phil. Maybe we can get them to agree for one of them to be around when one of them needs to be gone?"

"Why don't we hire one of these Mexican ladies to come up and help you with the kids, just like we did when we first had Philip?"

"Okay, let's do that," I agreed.

PHIL

The next day, I went down to the mine office and put the word out that we were looking for someone to come work for us at the store. Pretty soon, a young guy came up to me. I recognized him as one of the men who worked on leveling the ground for the new store. Morales was his name. He said he has two sisters who could do what we needed, so I told him to send them up to see me or Gipsy.

Within just a couple of days, two young girls around eighteen years old came to the store. They were from the Morales family down the Gulch a little ways. The father worked in the mines along with his two sons. After talking to them for a while, Gipsy decided to hire Francisca. She was the older of the two. But we told her sister, Sofia, that we would use her a little later. That gave me a bit of relief. I could be a little less anxious about Gip's safety when I had to be gone.

About the middle of the year, The Goldfield Company decided the prospects for success in Ruby were good enough to start operations in full force, so as the year moved into the fall, the Company was hiring more people, and they had started building a new mill that would use a new process called flotation. As the calendar moved into 1917, the mine was producing ore worth thousands of dollars, and soon they were milling over a million pounds of lead and zinc and thousands of dollars of gold and silver.

More people began to arrive. The prospects for work were better than ever, and business for the store grew more rapidly. It was a good time to be in the mercantile business in Ruby. The wooden shacks and tents began to disappear and, in their place came new adobe homes.

Unfortunately, there was still great risk of bandit and rebel activity and raids along the border, but most my main concern was our cattle running loose down in the Gulch. Luis and I are riding almost every day now, mainly trying to keep the cattle north of the line.

The Yaquis have continued to buy guns and ammunition up north and smuggle them across the line to their fellow Indians in Mexico. And along the way, they are stealing cattle, taking them across the border, and slaughtering them for the beef. As a result, the Army now has detachments of soldiers located from Nogales to Arivaca to Sasabe. The soldiers are said to be checking the border every day, but so far, I haven't seen them. We have our guns ready just in case.

GIPSY

In recent weeks, Ginny hasn't been feeling very well and has developed a mysterious high fever. We can't seem to get her fever to go down or to start feeling better. She cries more than she used to and more than she should. Phil rocks and coddles her, but we can't seem to get her better. He's been staying close by as much as he can but, he still has to go out.

Yesterday, he suggested I take her over to Nogales to the hospital and have her checked, so I sent word down to Hank and Liz to see if they would ride along with me. They said they would. And, Phil said to leave Philip with him. Between Alex and John and Francisca, they could keep an eye on him.

Nogales is just about eighteen miles over mountains if you take the short route, but the road is not much more than a rutted wagon trail. But because I was in a hurry to get over there, that's the way we decided to go. We soon found out it takes as long as going down to Arivaca then to Amado and back south to Nogales.

The doctors at the hospital ran numerous tests to no avail. They just couldn't get this strange fever to break. I have been a nervous wreck. Hank has to get home, but Liz is staying with me. We have been sharing a hotel room, and she has been a big help, but it's been difficult for her. We've been here for almost two weeks now, and finally, the doctors have determined that she has been fighting the effects of typhoid fever. Fortunately, they have managed to hold her temperature steady for the last couple of days. Hopefully, we will be able to get back home in a couple of days.

Thanksgiving is just a week away, so I am really glad Ginny is being released tomorrow and we're going home. Word must have gotten back to Phil because that morning just on time, he arrived to take us all back. As we leave the hospital, he said that we were going to take the train to Amado, and Clemente was going to meet us with the automobile and take us the rest of the way.

CHAPTER 24

PHIL

Soon, we were back home and settling back into some normalcy. Francisca and the Frasers had done a very good job of keeping things running well. But two days later, Luis came to the store to say there was trouble starting over in Bear Valley with the Indians. And the soldiers from Nogales were being sent over to see what was going on.

For the past year or so, the Yaquis have been coming up from Mexico to work in the mines and on the ranches over in that area. And, after they earn enough money, they buy guns and ammunition and smuggle it back across the line to the Indians down there to help them with their battles against the revolutionaries. I'm sure when the soldiers confront them there is going to be a war.

In addition to the Yaqui issues, the rebels and bandidos have been raiding over there, and I can't find those twelve steers that have been grazing on that side of the mountain.

"What do you think, Luis? I think maybe somebody has stolen our steers. Have you heard anything from cowboys over there?"

"Si," he said, "They think maybe it's Reyes, that guy from down near the Casa Piedra. Or maybe it's the Yaquis."

I said, "No, I don't think so, Luis. I don't think the Yaquis will steal the Bar-V-Bar. Maybe it's Camargo and his renegades. Go down to Billie's and get Buck and Slim. Get some food and water, and we'll go to Bear Valley today and find our steers."

"Okay, Felipe. I be back muy pronto."

I told Gipsy what has come up and that we have to go find our steers and see what's going on. "I'll try to be back in just a day or two. If you get to expecting trouble, try to get the kids and yourself down to Marteney's, okay?"

The boys were back in a couple of hours, and we headed up the old road toward Bear Valley, about seven miles east over the hills. Just as we were dropping out of the hills, we heard gunfire.

"Let's go, boys. We have to see what's happening!" I yelled.

It took us a while to work our way through the brush and trees, but all the while, the exchange of gunfire continued nonstop. Soon, I could see the soldiers on horses and Indians on foot chasing each other around through the oak trees and brush firing randomly at anything that was moving.

After only a couple of hours of exchanging fire, the battle came to a stop. As we approached, we could see that the Indians had suffered many casualties and that a number were being rounded up by the soldiers. I approached the captain and asked what happened.

He said, "We had a report that the Indians were coming out of Peña Blanca with bundles of firearms and ammunition on their way down to the border. We're part of the 10th Cavalry from Nogales, and evidently, this Indian over here says they mistook us black soldiers for Mexicans rebels, and that's why they opened fire on us. They have some wounded here, and we've got ten of them under arrest. So, now I'm going to have to take them back to Nogales."

"Excuse me, captain. I'm friendly with some of these people. Why don't you just let me take them down to the border? I could use their help. You see, I've lost several my steers, and I'm heading over toward the rock house to find them. If I run into Reyes or Camargo and their banditos, I could use these people to help us."

"I don't think I should consider doing that, sir," he said.

"Oh hell, captain, they paid for these guns, and they're just taking them across the line so their brothers over there can protect themselves from those crooked Mexican soldiers."

"Uh, okay, sir. Get them out of here."

"Clarke's my name, captain. I have the mercantile store over in Ruby. If you get over that way sometime, stop in for a soda or maybe a beer."

"Thank you, Clarke. I will."

"Luis, let's get these people rounded up and go find our steers."

"Si, señor," he said.

I rode over to the group of Indians, and to my surprise, there stood Tomas, my adobe maker.

"Tomas," I said. "Como esta?"

"Not so good today, Patron Felipe, but you make it more better. We go to Mexico?"

"Si, Tomas, but I need some help finding my steers. You help me, okay?"

"Oh, si, si, patron."

"Anybody dead?"

"No, señor, many wounded. I want to send them back to Peña Blanca. Is okay?"

"Okay, Tomas, let's go!"

Soon, we were on our way toward the border.

"Buck and Slim, you two cut over the south end of the hills. Luis and I will follow the line west to the rock house. We'll meet there. If you see the steers, come down and get me, okay?"

We moved west along the border, very slowly because the Indians were walking, and we were both looking for the steers but also watching for bandits.

Night came along, and I decided to stop. The Indians needed rest, and we couldn't see much. I thought, *Better to stop, have something to eat, and just listen.*

After an hour or so, we moved on. About midnight, we neared what is known as the Ora Pass, a short narrow gap in the southern end of the mountains and just a short way from the line. Soon, I heard horses and stopped. "Quiet," I said to everybody.

A full moon was over the eastern edge of the mountains, and I saw a single rider coming slowly and cautiously. I moved over to the edge of our group and soon saw I was looking up the barrel of

Buck's new Winchester .30-30 rifle. Lucky for me, he saw me at the same time. We smiled at each other and then laughed. He came on and dismounted.

"How you doing?" I asked.

"Good. Slim's up above following a small group of Mex's moving a herd of about thirty head. Can't tell the brand because of the dark, but I think they're all Bar-V-Bar."

"Go get Slim and the two of you hightail it to the pass. We'll meet you there, and if there too many of them, we'll take care of them pronto and head north with the whole herd."

But we were too late, they had just gone through the gap by the time we arrived. I wanted to get after them right them, but Buck said there were six or eight of them. He pointed out that we were out in the open, and that little herd was scattered all over. He said it would be better for us to wait until they got settled down and then wipe out the whole nest of those dirty skunks.

"You're right, Buck. The time has come to clean up this whole mess of dirty rebels and coyote Mexican soldiers. Before we left the store for Bear Valley, I heard that bunch of cavalry from Arivaca would be heading for the line here pretty soon."

"Well," Slim said, "It's going to take a hell of a lot more than that cavalry to scare us off. You can bet your life that whatever we get done here tonight ain't going to get out. Are we going risk it?"

All three of them said, "Yes!"

I just kind of nodded my head, not real sure about what these boys would be risking. In the stillness and blackness of the night, the four of them rode down to within sight of the house, dismounted, hid the horses in the gully nearby, and went forward on foot. When they knew everyone inside was asleep, they crawled on their hands and knees through the chaparral and rocks up to the first wall the house.

I said, "Buck, get that stick of dynamite we brought and put it in that wall."

We crawled back to the rocks and crouched behind them while I lit the fuse. "Get ready," I said.

When the blast went off, it started a major panic inside the stone house. There was screaming and screeching and different men yelling orders. Soon, men were scattering in every direction out into the darkness.

Before any of them realized what was happening, we opened fire and shot at will at everything moving inside. I heard screams of pain and yells of agony. I soon heard one injured man yelling and cussing, referring to us as Mexican soldiers. They evidently thought we were government troops.

The shooting only lasted about five minutes, but when it was over and the light of the new day approached, we could see bodies lying on the ground. Whoever didn't get shot had run off. As I walked among the bodies, I was amazed at what we had done. Suddenly, a fit of nausea seized me, and I put my arms across my eyes to conceal what a moment ago had given me great pleasure. This revenge thing was not very sweet today. For me, it had turned loathsome. I just want to get our cattle and get away.

"Come on, let's get out of here. Those soldiers from Arivaca surely heard all that shooting and will head here soon."

They hurried back to their horses, mounted up, and quickly began gathering all the cattle. In all the rush, I had almost forgotten about Tomas and the rest of the Indians. But they were right there, helping us get them all grouped up. I stopped and called Tomas over as we were beginning to move. "Tomas, you go now. You take three or four steers and go south."

"Okay," he said. "Muchas gracias, patron."

"De nada, Tomas. Gracias to you and your brothers for helping us. Vaya con Dios, amigo."

It turned out there were nearly a hundred head there, but we could get them all put together and start up the Gulch. Pretty soon, I realized that Luis and I were moving all those steers and cows by ourselves. It wasn't until an hour or so later that Buck and Slim were right alongside of us on the other side of the herd. I asked where they had been and Slim said, "We just hung back to make sure we had everything we came after."

"What else did you find?"

They each reached for bundles they had tied on behind. "We found a bunch of hides piled up in back there along with six carcasses they had hanging in the trees. Likely getting ready to cut up into meat for their people. Phil, a bunch of these hides have the Bar-V-Bar on them."

Luis looked at me and said, "I'm sorry, patron. I tried to find them."

"Luis, it's all good. We got way more than we lost. If we don't find any brands, we'll figure they are Mexican cattle stolen from ranches in Mexico and we'll put the Bar-V-Bar on them."

When we got back, I was ready to see my family

"Gipsy, we traveled over to Bear Valley and witnessed a skirmish of Yaquis and American soldiers over guns the Indians were trying to smuggle down to their brothers in Mexico to chasing renegade bandits across the border. We ended up in a shootout with them at that old stone house that the Reyes family used to own. We found that they had stolen our twelve steers, and we found six hides with the Bar-V-Bar on them. But Gip, we also brought nearly a hundred head of Mexican steers and cows back that we'll put the Bar-V-Bar on in the next day or so."

Gipsy asked, "Phil, where are you going to put all these cattle?"

"I think I'll go down to Billie's and see if he wants to partner on these animals in exchange for some of his Forest ground."

We shoved all the cattle into the corrals we had, but I knew I could only keep them there for a day or so, so I headed down to Billie's the next day. As I neared Oro Blanco, Billie and the boys were approaching. We got alongside each other, and Billie said, "Yeah, that's a good idea. Let's go get them."

I said, "What the hell you talking about, Billie."

"I'm talking about your idea, Phil," he said and laughed. "When the boys told me about what had happened, I knew you were going to come down and talk to me about this idea. I've got an open pasture up on the Coronado forest east of my home place. Let's go put some brands on them and get them moved up there."

"Well, by golly," I said. "Thanks, Billie. Let's go."

As we were turning to head back up to the corrals at Ruby, I saw a detachment of soldiers approaching from the west. I pointed them out to the boys, and Billie commented that they were probably just making their rounds. As they approached, I looked at them questioningly, fearing reports of our trip to the border would not be good for the boys and me. I was quickly putting together a plan of explanation and self-defense for what happened.

I was about to speak when the lieutenant paused and looked at me and then said, "Have you heard the news?"

"What?" I asked.

"The revolutionary Army went to the Casa Piedra and attacked Carranza's men a couple of days ago. Killed all of them. At least all that was still there. Then they hung six of in the trees. It looks like exactly what happened over in Nogales two weeks ago. We're expecting reinforcements at Arivaca anytime, and we'll guard the entire strip from Sasabe to Nogales and station an entire camp at the Stone House."

My mouth dropped open, and my eyes bulged out, and all I could think to say was, "Well, I'll be goddamned!"

Buck, Slim, and I rode back up the road to Ruby with hardly a word from any of us. But I sure wasn't missing the strange looks we were getting from Billie. I'll need a pretty good story for him, I'm sure.

It took us about three days to get all those cattle branded and moved, but we got it done without incident. When we were done and about ready to head home, Billie asked me about Yaquis we had picked up in Bear Valley. I told him how they had come over the hills with us that night and helped us with our little skirmish, and when we were getting ready to head back up the Gulch, I told Tomas to take a few steers with him and head on down to his people in Mexico.

He said, "I wouldn't be surprised if those Indians hung those bandits before they left. What do you think?"

I looked at Buck and Slim for a moment and said, "Yeah, Billie, I'll bet they did."

And we smiled at each other.

CHAPTER 25

The first couple of months of the new year were fairly quiet from the standpoint of problems along the border. We didn't lose any more cattle down there, so wondered if the rebels and bandits moved on to other areas along the line. The Army has patrols moving around all along there, now.

One evening in early February, Gipsy came up to me and gave me a big hug and said, "Phil, I have another surprise for you." I smiled because I knew by the way she hugged me and looked at me what she was going to say. "Yes," she said. "I'm pregnant again. I've been pretty sure for a month or so. I think we should be expecting the arrival about late summer."

She continued, "You know, Minnie has been talking about coming out to visit us for a couple of years. If she could come this summer, she might come when the baby is due, and she could be a big help."

"Sure," I said. "Why don't you try to put that plan together? Thank goodness we have Alex and John available to help in the store, and Francesca for you."

Between remodeling and repairing little issues that come up after building a new building, there was no end to projects around the place. With the Frasers here, it makes it a lot easier for me to deal with the cattle business. One day, I was working outside near the front door, and it occurred to me that when the monsoons come in late summer, we had huge amounts of rainfall through here, but we didn't have any means of measuring how much falls. I called Alex, who was working just inside the door and asked him if he remembered those long, plastic tubes that our gun powder came in.

"Yeah, I think we saved some of them, and we put them behind the counter."

"Bring me one; would you, Alex?"

He brought one outside and asked what I was up to.

"I'm going to rig up a little gadget with this tube to measure how much rainfall we get when the monsoon rains come. What do you think the size is? Maybe two to three feet long and about three inches across?"

"Yeah, I think so."

"Well, I think I can just drive this long rod into the ground and mount this tube to it and run some copper wire from the bottom down into the ground to create a ground wire for safety when we get lightning storms. We can mark off some measurements, so when it rains, we'll know how much has fallen."

Alex just thought that was the neatest idea he had seen. We probably had the only true rain gauge in the valley.

I was riding through Oro Blanco a few days later, on my way down to see Hank, and ran into Arthur Noon. He was at the little blacksmith shop getting some work done on one of his wagons.

Arthur's family has been around these parts for nearly fifty years or so. I think his father, Dr. Adolphus Noon, came into these parts way back in the 1870s or so and started doing a little mining and later running a few head of cattle. Arthur once told me that of all his siblings, he was probably the one with the most interest in the cattle business. After he went to Mexico and worked in mines for a few years, he came back here and has been taking care of the Noon ranches.

We've known each other well throughout the years, but he's a bit older than me, and he had spent most of his time on the ranch while I was working for The Company in town. I've always considered him a good friend and an honorable man. We said hello to each other and visited for a while. I was just getting ready to go on, and he stopped me and said, "Hey Phil, have you heard about the Forest people talking about splitting up the district."

I told him that I hadn't and asked what it would mean to our ranges.

"Well," he said, "As I understand it, they're thinking about creating an Oro Blanco district to the west of the road here and a Montana district on the east."

I asked if that would be a problem for the Noon's.

He said, "Not really, but it would be better for us if all our allotments are in the same district."

"Well, I can understand that. Maybe I'm wrong, Arthur, but doesn't your mother or aunt have a couple of patents on the east side along here?"

"Yes, and we will probably want to sell them and replace them with one or so of these Bartlett or Hardy parcels across the road sometime if that happens."

"Well, Arthur, you know I've acquired several parcels down in the Gulch in the last couple of years but really hope to have an opportunity to run my cattle further up north here and further from the border. I appreciate the information on the Forest; I'll keep an eye on what they're doing."

"Sure Phil. How are Gipsy and the kids?"

"They're all doing good. Thanks, and by the way, we're expecting another at the end of the summer."

"Well, good for you. You and Gipsy stop by anytime you come through here."

"Thanks Arthur. We will."

I left and headed on down toward Hanks. But my mind was full of ideas now. I thought that if the Noons were going to sell some of their parcels, I would sure like to have a chance at acquiring them. I thought I should talk to Billie and see what he knew.

I got to Hank and Liz's early in the afternoon. Hank met me and asked, "What brings you down here, Phil?"

"Well, Hank, Billie's boys and I were in a little shootout with some Mexicans last week down at the casa piedra, and I want to talk to the commandant of the detachment. I want to learn as much as I can about what they're going to do down there. The lieutenant we saw last week said they were putting a camp in, but so far, we haven't seen any sign of it."

"Yeah, word has it you went down to find some lost cattle and got into a little squabble."

"Yeah, well, it was more than just a little squabble for sure. Got my family and the Frasers all upset over it, too."

"Well, actually Phil, there's word out that Camargo has his group still running around making trouble down in Tres Bellotas and Sasabe area—stealing cattle, mostly. I guess lots of mouths to feed with this war going on. Sure would like to see it all come to an end."

"For sure," I agreed. "Well, I think I'll wander over to the store and say hello to Dink. And maybe see Annalee too. How are they doing?"

"I think okay, Phil. By the way, did you hear that Jack is packing up and heading back east with his Julie?"

"No, I didn't."

"Well, we all know she never did want to live out there on that place, and she didn't want to be at the Jarillas either. I think she and Uncle Johnnie clashed a bit."

"Well, I guess that means Dink will be living back here in the village again?"

"Yeah, probably so."

"Okay, good seeing you. Hi to Liz."

I went across the street, found Dink doing the same stuff I did for six years—sorting mail and putting goods on the shelves.

"Hey Dink, how you doing?"

"Phil, good to see you. As you can see, I'm just like you used to be—busy, busy all the time. The Company always has something more for me to do."

"Well, I just came down to see the commandant at the camp. Visited a little with Hank and Liz and thought I'd see how you are."

"We're pretty good, Phil. Did you hear, Jack's packing up and going back east with Julie?"

"Yeah, what's he going to do with his homestead?"

"I'm not sure, but I think Johnnie thinks he should give it to the Company."

"Well, I'll be damned. Good ol' Johnnie. Any chance you could get it?"

"No. I really would like to have it, Phil. You know, I only have a few head that Jack lets me keep out there, but the place is eighty acres and has an allotment for thirty-eight head, I think. Maybe it's more. But Johnnie would never let me have it. I'll just be moving back down here. That'll make Annalee happy, anyway."

"By the way, Gipsy is expecting again. Probably near the end of the summer. Maybe another boy this time."

"Well, good luck with everything Phil. Annalee's been trying for darn near a year now. We'll just keep trying."

"That's about all you can do, Dink. Just keep trying. So, take care. You two come out and see us sometime soon."

I left, thinking I probably had learned all the Army's plans for the border that I was going to.

I detoured over to Billie's on my way home. "Billie," I said when I found him out by the corrals, "I just came from the village. I saw Hank and Dink and thought I would stop by here on my way home."

"Damn, Phil, don't you have any work to do?"

"Yeah, I do, but I'm trying to find out if the Army is going to put a camp down at the rock house."

"Doesn't look like it, so I guess that means I'll be back to taking care of that area by myself again. Heard in town just now that Jack's packing up and taking Julie back east. Wonder what he's going to do with his homestead. Can't imagine he'd just walk from it. Be good for one of us to get it."

"Yeah," he said. "I'm going to look into it."

"Okay, I just thought I'd swing by, but I have to get back to work," I said with a smile.

Spring moved into summer, then one day in June, a neighbor to the north and a good friend of ours, John Lyttle, came to the store to see me. I was just getting ready to head south to check on the steers when he arrived. After we had visited for a while, I told John that I needed to get going if I was to make it home in time for supper.

He said, "Sorry, Phil, but I have something important to ask you."

"What can I do for you?"

"Well, Phil, you know I have some patents up near Oro Blanco. The border troubles are a little concern for us, and we're talking about selling out and moving north someplace a bit more peaceful. I happened to be telling Arthur this the other day, and he said he had heard you might have some interest."

I thought for a minute or so. I surely wanted some property up north, and his would be a great start for us up that way. "Well, John, yeah. I have some interest, and I do need more pasture than I have now. Care to tell me what your permits look like?"

"Of course, Phil. Mine are likely as generous as any in the district. My deeds total two eighties and three forties. And right now, there are a couple thousand acres in permits, and they allow for a couple hundred head, but we've been running a few more than that the last couple of years since it's mostly steers we run."

"I'm sure interested, John. If we can make it work for us, I'd do it."

"Well," he said, "I'll make it work. Can we get together in the next couple days?"

"Sure."

I rode the Gulch most of the rest of that day. It gave me a good bit of time to think John's deal through. I just needed to meet with him and try to get it done. He had a sizable operation, and I wasn't sure we were strong enough yet to make it work.

The next day, I rode down to his place, and we sat down. He was anxious to make the deal work. We worked out a few details worked in some cash for his cattle and some time for the deeds, and ended up with a good deal for both of us.

That evening, we were sitting on the porch looking out over the lake and up toward the peak. I had just finished telling Gipsy about our latest transaction. She was really thrilled, and she said, "Phil, wait right here. I want to show you something." She went inside and when she came back out, she had a new painting. "Phil, just look at this. I painted it today and didn't even know what you were doing."

She held up the picture. As I looked at it, I noticed Montana Peak was in the background. "Phil, look at all the colors. I did it this afternoon when the sun was just right, just before setting behind Baboquivari. Its rays magnify all the reds and oranges and purples in that beautiful peak. Phil, it's like all these colors are painted into the lands all through this district."

"Gipsy, that's a beautiful thought, and you're certainly right. This is a land of many colors, in nature and the real world."

Gipsy was well along with the pregnancy and increasingly uncomfortable. I asked her when Minnie was coming out because if she didn't get there pretty soon, she was going to miss out.

"She wanted to come long before now, but our sister Bert got sick, and Minnie felt she should stay until Bert was well again. She's planning for the middle of July. That should give her time to be here when the baby comes."

"What are her travel plans?"

"She's coming to Tucson, and I gave her instructions to get the Nogales train to Amado, and we would make arrangements to meet her there. I hope you can get her."

"Sure, Gip. And if I can't, we'll get somebody to pick her up. But I'll plan on it when you know her plans."

Times were good. There were lots of people working in the mines and on the surrounding ranches. The revolution in Mexico was winding down, but unfortunately, the fear and risk of robbery was still very great. Rebels and Mexican soldiers who deserted were still moving back and forth across the line, stealing and pillaging.

I had remained concerned ever since our encounter earlier down at the border, and one morning, a week or so later, an Army truck showed up at the store. The lieutenant from the Utah detachment stationed in Arivaca got out along with a half a dozen soldiers. All were heavily armed. He said they have been informed on good authority that General Camargo was somewhere between Sasabe and

Tres Bellotas and heading toward the stone house with plans to rob my store. They said that they were making rounds of the district to ask people to come down to the camp and wanted me to bring my family down.

"Do you have any idea when they will be in this area?" I asked.

"Maybe a week or so."

"Well, why don't you get some troops over here and take care of that guy?"

"We're trying. I just don't know if we can get them here in time."

Connecticut National Guard Camp in Arivaca, AZ

"Damn," I said to Gipsy, "They want us to leave our home and the store. They must think I'm not very smart. I'm not leaving this place. Everything we have and everything we've worked for is in that store and out in those corrals. I guarantee you, Gipsy, they will pay a hell of a price before they get their hands on any of it."

"Phil, why don't we go to California. I can get a hold of Jesse or Zehna Swift or even Bessie. I know Jesse is still at Redondo Beach, and I think the others are still there too. I'm sure I can get Minnie to go with us, to because she's supposed to be on her way here next week."

"Gip, those are all good ideas, but for now, let's see if you and the kids can go stay with Hank and Liz, or even Billie and Della.

"If that will work, I'll stay here and get things squared away with that scoundrel Camargo, and then we'll go to Tucson and meet Minnie and go to California. I think the mercantile in town has a phone, so you might be able to make arrangements that way. If you can get your stuff ready in the next day or so, I'll take you down."

Events happened fast over the next couple of days. Gip was able to get arrangements made with her friends at Redondo Beach and with Minnie, so we planned to meet Minnie in Tucson and go to California to have our baby. But not until I took care of General Camargo. We got Gipsy and the kids set up with Hank and Liz, but it would only be for a couple of days because Minnie would be in Tucson early the next week.

I was still at the store. I had told Alex and John that I was going to lock up so they could go back to their mine and take care of things there. Francisca got scared when the Army guys were here and left to go back to her mother's house down the valley.

I was getting ready to close up the store for the last day of business until this thing got resolved, and I was trying to get old Guzman and his burros loaded up. He picked a lousy time to come get his month's supplies because it always seemed to require both of his donkeys to haul everything he bought.

As he was settling up with me and getting ready to leave, he looked at my rain gauge and asked what it was. I was just starting to tell him when I had a strange idea pop in my head. I often kidded with Guzman because he was a very serious kind of guy, and he never knew when I was kidding with him.

He looked at me quizzically and asked, "Señor Felipe, what is that thing?"

I decided to try a story. "Well, Señor Guzman, this is a very dangerous machine."

I elaborated at length on the intricate wiring I had set up, pointing to the copper wire that ran up the side of the wall and down into the ground. I pointed to the wire and said, "This wire goes in to where

I sleep. There, I have a big button next to my bed. This big tube is filled with a deadly gas. If I press the button inside the house, it releases a big spray of the gas, enough to kill everything, people and horses, around for five hundred feet, soldiers, banditos—everything."

I showed him a big explosion with my hands and mouth as a demonstration of what it would do. He became very serious, more so than I had ever seen him and even scared. "Oh no, Señor Felipe. Be very careful." He backed away slowly and carefully until he was safely away.

He mounted his old horse, and as he was leaving I said, "If you see Camargo, you tell him about this thing. If he comes up here, he will not live. Do you understand?"

"Oh, si, Felipe. Muy bien," he said as he rode away down the gulch.

Our plan was for Gipsy to stay with Liz and Hank for a few days until Minnie arrived in Tucson, and I would get the store and house closed. Then I would go down and meet her, and I would send them on to California.

On my way to town, I met the lieutenant and some of his soldiers heading for Ruby and the camp and other mines in the area. I was surprised to see Hank riding along. "Good morning," I greeted the lieutenant.

He stopped and said, "Phil, we have word that Camargo is at the stone house already, and he is making lots of noise about going north to find Señor Felipe. You need to get out of here, Phil."

"I'm not going. Hank, please tell Gipsy that I'll see her in California."

Hank turned to the lieutenant and said, "Did you hear that? You tell Gipsy because I'm staying with Phil."

I looked at Hank and smiled. "Well, let's get back up there."

We gathered up all the rifles and pistols and ammunition we could carry, along with a few days' supply of food and water. We headed up to the rocks in front of the opening to the mine shaft. From there, we could see far down the Gulch and most of the area east and west.

"When he comes, I'll be ready for him. Hank," I said. "You know you shouldn't be here. Liz will skin you alive."

"Phil, no way would I let you try to protect this beautiful place by yourself."

"Well, you know, the odds sure aren't in our favor. If he comes up here with a hundred half-crazy coyotes, it's not going to be pretty."

"I know Phil, but let's just see what happens."

We sat up there in the rocks for three days and three nights, almost freezing to death at night and roasting through the day. But damned if I was going to let that guy sneak up on us.

On the fourth day, the lieutenant showed up with a whole platoon of his soldiers. He stopped in front of the store, looked around. Not seeing me or Hank anywhere surely worried him. He scattered his men all over with orders to find us and damned quick. I quickly came out from behind the rocks and yelled down to him that were okay.

When we got down to him, he quickly said he was so happy to see we were all right but asked if we had had any encounter with Camargo. I told him that we had not. When all the good news had passed around, he told us that Camargo only stayed at the stone house for a day or so then left with all of his troops and headed toward Nogales.

One of the miners who told them of this said he had heard that some old prospector came out of the Gulch and had some conversation with Camargo and soon after Camargo mounted up and headed east. At that point, they had a couple of platoons out of Nogales chasing him east toward Agua Prieta, over near Douglas. They didn't think they were going to see him back over this way, especially if they got him.

That was surely good news for all of us around here. "But I think I might have liked having a little encounter with the dirty rascal," I said.

"I hope you don't have the chance," he said. "He's a bad hombre."

Within a day or so, people started coming back around the camp. Alex and John had come back and offered to take care of the store if I was still inclined to go to California. I sure appreciated that.

I packed up my grip and headed down to the village to see about getting Gip and the kids ready to go, but first, I went to find Luis and make final plans for the cattle. We were not too far away from round-up time, and we needed to start bringing them together in the different areas. We already had it figured out, but I wanted to make sure he was still on. He was, and I reminded him Billie's boys were around if he needed any help with anything.

GIPSY

I was sure glad to see Phil, just as much as he was to see me and the kids. Hank had shared their story, so there wasn't too much more to tell. I said that Minnie was on her way tomorrow. She would stop in Kerrville for a night, then El Paso, then on to Tucson. We needed to meet her in two days.

Soon, we were all together and on our way to Redondo Beach. I was so glad to see so many of my old friends. Jesse and Zehna met us at the station, and we loaded up in Jesse's auto and drove out to her little place at the beach. I felt sure this was going to be a good idea.

Zehna's car

It turned out that I was much closer than we thought; it wasn't five days before I was in labor. I was at the medical center here Redondo Beach, right near Jesse's, so it was very convenient.

Unlike Philip and Virginia, this labor was very easy. After about six hours of labor on Aug 3, 1917, we had another baby boy. Both Phil and I were elated. He was very healthy, and I we both had been hoping for another boy.

"Well, Mr. Clarke, what do you have in mind for a name?" I asked.

"Gip, I've been thinking about this ever since Philly came along. You know, we named him after us and were both were proud of that. Do you have a name you would like?"

"No, but I think you have one in mind, and I think I know what it is, and if it is, I'll be very happy with it."

"Well, I'd like to name him Daniel."

"I like that," I said and added, "Since we had to come clear over here to the coast for his birth, for a middle name, what do you think of calling him Daniel West Coast Clarke? Or, maybe Daniel Out West Clarke?"

"Ah, Gipsy, your fooling with me, aren't you."

"Okay, how about just Daniel West?"

"Good! That will be his name."

CHAPTER 26

I recovered well and was up and around just in a matter of days. All was going well. Minnie was with us, and both the kids and I just loved being with her. Phil was going to be heading back to Arivaca soon, but we wanted to get a little vacation time in before he left.

We all loaded up in Zehna's big touring car, and she showed us all over Los Angeles. We went to the zoo and the orange groves and the cathedral that I talked so much about when Phil and I first met. And, of course, most of the time we spent at the beach. The kids love playing in the sand and trying to outrun the breakers as they crashed in the surf. We were having a great time and decided that the kids and I would stay for another few weeks. Minnie had talked to Frank, and all was well in Wharton, so she decided to stay, too.

PHIL

I left my family behind, and as I crossed the vast desert between the ocean and Tucson, I thought about much I was going to miss them. I planned to bring them back home in just a few short weeks, but what would I be bringing them back to? Was there still danger lurking everywhere along the border? Was it going to be safe for us there? I wondered if I should start thinking about moving someplace safer and secure. There was a lot for me to ponder.

In the meantime, I had a growing ranch with a bunch of cattle running around from the Forest of the Oro Blanco district all the way to the border, along with a mercantile store that continued to grow.

One day, I was visiting with Alex and John, mainly talking about how good we felt about the border problems seeming to have settled down a bit, when who should come up to the store but old man Guzman. I was afraid that if he had encountered Camargo, he surely would have been killed. But here he was.

After a short visit I asked if, by chance, he had seen Camargo after he left here last time. He looked at me and smiled and said that he had. Carmago had stopped him and asked what was going on up here at the camp. Specifically, he wanted to know about the store. He wanted to know if anyone was with Phil or if he was alone up here. And, he asked when the soldiers came by. He continued, "Señor, he was planning to come up here and rob you; I know."

"Well, what happened?"

"I tell him about your machine with the vapor. He just laughs at me. Pretty soon, I see him having an argument with some of his men, and then he takes my sacks from my burros, and they get on their horses and go toward the southeast. I don't see them again."

We all smiled, and I said, "Señor Guzman, I'm glad you are okay. I was afraid he would kill you, but you are very brave. Come in the store and have a nice refreshment."

"Thank you, Señor Felipe."

After a week or so working with Luis, we were getting pretty close to being ready, so when Ramon sent out word of the starting date and where it would start, we would be able to do our part. I decided to see Billie and learn what had been going on since we left nearly a month ago. I also wanted to learn what his plans were going to be for the round-up, especially if we might plan on working our outfits together.

On my way to his place, I ran into him and the boys in Chimney Canyon. They were doing exactly what Luis and I had been doing that last couple of weeks. He said he had heard our trip to California went well and asked about Gipsy and the kids.

"They are doing well. We're planning for them to come back around the first of October."

"Is she going to be okay down there with you gone quite a bit about then?"

"I'm not sure, Billie, but I think we'll be okay. Alex and John are around a good part of the time, and you know, things have quieted down quite a bit since Camargo took off. I think they'll be okay. By the way, whatever happened with Jack's place?"

"Well, Johnnie kept telling Jack he needed to give that parcel to the Company, and Jack wasn't liking that pressure much. He wanted to sell it to Dink, but Dink couldn't handle it, plus Jack only had a couple of old steers out there and no Forest permit. So, I said, Jack, just sell it to me, and I'll work a deal with Dink so he can stay on it.

"We did that, and I got a hold of Dink and worked out a deal where he could buy it from me when the prove-ups were completed. I also made a deal on some steers with him. I told him I had recently picked up some Mexican steers at a good price, and I would sell about thirty of them to him to take care of until spring round-up. I'd help him get a permit for them, then we would sell them, and he could pay me and keep the rest. I figure that would give him and Annalee a fair chance to get started on their own."

"Good for you Billie, always wanting to help the guy out. I hope it works out for them."

Gipsy and the kids arrived back in early October, and we quickly settled back into some element of normalcy. The store was busy as ever, and Alex and John were as helpful as ever, even though they were getting more involved in their mining operation again and were only at the store during the day.

The Goldfield Mining Company did just as they had indicated they would. New mills were built, more people were moving in and being hired, more homes were being built, and Ruby was turning back into a promising and prospering little village.

And even though the village was in a peaceful situation now, trouble still continued along the border. The Mexican revolution was coming to an end, but rebels, revolutionaries, and bandits were continuing to steal and raid ranches and homesteaders from Texas to

California. The cavalry continued its presence at key locations and was managing to maintain a good element of law and order in our area and up north toward Oro Blanco and Arivaca.

GIPSY

The end of the year came and went in a flash, just as previous ones had. With so much going on, we didn't slow down much. The kids were growing like weeds and doing well. The summer monsoons came early in 1918. They brought lots of moisture, and the pastures in the forests and valleys were green like they hadn't been for many years.

Phil continued to take advantage of opportunities to purchase additional ranches farther north between here and Oro Blanco, and along with these acquisitions comes more cattle. Our herds now number into the hundreds and require more of Phil's time. In addition to taking care of the cattle and the ranches, he also is gone a considerable amount of time on buying trips for the store. Sometimes, he only goes to Tucson, but there have been occasions when he goes to Phoenix as well.

Fall arrived and took us into round-up time. We prepared for Phil being gone quite a bit during this time, but he is trying to get back as often as he can. Even so, it is so lonesome when he's gone. The kids keep good company, and Francisca lives around back in the little house. However, I don't see her after she leaves when supper is done and the kids are settled down for the night. Her worthless boyfriend, Ezequiel Lara, comes around most every night, so she is never any company. Even though Liz and Hank do come down often, it's still scary for me being here at night by myself.

PHIL

The round-up is moving along in good order, and we're hoping to be done and on our way to Tucson in a week or so. That will be good. The cattle will get sold, and everybody will head back to their ranches, and another season will be ready to begin.

Billie approached me one evening as a group of us were sitting around discussing markets and prospects for the coming year and said he had an idea for me. I said, "Is everything okay?"

"He said, "I just have an idea for you to consider. "You know I'm a bit older than you, and I've been doing this for a long time."

"Sure, Billie, I know, and you know I think the world of you."

"That's why I want to talk to you about you buying me out."

"What are you talking about?"

"What I'm talking about is that Della and I want to move to Tucson. You know, I own some property there, and I'd like to slow down a bit and maybe build some apartments on some of them. You're the one person in this district I'd feel good about turning this place over to."

"Billie, your place is mighty big. I'd sure like to be able to get down into that cienega area and do some farming, too. Do you have ideas of how we can put this together?"

"I do," he said, "but for now, I just want to know if you are interested."

"Yes, Billie, for sure I am."

"Okay, when we get back from round-up let's get together and talk it over."

Wow, I thought. *What an opportunity. This will be great news for Gipsy. She will surely think this is our opportunity to get closer to town.*

Round up ended in Tucson just before Thanksgiving, and soon after, most everybody left for their ranches. Billie suggested he and I stay an extra day so we could visit more.

We went to El Charro cafe for lunch, and he told me that he and Della had been talking for some time about changing their life. They had spent nearly fifty years in the area, and they wanted to move to the city. He said, "We've talked about this for a long time, Phil, but there never has been the right person to approach about it. We have watched you and Gipsy since the beginning. You have shown you are a good businessman and have done very well with the store and your land and cattle acquisitions. And I just remembered, you also have a couple of mines that have done okay for you."

"All of that is true, Billie, we have done well. Thank you for thinking that."

"We want to sell the entire ranch, including all the buildings, equipment, and the livestock. Are you still interested?"

"I am, but I only know what I think I know about your ranch. I know it's very large and consists of many homesteads and other deeded parcels. And I believe they are scattered from just north of Ruby all the way to the Company's south line. And, of course, the Forest permits that run with these parcels. I think we need to determine if Gipsy and I are able to make it work."

"I assure you, Phil," he said, "We can make it work."

Within three months, in early spring of 1919, we had bought the Marteney ranch, which included a vast checkerboard of deeded parcels, including part of the late John Maloney's homestead and the John Lyle homestead near Oro Blanco, Bertolo Caviglia's homestead, the William Tonkin homestead, and also, the Perry homestead just east of Oro Blanco. Along with each of these parcels came thousands of acres of Coronado National Forest grazing permits. The purchase included hundreds of head of his cattle, many horses and, most importantly, Buck and Slim.

Additionally, Billie insisted that we honor the agreement he had made with Dink the year before where he could purchase Jack's homestead and run up to thirty head on the Forest if he wanted to. He knew I would be happy to do that. The terms were simple— some cash, some gold, and a little time on contract. It was a great celebration for us and the Marteneys.

We had to decide what we would or could do with the mercantile because I had become more involved in the cattle operations. This acquisition more than doubled our ranch size, and as a result, I was gone much more than I wanted and am not spending near enough time at home and the store. Every time I left, I had a lot of anxiety knowing Gipsy and the kids were essentially alone every night.

Late one night in early June, I had just had a smoke and cup of coffee when I heard a horse approaching at a fast clip. I wasn't concerned there could be danger, and when I stood up, Slim came sliding into my little camp.

"Phil!" he yelled, "There's been trouble at the store. Luis came down and told us somebody tried to break in."

"Oh, hell," I said as I hurried to get Payaso saddled up.

Slim said, "Don't worry about your grip, Phil. I'll get it tomorrow."

The two of us were on our way up to Ruby and were there within an hour. Many people were milling around, and I quickly found Gipsy inside the store.

"Gip, are you okay? What happened? Is anybody hurt?"

"I'm okay, Phil. I'm just scared."

"Well, can you tell me what happened?"

"I was in bed, but not yet asleep, when I heard a noise outside on the porch. I sat up and heard steps moving along the porch and then I saw a shadow of a man out there. He was rattling the windows as he walked toward the front. I got up quickly, grabbed two pistols from the corner cabinet, and headed for the store. When I went down the steps, I saw he was trying the front window, so I shot at him. You can see the window is shot out.

"What happened next?"

"He ran around toward the front door, and I ran there myself. When I heard he was trying the door, I shot again, and the door came open. I went to the door and saw him running off down the road, so I fired off two more rounds and heard him scream and fall down. But he got up and ran off. I just stood here, Phil. Too scared to move."

"Come here, Gip," I said as I gave her a big hug. "Come over and sit down."

She continued, "Señora Guitieriz from down by the lake is outside, Phil. She said she saw him running down the road to where he had left his horse and recognized him. She said it was Lara, Francisca's boyfriend. And he was running with a bad limp."

"That goddamned worthless coyote! Tomorrow, I'll find him and bring him back up here so you can finish him off!"

The neighbors were still around, and I asked different ones if they saw where he went. Most said he was limping, and that he had a lot of trouble getting on his horse before he lit out for the border. The next day, I took Luis, and we went all the way down the Gulch to the line and found traces of blood.

When word spread around the village and through the district that Gipsy had likely shot and maybe killed the intruder, she became a hero. But I was feeling differently.

I sat Gipsy down later that day and said, "It's time we got out of here. We need to move down to the Marteney house at Oro Blanco."

"Yes," she agreed.

"Tomorrow let's talk about the store and what we're going to do about it."

After a couple of days, Alex and John approached me, wanting to know if we were planning to make any changes regarding the store. I told them that after what happened the other night, we needed to move to a safer place and that we discussed moving down to Oro Blanco to the Marteney place. John asked if we were going to do anything with the store and were we going to want them to stay on.

I said, "John, what do you and Alex want to do?"

He said, "Well Phil, as you know, Alex and I have the eight little mines over at Los Alamos that we have had for the past sixteen years. You also know that for the past two years, Alex has been helping Goldfield develop and check out the new milling operation, and they are about ready to begin serious lead and zinc mining here in the Montana mine. His work with them is about over now, and we've been thinking, we are both in our fifties now, and perhaps, we should move out of the area and look for some new opportunities. But with what has happened recently and with you planning to move, this wouldn't be a good time for us to leave you. That is, if you would want us to stay on for a while."

"Well, John, and you too, Alex, we don't want you to leave. This store needs to stay open and operating. It's too important and essential to this community. If you're not in a big hurry to leave, maybe we should work out an agreement where you could effectively take over. We could make an agreement that would allow you an option to purchase it in a year or so, if you wanted to.

John and Alex looked at each other, then John turned back to me and said, "Let us talk about this for a day or so Phil, okay?"

I said, "Sure, and I'll talk with Gipsy as well."

Alex and John were born in Nova Scotia, Canada in the early 1860s and emigrated to the United States as children. In the 1880s, they went West and began a long mining career together in Colorado. Their search for gold in Colorado continued into the early years of the 1900s. Having not experienced any significant success, they decided to leave.

They had been told of large success being had in a large area in southern Arizona. In 1903, they arrived in Oro Blanco. After about a year, they discovered eight contiguous mines located in an area known as Los Alamos, and they always referred to them as their Los Alamos mines. These mines would become the center of their life for the next sixteen years. They had tried to earn a decent living with their mines but had never been able to achieve any significant success. The thought of being able to take over the very successful Ruby Mercantile had much appeal and might just be the answer.

Within a week, a lease agreement was put in place and the Frasers became official proprietors of the Ruby Mercantile. Gipsy and I would continue to help and be as active as we could for a period of six months and would retain the residence until we completed our move to Oro Blanco and then the Frasers could occupy however they chose. A purchase of the business could take place after six months of them running it successfully.

By the middle of the summer, we had moved most of our personal property out, and Alex and John moved in. John was anxious to get his wife, Ines, and their children moved over from San Diego.

CHAPTER 27

We spent a good part of the rest of the year settling into the Marteney place and getting set up with our new ranch. Slim and Buck agreed to stay on with us, and Luis would stay up at Ruby and help me take care of the ranch south to the border.

I was anxious to get over to Jack's old place and see how Dink and Annalee were doing. One of the last times I talked to Billie about Dink, he indicated he thought Dink might be getting restless and maybe missing the rodeo life. Annalee was pregnant, and they some stress going on with that.

One day in early September, I suggested that we hook up the buggy and go over to see them. We arrived on a pretty Sunday afternoon and were glad they both were home. Annalee was still teaching but had been pregnant for nearly eight months, and I learned later from Gip that she'd been having difficulty with her pregnancy. I suggested that Gip keep in close touch with her.

Dink mentioned the war in Europe a little. I asked what his thoughts were about it. "You know, Dink, we're a long ways from that conflict here and have plenty of problems with the border issues ourselves."

"Yeah," he said, "but sometimes I think I should take a look at that."

"Dink, you've got plenty going on right here. Annalee's about to have a baby, and you've got cattle to take care of. Anything you want me to know about?"

"No, Phil. Everything's fine."

"Okay, just let me know if you need anything from us. How are the cattle doing?"

"They're fine; they're up in the Forest now. I haven't seen them for a while, but they were doing well when last I saw them."

"Maybe we should ride up and look them over one of these days. You want to do that?"

"Sure, Phil. Anytime!"

We stayed for a while longer and enjoyed catching up. On the way home, I told Gip I was a little worried about some things with them. She said she was, too.

"Let's keep close to them, at least until she gets ready for the baby's arrival. Is she going to town for the birth?"

"No, she says one of the wives from the Company is looking out for her."

"Yeah, well, we need to look out for her, too."

"I will, Phil."

About a week later, I said, "Gip, I think I need to go get Dink and get up in the Forest and check those steers he's supposed to be taking care of. I think you should take the auto and go check on Annalee."

I rode over to Jack's old place but didn't find Dink and didn't see any sign of him. His horse was there and some of the steers. I could see they hadn't been watered for a while or the horses fed for a while. I looked all around but didn't find him, so I took off for Arivaca. I arrived at the house and saw Gipsy and Liz and a few other ladies talking. "What's happened?" I asked.

"Oh, Phil," Gip came over to me. "Annalee had her baby last week, and yesterday, she and Dink packed up and left for Tucson. According to Liz, Annalee is going to catch a train for her home in Kansas, and Dink is going to Texas to join the Army. Says he's going to go fight the Germans in Europe."

"Well, I'll be damned." I was dumbstruck. I didn't know what to say. I just knew I needed to get back out to Jack's place and get the livestock taken care of.

"Gip, I'll probably be gone a bit. I'll need to get Slim or Buck to go with me up into the Forest. And maybe you do what you can here, but shoot, you need to get home, too. I'll be there as soon as I can."

"Okay," she agreed.

It was like a state of shock for everybody, including me, but I had things to take of right then.

Thanksgiving was approaching soon, and one day, we were all working at the store, and Alex and John said they'd like to talk about the option on the store. John said, "It's been close to six months, Phil, and we think we're doing well here.

"You are," I agreed. "What's on your mind?"

"Well, we want to complete the purchase if you're still willing."

"I'm willing, so there shouldn't be any reason not to go ahead with it."

"Well, good. We've been trying to interest Ines's brother in coming in on the deal with us, but we've been unsuccessful, so we've agreed to go ahead on our own."

John continued, "I'm going over to San Diego next week for the birth of our daughter. I plan to be back in early January and would like to move quickly to close the deal."

"Well, if we get started on it, we should be able to have it done by early January."

"Good. Let's get started right after Thanksgiving."

We had a grand Thanksgiving at our place with the Frasers and Liz and Hank and even Beanie and Ples came down. We had the music going on the phonograph, and lots of Irish songs were sung.

Though the final papers had not yet been signed by mid-January, we agreed to have everything remaining moved out and the Fraser's moved in and in full ownership operation. On February 16, the deal was fully closed with the first payment of $765 due April first.

The Fraser brothers were off and running as full owners and operators of the Ruby Mercantile, and within a week, they had their own sign up and letterhead with their name on it. They had purchased all the inventory with the transaction and had already ordered their first shipment of goods. John was very excited, anxiously waiting for the day when Ines and the kids would join him in Ruby. He was busy planting flowers around the store and vegetables in the garden.

But, on February 27, 1920, only eleven days after completing the closing on the store, both Alexander and John Fraser were robbed and brutally murdered by Mexican bandits. I likely would not have gotten so closely involved in what happened if Jack Morgan, an ex-Indian fighter from Oklahoma, hadn't sent young Jose Gutierrez down to the ranch to get me. Jose quickly told me that he had gone to the store at about 11:00, but it wasn't open yet, so he looked in the window and "saw lots and lots of blood all over the place. He could only think of running down the hill to tell Morgan.

I didn't waste any time asking the kid a bunch of questions. I saddled up as fast as I could and was at the store in less than an hour. There were a lot of people milling around outside, but I went right in and saw Morgan over by the counter trying to help John sit up. He was bleeding profusely, moaning, and obviously mortally wounded. Off to the side, in the middle of the room, I saw Alex lying face down with in a large pool of blood. I leaned down to check him as best I could, but he was dead.

The place was a mess, and everything was in shambles. Merchandise was scattered everywhere. I couldn't believe the grisly scene. I stood and looked over to where John was now sitting, and went over to him and Morgan. John had a hole in his eye and blood all over the back of his head. But unbelievably, he seemed coherent. I got very close to him and quietly asked him if he could tell us what happened.

Just then, I heard a scream from the door and heard Jose scream again, "Madre de Dios!" and cross himself as he fell to the floor crying. I yelled at him to get over here. "Jack, tell him to take your horse and get over to Nogales to get the sheriff and send somebody to Arivaca to get the soldiers up here, too."

Jack said. "Go do it, Jose, and pronto. Take my horse and ride like hell, tell the sheriff the Frasers have been shot—murdered. Now get going!"

John was able to talk, but just barely. "We had just finished breakfast in the kitchen," he said, "and Alex went down to the store to begin re-arranging some of the shelves and putting some of our new orders away. I stayed in the kitchen to clean up before going down to help him.

"Pretty soon, I heard the front door open, and the two Mexicans came in. It was Francisca's boyfriend, Lara, and that Garcia guy from Arivaca. Almost immediately, I heard gunshots, and before I could react, I heard the cash register ring. I don't know what I was thinking, Phil. For as long as I've lived around here, I should have known better. I rushed out of the kitchen without getting a gun.

"As soon as I went down the steps and into the store, I saw Lara standing over Alex with his pistol still smoking in his hand. Alex was lying on the floor, apparently dead from a bullet wound in his head. Before I knew what was happening, Lara grabbed me by the throat while Garcia covered him with another pistol. He demanded I open the safe, which I did. They both rummaged around in it for a while and after they had removed all the valuables and everything else that they wanted, Lara turned to me. He just looked at me and smiled. I saw the flame from his pistol, but all I know now is that my head hurts, Phil."

"John, I'm going to get these bastards for you and Alex. I promise you."

John soon lapsed into unconsciousness. He had been shot point blank in the eye, and the bullet had exited out the back of his head. He had lost an enormous amount of blood, and I couldn't believe he was still alive.

Soon, a military ambulance and a platoon of soldiers arrived from the camp in Arivaca, and the Alex and John were placed inside the ambulance and rushed to the military hospital in Nogales. The soldiers quickly began a search of all the buildings around the camp, but soon after, Mexican women approached and told Jack and me that they saw the two leave the store. They told us they saw them get on one horse and ride up the hill going east.

I sent one of the miners down to get Slim and Buck while I located Luis. By late afternoon, we had our little posse together, and along with the soldiers from Arivaca, we took off in the direction the women had told us Lara and Garcia had gone. We rode with the soldiers to the border, but when we got there, the captain refused to cross, saying that because of the recent settlement of the war, it would cause serious political issues with the governments. It was dark by then, so we turned back where I had to turn my attention back to reopening the store as soon as I could.

The next morning, we formed up again. Only this time, it was just our little posse and Frank Murphy, the chief of police from Tucson. He had come down during the night and had brought a couple of bloodhounds along.

We found several signs of their trail. First, we found where they had cut the telephone lines and later where they had stopped to eat. The hounds took to the scent right away, and we soon found a spot where Lara had dropped an old blue sweater we had seen him wear so many times, along with an empty cartridge box.

We followed the trail all the way through Bear Valley. This was obviously the longest route to the border but also one that is almost entirely deserted. We could tell they only had the one horse and had been taking turns riding, and sometimes, they tried both riding at the same time. We learned that the horse must have given out before they reached the line because they camped last night on this side up on a hillside where they could see if they were being followed.

We must have been about twenty-four hours behind them because we came across a second camp they had made, and the ashes had cooled by then. The dogs were not very effective after so many miles, so tracking was pretty slow. We followed them all the way to Cumeral and a little ranch house about seven miles below the line but lost track of them. We talked to a Mexican there, and he told us he had seen them go through earlier in the day, but he didn't know about the murders, so we had no choice but to return.

When we returned to the camp, we told the captain, and he sent word to notify the Mexican army to take up the search. I remained angry at the Army captain for refusing to cross over. We were so close behind the murderers last night that, had we crossed, we would have had them just a quarter of a mile below the line where we found the remains of their campfire. The Mexican army was put into the field to continue the search for the killers, but they were unsuccessful, and the hunt was soon given up.

I learned that John remained conscious through the night and that Sheriff Earhart in Nogales had wired Ines Fraser in San Diego that Alexander had been shot and killed and John had also been shot but was expected to recover as he was resting easy. Additionally, he requested that she come at once. He told her that the Ruby store was robbed, and he had been wounded.

John remained conscious until late Saturday morning, continually asking about his brother until the doctor told him of Alex's death. When he was told this, he laid back, and the blood rushed to his head. It rapidly swelled and discolored, and his life soon went out.

Ines, her three-month-old infant, and her sister arrived Monday afternoon. Alexander and John Fraser were buried in Nogales on March 6, the bodies of both having been held, awaiting the arrival of their sister Annie from Boston.

Ines and Annie wasted little time after the funerals. On March 12, they went over to Ruby to look after the brothers' affairs and the status of their interests in the store. After determining that the extent of the brothers' worth was essentially in inventory and property, which all was mortgaged to us, and that there just wasn't enough worth to deal with, Ines came to me and turned the problem of what to do with the store over to me. On March 19, she departed for her home in San Diego. But before she left, I had the opportunity to share with her what I told John while he was still conscious.

"Ines," I said, "I promised John that I would find these people, and I promise you that justice will come to them." She merely smiled at me and thanked me.

In the months that followed, the investigation and search for Lara and Garcia persisted diligently by Sheriff Earhart. He had scattered the entire district from the Altar valley to Patagonia and Sonoita with numerous wanted posters and flyers. Many suspects were arrested and questioned, but no charges were ever filed against any of them. All through the spring, word would trickle across the border that they both had been spotted, and the Mexican authorities continued to issue statements that both were wanted in Mexico for various crimes committed down there. Fortunately, the search continued throughout the district.

In the meantime, Gipsy and I had been trying to get the store back in order. We really didn't want to go back in there and run it again. We hired many people to help us get it cleaned up and repainted, so we could decide whether to sell all the inventory and then the buildings or do something else. I thought that if the building was repainted and cleaned up, the Goldfield people would have use for it. We thought it could make a good school building or a warehouse for them.

Less than a month had passed since the tragedy, but by the end of March, we had the store open again, and Gipsy and I had been going down every day to run it. On a Tuesday morning, about the first of April, Frank Pearson came in and approached me about buying the store. He wanted to know if the Fraser estate owned it or if we did and many other details. I immediately said, "Frank, whoa, slow down here. Who owns it right now doesn't matter. You need to know that we are not anxious to turn this place over to anyone after what happened. We're just trying to get it cleaned up and try to put what happened behind us."

"Phil," he said, "You and Gipsy, and the Andrews before you, lived through the absolute worst time in this part of the country, and another tragedy like what happened to the Frasers isn't likely to happen again. You have to understand, Phil, we are a very religious family, and I just don't believe that, as the saying goes, that lighting will strike twice in the same place."

Again, I tried to dissuade him, but he stopped me and said, "Phil, let me tell you a bit about us that you surely don't know. Myrtle and I have only been in the area for about a year. That you do know. Myrtle has been teaching at the school in Arivaca since Annalee left, and I've been in the store since Dink left to join the Army. But we were originally from Texas, small towns around San Antonio. Our families are farmers and ranchers, mostly growing cotton and hay and running a few head of those old longhorn steers. When I was quite a bit younger, I worked in a store that was a combination mercantile and post office. While there doing that, I met Myrtle, and we soon got married.

"She taught, and I worked in the store, but then I got tuberculosis, and we decided we needed a drier climate. We thought New Mexico might work so I could be healed. I got a job as a cowboy on a ranch near Carrizoza. Since Myrtle was a college girl and had taught at various schools in Texas, she was able to get a job there.

"I cowboyed there for a couple of years but wasn't getting better, so we moved to Bisbee. I was working in the mines, and she was teaching. But, Phil, let me tell you, working in the mines is not a good place for a fella with TB. By chance, we heard there was an opening for a clerk and postmaster and a schoolteacher over here in Arivaca. Well, shoot, Phil, we couldn't resist the opportunity. So, now you know the whole story. We are very determined. We've been through hard times and we're tough. We know we can make this work for us, and the climate is just right for my TB."

I said, "Frank, I'll talk to Gipsy. And please come down tomorrow."

They left, and I went to find Gip.

We sat and talked for a while. "Gip, I told him we didn't want to do anything with the place right now, and I really tried to talk him out of it, but he's persistent. I just can't help but like this guy. I know we've known them for a while but not very well. I believe they can take care of themselves here, at least, for sure as well as anybody."

"I agree, Phil. This place needs a store and certainly the postal service wants a post office. What do we have to do to get them in here?"

"Well, we have to clear up the debt with the Fraser estate and then start over with the Pearsons, probably with the same terms we had with the Frasers."

"That shouldn't be too difficult."

"You're right. I asked Frank to come back tomorrow."

"Good thing we have an auto now!" We both chuckled at that.

So, surprising to all, just over a month after the Fraser murders, the Pearson's purchased the store from the Fraser estate through the help of us renegotiating the debt and mortgage we had with the Frasers. Before the Frasers moved in, we were able to get the running water system working so that the building had water available throughout, as well as a telephone.

Months passed without additional incidents in Ruby. Unfortunately, no new leads had surfaced regarding Lara and Garcia. The Pearson's had settled in and were doing a good job with the store and post office, and Myrtle had started teaching in the small building just down the hill from the store.

In October, we got a break in the search for the two murderers. Sheriff Earhart had learned that Lara and Garcia had been working at the mines south of Tucson, near Twin Buttes, not long before they came to Ruby. The sheriff was notified by a lead coming from over near Sasabe that the two had been spotted in that area just days before. He sent two of his deputies from Nogales to try to locate them. They soon came through Ruby and said they had learned that they both men were heading back up north to go back to work in the mines. I said, "I'm going with you, and I'll catch up north of Sasabe."

Deputies Lowry and Holliday and I worked our way up through the Altar valley, and from leads obtained on the way, we learned that Lara and Garcia were staying at a ranch just west of the mines. Deciding to use the cover of darkness, we waited until that night to make our move.

As we approached the ranch, we found both men out at the corral saddling their horses and obviously getting ready to leave. When we approached, Garcia drew his pistol and dropped behind a water trough and let off two or three shots before the deputies and I knew what was happening. At the same time, Lara had mounted and taken off into the dark of night. I was still mounted, so I took off after him, but in the darkness, I soon lost any sign. I turned to go back and help the deputies when I realized that the shooting had stopped. I hurried along but didn't get back until the short battle was over.

The exchange with Garcia had lasted only a matter of minutes. But as Lowry had rushed the water trough, two of Garcia's shots had hit him, and he was down. In the continuing exchange, Holliday hit Garcia twice, once on each side of his chest. He stood for an instant then fell dead, only ten feet from where deputy Lowry lay.

Lowry was seriously wounded. One bullet went through his right side, exiting his back not far from the area of his spine and another through his upper right shoulder. Neither Holliday nor I were hurt, so I told Holliday to hurry over to the mine at Twin Buttes and get some help. "I'm going to stay here with Lowry until you get back, then I'm going after that damned Lara," I said.

Early the next morning, around 2:00, an auto with a bed in the back arrived with Holliday and some others. They put Lowry in the bed and left. I couldn't do much in the dark, so I waited until sunup before chasing down Lara. For two days, I tracked and followed leads from people along the way until I arrived at the border crossing at Sasabe. Lara had obviously crossed because I was close behind him, but I wasn't fast enough.

Perhaps we had fulfilled part of my promise to Ines, but the most important one, for me anyway, was still on the loose. I was committed to continue looking for him until I found him and put him down or I knew he was dead.

For quite some time, we all feared Lowry wouldn't survive. He was critically injured and even experienced moderate paralysis for a short time. But after a month or so, he was up and back in the sheriff's office in Nogales. I was in Nogales a month or so later and stopped to see how he was doing. He told me he had received a nice letter from Ines, expressing her thanks for his efforts and wishing him a full recovery. He said, "I replied to her and told her I was near full recovery, just a little weak. I told her we were all glad that at least Garcia was down and won't hurt anyone else. I wrote, please rest assured, if Lara is ever heard from in this country again, this sheriff's office will do all in its power to capture or kill him."

To our knowledge, Lara never did come back across the line. Later, in early August 1921, we heard he had been arrested and convicted of murdering an oriental man in Ures, Sonora and was sentenced to hang in the prison in Hermosillo.

Athough Lara was never caught, arrested, and convicted for murdering the Fraser brothers, his imprisonment and hanging ended this tragic story.

CHAPTER 28

When I got back to the ranch, Gipsy said, "Phil, we need to talk about some things."

"What are you thinking?" I asked.

"You know a lot of things are changing in our lives and pretty darn fast. We now have three little kids, and Philip is eight years old and barely knows how to speak English. Ginny continues to have those fever spells that she gets. I think it's time for us to think of following the Marteneys to Tucson so we can get these kids into some good schooling and closer to doctors."

"Gipsy, we've only been here in Marteney's place for a year, and we're just getting settled in."

"I know that, Phil, but we also have to think about the events that have happened in the last couple of years. It's hard for me to get the terrible events from Ruby out of my mind."

"You're not talking about selling the ranch, are you?"

"Oh my gosh, no Phil! Never would I think of that. I'm just thinking that if we go to Tucson and rent a little place to be during the week, we could still make the ranch our main house. You could come and go back and forth as you need to. I'm thinking more about safety for the kids and me."

"Gip, let's talk about this tomorrow. You make some really good points, but you've surprised me. I need to think about it."

It didn't take long for me to realize Gipsy was absolutely right, and soon, we were in Tucson looking for a place. I had asked Gipsy if she had an idea of what area of town she wanted to live in, and she said she had been keeping in touch with Nita and Doña Josepha and would like to be near them if we could and also the university and schools.

By early fall, we had a place near 5th Avenue and East 7th Street, almost right next door to Nita and her mother. The place was perfect. Nita and Gip could get their friendship started back up and maybe Doña will be of some help to Gip when I'm at the ranch.

On the other side of our house was the Bustamente family. It didn't take long for us to get well acquainted with them. They are a wonderful family—very friendly and always wanting to help with something, especially when Phil is gone. Alfredo and Mary Louise and I think they have four or five kids. They know that I'm pregnant, and I think that makes Mary Louise want to do more for me.

Phil and Gipsy's house on 5th Avenue

PHIL

At the time, Tucson had a population of about 20,000. The city had been in a little depression for a while, but it showed great promise in a lot of ways. This move offered a lot of opportunities for Gipsy to pursue many of the things she had always loved. The university was not far away, and the public library was right downtown. I could imagine Gipsy getting her painting materials out again, and she can start writing more.

Though the little house in Tucson soon became Gipsy's main place to live, I continued to stay busy with the ranch. A couple of months ago, we set the boys up in one of the ranch houses down near the Oro Blanco stage station and fixed it up as a pretty nice bunk house for them. Our thinking was that this put them closer to being halfway between the Gulch places south of Ruby and the Marteney ranch north toward the Company's south line.

In early December, I had just returned from a week at the ranch, and Gip surprised me again.

"Phil, guess what? I'm expecting again!"

Well, I thought, *Philip is nine now, Ginny is almost six, and Dan is three.*

"Wow, where has the time gone?" I asked. "What is the expected date for this one?"

She replied, "June or July, I think."

"Well, well, an early Christmas present. We better have a celebration. Maybe we can get together with old friends during the holidays."

And we did. The holidays were a great time, and before I knew it, I was back at the ranch, and Gip was busy with school stuff with the kids. I found that there were more activities taking place in the city on than I ever thought about before. Politics, civic involvement, and cultural events now occupied more of our conversations. As the year has moved along, I met more people involved in the cattle industry, as well as people in banking, people involved in buying and selling cattle, and people from the political and legal arenas. There are so many industries I hadn't had much knowledge of or much to do with before.

Early June came around. I was at the ranch when Gipsy called to tell me her time had arrived. I told her I would be on my way right away. She told me Nita, who at that time was a grown-up young lady, would take her to St Mary's.

I arrived about three hours later and learned that Gipsy was having problems with this delivery. All the previous ones had been pretty easy for her. Late that night, after a very difficult time, we had another little boy. But the prognosis for this baby was not good. He was not breathing well, and the doctors were having difficulty.

We waited for what seemed like hours for information, and while we were waiting, Gipsy asked about a name. "Well, Gip, I named Daniel. Why don't you come up with one for this boy?"

"Okay, I'd like a name from my family, and I also like the name James from the Bible. What do you think of James Harper?"

" I like that!"

We waited more for the doctors. Just before 11:00 or so, a couple of doctors came to our room and sat down. One of them told us that James was weak from the start and had difficulty breathing and just wasn't strong enough to make it through the night. He was sorry, but he told us they lost our new baby boy. Gipsy just broke down and cried and cried. I was so afraid she was going to have a breakdown. There would be no James Harper.

The next month or was very difficult. Gipsy was very depressed and despondent.Nita and Doña encouraged her to talk to their priest, and she had some visits with the pastor from a Southern Baptist church. I think she'll be okay, but it was a very difficult time for all of us.

CHAPTER 29

It was late August, and we were all trying to work through a difficult dry season. The monsoons had not come yet, and it was getting close to being too late for them to do us any good. If we didn't get some good rains soon, it would be necessary for many of us to start selling off some of our cattle. After the hot, dry summer, there was barely enough grass in the hills to feed them. We worked hard every day just to keep enough water in the ponds for them. We all know droughts come every few years, but this one could be costly. We just had to keep doing what we could.

I was working on a stock pond with Buck and Slim near the mouth of Chimney Canyon. It had barely been eighteen months since the murder of Alexander and John Fraser, and we learned that lightning does strike again. Seven Mexican bandits robbed the Ruby store and murdered Frank and Myrtle Pearson and wounded Myrtle's sister, Elizabeth Purcell, who had been visiting from Texas. I told Buck and Slim, "I'm going up to Ruby. I'll leave the truck here with you. I might need the horse."

I rode as fast as I could and arrived at the store that evening shortly after Oliver Palmer, the Arizona Ranger for the Santa Cruz district, and George White, the county sheriff arrived. We entered the store through the front door and what we saw was the most gruesome sight. Blood was splattered all over the floor, on the countertop, on the walls, all over the safe, while chairs were overturned, and boxes, canned goods, bottles, and articles from the shelves were scattered everywhere.

Palmer tried to tell me that he and the sheriff had just interviewed Irene Pearson, Frank's young sister, who was in the house when this happened. He said, "She's obviously is in a serious state of shock right now, but this is about how she remembers it."

"My aunt Elizabeth, or Lizzie as she is called, and I recently came out from west Texas to visit my brother, Frank and Myrtle. Frank and Myrtle, along with little Margie, went for a horseback ride up in the hills behind us. They left Lizzie and I here to watch the store. At about 9:00, a Mexican man came in and asked if my brother was here. I told him that he and Myrtle and their little girl went for a ride. He asked me when they would be back. I told him, in about an hour, around noon."

Palmer said he asked Irene if the guy spoke English well enough to understand her, and he said she said he spoke pretty good English.

"The man said he would just wait, and he went outside, but I don't know where he went.

"They got back just before noon, put the horses away, and came to the store. Before they came into the store, I went upstairs to the living rooms and was getting some cold tea for them. Margie came up the stairs, and Lizzie and I were asking about their ride when we heard gunshots, many of them, along with screams and yelling.

"Lizzie ran to the door at the top of the stairs, looked down, and later told me that what she saw was a terrifying scene. She said it looked like three men were standing over my brother. There was blood all over the floor where he was lying and then another one grabbed Myrtle and dragged her over toward the safe. They told her to open it, and when she said she couldn't, one of them pulled out a double-edged hatchet and started beating on the safe door. When he couldn't get it open, he turned in anger and shot Myrtle two or three times and then bashed her in the face with the butt of his rifle. He continued to beat on the safe, and eventually, it opened.

"One of them pushed Myrtle off to the side while they all started grabbing what they could take. They took all the money and all of Frank's guns. It looked to me like they were loading up armloads of clothes and other goods from the shelves. At the last minute, one turned to Myrtle and knocked out all her gold teeth and put them in his pockets.

"Lizzie said she saw a gun laying on a table down there, so she reached for it. I don't know why she did it because she doesn't know how to use one, but she raised it and pulled the trigger many times. She didn't hit anybody, but one of the bandits turned toward her and raised his gun. She held up her hand to protect herself and then he shot her. Her hand was against her forehead and his bullet hit her hand. Blood gushed out, and I thought she was dead, but she must have just fainted. He must have also thought she was dead because he turned and left her where she laid. She came to quickly and turned and ran for the back door, grabbing Margie as she went. I quickly joined them.

"There is that old screen door along the back porch. We all ran along the porch. I tripped on something and fell spread eagle on the deck, and Liz and Margie kept running, trying to get to the woodshed out back. Two of the bandits were chasing us and firing their guns. I could hear their spurs jangling and their chaps slapping on their pants and their boots stomping on the deck. For some reason, when they saw me fall down, they stopped, looked at me, and turned around and went back inside. I don't know why, unless they thought they had shot me.

"As soon as they were out of sight, I got up and ran out to the woodshed where Liz and Margie were hiding. We hid there for quite some time and then came out and ran up into the hills behind us there. We hid behind some rocks, and I saw that Lizzie's pretty blue and white checked dress was covered with blood. So, we tore a big piece out of it and wrapped her hand to try to stop the bleeding.

"I think we were up there for about two hours, but when we heard other voices down here, we came out and came down. There were lots of people milling around but not doing anything. Margie was hysterical, Lizzie was in much pain, and I guess I have been in shock because I don't think I really know what happened. But an old local neighbor lady named Doña Paz came over and took us away to someplace over there," she said, pointing to one of the homes down the hill.

"When we arrived a while ago, Phil, Doña Paz, came over and told us she knows two of the bandits and identified them as Placido Silvas and Manuel Martinez. I told Palmer and White that I know those two scoundrels. That Silvas guy had been living and working in Arivaca for quite some time, and he and Martinez had been working different ranches around the district."

"Sheriff, I wonder if we might pick up some information on their whereabouts if we sent some wanted notices around to all the ranches in the district."

"Yeah, Phil, of course we'll be doing that. As soon as we figure out exactly what happened here."

I asked Sheriff White what he was going to do with the family?

"I've got an ambulance on its way over from Nogales. It will probably take some time to get here, though. It's coming around through Amado and Arivaca because of the washouts on this old wagon road between here and Nogales."

"Okay, do you have enough help here for a while?"

"There's just me and Palmer until we get some people over from Nogales. Can you stick around for a while?"

I said, "Of course, sheriff. It looks like it's going to be my store again, so I'm going to find Worthington, and after you have done what you have to do, I'll see if he can gather some people to help me start getting things straightened with it. In the meantime, I'll run down to the ranch and get a little grip put together and give Gipsy a call to let her know what has happened. You know, I got pretty close to the Pearson's, and I think I'll see what I might be able to do to help them out when they get to Nogales."

"Whatever you need to do, Phil. This is going to be a hell of a mess to straighten out. You go on and do what you need to."

I found Worthington down by the Gutiérrez home and talked to him for a bit. He said he was on his way up to the store when all those Mexicans showed up.

"And just before I got to the store, the shooting and yelling and screaming started. I'm sorry, Phil. I got so scared that I didn't know what to do, so I just ran back down here to hide. They were in there for about another hour before they finally came out and loaded up everything.

"I went up there after they all had left and saw Frank and Myrtle, but the girls weren't there. I found them coming down from up above, and they told me part of what happened. Damn, Phil, it's just terrible in there. It looks like they just went on a rampage."

"I know it is, Al, but we're going to have to get it cleaned up again. Will you be able to help me?"

"Sure, what do you need help with?"

"I want you to gather up some people who will help us. Probably tomorrow; the sheriff has plenty to do right now. I'm going down to the ranch to call Gipsy and get some stuff, and I'll be back later."

"Okay, I'll get some folks lined up."

I went to the ranch and told those who were around what had happened and how bad it was. I called Gipsy. We talked for a while, and I told her I was planning to go to Nogales with the girls to try to be of help there. "Then I'm going back to Ruby to try to get Al and some people to help me clean up." After a pause I said, "You know, Gip, do you think you might feel up to coming down to be with the family for a while? Maybe Nita can get away and go with you?"

She hesitated then said, "Yes, Phil. I really should do that."

"Okay, I'll see you there."

I quickly gathered up a little grip and threw it in the truck, choosing it rather than taking the horse back, thinking I might be going over that road to Nogales. I stopped at the bunkhouse when I passed Oro Blanco and talked to the boys for a while.

"I don't know how long I'll be, but you guys can take care of things," I said.

"Sure," Buck said. "And Phil, do you remember Tony Aros from Sasabe?"

"Yeah."

"Well, he's been asking if we might be needing another cowboy. I told him I would talk to you about it."

"Sure," I said. "With what I'm going to be dealing with for the next bit of time, I think it might be a good idea. But Buck, I haven't been around Tony much. Are you sure you're okay with him and what he can do?"

"Yeah, Phil. He's turned into a good hand over at the King place. I think we can depend on him."

"Okay. I'll see you guys later and be sure to keep in touch with Luis. He's down there all by himself."

I got back to Ruby late that afternoon, and the ambulance from Nogales was getting ready to head back. Frank and Myrtle would be transported in it, and Ranger Palmer would take the girls over. Liz's hand had been treated and wrapped, and it was determined she would be able to ride with them. I walked over to his vehicle and said a few words to them and told them Gipsy would be on her way down to Nogales tomorrow, and I would be over later tonight. "Mr. Palmer will help you get situated for tonight, and I'll be over to help you contact each of your family members, okay?"

"Thank you, Mr. Clarke," Irene responded.

We all arrived in Nogales late Friday night. Oliver Palmer quickly got the three girls situated in a nice place in the plaza, not far from the sheriff's office, and Palmer told me I could stay with him. When we were all settled in, we gathered at the sheriff's office so we could start the sad process of contacting family. Irene wired the bad news to her and Frank's father, J. W. Pearson in Liberty Hill, Texas, which was a short distance from Fort Worth. We also sent a wire to Myrtle and Liz's brother, William Purcell, in San Marcos, Texas.

The wires briefly explained what had happened that day and that Frank and Myrtle were being transported here to Nogales and were expected later that night. Replies soon began to arrive, obviously expressing much sorrow and sadness. Mr. Purcell advised us that they would like the bodies embalmed because they would be transporting them back to Texas and that he and the rest would be leaving immediately for Nogales.

The ambulance didn't arrive until early Saturday morning. They had tried to come over the mountains between here and Ruby, but torrential rains had fallen in the area shortly after we had come through earlier and made the road tortuous and impassable, so they had to turn back and go through Arivaca and Amado.

That Saturday, Gipsy and Nita arrived and assisted me and the others who were trying to comfort the girls. It turned out to be a great idea because, even though it was a very sad time, it was really good for Gip to be able to set her emotional distress aside for a while. Having the opportunity to provide comfort and solace to these young ladies and little Margaret turned out to be as therapeutic for her as for them. It was a long wait, so we sent Nita back to Tucson on the train. It was a good idea for her to come down with Gipsy. Not only is she a rock for Gipsy, but also, at her young age, she could provide strength to these girls.

The family members didn't arrive until the middle of the following week, and after all arrangements had been completed, the bodies of Frank and Myrtle along with all family members, including Irene, Elizabeth, and little Margaret, started their long and sad journey back to Liberty Hill for the burial.

Gipsy and I stayed in Nogales one more day; I thought it would be good for both of us to be away from all that had happened for a while. I still wondered how she was doing. I think just being there, helping the others with the needs of the two older girls and especially little Margaret, had been good for her.

"Phil, I think me coming down here has been a good thing. I just lost a baby I will never know, but I think I got so much out of being with little Margie and the two sisters. It helps me better understand God's plan. I think He plans for us to have at least one more child and maybe not so far in the future. As I continue to think of a brother or sister for Philip and Dan and Ginny, I feel much better. I think I can go back to Tucson unless you think I should come to Ruby to help you."

"Naw, Gipsy. I just feel so much better about you right now. I'll be okay down there with Worthington."

"What do you think we're going to have to do, Phil?"

"Gip, I think we need to give Al a little time with the place, keep a close eye on things and go from there. We both know we have plenty going in our lives now; we don't need another one of these events."

"Yes, I agree. You know, I just never would have expected something like this to happen once, let alone twice in such a short period."

"I don't know, Gip."

"One day, we will figure out what these tragedies were really all about and why they even happened."

In the meantime, Sheriff White formed a large posse and a massive manhunt was underway. They immediately headed for the border area south of Ruby, thinking that would be the most likely direction the murdering bandits would have gone. The Mexican military was brought in to help search south of the border, and even an airplane from the army in Nogales was being used—the first airplane ever used in Arizona for a manhunt. But there are no positive results so far. Travel is difficult, mostly all by horseback. Most roads are useless for autos, so there have been many days in the saddles and nights under the stars for these deputies.

Finally, just about two weeks after the murders, there came a report from Bisbee, over a hundred miles to the east, that Mexican soldiers had located and captured a number of suspects and taken them to the border at Agua Prieta, just across the line from Douglas. Sheriff White and several members of his posse left Nogales immediately.

Two days later, Placido Silvas was taken into custody. Three others were held, but none was Martinez, and were released because the sheriff didn't have enough evidence to hold them. Silvas was brought back to Nogales and went on trial in the Nogales Superior Court on December 15.

Testimony was heard over the course of the next few days. Three locals from Ruby testified and identified Silvas as one of the bandits. They had seen him go into the store just before the shooting began. Plus, as we know, Irene Pearson told Sheriff White that day that Silvas was the second one to enter the store and that he was the one who fired the shots that killed her brother. The case went to the jury on Christmas Eve and returned with a verdict shortly after.

He was declared guilty of the murder of Frank Pearson and Myrtle Pearson and the attempted murder of Elizabeth Purcell. Interestingly, the death sentence was not imposed, but a sentence of life imprisonment was.

While Silvas was being held in Nogales before being transported to the state prison in Florence, word came that Manuel Martinez had been arrested in Saric, Sonora four days earlier and was being deported to the United States by order of President Obregon. After Sheriff White picked him up at the border at Sasabe and arrested him, he was brought back to Nogales, and in the office of the Santa Cruz county attorney, he made a complete confession. He named himself as the leader and Silvas as his partner but he didn't name others.

Four and a half months later, Martinez went on trial for the same charges that Silvas had earlier, the murder of the Pearson's and attempted murder of Elizabeth Purcell. The same eyewitness testimonies and accounts that had been given to the Silvas jury the previous December were presented to the Martinez jury. The jury's deliberation only took three days, and they returned a verdict of guilty in the first degree with a fixed penalty of death by hanging. His execution was set for August 18, 1922, at the state prison.

The very next day, Sheriff White and his deputy, Larry Smith, left Nogales by automobile with the prisoners Placido Silvas and Manuel Martinez. The sheriff and deputy rode in the front and the two prisoners, handcuffed to each other, were put in the back They were taking the two to the state prison in Florence for their sentences to be carried out. They had tire trouble near Tubac and had to call Nogales for another vehicle to be sent to them. With the new auto, they resumed the trip, with Sheriff White driving at a high rate of speed, trying to make up time lost with the tire trouble in Tubac. As Deputy Smith later told it when he was in the hospital, near Continental, the car drove into a wash with lots of sand across the highway and started swerving side to side on the highway. Soon the sheriff completely lost control, and the car went into a deep ditch bordering the highway and overturned several times.

Sheriff White was killed instantly, and Deputy Smith sustained numerous and serious injuries, but when help arrived, he was still alive. Silvas and Martinez survived the crash with no serious injuries and escaped into the desert, still handcuffed together.

By the next day, several posses had been formed, and soldiers from Arivaca were activated and sent toward the Tumacacori Mountains between Arivaca and Continental, the site of the crash. Footprints were found near the crash site and indicated the two were likely still handcuffed together.

Silvas and Martinez

On July 16, Harry Saxon was appointed sheriff to fill in for Sheriff White, and the next day, Deputy Smith died from his injuries suffered in the crash.

Finally, after being on the loose for four days, and just before noon on the 18th, the two prisoners were located and recaptured.

They were found weak and exhausted, hiding in some rocks only about two and a half miles south of Amado. Neither had eaten for days; they traveled at night and hid during the day but had only gone about twelve miles from the crash site.

The prisoners were returned to Nogales, but only for a day or two before being delivered to the prison by Sheriff Saxon without incident. After a number of appeals to save Martinez failed, he was hanged at the federal prison in Florence. His body was not claimed by his family, so his body was buried in the prison cemetery. Meanwhile, Placido Silvas had started serving his life sentence in the prison. The search for the other five murderers continued with the new Sheriff Saxon continuing to follow up on leads daily. Shortly after the funeral, Purcell and the Pearson family left for Texas. Gipsy and I went to Tucson. I stayed in town with her for a couple of days to be sure she was going to be okay. After a couple of days, I felt she was doing well. I needed to get back south, so I decided to return to the ranch for a while and help the men out. However, my objective was to go to Ruby and figure out what to do with what was left of the mercantile. I planned to talk to Worthington a little to see what his plans were and then decide what to do.

I arrived at the store the next morning, expecting the mess to have been cleaned up and the scattered merchandise put back on the shelves. I walked in and saw that nothing had been done. "Worthington," I said to him. "What the hell is going on here? I thought you would get this taken care of."

"I tried, Phil, but I had trouble finding anybody who would come in here."

I went in and slowly walked around. Everywhere I looked, there was evidence of what had happened. Dried blood was everywhere. Merchandise was scattered all over the place. Just a couple of weeks ago, this was a wonderful place. Happy people were coming and going. Friends and relatives visited these two wonderful people. And then, in a heartbeat, for no logical reason, bad people came in here and destroyed so many lives and this wonderful place that had given Gipsy and me so many good times and memories.

I couldn't stand to be there any longer. I turned, pushed Al out of my way, went out the door and around the corner, got sick to my stomach, and cried again, for what I think was only the second time in my life. As I stood there, trying to get composed, I thought, *Oh, Lord, how could you allow something so tragic and cruel to happen to those four wonderful, happy people? Lord, the ways of your workings will be a puzzle to me for the rest of my days.*

I walked over to my truck, turned, and looked up at the building for an instant and drove down to the Goldfield Mining Company office to see George Wingfield, the manager in charge of this whole operation. "George, I need to talk to you."

"Phil, I'm so sorry about what has happened again. What can we do to help you?"

"Well, George, I want to sell the store and the business to you or the Company, doesn't matter to me."

"I don't know, Phil. Running a store isn't something we do."

"It doesn't matter, George. You know as well as I do that this village needs that store and post office."

"Yes, I do know that. What do you think you want?"

"George, I know what I want. I don't want anything but just enough to settle up with the Pearson estate. There's nearly $8,000 worth of merchandise up there in that place. You pay me a thousand dollars so I can take care of the Pearson's, and you can have the inventory. I'll transfer the deed to all the buildings to you, excluding the Excelsior mine. I'm going to keep that."

He looked at me for just a minute, then said, "This saddens me even more, Phil. What you and Gipsy did with that place and what it has meant to these people, not just here, but people from all over the district, has made Montana Camp what it is. I'll do your deal, Phil. I don't have any idea who we can get to take care of it, but we'll get somebody."

I said, "Try Al Worthington. He's been working for Frank for a while. He'd be better than somebody who doesn't know anything."

"Okay, Phil. Get your paperwork done, and we'll get this done."

"Okay, George. I'm done here for now. I'll lock the doors on my way back to the ranch, and I'll call you in a few days." I drove back up to the store, placed the key inside on a shelf, turned, and pulled the door closed behind me. I then vowed that I'd never set foot in that place again.

I went down to the ranch and called Gipsy. "Hello, my dear Gip. I'm at the ranch right now. Just got here a little while ago but wanted to call as soon as I could. I've been down at Ruby pretty much since I came back from town. Gip, I just have to tell you, I didn't do well there. Worthington didn't get anybody into the store, so it's just like it was over a week ago. I wanted to turn around and go back to Tucson and be with you, but I know I couldn't do that.

"I left the store and went directly down the hill to the Goldfield offices and talked to George. I told him we weren't coming back, and I was able to negotiate a deal for the company to buy us out. I told him all we want is enough to settle the Pearson's estate, and we would give them everything. He accepted that proposition, and I told him I would get Sam Noon over in Nogales to get the papers ready.

"I'm sorry I didn't talk to you about this, but when I went back in the store, I couldn't see how I could ever go back. It just made me sick. I'm so sorry."

"It's okay, Phil. I wanted to tell you I was having those same feelings. I'm glad you did that. I don't want to go back there, either."

"Okay, my darling. I'm coming back to town tomorrow, but I need to stop in Amado and see Bud Parker. Buck told me he's called a couple of times."

The next day, I drove to Amado to see Bud. His ranch was right along the Santa Cruz River, so there were numerous cottonwood trees everywhere around his place. I arrived about mid-morning, and Bud was right there to meet me.

"Hey Phil, how are you?"

"It's really good to see you, Bud. I think it's been about a year, and as you sure as hell know, a lot of things have happened."

"Phil, I can't believe what's happened to you and Gipsy. Another tragedy at the store is just so awful, and I guarantee you there isn't anybody around who isn't really feeling for you."

"Thanks, Bud. We're going to be okay, though. We're moving on and have plenty of new stuff going on. After the Frasers were killed, we moved to Tucson and got a little house rented. That's turning out to be really good for Gip, and it's not too bad for me. I've been going back and forth quite a bit, especially in the last week or so. But you know that I bought Billie Marteney's places, right?"

"I knew that. With what you've already put together down south in the gulch, the Marteney deal gives you a sizable operation, doesn't it?" Bud said.

"It sure does," I replied. But I've got a good crew. Buck's doing a good job keeping things running smoothly so far. This damned drought has really made things tough, though. Not only is the grass poor, but also keeping water where it needs to be isn't easy. We've got a lot of head running on a lot of Forest ground. You know, I haven't run an outfit this size before, and it's taking me a bit of time getting it all figured out. Good thing I've got lots of friends like you around."

I said, "I guess the Arivaca Ranch isn't immune to these troubling times, either. I've heard they've lost quite a few cows to this drought and even gave Arthur a bunch of little calves because they had lost their mamas. During the early years, when Nonie had been managing the place, he had more than his share of personal problems too. You probably know that his wife Mary got sick with the flu a year or so ago and passed away. And that same year, Pusch had a stroke and is incapacitated, and Uncle Johnnie's getting' along in age and spending most of his time in Tucson.

"And since the Forest service started dividing up the range into specific grazing allotments, it's hurt the company quite a bit. And Johnnie's Bear Valley ranch, down by the border, is now part of the Company, and he's losing quite a few head to the bandits. I've even heard recently that Nonie might be getting ready to pack up his little girl and move to California. Could be that the Bernard era in Arivaca could be coming to an end pretty soon. And, as you know, when an outfit looks like it might be in trouble, there will be interested parties asking around."

"I wonder, Phil; does this story have anything to do with that guy from back East? I think his name was Jack McVey?"

"Yeah, it does. He's about Nonie's age, and has lots of money. He came out here to go to school at the University back in about '14 but had always wanted the cowboy life. He learned about Arivaca from Nonie at one of Nonie's parties in town and actually got a hold of a friend of his back east, name of Forbes Talcott, also a guy with lots of money, and had him come out and help him acquire the Las Jarrillas, then after that, they bought the Tres Bellotas.

"Unfortunately, shortly after that, they experienced a tragic accident. Jack had gone back East to marry his fiancé, Anna, and while he was gone, Talcott took a new horse out for a ride. The horse was green and started acting up, and Talcott got thrown, landed on his back, and broke his neck. He was taken to Tucson but passed shortly after. Jack returned with his new wife and kept on with the ranches and started buying up homesteads along the Arivaca Creek.

"Soon, all this activity brought on financial difficulties he didn't expect, and he had to mortgage the ranches. About that time, another newcomer to the area arrived, a guy by the name of Gene Shepherd. Evidently, another man with plenty of money.

"I hear he was orphaned when he was about fourteen and started working as a cowboy over in California. Soon, he and his family were in the cattle business in California and Arizona, near Winkelman. He sold out up there in about '19 and came down here and hooked up with McVey and bought an interest in the two ranches from Jack. As it has turned out, he got in here at a bad time. It wasn't but just a year or so ago that they merged the two ranches in with the Arivaca Ranch. Well, this consolidation didn't help either of them financially because, as we know, Mother Nature stepped in and brought us this terrible drought we've been experiencing.

"Now, I come to the point of my story. It appears that McVey and Shepherd got this idea of getting themselves and others out of this financial predicament by putting together a proposal to consolidate all the major ranches in the district, including my Bar-V-Bar and Arthur Noon's Ranches into what they are going to call the "Arizona Land and Cattle Company," a major Arizona corporation with a capital of about $3,000,000, with an issue of about 30,000 shares of stock.

"The purpose of this organization will be the consolidation and purchase of all the interests of the La Osa Livestock and Loan company, the Arivaca Land and Livestock Company, the Las Jarrillas Cattle Company, the Paso Verde Cattle Company, my Bar-V-Bar, and the Noon Cattle and Land properties. All these ranches adjoin, and their consolidation would create control of all the cattle operations for about forty miles in all directions. It could include everything from the border to the south, to the Atascosas and Tumacacori to the east, the Cerro Colorado's north, and even some of the Altar valley west—over one million acres of land. It will consist of over 215,000 acres of patented land and over a million acres of state and federal grazing land. Their proposal claims that all these ranges will, conservatively, sustain over 50,000 head of cattle, meaning only one animal per every 20 acres. They claim this doesn't mean all the cattle would graze over the whole property but would be moved around from various pastures as the feed is consumed.

One last thing you might be interested in is, the organization plan for management is that the corporate board will consist of seven people, five would be owners and two would be bond holders. Three of the officers will be ranch managers, and the plan is that Shepherd will run the Arivaca, Jack McVey the La Osa and, get this, Ramon will be moved to the Paso Verde."

"Wow, Phil, what a story. I've heard little of this over the last couple of months but didn't really think much would come of it. What are your thoughts?"

"My thoughts aren't good, Bud. The way I see it is that Arthur and I would be in a lose-lose situation. Both of our places together would only make up a small part of the whole thing, and we would be very small shareholders, working for somebody else if we choose to stay on our places. I haven't talked to Arthur yet, but for me, you know,

I just barely got my ranch put together and am not too interested in turning it over to that bunch from the Company any time soon.

"The problem, Bud, is if I don't go along with them, they will likely make my life tough going forward. And they would pretty much have me surrounded. I talked to Johnnie about that very issue a couple of weeks ago, and he told me I wouldn't have to go all the way around Arivaca up the Ruby road to my road across the cienega to get to my place anymore because the Company was cutting a road through the Arivaca ranch to the north boundary of my place. Said they were doing that, so when this deal got done, they all would have direct access to my place and the north side of the cienega.

"So, in the event either I don't go along with this deal, or even if I do, I'll have a hell of a lot better way into my place. Might even move that little house we're living in up to that bluff above the cienega someday. But you know, Bud, times are tough right now, so I'm not sure that it will work out. I guess we'll just wait and see."

"Phil, one of the reasons I've been calling you is I've got another good story to talk about. One, I think you're going to like to hear. I bank at the Consolidated National Bank in Tucson, as you know."

"Yes, I do."

"Well, how well do you know Albert Steinfeld or any of the his management people?"

"Well, I've met Steinfeld once or twice. I know he's got something to do with the Company in Arivaca, but I don't know him real well. Seems like an okay guy, though."

"He knows a lot about you and what you've managed to put together down south. He talked to me and Billie a little about something he's got going, and he asked me if I'd talk to you about it."

"Okay, Bud, what's up?"

"The bank is really growing, especially in agriculture and livestock business, and they want a top-notch kind of guy to come in and head up their loan inspector operation. And Albert told me he would like you to be that guy and asked if I would just throw the idea at you."

"No, Bud; I'm a cattleman, full-time now. I've never even thought about having another job, working for somebody else. I'm surprised you'd even ask with what I've got going on now."

"I asked because I think I might know you better than you do yourself. You're sharp, Phil. Look what you've done in the last ten or so years. Hell, when you first got here, you could hardly keep the books at the Arivaca store. Now look, you're damn near a self-made lawyer and accountant, and you sure are a good businessman. The reason I want you to do this is because of what it can do for you, and maybe us together some day in the future."

"What do you mean?"

"Phil, if you get into this job, think of the people you'll meet and the experiences it will give you. You'll be able to make new contacts with big people in all different kinds of industries, including politics and civic activities. Think about it. I told Albert I'd like to do it, and he said, 'Not until I have a chance to talk to Phil Clarke first.'"

"Bud, this is too quick. I'm heading home. I'll talk to Gipsy and think about it some, and I'll give Mr. Steinfeld a call before I go back to the ranch. Is that fair enough? But what did you mean a while ago when you said, 'and maybe us together someday?'"

"Phil, what if you and I become partners and start feeding and moving steers back and forth across the line. Think of the numbers we could do together."

"That could be a good idea someday, but I have to think about it. I'll call in a day or so."

When I got home, Gipsy came to the door and gave me a big hug and said something to the effect of how bad she felt about what I had gone through in Ruby. I told her I was just glad she didn't have to be there and see all of what remained of that day. I continued, "I don't think there's a chance in hell that Worthington will make that place work, and before you know it, Ruby will be without a post office and mercantile. We'll see.

"And it's hard to believe we have three kids, now."

"Phil," Gipsy said, "Are you ready for the next one?"

"Oh my goodness, Gip. For sure?"

"Yes, I just learned a week or so ago, so we have to think probably around June or July."

"Well, that didn't take the good Lord long to help us with the loss of our little boy. Are you doing okay, Gip?"

"I'm really doing well, and I'm very excited about this."

"So am I. There's something else, Gip. Yesterday, Bud told me Albert Steinfeld, the president of the bank, wants to talk to me about working for the bank. It's something to do with inspecting cattle and other livestock that is used as collateral on loans. I told him I didn't have any interest in working for somebody again and that we have plenty going on in our lives already. What do you think?"

"How can you do something like that and take proper care of the ranch?"

"I'm not sure, Gip, but I feel like I need to at least give him the call since he asked Bud to ask me to."

The next day, I called the bank, told the receptionist who I was and that I was returning a call to Mr. Steinfeld. When he answered, I said, "Mr. Steinfeld, my name is Phil Clarke. Bud Parker asked me to call you."

"Yes, sir," he said. "Phil, first, thanks for getting back to me. Can you come in and visit with us in the next couple of days?"

I said, "Sure I can, but what is this all about?"

"Phil, the bank has a need for an agriculture loan officer and livestock inspector, and we want to inquire as to whether you might be interested in working for the bank."

"Well, Mr. Steinfeld, I haven't given any thought to the idea of having a job since I left working for the Company in Arivaca years ago, but Bud Parker is a good friend of mine, and because of that, I would be more than happy to come in and visit."

"That is all we can ask of you, and we would appreciate it. Would you be available to come in tomorrow?"

The next day, I arrived at the bank and was met by Mr. Steinfeld. We went into the bank's meeting room, and there were three other people there as well.

"First, Phil, please call me Albert. This gentleman is George Stonecypher, our senior vice president, this is Charles Walker, and this is Bob Butler, both assistant vice presidents." We all shook hands and said we were glad to meet each other.

"We make up the management team of the bank," Albert continued. "The Tucson Cattle Loan Company, as a division of the bank, has numerous agricultural loans all over the southwest and a few are as far east as Kansas City and Chicago, and many of these are secured with livestock.

"You may not know much about us, Phil, but we know a great deal about you. You've accomplished quite a bit in your short time here, and you have developed a reputation for honesty and high integrity, and just as important to us is your reputation among most, if not all, cattle people in the district regarding your capabilities with and knowledge of cattle and horses.

"Our need is for an individual with your credentials to represent the bank's interest, as our agricultural loan officer and livestock inspector in building and expanding the bank's business throughout the livestock industry."

"Well, Albert, as I told you yesterday, I have not given any thought about the possibility of having a job. As you know, we recently had to deal with a couple of tragic events in Ruby and I continue to be more involved with my growing ranch and herd. However, I'm intrigued by the thought of being able to continue to be more involved in the cattle industry and meet other cattle people. I am interested, but I'm sorry. I don't believe I can accept due to my responsibilities with my ranch."

"We understand that Phil," Albert said, "And we are prepared to accommodate those needs as much as possible. We would like to share your time with the ranch. If you can split your time at the ranch with time working for the bank, we believe a relationship like that would be acceptable."

"You know, I believe I could make that work. I'd like to spend some time with my wife, Gipsy, and share this conversation with her, and I'll provide you a response within a day or two if that's okay."

Albert said that would be good.

Gipsy and I discussed this as an opportunity more than a job. We agreed I didn't need a job, but the opportunity for us to grow was really too much to pass on, so we decided to give it a chance. I notified Albert within a couple of days.

It was getting close to the end of the year, so we agreed I would start at the first of the year, and between now and then, I would spend time in the bank getting familiar with what I would be doing and with who and where. Bob Butler, one of the assistant vice presidents who was also responsible for business and loan account development, provided me with a portfolio of all the bank's agricultural and livestock loans. It would be my responsibility to do a physical inspection of these loans and confirm the status and condition of the collateral, be it equipment or livestock. If the collateral was livestock, I would need to verify the numbers and visibly inspect the condition of the herds.

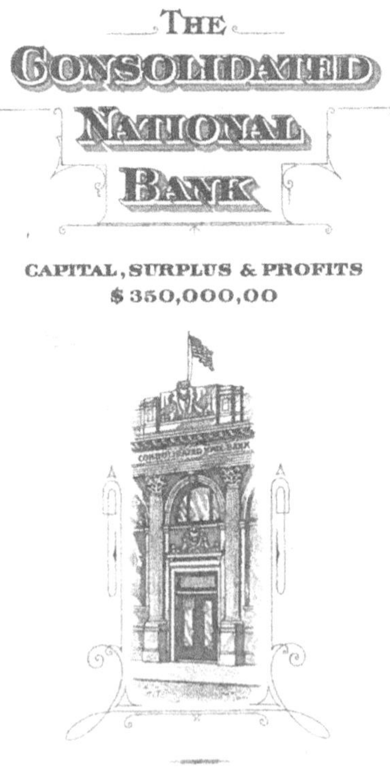

In early 1922, I started my new adventure. I soon learned, much to Gipsy's displeasure, that I would be traveling quite a bit, mostly around Arizona but also throughout the southwestern states. I started mostly around the local, southern Arizona cattle operations, which included, not only my own operation, but also the Arivaca Land and Cattle Company.

That turned out to be an all-day project. Ramon was still pretty much the main guy there, but the operation of the company had dramatically changed in the last four or five years. Nonie had packed up his little girl and moved to California, and Johnnie didn't come around much. Ramon and I spent a good day checking the herds and the pastures throughout the ranch.

When we left the headquarters, we headed south on the new road to the Bar-V-Bar. It was my first chance to talk to anybody about it, so I mentioned to Ramon that I sure liked having this new access to my place. He said he was glad when Johnnie told him to put it in. He said he had talked to Johnnie for a long time to let him do it, but Johnnie always said no—until there was this talk about consolidating. Then Johnnie told him to go build it.

"We're going to need to be able to get to the cienega from this side when this deal is done. It's a good road, eh, Felipe?"

"Yes," I said, "Right through the ranch."

I asked him if there were any new developments with the consolidation in the last couple of weeks, and he surprised me by saying there was nothing new, and he really was beginning to think it wasn't going to happen any time soon. *That's good,* I thought to myself.

This relationship had turned out to be a great opportunity for me. I could spend a couple of days a week at the Bar-V-Bar and the rest developing new loans and doing inspections. I continued to make many new acquaintances all over the state and throughout the southwest.

CHAPTER 30

Summer moved into the monsoon season, and the cooler weather came at just the right time, especially for Gip. Our new baby arrived, and we had another girl we named Patsy. Both she and Gipsy did very well with the birth, and as the year has moved along, both were doing very well.

Soon, we were into 1923. Business at the bank continued to be very enjoyable for me. Our number of new loans grew every month, and the performance of our existing loans were much stronger than in years past. And I tried to stay closer to home as much as possible to help Gipsy as much as I could with the kids. Patsy was nearly a year old, so Gipsy was taking care of four and was even talking about wanting another soon.

Early in 1923, Gip and I started talking more about our living arrangements, or really, more about what we should do. We had four children, and Gipsy recently let me know we were expecting again in December, so we decided to look for another place in Tucson. But I also had been thinking about moving the ranch headquarters farther north from Oro Blanco to be closer to Arivaca, and with the road through the ranch, it was easier to get to and from Tucson. It was not a good time to think about building something down there.

We talked about different ideas for a couple of weeks. Gipsy wanted something bigger and more functional for us, and one day, a thought came to mind.

"Why don't we move the Oro Blanco house down to that bluff that overlooks all the cienega that our ranch is part of?"

"That's a good idea," Gipsy asked. "But how do you plan to move it?"

I said, "You know, it's really not much more than a little shack, and I think, with some help and some wagons or trucks, we can take it apart, move it, and put it back together there. And while we're putting it back together, we can add more to it, maybe a couple of rooms and make the kitchen larger."

As I got more serious about the idea of moving the place, I kept coming back to the thoughts I'd had for the past couple of years about the road through the ranch. Somehow, I had to get permanent use of it. If we moved the house, and even thought about building in the future, we would need that road in our name.

A couple of days later, Albert and I were in my office discussing some business about the Las Jarrillas ranch when the consolidation and "my" road came into the conversation.

"Albert," I asked, "You're involved with the Arivaca Ranch in some capacity, aren't you?"

"Well, yes. I serve on the board on behalf of John Zellweger on occasion when he's not available. Why do you ask?"

"There's this proposed consolidation that's been going on for months. It seems to be very difficult for some of us to keep abreast of what's happening or not. Would you mind sharing what you know?"

"Of course, Phil. I'm sorry I haven't been having conversations with you all along. It appears conditions in the cattle industry over the last year or so have cooled the idea of consolidation to just about a standstill, to the point that none of us believe it will happen soon, if ever."

"Well, that's pretty much the feeling some of us have been getting also, and you've known all along that I haven't been very supportive of it."

"I know," he said. "And I've always thought it to be in the bank's best interest for it not to happen."

"Albert, perhaps you might have an idea of how I might approach a little challenge I'm dealing with personally."

"Sure, Phil. What is it?"

"It's my road, Albert."

"Your road? Phil, what are you talking about?"

"Two years ago when McVey and Shepherd started this talk about consolidation, a lot of the ranch people kind of jumped the gun a little and did some things they maybe shouldn't have."

"What things, Phil?"

"My road, Albert! Johnnie got all excited about the merger of the Bar-V-Bar with the company ranch, and having access to the north end of the Bar-V-Bar prompted him to have Ramon go in and build a road from the ranch headquarters to my line. It's only a mile or so, but it's still a road on company property, and I need to get permanent use of it somehow."

"Phil, I'll get that taken care of. We need to get you a permanent easement or sell you a 'right of way' from the headquarters to your border. If Johnnie balks at that, I'll get Zellweger or Pusch to get it done."

Phil Clarke

In two weeks, it was done. A permanent easement to me and my heirs, off of the Tucson-Arivaca road, around the north side of the ranch headquarters and on to our north boundary.

It took over a month, but by late summer, we had the little house moved and rebuilt. And we did add a couple of rooms. Gipsy was really happy with the way it turned out. We had to build a large water storage tank that we could use to catch rainwater during the monsoon season, but we would still need to haul water from town—at least for a while. I told Gipsy we would drill a well early next year.

Phil and Gipsy's house on Tyndall Avenue

The year has been very hot. Temperatures in August and September reached as high as 118 degrees. We took numerous trips, mostly to avoid some of the heat. We spent three days up at Mt. Lemon up above Tucson, where it was 20 degrees cooler than here in town, and Gip and I went to the beach for a couple of weeks and were able to leave the kids with Mrs. Beetson.

Our next baby, Michael Bruce, was born on December 19, so we had an exciting and busy Christmas this year. When the holidays were past, and we were into the new year, 1924, it began to be apparent that we were going to need more space. We decided to look for a larger home, and I let the word out at the bank to that effect. Pretty soon, we had many people trying to help us find a place.

One day in early 1924, Albert came into my office and said, "Phil, I have an idea for your house. We just recently decided to move further out east to that new area called El Encanto out on Broadway, and you know our home over on Tyndall Avenue?"

"Well, yes, we sure do. It's a beautiful place."

"Well, Phil, Lois and I thought maybe you and Gipsy might like it. It's only a year old and is plenty large enough for your growing family. If you think you might be interested, I'm sure we could work out a favorable arrangement for you to purchase it."

"Well, of course, Albert. I'll talk to Gip tonight."

Albert Steinfeld was not only the president of the bank but also actively invested in many commercial and real estate properties. He got his start in Tucson many years ago when his family moved here from back East in Illinois. They started in business here with the opening of the Steinfeld department stores, which have now grown to numerous stores throughout the state. We had become close friends as well as mutually involved in the bank, so it doesn't surprise me that he and Lois's social life and activities would also include a residential move to a more upscale area in the growing city.

Gipsy and I discussed the proposal he had presented and concluded it would be both foolish and senseless to reject his very generous offer. By early summer, we had acquired the Steinfeld's beautiful two-story home right next to the university. We got moved in, and by fall, we were pretty well settled and enjoying everything about it. One day, I came home at noon for lunch and Gipsy said, "Phil, I have a late housewarming surprise for you. We're going to have another baby."

"Oh my gosh, I said. That's great news. Do you know when?"

"Probably late spring or early summer."

Albert was influential in getting us more involved in not only civic and business affairs but also the social activities of the city. Gipsy became active in a writers group and the Tucson Artists Association, the PTA, the Cowbelles (which was a group made up of women who were closely involved in the cattle industry), and, one of her favorites, the Arizona Pioneer Historical Society. For Christmas last year, I enrolled her in a correspondence writing course offered by Columbia University. Soon after, she was attending writing and painting classes at the University of Arizona as well.

While Gipsy was getting more involved in her activities, Albert was introducing me to many interesting activities that I previously knew very little about. He got me involved in the Arizona Bankers Association, The Arizona Cattlemen's Association, the Rotary Club, the Catalina Council of Boy Scouts, and other civic organizations.

However, the most amazing introduction was to the game of golf. I had never had a golf club in my hands and knew nothing about the game. He soon started encouraging me to come along with him on his weekly outings to the courses he played. Pretty soon, I was taking lessons, and to my surprise, I became a fair player. There were no courses with grass in Tucson.

One day, we were playing on a course on the west side of town, and Albert said, "You know, Phil, this old, dusty place would be a pretty nice course if it had grass. I think we should think about doing something about that."

"I agree, Albert. Maybe the bank could put a finance program together for somebody."

"Hell, Phil, let's do it ourselves. I haven't said much to you about this, but I'm not going to stay with the bank much longer. You know, I have numerous other projects I'm involved with besides the department stores, and I'm getting to a point where I think I want to have a little more freedom to work with them. With that in mind, the timing for this golf course project is perfect for me. I'll get with you in the next few days and talk some more about this.

I don't know why I haven't thought about this before. It will be a first for the city, and it could be ours. We could make it a heck of an addition to the city."

"That would be great, Albert, but I'm not very happy about you leaving the bank."

"Don't worry, Phil. It won't be for a while, and when I do decide, I'm sure George will take my place, so you'll be fine."

"Ah, well, okay," I said with a frown on my face.

A couple of days later, he came into the office with a big smile on his face and said, "Phil, I've got this golf club idea all figured out. I'm going to work out a way we can make you a major part of it, if you would like.

"We'll create a club with memberships purchased by investors to finance construction and landscaping. And when it's done, we'll charge dues from the memberships to fund the upkeep and operation of it."

Within just a couple of months, the new El Rio Golf and Country Club was being created over the old dusty dirt and weeds course that we all had been playing on for so long. I really enjoyed watching the big machines move the dirt around and create ponds for water and holes for sand traps. This would be a beautiful course.

One day toward the end of the year, Albert called me into his office and said, "Phil, the time has come a little sooner than I had planned, so I need to tell you about some additional changes that will be made when I leave.

"First, as I told you, George will replace me as president, but Charles Barker is leaving the bank for personal reasons. Because of that, the board wants to move you from the Cattle Loan Company into the bank as assistant vice president. Your responsibilities will be to support George as president as you all continue to grow the bank's entire operation. You'll still have hands-on management of the Cattle Loan Company as well. As part of this change, it will be essential for you to get more involved in the Cattlemen's Association's activities."

I sat still for a moment, trying to figure how things would be without Albert around, but as we all know with things like this, time moves on, and we would too.

As we moved into 1925, I became more involved in the day-to-day operations of the bank, assisting George, as he was out of the office much more often. I was also required to continue my inspections of collateral all over the country just as before. In May, I made a trip to San Francisco to attend the National Bankers Association Convention and quickly left there for Kansas City and Hominy, Oklahoma on loan inspections where it was necessary for me to help with the shipment of over one thousand head of cattle.

I recall writing to Gipsy from Hominy, telling her of one week's work. I wrote:

> *I've been out on ranches most of this week and succeeded in delivering over 1,000 head. Despite the cold, miserable weather, I have done more actual cow work, such as branding, sorting, and working cattle than I have since we left the ranch. And every night, I have been just as tired and sore as I used to be. We gather at the main house and eat hominy, salt pork, beans, and hot bread. Just like the days not so long ago at Arivaca.*
>
> *Worlds of love to you, my sweet Gip."*

I had been gone for nearly a month on that trip, and despite maintaining contact with Gip regularly, I knew she was beginning to feel anxious about my long trips. One night, after coming in from working cattle, I decided to call her instead of writing as I usually did. Early in the conversation, she said, "Phil, you better be getting yourself back here pretty soon."

I said "Is it time?"

"Pretty close. I think it's likely just a few days."

I said, "Okay, I'm going to catch a train tomorrow. And as soon as I get my ticket, I'll call and let you know my plans." At that time, I committed to changing my travel plans dramatically very soon.

Shortly after I got back to Tucson, we had another baby girl—a very healthy and happy little girl we named Nancy. Both mother and baby were healthy, and Gip was up and around quickly.

However, despite my well laid out plans to cut back, bank and cattle business continued to require my presence around the country. And though I had been able to stay close to home after Nancy was born, in October, I had to go to Washington, D.C. on behalf of the Cattle Growers Association to meet with the director of the Department of Agriculture to discuss ongoing discrepancies within the Agriculture Credit Act.

This act was created in 1923 with the intent of providing farmers and livestock people access to financing that had not been available as intended. I was in Washington for two days and was able to meet with several people in the department, and I believe I obtained very positive results regarding how this act would be administered in the future. I looked forward to passing it along to the various associations around the country.

It seemed like I had just got back from Washington, but in late November, I was working in my office, and Bud came in for a little visit. We had kept in pretty close contact ever since we moved to Tucson, and since I had been making frequent trips down to the ranch, I would often stop at his place in Amado and just shoot the breeze about different things.

That day, he said, "Phil, I've come up with an idea for us. I've just learned that the Baca Float land is available to lease, and I'm thinking you and I should partner up and start running some cattle on it."

"Damn, Bud, that's a good idea."

"As you know," Phil, "the Baca Float is really big. It's about 10,000 acres, and it originated when all that Spanish land grant business was taking place all over the southwest about 200 years ago. And this piece came because of some splits in that old Baca family land grant from over in New Mexico. We can take a long-term lease on the whole thing for hardly any hard cash if we're willing to share a small percentage of proceeds from the sale of cattle."

Within a month, we had put the lease in place and had started buying steers down in Sonora and other areas in Mexico where we could find them. It turned out there were numerous head running loose down there that were abandoned when the revolution ended.

Over the next few months, Bud and I and our cowboys made several trips to Sonora and started bringing back herds ranging in size from one hundred to five hundred. Over the next few months, we were able to move nearly a thousand head. There was plenty of pasture and lots of land to run them on. And we think as we keep going and continue to find cattle and the domestic beef market continues strong, we should be able to move numbers into the thousands, either to the domestic market or back into Mexico.

CHAPTER 31

The new year arrived, and even though we had a great holiday season with friends and all our kids at home, I needed to get back out around the state and start on inspections again. My plan was to go over to Cochise County and work my way back west. But just before I left, I got a call from Buck at the ranch. My first thought was something wasn't right down there, and he said, "Phil, I don't know if you've heard, but I just talked to Ricardo over at the Arivaca. It seems that Ramon passed away yesterday at his home in Tucson."

Oh no, I thought. I heard that he had stepped down at the ranch and had moved to town, but I thought he was doing well health-wise. "How old was he, Buck?"

"Only 53, Phil, but you know, he'd had a damned hard life, and people think he just wore out."

Ramon Ahumada was a legend throughout the cattle country of Arizona and beyond. For me, this was a big loss. He was not only my mentor, but he also became one of my best friends. I didn't think there was any way I could count how much he and his wife, Virginia, did for Gipsy and me over the years. *Oh, this is just going to break Gipsy's heart, as it will many in this community.*

One day in early spring, George came into my office, closed the door behind him, and said, "Phil, I have something to tell you. I received a letter from T. N. McCauley, who is the president and sole owner of the Central Copper Company down at Dos Cabezas, near Willcox."

"I know of him," George, "but haven't met him. Isn't that company one of the largest mining operations in the country?"

"That's right, Phil. And here's the deal. He's interested in acquiring our bank and wants to know if we will entertain his inquiry."

"George, thanks for sharing this with me, but you know, this is for you and the board to decide. I work for you, and I'll support and help you with whatever you decide you want to do."

I called Gipsy soon after that visit and told her what George had told me and said I was coming home early so we could talk about it. According to George, McCauley was moving the Central Copper headquarters to Tucson. The company currently had in excess of $2,500,000 invested in the various banks in the city. He was a man with a great amount of initiative and believed acquiring a local bank was an important move for him personally and for the company as well.

Gipsy stopped me for a minute and said, "He sounds a lot like you!"

"Well, I don't know about that," I replied. "He obviously has a large amount of financial strength and has indicated to George that he will be putting that power to work in favorable ways in the further development of our city. He told George he considers this bank to be one of the great banking landmarks in the Western states and that this bank is one of the better institutions in the city. He has watched it enjoy a very admirable and honorable history. He believes that with the infusion of new leadership and many more dollars, this bank can do much more for the benefit of Tucson. I told George I would be supportive of whatever they decide to do."

"Well, where will that leave you, Phil?"

"Gipsy, I'll probably become a full-time cowboy again. You know, with what Bud and I have going on now, I probably really don't need to be in the banking business, anyway."

"Sure," she said, "but we both know you've really developed a love for it and the opportunities it has provided us."

"Well, sure. I guess we'll just see how things work out."

Only a short time passed before Mr. McCauley told George he wanted to talk to me. When George told me, he also suggested that, before I met with him, we should sit down so he could apprise me of how everything was progressing and how it all would work out. I agreed.

"It looks like his acquisition is going to take place, and probably sooner than we expected. He has his own man, George Ramsey, who will replace me as president, so I'll be moving on. It is my belief, though, that he wants to talk to you about staying on in some management capacity. And, Phil, don't be concerned about me. As you know, I have numerous other involvements in the city, so I'll be just fine."

Within a couple of days, Mr. McCauley called and asked to talk to me, and he came to my office later that day. We shook hands, and he said, "Phil you are well known throughout the banking industry, and as I have become increasingly interested in acquiring the Consolidated Bank, I have felt it would be essential to have you remain with the bank.

"I believe we will consummate this purchase very quickly, and just so you know, I have asked my good friend and associate George Ramsey to replace George Stonecypher as president, who, incidentally, will be compensated very generously upon his departure. Additionally, Mr. Stonecypher will be asked to join our board, as will you and Mr. Hermes.

"George Ramsey has had a prominent and successful history in the banking and financial management fields for many years. I was fortunate to induce him to join us at the Central Copper Company a number of years ago. We share a similar philosophy regarding management of employees and relationships with the community, and now I am asking him to come here to Tucson with us.

"He has agreed, and perhaps equally as important, he agrees with me that we must encourage you to stay with the bank. Not in the same capacity as now, but rather as vice president, second in responsibility only to George."

"Thank you for your interest in me," I said, "but there are a couple of items I would like us to be clear on. You surely are aware that I have and operate a large ranch of my own down in Arivaca, and even though I have good hands and a good manager down there, I still devote about twenty percent of my time to that. And, please, help me be clear about what you believe my value and contributions will be to you."

"Phil, yes, we are aware of your ranch and the arrangements you have had and intend to encourage you to continue with that, as you see necessary. I have followed your banking career for many years. I know you first came to the bank in 1922, and because of your very successful experience in the cattle business were asked to manage the old Tucson Cattle Loan Company, in which administration you made an enviable record of care, caution, and conservative handling of the affairs of not only the bank but our customers as well. And it is well known now that you are one of the most respected and able cattlemen in the Southwest as well as into the Midwest. You are looked upon as a very eminent authority in all livestock matters. Phil, a man with those credentials is essential to the continued success of our livestock business.

"We believe our values and cultural goals and objectives are consistent with those that you have demonstrated over the years. We stress the value of cooperation, both with our relationships with employees as well as the community. We stress the importance of employee personal interest not only in the bank but also in the business and civic welfare of Tucson, as well.

"Also, Phil, you know we are well funded. At the time of purchase, we will increase the capital stock from $100,000 to $300,000, and I am making a personal contribution of an additional $100,000. Furthermore, I have committed to the directors that I will take no salary or bonuses for the first five years. As such Phil, we will offer you a salary of $15,000 per year with the opportunity to earn an additional amount in incentive-based bonuses.

"Understanding you likely will want to discuss this with Gipsy, perhaps we could expect a response by the end of the week?"

"Yes, of course. I appreciate all you have shared with me and am comfortable with that. I suspect that I will have a positive answer soon," I said.

Gipsy and I discussed the new opportunity more that evening. The key part for me was what Mr. McCauley said about cooperation and cooperative thinking as it relates to our relationships with our employees as well as our customers. That, obviously, had been a key position that Albert, George, and I believed in all along. We determined that, with that kind of philosophy, this would be a good move for us to make."

I got back to Mr. McCauley the next day and told him I was happy to accept his offer and looked forward to moving ahead with him and Mr. Ramsey.

In early October, the ownership of the bank passed into the hands of Mr. T. N. McCauley. I also learned that he had acquired ownership of the Santa Rita Hotel and the Tucson Realty Company at about the same time.

For the most part, I continued to function in a similar capacity as I had with Albert and George. Mr. Ramsey and Mr. McCauley were both serious and professional businessmen. Unlike my more relaxed relationships with Albert and George, we were, for the most part, strictly business.

One of his first directives to me was to develop a full and complete analysis of the bank's financial status as of the day he closed on the acquisition. I thought that to be a little strange since it was very close and similar to what I had prepared for him only a month or two previously.

Shortly after, we were open again. Under our new management structure and ownership, Mr. McCauley advised me we would be tendering all the employees of the bank and the Tucson Realty Company a banquet in the main dining room of the plush and new Santa Rita Hotel the last week of October. He wanted an opportunity for him and Mr. Ramsey to meet all the employees in a social way and become better acquainted with as many as possible.

In their respective talks, they each addressed the value of cooperation and cooperative work, stressing not only their personal interest in their work but also in their potential involvement in the civic welfare of Tucson. They each asked all to pledge themselves to the betterment of the city as well as themselves. Most all employees were attentive and interested but perhaps a little dismayed at their approach to acquiring loyalty and commitment.

Moving into 1927, Gipsy and I continued to have ongoing conversations about our house on the bluff. We were very happy with the changes and additions we made to the little bunkhouse, but we both knew we were going to need something larger. Since we had access to the bluff from the north on the new road through the ranch, we decided to build a new home right next to the other one but closer to the edge of the bluff with an even better view of the pastures in the cienega than before. We decided we would build the home out of adobe, mainly for heat in the winter and because adobe is much cooler in the summer.

Gipsy designed the home to have an east-facing patio so we could sit out in the summer evenings in the cool of the shade and still have the warmth of the winter sun. One day, during construction of the new house, I took Gipsy and the kids out for an inspection and to give her an opportunity to make sure it was coming along the way she wanted it to. Everybody enjoyed watching the laborers mixing mud and straw with shovels and putting the mixture in the wood mold to form adobes. The molds looked like ladders lying on the ground, and when the mud dried, the molds were removed and the adobes were stacked like bricks to make the walls of the house. The house would have three nice-sized bedrooms, a large kitchen with a back porch, and a large front room with a dining area at one end. By the middle of the summer, the home was finished, and we began moving some furniture and other items in. Just before the monsoon season began, we were in.

Right from the beginning, this became a special place for us. We would come down here, and I would help the cowboys with the cattle and ride the ranch with Buck and Slim, checking the fence lines and the cattle as we rode down through the Gulch all the way to the border. I was always amazed at how good riding the ranch made me feel after spending day after day at the bank.

While I was doing that, Gip was busy getting the home fixed up. She planted flowers and even started a little garden with late summer vegetables. But while we have surely been enjoying the new place, it was becoming increasingly apparent that we needed water available without having to continue hauling it in from the springs below.

One day, I said, Gip, "I think I'm going to look into putting a well down below us in the cienega. The water table isn't but just a few feet deep down there, and I've been thinking about building a concrete water tank down, anyway. Power is available in Arivaca now, and I think the Company has it into the headquarters place, so I think it shouldn't take much to be able to bring it on over here to our place. If I can get that done, we can pump water up here to our big tank out there in the back. You would have running water whenever you needed it."

"Oh, my gosh," she said. "Wouldn't that just make this place so much better?"

As the year moved on, we began to look forward to getting down there and enjoying it like we did when we lived there full time. The good news was that it didn't take much to get the power extended to our place, and the well only went a few feet deep before we reached plenty of water to keep a stock tank and our house tank full most of the time.

Toward the end of the year, I began to feel less comfortable in my role. I had become an active member of the Arizona Cattle Growers' Association. I attended their numerous meetings around the state and was even invited to speak at the national convention in October. I'd also been quite involved with the Arizona Bankers Association and participated on many committees discussing statewide issues in the industry.

But Mr. McCauley, Mr. Ramsey, and I seemed to be lacking something in our relationship. We got along just fine, but I sensed a disconnect regarding cooperation and cooperative thinking. Both men were very driven and community oriented, to the point of almost overdoing their financial involvement in the city, not with bank resources so much, but perhaps with funding Mr. McCauley developed from sales of his mining company stocks to investors back East. I didn't complain or say anything, and I didn't intend to. They were very generous and compassionate toward everyone. It simply wasn't the direction I had hoped the bank would go.

And of course, Bud and our Baca Float operation continued to do very well for us. During the previous six months, we had moved close to 3,000 fat steers, either into Mexico or into Texas and California. I usually met up with him every time I went down to our ranch, which was two to three times a month.

I noticed Buck and Slim were getting older, so I planned to talk to them about their plans going forward. They both had been with us for over fifteen years. Luis was still taking care of the little mine at Ruby and the cattle down in the Gulch, and he was getting close to forty years old himself. I thought we may need to look at bringing in a couple of young cowboys we could train to fill in for them.

After spending a good part of Christmas at the ranch with Gip and the kids and going back and forth to Amado to see Bud, we headed back to Tucson and our activities there. Gip went back to writing and painting and to her bridge games with her friends, and I went back to the bank. Early in the month, Mr. McCauley called me in to let me know he was making major changes in our management staff. He said George Ramsey had left and that he would replace him as president.

I thought, *Uh oh, I must be next!* Apart from me, he was dismissing the entire set of officers. Most important to me though was, my good friend, Fred Hermes, was replaced as vice president by George Bedell, who was cashier. I asked why Mr. Ramsey had left, but he chose not to discuss that with me and moved on to why he was doing all this.

He explained he was making these changes to reduce expenses and that there would be other reductions made soon. He said that this was about a plan he had for the near future to increase the bank's revenue. He believed this plan would enable us to increase our undivided profits to more than $70,000.

Surprisingly, he increased my salary by $5,000 and promised a bonus if we achieved these profits. Furthermore, he told me to keep all this absolutely confidential. Of course, I planned to tell Albert if he didn't already know. It was McCauley's belief that we needed to maintain a complete understanding of our objectives, and that, moving forward, I would be serving in more of an advisory capacity to him.

I discussed all this with Gipsy that evening, and she looked at me with her jaw wide open. I said, "Gip, close your mouth. A fly might get in there." She smiled a little and shook her head. I continued, "You know, Gip, maybe I'm just meant to be a cowboy again."

"That may be," she agreed.

Unfortunately, the new arrangement didn't work out very well for either of us, and as the end of February neared, I decided I was going to leave the bank and go back to the ranch. I drafted a resignation letter as eloquently as I could. I addressed it to the Board: Attention, T. J. McCauley, and it said:

There has been a total lack of harmony for the last few weeks, and I am not in accord with certain plans and policies you have put in place for the bank. Where there is a lack of harmony, there can be no unity of purpose, and without a unity of purpose, there can be no cooperation, a thing I know you desire and which I feel I cannot give you under your present arrangements and plans.

My personal business is constantly growing and of such a nature that I believe I can devote all my time more advantageously to my affairs, and as such, I regret to ask that you please accept my resignation as vice president and director of the Consolidated National Bank as soon as convenient but not later than March 1, 1928.

I have given this considerable thought, and salary is no object. I ask that you please not request me to reverse my decision.

In asking you to accept my resignation, I want you to feel that I have the most profound regard and consideration for all that Mr. McCauley has done for the bank, as well as the community, and want to further assure you that you will continue to have my best wishes for the continued healthy progress of the Consolidated National Bank.

Sincerely,
P. M. Clarke

I hand delivered the letter to Mr. McCauley's secretary that day, and within an hour, he was in my office. We talked briefly. I provided him with an additional explanation of my thoughts and was happy he only expressed disappointment. We concluded this would be an amicable separation and ultimately would be best for both of us. I told him I would leave immediately but would return prior to the first to finalize my departure.

I left immediately. I went home and suggested to Gipsy that if she could get away, it would be good for me to go to the ranch. She said, "Phil, I have been pretty sure this is what you would do, and I am in full support, but I have a variety of things going on in town the next couple of days. Why don't you go on ahead, and I'll come down with the kids in a few days."

I collected some things and left for the ranch and stopped to see Bud on the way down. Even though I knew he knew this would likely happen, I didn't think he thought it would be this soon, and I didn't want him to hear about it from others.

I caught him just as he was leaving to go down to Nogales, and he wasn't surprised. He simply said that he expected it. He continued, "Now, let's get you back into the cattle business."

I said, "Well, I'm going to be at the ranch for a while. I told McCauley I would be back in before the first to settle our unfinished business, so let's go down to the Baca Float one day to give me a chance to look things over again."

Phil Clarke

CHAPTER 32

I went down to the ranch, settled in, and since we had gotten phone service to the ranch, I began making calls. I called Albert first and was glad I reached him. He surprised me when he told me he had already heard the news.

"I was hoping I could let you know before you heard from other sources," I said.

"Don't worry, Phil. I've actually been fearful this would be happening for quite some time. I hated to see Stonecypher set aside when McCauley took over, and when word got out that he was bringing in his own man, I was concerned the two of them just wouldn't have a clear understanding how we had attained the success that we had. But, Phil, it will all be for the good going forward. So, what are your plans?"

"I think I'll start playing a little more golf on our new golf course. It sure has turned out nice and is becoming very popular in the community. I'm really glad you encouraged me to invest in it."

Next, I called my friend, Fred Hermes, who had been the vice president for years under Albert.

"Fred, I just want to let you know I submitted my resignation yesterday. I don't need to get into details now, but I wanted you to know. I'm down at the ranch now."

"Thanks for telling me, Phil. I'm sorry for you and Gipsy. Do you have any specific plans, now, other than the ranch?"

"Actually, I'm planning to get more involved with the cattle here and become more of a help to my cowboys. I stopped and saw Bud on my way down today, and we were talking about my guys, and maybe I might need to look around for some younger cowboys to help them out some. Hell, Fred, sometimes I forget just what I've got going here. You know, in the last couple of years alone, we've acquired six more allotments down near Oro Blanco, and right now, we're running about 700 steers and some 350 mother cows. That's quite a bit for my four cowboys, so I guess I better get my boots on and get ready to get back in the saddle . Might be time for me to remember what Billie once told me. He said, 'The eye of the master is what fattens the ox.' I need to get my eyes back on my oxen."

"Listen, Phil. I've been keeping my eyes and ears open since I left the bank, and recently, I was talking to Harry DeFord over at The United Bank and Trust. This is confidential, but he told me that the bank is in pretty serious trouble and may be looking for a resolution in the near future."

"What do you mean by resolution, Fred?"

"Not sure, Phil, but I think he was trying to tell me they may be needing to find a buyer pretty soon."

"That's really interesting. Fred, are you thinking you might have some interest in that?"

"Maybe, Phil, but only if you do."

"Hell, Fred. I just finished telling you that I'm ready to be a cowboy again."

"Okay, just thought you should know."

"Well, thanks. And I guess you better keep me apprised of things."

"I will. Talk to you soon!"

I am really glad that I made all those calls because it only took two days for the story to make headlines in the large local newspaper, *The Tucson Citizen*. The story headlined, "Clarke resigns post with bank and plans to devote time to his own cattle business."

The article continued:

His personal cattle business has now grown to such an extent that he needs to give it his full time and attention. He has extensive cattle interests in the Arivaca and Ruby areas as well as cattle brokerage and feeding activities in other areas of the state as well.

He was born in Dublin, Ireland and came to Arizona after spending his youth on the streets of New York. When he first arrived in Arizona, he was hired as a greenhorn cowpuncher and storekeeper for the old Arivaca Land and Cattle Company and later started acquiring cattle of his own after he and his wife Gipsy purchased the old mercantile store in Ruby. Over the past fifteen years, he has acquired numerous old homesteads in the Arivaca district and has continued to expand his cattle interest in the area. For two years, he was the manager of the Tucson Cattle Loan Company and later became vice president of the Consolidated National Bank, a position he has held for the past four years.

The next day, I met with Buck and Slim, and Tony was with them. We got a big pot of coffee going and sat around a table and started making plans. They all had been busy for the previous month. Calving season started in February, and when the calves start coming, it was an around-the-clock job to make sure all mommas and babies were doing okay. I asked Buck if he had contact with Luis, and he said he saw him the week before, and the cows were doing good down there, too.

I said, "Why don't one of you ride down there with me tomorrow? Tony, why don't you go with me?"

"Si, Felipe. That would be good."

We all talked some more—about water and fences and summer pastures and where we were going to put all the cattle for the summer. While we talked, I thought we should talk about them as well.

"How are all of you guys doing? You are all getting older. You've been with me for a lot of years! You think we should look for some young cowboys to help us when roundup time comes around this fall?"

They were all quiet for a minute, but then Buck said, "Yeah, we should, but Phil, we're all okay. I'm only 38, and Slim, what are you? 42? And Tony is only 40."

"Okay," I said. "I think we should build a bunk house up here near the house and move that big barn up here from Marteney's place. I think it's time we get our whole operation up here close and have most everything together. What do you think?"

They all thought it would be a good idea, so I said, "You all think about the bunk house idea and tell me how we should do it so we can have all of you here or close by here. Look at that big barn and let me know what you think about moving it."

The next morning, Tony and I saddled up and headed across the east end of the cienega and up toward the Tonkin Well before going over the hill and up Chimney Canyon south to Ruby. I first wanted to go by the mine and see what recent progress Luis had been making. It had been a couple of months since we sent our last load of ore down to the smelter, so I want to see if he and his crew had pulled more out since then.

When we got there, two of Luis's helpers were digging, but they told me Luis had gone down into the Gulch today. So, we left and continued ourselves. As we rode along, Tony and I began to visit about the old days, especially back to the night at the campfire during the roundup of 1909. I asked if he remembered that night, and he said, "Oh, si, Felipe. I remember well."

"You never had any bad feelings toward me?"

"No, no, Felipe. After that night, I learn from all the cowboys around you are muy bien hombre, and I always tell Ramon that someday I want to work for you."

"Well, Tony, you've been working for me for about ten years, and you are one of the best cowboys in this whole district."

"Muchas gracias, patron."

"De nada, Tony. I hope you stay at the Bar-V-Bar for a long time."

We rode along, checking the cows and their calves as we moved south, looking for Luis. Shortly after noon, we came up on a cow and her calf. Tony pulled us to a stop and said, "Patron, this calf is in trouble."

"I said. "I see that. This little baby looks to have an infection around the shoulder. We better get him down and see what's going on."

Tony reached for his lariat, and I said, "Wait, Tony. let me get this one." I got my rope off the strap, made my loop, and as I took a couple swings, the little calf spooked and started running away. I trotted after him a little and threw the loop and missed him completely. Oh, did Tony start laughing. So, I made another loop, threw it again, hit the little bugger on the shoulder but still didn't get the loop over his head. I turned to Tony, watched him laugh some more and said, "Uno mas, Tony." The next loop made the mark. We got him down and saw he had a little cut in his left shoulder, probably from a tree branch or broken limb. We put some iodine on it and some packing and turned him back to his mama.

As we rode on, Tony just kept that big smile on his face. Finally I said, "Okay, Tony, it's been a while since I did this."

"Si, patron," he said and chuckled.

Shortly after, we met up with Luis and talked for a while. He told us the cows and steers were all doing well. He hadn't had any problems across the border, either. Also, he thought he would have another load of ore ready in another month or so. I said that would be good and told him I would be around the ranch pretty much full-time from now on. I also told him that I wasn't working at the bank anymore.

"Is okay, Patron?" he asked.

"It's okay, Luis. It's good for me to be here."

He seemed to be pleased that I would be on the ranch more.

We started on our way back north when the thought came to my mind that I hadn't been by the mercantile for six or seven years. I had been to Ruby on occasion, but intentionally avoided the old store. But I was feeling good that day, so I told Tony we should go back by there.

The old store had changed quite a bit. I learned that Worthington only lasted a few months after we left, and the new mining company had opened what was currently there. The building pretty much looked the same, but they had gas pumps out front where once there was only a hitching post. And they put in parking spaces for the numerous autos that moved around the mines and district. Bad memories don't leave us very easily, and they hadn't for me either, but I felt okay as we moved on back toward the ranch. It had been a good day for me, and I was ready to move on.

I stayed busy most of March and only went to Tucson twice. I realized I greatly enjoyed being back at the ranch and working with the cattle again. But in early April, Fred called with an update on the United Bank situation.

He said, "Phil, Harry says they're getting ready to go down. The Arizona State Banking commission just completed a thorough examination of the bank's condition and rendered a report that the bank is hopelessly insolvent. As a result of this examination, the Commission levied an assessment against all the stockholders. But lo and behold, all the stock is held by the Tucson Cooperative Association, and because of this, it was determined that it would essentially be impossible to collect on the assessment."

"Well, Fred, are you suggesting or proposing something?"

"I sure am. If you are interested, I think we could put together a small group and purchase that stock at a very attractive price."

"Fred, do you have a contact?"

"That would be Harry."

"Okay, Fred. Do you think you can get a hold of him and have him agree to meet with us? If you can, it would be good if we could meet, maybe at Albert's. What do you think?"

"I agree, Phil. And we need this meeting to be in strict confidence."

I called Gipsy that night and told her about my day and about my conversations with Fred and that I was coming to town today to have the meeting. I could tell she was laughing, so I asked her what was so funny. "You roping that calf. You used to never miss!" she replied.

"I know, Gip, but it's been a while. Tony couldn't resist telling the rest of the guys, and they had a big laugh too. I'm planning to stay in town for a couple of days and see how this thing works out. I'll see you this evening. All the kids okay and missing their daddy?"

"Yes. They'll be glad to see you."

We met at Albert's store, just a ways down from the bank, and went to his office in the back. Fred and Harry were there as well. We discussed this thing for a while, and eventually, I said, "Harry, why don't you tell us what you think and what you know, and how you might feel about this idea that Fred has?"

"Sure. First, you know I am the vice president and cashier at the bank and am also acting president of the Tucson Cooperative Association, and as such, I am privy to most everything that has transpired in the last month or so. Due to the latest developments, I feel I am acting in good faith with the bank and am cooperative in having this discussion with you. And frankly, anyone else, as well."

"We understand, Harry, and thanks for making that clear to us. Go ahead, please."

"The reality, gentlemen, is that the bank is defunct and needs to be liquidated quickly to avoid numerous legal actions. All the stock is owned by the Tucson Cooperative Association. Par value of the stock was between $150,000 and $175,000. Today, I would encourage the board to accept any kind of offer around $100,000. We can discuss many of the numerous particulars you would like, but essentially, this is where we will be starting at to effect a change of ownership."

"Very good, Harry," I said. "We appreciate you sharing this with us. I'm pretty sure Fred is sharing a similar interest to me. We will discuss this as well with other acquaintances we think could have interest. Incidentally Harry, might I ask that, if this would come to pass, would you have interest in being a part of the group?"

"Thanks, Phil. Yes, I would."

"Very good, Harry. We'll be in touch soon"

Over the next few days, Fred and I contacted my good friend from Australia, Julius Kruttschnitt, a renowned mining engineer who had been active locally for many years, and Bill Gurnee, a former capitalist who had recently retired from his vast investment activities. I also talked to Bud and Albert, Frank Brophy, Tom Peters , Harold Thurber, and John Goodman, both well-known and active cattlemen in southern Arizona. When I talked to Fred again, he said he had talked to Henry Boice down at the Empire ranch near Sonoita. He told Fred he could be interested, but not at this time.

In mid-April, I received a letter from Mr. Donald Beales, a vice president with the Interstate National Bank in St. Louis. In reply to my inquiry of financing this venture, he was very positive and interested in his bank being involved, especially in livestock financing here in Arizona.

I told Fred that this could also be of interest to us. He commented to the effect that they knew it was very difficult at that time to buy a bank that was clean, but when you have an opportunity to buy one that has been declared insolvent by the State Banking Commission, it put an entirely different look to it.

"Fred, I think we have an additional option to package the cash for this," I replied.

One evening I told Gipsy, "It looks like this thing is going to come together, and the way I am structuring it, we will be acquiring the majority interest in it and be joined by Fred and Julius. I also believe Bill Gurnee will join us, as well as Harry DeFord, who is currently with the bank and is the president of the cooperative association. We're going to meet the first of the week and present an offer."

After nearly a month of back-and-forth discussions with the officers of the cooperative, they called a special meeting of their directors. The meeting was to determine the resolution of the offer from Mr. P. M. Clarke and his associates. A copy of the minutes of that meeting were acquired and read as follows:

After discussion of the offer, it was moved by Mr. Murphy and seconded by Mr. Jackson that the offer be accepted and that an executed contract be written and signed by the president and secretary under its corporate seal and that the matter be presented to the stockholders at the annual meeting next week.

The Chairman put this motion to a vote, and it was unanimously carried.

The resolution was certified as true and complete and was signed by the president, Harry DeFord.

To my dismay, in next Monday's mail was a letter from Billie Marteney. I couldn't believe it. He wanted me to partner with him in purchasing the Robles Ranches out at Three Points, near the north end of the Altar valley. I read the letter three times, and when I got home later, I read it again to Gipsy.

Dear Philippe (as he has always spelled my name),

Last night, I could not sleep and kept thinking about how things were at the bank. I made up my mind to write to you. My idea is for you to buy my paper out of the bank and, individually, hold the mortgage on the ranch. We could then form a new company and stock the ranch, and in three years, we could make enough to pay off the debt.

If we have the notes out of the bank, and I think you can buy them all for about $30,000, we could form a new company and borrow enough to put in two to three thousand steers. If you have the notes, we could have a pretty strong company by doing this. I can't see why in any way it would interfere with your loyalty to the bank or your work in the bank.

You know that a man invested in a ranch is worth two or three fellows working for wages. I think we could operate the Robles Ranch with success and harmony.

There is no doubt in my mind that in a few years you will be the largest rancher in the Arivaca district, and if you are also an owner in the Robles Ranches, it will make you one of the largest ranch owners in the whole state of Arizona. In Bud Parker, you have an ideal partner for the Santa Cruz and Arivaca, and in myself, you would have another in the Robles. The Robles ranches are outfits that can be run very inexpensively if we have the proper number of cattle and the range is kept in good shape. These ranches, if administered correctly and with a few good seasons, will make us all well-to-do men.

What do you say?

After you read this, I am coming in to see you.

Sincerely,
Billie Marteney

Before I could even call Billie back in the morning paper, *The Arizona Daily Star*, the headlines read: "Clarke and Hermes Purchase United Bank and Trust Co." The article continued:

The bank was purchased by Clarke and Hermes and other unnamed associates, following the completion of negotiations, which have been under consideration for some time. They will take control of the institution this morning at the bank's offices on the corner of Stone Ave. and Broadway.

The article continued with brief resumes of Mr. Hermes and Mr. Deford and proceeded to disclose that the purchase required the acquisition of all the capital stock of the old institution and that it was the intention of the new ownership's management to increase that capital substantially.

I quickly called Billie, but as I suspected he had read the article that morning. But, true to Billie's persona, he was only as happy for me as he could be. We talked for more than an hour, and I covered everything that had happened in the last month or so as best as I could. We discussed his proposal at length, too. It was very difficult for me.

I told Billie that on one hand, I was sorry I didn't get his letter two months sooner, but I also had to be sure he understood I couldn't do both. I knew I would look back on that day and wonder many times if I missed what might have been the greatest opportunity of my life. All the while, he knew the banking business was something I had realized enormous rewards from over the past six or so years. I assured him I would be keeping close watch on The Robles and him as well. We made plans to get together for lunch the following week.

About a week later, early in July, *The Tucson Citizen* followed *The Daily Star's* article of the previous week with a headline on their evening paper.

Their article briefly noted that we had elected our officers, and with my purchase of approximately 70 percent of the stock, I was elected president with Fred Hermes as vice president and Harry DeFord secretary, along with Julius Kruttschnitt and W. S. Gurnee as directors.

In a short interview, I was quoted as saying, "I feel complimented to be associated with such a well-rounded board of directors. All these directors are men who can and will direct the affairs of this institution and will not be directors in name only. They all are men of broad and varied experience, and they represent the highest level of character, integrity, and honesty. Their records are open books and will stand up very favorably under the closest scrutiny."

I said, "I feel that with this board, this institution is in a position to take care of the reasonable credit requirements of every individual, business, and industry in a manner consistent with sound banking principles.

"It will be our policy to conduct a safe and sound banking business and create a reputation for just and impartial treatment for all our customers. We believe that our character and integrity are at the top of the list of assets we bring to this institution. This is a distinction this bank has enjoyed for years, and we will strive to maintain that distinction.

"Before taking over this bank, we absolutely satisfied ourselves as to the condition of the bank, and we believe that though we may not be the largest banks in Tucson, we are one of the most liquid in the State.

"On day one, we are in a position to serve this community efficiently on the basis of financial responsibility, integrity, honesty, experience, and a complete knowledge and understanding of local conditions."

The article concluded by stating that both Fred and I were former executives at the Consolidated National Bank and that Fred has been in the banking business practically all of his life. It said that he was an expert in bonds and securities and that I was with the Consolidated Bank for over six years, was the executive vice president prior to leaving that bank earlier this year, and that I had extensive experience in the cattle business.

CHAPTER 33

We opened for business immediately and experienced enormous interest from the city. Many depositors came over from Consolidated, which I was enjoying immensely, and we had numerous inquiries about the services we would be offering.

Bud called and wanted to know if I had lost my mind. He said, "I thought you were glad to be out of the bank and excited to be back at the ranch!"

I said, "Bud, I haven't lost my mind, but yes, I'm glad to be out from across the street and am glad to be back in the saddle, so to speak."

Bud, I said, "I've got to make a quick trip to Winslow in the next day or so but will be going to the ranch as soon as I get back."

"I have lots to talk to you about. One thing is why I chose to get back in a bank. I'll call ahead so we can plan to spend some time together."

A couple of days later, Fred and I went up to Winslow. The cooperative owners had purchased that bank a few years before, and we believed it was one of the reasons the United got in trouble. We decided a month or so before that we would be best served if we sold it to some local interests up there. Many issues factored into our decision, distance being one, a challenging facility up there was another, but mainly that it was located in an entirely different market than ours in Tucson. Two family interests were purchasing it from us, and they were changing the name to Citizens Bank of Winslow.

After a couple of days, with all particulars agreed to, I left for Tucson. Fred would stay and finish up the closing, or as close to it as he could before he came back.

I got back to town, and after a quick stop at the bank, I went home. Gipsy and I had planned to take the kids to the ranch for a while, but I told her I had to go see Bud and was going to go to Amado for a couple of days.

I called Bud that night to see how his next couple of days looked for a visit. He said, "Phil, I've got a hell of a lot more to do than you do, but I'll set it all aside just to spend a couple of days with you." I'm glad he chuckled after he said that because I know he's damn right about it. He was, in fact, a hell of a lot busier than me, doing what we both love to do.

I went to Amado the next day and met Bud. We spent most of the morning going over our steer books and talking about plans for the fall and next year. Sometimes, I stop what I'm doing when I'm with him and wonder about how I miss what he does every day and how much fun we'd had the past few years. And right on time, he straightens up and says, "Okay, Phil, tell me where your mind has gone."

That day, I shook my head back and forth a little as I smiled and said, "Bud, you're a mind reader."

"I told you a long time ago, I might know you better than you know yourself," he said.

"Let's go down south, Bud, and I'll try to explain why I've done this new bank deal. Do you remember back in about 1921 or '22 when you called to tell me Albert wanted to see me?

"As you know, Albert hired me to help with their livestock loan business. Right after I started working for them, Albert took me aside one day and started what would turn out to be one of the most valuable educations I could ever have.

"He started off one day by saying, 'Phil, I want to tell you a little about the value of money. You see, Phil, money is like steers or milk or clothes or automobiles. It's a commodity, a product, to be bought and sold. Think of it as you do when you are discussing the price of cows or steers you want to buy or sell. If you're buying, you want the price to be as low as you can get it so that when you're ready to sell them, you want your price to be as high as possible. It's all about maximizing your return on your investment by maximizing your gross profit by as large a percentage as you can.'

"We buy steers," Bud, "for a price we hope will allow us to double our investment. For example, we buy a steer for $10 or $12 and expect to put enough weight on him to sell him for $25 to $30 in eight to twelve months—maybe even in a shorter time than that. And, if we're able to do that, we're going to realize a gross profit of 100 percent, right?"

"But here's the deal about the banking business. It's possible for us to make five, six, or seven times that much!"

"How in the hell can you do that?" Bud asked.

"Bud, it's about deposits and loans. If you deposit $100 in my bank, I'm going to pay you about one percent on your money. Now, I'm going to turn around and loan you depositor money to buy steers at a rate of about seven percent today, right? That's seven hundred percent gross return on that depositor money. Additionally, a bank can buy money from the federal reserves for just a fraction above prime to use for installment loans and mortgage loans and numerous other investment opportunities with intentions to also return to the bank seven percent. When the country's economy is stable, as it has been for the past ten years or so, the banking industry has realized great returns as, I might add, you saw happen for us at Consolidated the last four years or so.

"So Bud, Albert continued to hammer that into my cowboy brain over and over during my early days with the bank. And that explains why I worked so hard to create and maintain as many new loans as I could. And, I guess, just to finish up my little story here, it is why you and I, and many other cattle people, don't mind paying the bank seven percent. Why should we if we expect to realize a much higher return than that? And, Bud, now you know why it was too difficult for me to say no to this opportunity.

"This bank is a small bank, Bud. And that's why I see such a great opportunity for growth, both in depositor money as well as in loan business, especially if I can bring a good number of my old customers over from Consolidated."

We continued to have a very good day. We drove around most of our pasture on the Baca Float and talked about the success we'd enjoyed the last couple of years. We didn't talk much about how much we've earned because neither of us knows for sure how much. We had a good time catching up, and I assured him that there would be no decrease in my involvement with him and our business together.

The bank got off to a very good start, and in August, Gipsy and I decided that her and the kids would go to Hermosa Beach for a couple of weeks before school got started up again. As we always had done when going to the coast in the summer, we loaded up the big Studebaker touring car early in the morning, before the sun came up, and headed across the desert, trying to get to the cooler Pacific breezes before it got too hot. It was my plan to stay for a week or so and enjoy a little time away with the family, but after only being on the beach for a day, I received a telegram from Fred.

Am informed by Sykes that Arivaca was being offered by bank at $165,000. Cattle to be sold separately. One Texas outfit seriously considering purchase. Eastern concern also interested. Sykes thought this information would be of interest to you and suggested I wire you.

I thought, *I can't believe this. Two big ranches are available for the taking within just a couple of months of each other, and I don't have the ability to pursue either one of them.* I had no choice but to respond back to Fred.

Doubt my ability to be able to place a five-year loan. Best we can do is the first proposition of $30,000. Tell Sykes to deal with the Texas outfit. I can't be interested.

I was interested to know who the Texas outfit and Eastern concern were, so I decided to wire Fred back and ask him to ask Sykes to try to find out who they are. I stayed at the beach with Gipsy and the kids for another few days and was enjoying the little vacation a great deal but decided I needed to get back to work. I told Gip to stay a couple of more weeks, and I would come back and pick them up.

Shortly after I returned to the bank, I was reading the newspaper and saw the headline on the third page: "Ruby murderer Placido Silvas escapes from prison." I came right to attention and called Fred into my office. Fred, listen to this.

According to prison records, by February, 1926, Placido Silvas had earned a position of trustee due to having served three years of his life sentence for murder of the Pearson family in Ruby in 1921 for good behavior. On December 13, he was returned to the general yard for incidents that had taken place on the trustee farm, and he was removed from the trustee list. However, in April 1928, he was returned to the trustee list and sent to what they call the trustee ranch outside of the general yard. But, two days ago, on August 30, this paper learned that he escaped from the trustee ranch. Though numerous attempts are underway to locate the escapee, he is still at large and presumed to be heading toward Mexico and, likely, through the Altar valley to Sasabe.

"Damn, Fred," was all I could think of to say. After a short time, I told Fred I needed to go see Billie at the Robles ranch at Three Points, and I might even need to go down to see Manuel King at the Anvil ranch. I might be gone for a couple of days. I looked back at him and said, Fred, I have unfinished business out there.

I was on my way by early afternoon after going to the house for a change of clothes. I went and saw Billie and Manuel and visited with both for a while. They both wondered if I was there to do inspections, and I said, "No, I just need to make a quick count on account I might have missed some last time. By the way Manuel, do you think I can borrow a horse for a while?"

He said, "Sure."

"Don't worry about an outfit, Manuel. I've got my own rig."

I got saddled up and ready to go and Manuel looked at my rig and asked, "What do you have all that firepower for, Phil?"

I said, "Manuel, I've heard there are still bandidos running around out here."

"Yeah, some, I guess," he said. "I saw in the paper today that Silvas guy escaped from the prison recently."

I replied, "Yeah, I saw that, too. Thanks for the horse; I'll be back soon."

Folks thought it was a little strange that I went out on inspections so soon after returning from the beach. I just said there was some unfinished business at a couple of ranches and left it at that.

Over the next eight to ten months and into the spring of 1929, we continued to grow. In the latter part of 1928, we infused an additional $50,000 of capital to help support our rapidly growing demands.

On the home front, Gipsy and the kids all stayed busy as well. Gipsy continued with her paintings and writings. Additionally, she continued with her schooling at the university. Phil was darn near grown up—almost eighteen years old and busy with sports at Tucson High school. I always enjoyed it when I had a chance to go by the school when the football team was practicing. He had become an excellent football player and continued to receive accolades from all over the state.

Ginny and Danny were busy with their activities as well. Ginny was nearly sixteen and was boy crazy. She and her friends talked about traveling the world as soon as they got out of school. And Danny had taken to raising a flock of homing pigeons. He recently finished building a sizable hutch up above the garage and had a great time sending his birds off in different directions and being able to bring them back.

The younger kids were busy being younger kids, but they were still at an age where I could have a great time with them when I was home. They all always had new and exciting things to tell their daddy.

As we moved on through our second year, we began to feel more comfortable with our progress and how we were doing. When we closed on the sale of the branch in Winslow the year before, I advised the new buyers that the Hash Knife ranch outside of Winslow was going to move their loan with us to our new operation in Tucson. I stayed pretty close to their operation there and worked closely with the old patriarch of the ranch, Miguel O'Haco.

He called me a while back and asked if I could come up and help him work out some ideas he had for his herd management going forward over the next few years, so right about in the middle of the year, I went to the Hash Knife and spent a couple of weeks up there with him. It was a very large ranch and required good cowboys and management for it to be successful. When I left, I felt good that I could contribute input for Miguel that would be helpful for them to continue to be successful.

Albert and George Stonecypher remained in contact with me since my change from Consolidated, and we and our wives became quite involved in a lot of civic activities over the past couple of years. Albert was quite active socially and invited Gipsy and I to many "gala balls," as Gipsy likes to call them. I guess they are galas because I always have to dress up in a black tuxedo, and Gipsy gets to dress up in a beautiful orange formal gown that she loves.

I now belong to the Tucson Rotary Club and have come to enjoy the community service that we get into in that club. It seems that as time continues to move along, I find that both Gipsy and I became more involved in what was going on in the city. Gipsy was very active in PTA and academics for all ages of kids. I'm sure it was partly because our kids' ages are spread all over, but likely more because she always had such a strong belief in the value and need for a solid education. I can look back twenty years to 1910 when she so emphatically encouraged me to get involved with all those correspondence courses I took. I'm sure it's the reason all our children are performing very well academically.

For the remainder of 1928 and through much of 1929, the bank's performance had been as much or even more that we had expected or hoped for. We had been able to bring many of the livestock loans over from Consolidated and our deposits increased substantially as well.

As we have moved into 1930, we began to notice changes in the national economic picture. Fred and I have been watching it closely, and even recently, other members of the ownership have been inquiring if we're concerned at all. "Not yet," we tell them.

Fred and I were sitting in my office one day recently when the phone rang. I answered, and Sykes was on the other end. "Just wondering if you've heard about the Arivaca, and if you haven't, I'm going to tell you."

Both Fred and I came to attention right quick. I said, "Sykes, let me get Fred on speaker here with me." When I had brought Fred to my office, I said, "Now tell us what's happening."

"You know the Arivaca has had questionable management for the last eight or ten years, especially after Nonie took over. Ramon sure did the best he could, but he wasn't getting any help, so it was only a matter of time before it came to this. And, you remember, Phil, just two years ago, I told you there was a good chance you could get it pretty reasonably."

"I know, Sykes. So, who are the new people?"

"It looks like Henry Boice and the Chiricahua Cattle Company are the most recent buyers. The way I have it figured," he said, "When Ramon died, the Tucson Realty and Trust Company took the mortgage for a time, then soon after, the War Finance Corporation held it for a while. Next, the Border Land and Cattle company from over in southern New Mexico came over and bought Arivaca and Las Jarrillas, but that was only temporary. Maybe they were just getting it set up for the Boices.

"Well, back about 1920 or so, Henry Boice passed away and left the whole thing to his three boys: Henry, Frank, and Charley. Henry had been running lots of cattle up on the Apache reservation in the White Mountains, but when the tribe decided to run their own cattle up there, the brothers had to take their cows off and find more land to put them on.

"Henry had been instrumental in developing the Hereford breed, so they surely didn't want to leave them up there, and they didn't want to sell their herd off. So, they started looking for another ranch or even more to move them to. Within six years, they had acquired the Eureka, north of Willcox and the Empire and Rail X, between

Sonoita and Patagonia. They have wanted the Arivaca for some time now, for a couple of reasons.

"First, it's large. It includes the Tres Bellotas, Las Jarillas, and the Bear Valley, and the Fresnel and Sardina allotments. But the main reason they want Arivaca is the range. This range offers a more diversified soil and grass varieties than what they have over in the Sulphur Springs Valley. The climate is much more suitable for running cows with calves and big steers as well. With all these ranches, the Chiricahua Cattle Company would be permitted nearly 6,500 head over a good part of southern Arizona.

"This acquisition works perfectly for these brothers. Although they have worked together all these years up in the mountains and in the Sulphur Springs Valley, this will enable them to put one of them on each place. It's my understanding that Frank will stay over at Willcox, Henry will run the Empire and Patagonia, and Charlie will come over here and run things here.

"We know these Boice brothers well, and I think very highly of all of them. I think they're a bit younger than us but close to the same age. And, for me personally, it's going to be good having Charlie down there as my next-door neighbor. I think he has a couple of kids and nephews about the same age as my younger ones. So, we should be good neighbors and work well together."

CHAPTER 34

I sometimes think I have let myself become involved in too many business and civic events. I have been on the board of the Arizona Bankers Association since we opened the bank a year and a half ago. And, for the past six months, I have been serving as the executive director of the Board. Gipsy and I just returned from a semi-annual meeting of the membership and the talk for most of the three-day meeting was about President Hoover's introduction to Congress of his proposal for a relief action for financial institutions across the country. At this point, we don't know much about it, but it sure has the attention of all of us who operate small, marginal banks. I told Fred about all I know when I got back. We will surely keep our eyes on how this might develop.

Gipsy and I attended a Boy Scout award ceremony last night. Danny was receiving the Star award on his way to reaching the rank of Eagle, and we wanted to be there for him. When he was getting the badge pinned to his chest, it was a proud moment for both of us. It seems all our kids are excelling in one thing or another. The boys are all into sports, and the girls are into art and music. Ginny is very involved in the school paper. She sells advertising for the university paper and seems to really like doing that. We think it's mostly about giving her more opportunities to meet boys, though.

As we were driving home, Gipsy started a conversation about all the groups I belonged to. She suggested maybe I should think about eliminating some of them. I said, "Gip, let's start at the top of the list to see which ones we should drop out of.

"The Elks Club?"

"Maybe."

"The El Rio Golf Club?"

"No way. Gipsy, that's my escape from everything."

"Well, just list as many as you can."

"Okay, Rotary Club, Boy Scout Council, the Arizona Cattlemen's Association, The Board of the Arizona Livestock Association, The Arizona Bankers Association, and, let's not forget, the little nature study camp school up in the Catalinas near Summer haven. Unfortunately, most of them are important to the betterment of the bank, and a lot of them are important to our social life."

"Yes, I know, Phil. But I think when this financial dilemma passes, you should step back from most of those business groups."

"I will, Gip," I responded hesitantly.

We just returned home when the phone rang, and it was Bud. I answered and asked if everything is okay. "Phil, Billie died this afternoon. I just heard from Della. Evidently, he was working a new colt out in the big round pen, and he just collapsed. His cowboy Diego ran to the house to get her, and she called the sheriff. They both ran down to the corral, but I guess he was dead when they got there. When the sheriff arrived, he determined that he likely had a heart attack and probably died immediately. His lasso was still in his hands, and his hat was still on his head."

"Oh, Bud, this is just too much. It's like if I were to lose you. He was one of my very best friends."

"I know, Phil. Come down to the mission tomorrow morning and meet me, and we'll go out to Three Points and see Della"

The next day, Bud and I were on our way early. I talked about how recently he asked me to partner with him. Billie was a highly respected cattleman and man. He was only sixty-four years old and was in good health. Everybody loved him. We had a large funeral and hundreds of people attended from all over the state. I assured Della that I would help her with all of her estate issues and anything else she needed from Gipsy and I.

A couple of days after the funeral, Harry came into my office and told me how sorry he was for all of our loss, then, sat down and started talking about the school board and some of the issues it will be facing in the upcoming months. In a short while, Harry said, "Phil, I will be resigning from the board very soon."

"I expected that since you were just elected to the City council," I said.

"I think you should take my place, Phil, and I'm pretty sure Assistant Superintendent Rose would be pleased if you were on the board as well."

"You know I'm very interested in our schools, and if they think I could make a contribution, I would express an interest in replacing you," I said.

At the next meeting, I was appointed to replace Harry, and Mrs. Daniels, the current president, asked for my thoughts.

"A lot has been accomplished in the year, and I hope to fit into the board membership and work in harmony with other board members for further development of the schools in the city. I plan to work along the same lines that have proven successful in the past, keeping in mind always that the welfare of the schools is paramount."

Six months later, Mrs. Daniels' term expired, and for reasons I don't understand, I was elected president and quickly became more involved than I ever thought I would. One major effort facing me is to reduce expenses. It is clear the boards over the years have been negligent in controlling the rapid escalation. Fortunately, we have been able to restructure the fiscal budget for the district by approximately $65,000 even while attendance has increased significantly. My challenge appears to be a need to rally some of the other supervisors to be more supportive of the reduction in expenses budgeted for the same period. I am enjoying the challenges and continue to be enthusiastic about dealing with them.

But, as we move into 1931, the national picture continues to look as though we may very well be heading toward what we call another correction. Simply put, supply and demand of products produced and dollars spent on these products are out of balance. What then happens in the banking world is depositors begin to lose confidence in their ability to save, borrow, and spend their hard-earned dollars.

Soon after, the economy depresses to the point where manufacturing and production of new products comes to a halt. And then, the cycle begins—no products to buy, no jobs for workers, and no money earned to spend. The whole free enterprise system shuts down.

As we moved through 1931, we, in our little bank, noticed this potential shutdown sooner than larger banks. We observed many of our depositors pulling their savings and closing their accounts, and our lending applications were almost non-existent. With this, many of our loans were becoming delinquent or had already gone into default. And, of course, all of this resulted in our inability to perform our obligations.

It reminded me of a talk I had recently presented at the State Rotary Convention. It was a talk about credit and the importance and necessity of it in the successful function of our free enterprise system. In simple terms, credit moves money. When money is borrowed, it follows that it will be spent through investment or manufacturing or just simply purchasing goods and services. When money stops flowing and is taken out of circulation, the effect is the freezing of credit. When this happens, the business of our country comes to a stop and until this condition is remedied, we will continue to have stagnant business activities. By the end of the year, we knew we were in trouble, but as with everybody else, we saw no solution.

Early in 1932, the State Banking Commission levied a $50,000 assessment against the shareholders of the bank, which increased our total debt accrual from $165,000 to $215,000. Because I own approximately 70 percent of the stock, my share of this debt is nearly $140,000. I asked Fred to come to my office so we could attempt to develop a plan. We were both stymied and decided to call a special meeting of the stockholders.

Though the total number of owners is actually twelve, all but three of us own less than 150 shares of the 1,000 issued, so only Fred, Kruttschnitt, Gurnee, and I were present. After discussing what few options we had, we decided to take care of the assessment from the state personally—my share was about $35,000. The fact that virtually all of my money was tied up in cattle, I would have to take a short-term loan from one of my friends.

I wrapped up the meeting by saying, "As an addition to the minutes of this meeting, I want to state to the entire ownership group that I intend to make everybody who entrusted their dollars into this venture whole when it is all over. I am committed to all of you to be sure that happens."

We continued to battle the Depression as best we could throughout the remainder of the year, but on November 16, we determined we could not keep the doors open, and at the end of that day, we suspended operations. I walked out the door, alone, turned around, locked the doors, and closed the bank. We had no choice but to declare and file for bankruptcy relief—both for the bank and me personally. I had no idea what the remedies were going to be, but I knew the resolution laid squarely on my shoulders.

I immediately began searching for means for restitution, not only for the shareholders, but also the depositors. In the depths of a recession, there are not too many places a defunct bank can find money, so I knew this was going to be an uphill journey. I soon learned that President Hoover was planning a meeting of influential business leaders in October. I was anxious to hear the results of that, thinking that it could possibly be an opportunity for us.

I had borrowed my share of the assessment, $35,000, from my friend George Stonecypher, but had to give him a mortgage on our home and the big lot on north Stone Avenue and the forty acres out on East Broadway. All this free-and-clear property was worth much more than the loan, but the loan was short-term, and looking at it from George's view, I would probably want the same security. So, we had taken care of the assessment, and I had to figure out how to make the shareholders and depositors whole.

In October, President Hoover called together the industrial and business leaders from around the country. Because of the meeting, bankers formed what was known as the National Credit Corporation, which was making $500,000,000 available through subscriptions of bonds. When Congress met later, it immediately set out to relieve financial institutions of these stringent conditions and converted this Credit Corporation into what is known today as the Reconstruction Finance Corporation.

The bill creating this corporation was passed by Congress immediately. The $500,000,000 was capitalized and subscribed by the Federal Government and was authorized to sell bonds on the open market. The bonds would be a direct obligation of the corporation and guaranteed, both principal and interest, by the government. Plus, they are tax exempt.

The Reconstruction Finance Corporation was then authorized to make loans, on a secured basis, to banks, savings and loan associations, mortgage companies, trust companies, insurance companies, and Federal Intermediate Credit banks, as well as numerous others. These loans will enable banks and other financial institutions to sell their existing good, secure loans to the corporation, and receive enough funding in return to pay off their depositors in full. Fred and I determined to pursue loans through this avenue as soon as we could. If we could satisfy our depositor losses, it would then only leave my settlements to creditors.

I quickly contacted my friend HenryWatson at the Arizona Livestock Loan Company in Flagstaff. They were holding a large amount of my personal debt, and I wanted to discuss with Henry the options we might have available through this new corporation.

We immediately came up with a plan for the bank. Through the Reconstruction Finance Corporation, we could avoid the bankruptcy filing by sending our secured delinquent loans to the Intermediate Credit Bank in Berkley, CA, and generate sufficient funding to satisfy our depositor debts. For me personally, I needed to maneuver my personal estate around so I could make my shareholders whole and satisfy my creditors as well. We discussed this situation at length and developed a plan I thought had a good chance of working.

Our plan was to first protect the ranch and second to pay off the loans I had from personal friends. We developed a plan with the livestock company to rediscount the loans I had with them to the Intermediate Credit bank as well. This plan would pay off my big loan with them and also enable me to pay off George and regain the title to my house, the Stone Avenue property, and the East Broadway property. The presentation of this plan was such that, to avoid a complete default from me, it would enable all parties to realize satisfaction.

Rather than take this loss, the loan company agreed to refinance my operations and make a new loan with sufficient additional funds to pay the indebtedness to the creditors and provide me funds to purchase an additional six hundred head of cows to be placed on the ranch at Arivaca. The conditions, of course, were the creditors must be paid off, and the bank would have a lien on the ranch and all the livestock on the ranch.

I was only in agreement with giving a fifty percent lien on the ranch. I argued that the value of the ranch and all livestock were worth triple the amount of this new loan. In exchange, though, I agreed to mortgage our home and my interest in the El Dorado Resort on East Broadway. The entire contract was for only three years. That made me very uncomfortable, but I figured that with six hundred cows, which were carrying calves, plus the steers and cows on the ranch, we should be okay. Unfortunately, the Intermediate Bank wouldn't do the loan under these terms, so I would have to come back to them with a new idea.

Henry and I had been working on this for the past few months. We had been able to avoid bankruptcy for the bank through the Intermediate Credit Banks loan to the Reconstruction Finance Corporation, but I personally had not been able to. By late November, we determined that I had no capability to satisfy all my indebtedness and had to file for bankruptcy to avoid losing everything Gipsy and I had acquired over the years.

It's now been over a year since the signs of the Depression started showing their ugly faces, and both Fred and I are just about whipped. I can't remember ever having such feelings of defeat. And I know that Fred is having a much harder time with it all than I am. I see it every day when I'm with him, both in his eyes and in his demeanor.

I went home that night and sat down with Gipsy to talk this whole thing over. She was very depressed over the entire development, but she remained fully supportive of me all the way through it.

I said, "You know, Gip, I promised everybody I would make them all okay again, and I intend to keep that commitment. And even last night, Patsy came in and sat on my lap. I knew she was sad, so I asked what the trouble was. She said, 'Daddy, I heard you tell all those people at the bank that you were going to get all their money back.'

"I replied, 'I did, sweet Patsy. I plan to do just that.'

"And she said, 'Daddy, I have $2 in my savings account, but you don't have to get that back to me; you can use it to help somebody else.'

"I told her, 'Patsy, I will get your $2. back for you, too.'"

Telling Gip that little story put a smile on her face. And, she said, "Phil, you don't have to worry about me and the kids through all this. We know we'll be all right. The older kids all have jobs of one kind or other and are keeping themselves busy. We've always known that our kids were very resilient and know how to take care of things when they face problems."

"I know, Gip. You're so right, but what about you? You just keep plugging along and taking care of everything here all by yourself."

"Phil, I keep busy with my projects. I've been doing some painting, and just the other day, I went out to the San Xavier Mission south of town and set up my easel and started a picture of the Mission. It's on the porch here; let me show it to you."

We stepped out, and when I saw that painting, it lifted my heart. It was so pretty, and the thought that Gipsy went out there to paint that on canvas made me feel so bad for all I had brought on us. But she went on and told me that she had been writing more and more recently.

She said, "I have a story going right now about a family in south Texas during the revolution that took place between Texas and Mexico in the early 1830s. You remember the story of the battle of San Jacinto near where Houston is now?"

"Sure, I remember you talking about that a lot when we were down there."

"As I get further along with it, I'll tell you how it's going."

"Good, I'm anxious to hear about it."

"Phil, you've been keeping me aware of how things have been progressing, but maybe you should tell me what the whole thing looks like and just how serious it could be."

"Gipsy, yes, you need to know. And I'll tell you, but sweet Gip, you're not going to like it. A bankruptcy usually means a person loses everything they have. In our case, we must forfeit our properties and stocks and bonds and, of course, all our real estate."

"But not the ranch, Phil?"

"Yes, I am afraid that too, unless I can come up with a solution that I don't know about yet."

"Well, what does all this mean in terms of dollars?"

"Gipsy, here it is. We own 70 percent of the bank. We own property out on Stone Avenue, our home, our share of the resort on Speedway, the 40 acres east of the resort, a portfolio of stocks and bonds that a year ago were worth about $65,000 and today are worth zero. And then there's the ranch. It's worth about $85,000 and the livestock on it is another $35,000 or so. And, we know the bank has no value any longer, but my 70 percent share of the debt is nearly $145,000. In total, Gipsy, before the Depression, our worth was close to about $400,000.

"The bank has no value, but the remaining shareholders' interest is about $65,000. All told, Gipsy, the debt to be settled is that plus the amount that the depositors have lost. I don't know exactly what that amount is, but I'm committed to pay that back. The good news about that is we have a federal program that will deal with depositor losses, so if I can make that work, it will prevent filing bankruptcy for the bank. Regardless, the court will lien or sell enough of our personal worth to satisfy the personal debts we have outside of the bank. Right now, I am trying every angle I can think of to save as much of what we have as I can."

After a long, long pause, Gipsy looked at me and said, "Phil, we've been here before, just not this far; I guess. You know that, don't you?"

"Yes, back in 1910 in Arivaca we didn't have anything. And in Ruby, when we started the store. And when we started trading for those old raunchy steers and then the big jump to the bank. You're right."

"You'll get us out of this, Phil. I know you will."

"Well then, Gip, since we were talking about Texas a while ago, it makes me think. It's been a long time since you, or we, have been there. Do you think you might like to go down and spend some time with the family while I'm working through this mess?"

She paused for a minute, then said, "Yes, I would like to do that. But we'll have to wait until summer, so I can take the kids, or the ones who can get away. Besides, I want to stay here and help you get through this."

I got up and went around the table and gave her a big hug and kiss, and by golly, she got tears in her eyes. I looked at her and said, "I haven't seen you do that very often."

"No," she said, "You haven't."

CHAPTER 35

I remembered what Bud had told me years ago. "If you ever need anything from friends, Phil, there will be no end to the line of those of us who will be there to help you." I thought about that and wondered if Bud and I could expand on what we were doing. So, I called him and said, "Bud, I know you're aware that I've filed bankruptcy recently. I'm going to lose everything real soon unless I can get something going with someone other than a bank."

"Do you have something in mind?" he asked.

"Yes," I said. "I've heard that there are a bunch of feedlots sitting vacant out at Cortaro. We both know we lose our lease on the Baca Float this year, and we haven't made arrangements to continue on. I'm thinking we should keep our partnership going and stock that place up with all the steers we have and add enough more to fill it up. I believe we could both make a good piece, and it surely will help get me out of this bankruptcy a hell of a lot sooner."

"Phil, that's a great idea. We've got plenty in reserves, so we can afford a sizable bunch more right from the start."

"Okay, but we need to keep this a little under cover until I get something finalized with the court."

The next day, I contacted Henry and asked if he might have any new thoughts or ideas for what we might do to remove the bankruptcy. "Well," he said, "The bank wants the ranch, and you won't release fifty percent of it. But I have an idea that I think will work. If you personally sell me that other half for only a short term, say four or five years, I can then pledge it to the bank and put myself in second position on it, and I'm okay with that. I believe they'll do that, and we can make it work. Obviously, you're still giving up the whole thing, but it's not the same as the bank having a lien on the whole thing. With me owning half, we can use that half for your benefit."

"Okay," I said. "I'll do that with you. Let's get the details on paper. I'll look it over, and maybe we can put this terrible experience behind me. At least, as soon as I get everything paid back. Three or four years sure seems like a very long time right now, though."

"Hell, Phil, when you bought that store in Ruby, you didn't know what a long time looked like."

"Yeah," I said and laughed for the first time in a long time.

A couple of days passed before I heard back from Henry, but when I did, he was very upbeat. He said the bank had agreed to work with us on our plan, and if we could get the court to agree, we could put it together quickly. He continued, "If you can get away and come up here, we should be able to get this proposal together pretty quickly."

I left the very next day, and Henry and I got right on it. We drafted a letter from him to Judge Robert Simpson, who was the bankruptcy judge for the Superior court in Pima County. It was simple and to the point.

Dear Judge Simpson,

The bank and I have been working with Mr. Phil Clarke, who you know is the former president of the United Bank and Trust in Tucson. We have discussed an option of compromise of his liability to his creditors. I have investigated the facts that he has set forth to us and have concluded they are accurate. And as such, we believe that being the case, his proposal is eminently fair and equitable and will result in his creditors receiving a much more substantial amount from his estate than if we proceed with the bankruptcy. This would also allow him to borrow additional funds from our institution, which will enable him to get on his feet again.

It is our view of the matter that regardless of what others may suggest, it is our duty to investigate the facts and then do what we think is in the best interest of the creditors, of course, but also the debtor.

In this case, by Mr. Clarke accepting this compromise, we will be doing the very best possible thing for all the creditors, and it just so happens that in doing that, we will be giving Mr. Clarke a chance to get back on his feet and out from under his financial wreckage. If the bank's investigation by Mr. Entz shows that the facts stated by Mr. Clarke are true, and Mr. Entz so informs me, I will encourage you to approve and order this compromise to be made immediately.

Mr. Clarke is offering to give a mortgage of four years on his ranch in Arivaca as well as his other real estate properties, including his home in Tucson.

We would appreciate you giving this your careful consideration and subsequently agree that this is the course we should pursue.

Signed
Mr. H. C. Warson
Manager,
Arizona Livestock Loan Company

In February, the agreement was approved by the court, and my bankruptcy proceedings were vacated. The livestock loan company, through the cooperation of the Intermediate Credit Bank, agreed to refinance my operations and make a new loan with enough to pay off the indebtedness to all my creditors, which included the stockholders other than me. All these creditors agreed to accept this compromise settlement.

Terms of the refinance included a new mortgage on 50 percent of the ranch to the bank and Mr. H. Watson taking a second position on the other 50 percent. Both parties would also take as collateral all the cattle presently on the ranch, approximately 763 head, which was a mix of bred cows, bulls, and steers. Additionally, sufficient funds would be loaned to allow me to purchase up to 600 head of cows to place on the portions of his my allotments on the ranch that were not being used. By being able to purchase cows at that time, I would be able to buy springer (bred) cows, which could give me a calf crop the next spring of potentially 900 calves.

Out of the proceeds, enough money would be available to apply to my second mortgage and to set aside operating funds for the next year. In as much as I have shown I can operate my ranch for no more than $4,800 per year, it would assure that this arrangement would avert any loss to the bank and allow me to retain ownership of my ranch and remain in business.

In just a short time, people were calling from all over. People we had known for years and years wanting to tell us how happy they were for us. And, needless to say, Gipsy was back to her old self—just busy as can be.

"Phil," she asked, "Is this destiny, also?"

"Must be, Gip. It just must be."

One of my first calls was back to Bud. "Okay, Bud, we're good to go. The court signed off on my settlement proposal, and I guess that means I am now able to start over."

"So, start over, we will. Just let me know when you're ready," he said.

"I will, but I need to get back down to the ranch and see the boys. By the way, keep your eyes open for a couple of cowboys. My guys are getting older, and Slim is about ready to retire. I don't want to get surprised when I start putting all those new cows down there."

I called Albert next and said, "Albert, do you want to go play some golf?"

I could hear him laughing in the background. "I just heard the good news. Let's go. I'll see you at El Rio for lunch tomorrow."

We met at the club the next day and started with lunch, but as we started visiting, I began to wonder if golf was really the reason we were there. Albert said, "I don't have to ask you how you're doing. I know you got your bankruptcy vacated and hope to hear as much of that as you want to tell. However, I think I'm more interested in how you're doing since we lost Fred."

Our friend and my partner Fred Hermes had passed away just a month before from a surprise massive heart attack.

"Albert, Fred's passing has been very hard for me. I know he was very dear to you, too, and I know losing him has been very hard for you. Over the years, I have lost many good friends, many people who have been very close to me, but losing Fred when we did just completely broke my heart.

"When we closed the bank, he and I made the commitment to the court that we would make all of our depositors whole again. I always thought he was 100 percent okay with that commitment, but the more we negotiated with the Intermediate Credit Company, the more I began to notice changes. Albert, I think his heart just wasn't strong enough to deal with the terrible stress we had in front of us every day. And, as you know, he passed just two days before we got the deal settled."

"Yeah, I know, Phil. But it sure was a beautiful service, and I want to commend you for delivering such a wonderful eulogy. Everybody knew your words were truly from your heart, and there wasn't a dry eye in the church."

"Thanks Albert. Sometimes, it's easy to say things well when the words are coming from your heart."

"Now, how are you doing, Phil?"

"I'm doing good, now. The big load I've been carrying around for the last couple of years is gone. My entire estate is mortgaged, including my ranch, either to a bank or various other sources, but it's only for four years. As part of my settlement, I was able to get refinanced by the livestock loan company in Flagstaff. Part of that refinance is an operating line to purchase additional cattle for the ranch. Another bonus for me, I think, is that I heard a month or so ago that all those feedlots at Cortaro Farms are open, and since Bud and my lease on the Baca Float is over this year, we're going to move all our steers from there to the feedlots out there. I believe if we work this thing really hard, both of us should be in good shape in four to five years."

"Phil, in all of this, how did you keep the partnership with Bud out of your estate?"

"Strictly by accident. Bud and I never officially created a legal partnership, and officially, I've never been a part of that."

"And that steer deal has been pretty good for both of you, hasn't it?"

"It sure has. And Albert, would you keep your eyes open for a young cowboy or two for me? I think Slim wants to slow down and maybe move back to Texas where his family is, and Buck is still good, but he told me he wants to slow down a little."

"What about Tony?"

"Tony has been one of the best cowboys I've ever seen, but he's going back to Sasabe to take over that store and saloon for his pa."

"Actually, I think I know a couple. I'll let you know later, Phil."

When I got home later, I told Gipsy about my day, and we talked about what we were going to do next. She said, "Well Phil, I'm going to start painting more, and I have the manuscripts I've been working on and then I want to talk about either going over to Redondo Beach this summer or all of us going to south Texas instead."

"Okay, Gip, those are good ideas. Right now, though, I need to get down to the ranch and be a cowboy again."

"I know," she said. "I think that's going to be good for you."

"So do I, and say, I think I'll take Philip with me this time. What do you think of that?"

"I think it's a good idea, but you know, he's pretty busy with school and his sports."

"I know, but I'll talk to him and see if he's okay with pulling out of school for a couple of days. I think it would be good for us to get away together. I feel he doesn't have the interest in the ranch like I have hoped he would."

"Phil, I think a lot of that comes from the Ruby experience. He doesn't say much to me, but I think that maybe his feelings about being a cattleman are too connected to what happened down there. You know, for him, Ruby and the ranch are all one and the same, and we probably would be smart not to push him too hard in that direction. I think if he eventually decides that's what he wants, that will be good. For now, I think it's important for us to continue to encourage Dan and Mike in that direction. They're both still young, but Dan really likes it down there, and with you being able to spend more time there, it will be good for him, and Mike, too, as he gets older."

Philip did agree to pull out of school for a couple of days and go to the ranch later that week. On the way down, we talked a lot about school and all his other activities. He loved to talk about football and baseball. He was okay with his schoolwork, but I think, for him, school was more about the sports.

"Philip," I said, "I thought bringing you down to the ranch with me would give us both an idea of just how interested in the ranch you are."

"Well, Dad, I really like the ranch, but you know, I don't care that much about working with the cattle, and I'm not a very good cowboy."

"Well, you could be a good cowboy if you really wanted to."

"I know, Dad, but right now, I just want to play football and baseball. Is that okay with you?"

"Well sure, son. I've had plans that you would take over this place one day, but I understand your interest in sports. For now, why don't you just do that, and we'll see how things turn out."

I hadn't been down for over a month, and the last time I was at the ranch, I had asked the boys to think about moving the bunk house and barn from Oro Blanco. When we got together Friday at the bunkhouse in Oro Blanco, we got right down to business. First off, they wanted to hear the story of the settlement and what it would mean to them, of course, but also to the ranch going forward.

Right away, Slim said, "Phil, when you were here last time, we talked about our plans, and I've been thinking I'm want to leave soon and go on back down to Texas."

"I know, Slim. And Buck, what about you?"

"I'm okay, Phil, but I want to slow down soon."

"Okay, boys. And we know that Tony is going back to Sasabe. Tony, about how long can you stay with us?"

"Oh, Felipe, no hurry. I stay until you say go. Bien, Tony."

"I'll start looking for one or two younger guys. You boys help, okay?"

They all said, "Oh, si, si, Felipe."

"Now, tell me what we can do with the bunkhouse and barn."

Buck did most of the talking. "We think we can move the bunkhouse and put it down there near where you want to put the barn. Regarding the barn, we think only about half of that barn can be moved. Once it is moved, we should build a good room inside for the tack and medicine and then put a loft up above to store feed. And, for sure, we need to have good corrals next to the barn for our horses and some cattle when we must bring them in for doctoring or other problems."

"So," I said, "Can you guys do most of this, or do we need to get some help?"

Slim said, "We can do a lot, but it would be faster if we had some help."

"Okay, do you know people?"

"Si, patron. Tomas and his Indians over in Bear Valley."

"Sure, Slim. That's a perfect idea. We need to get going on that job right away. The big part of my settlement with the bank problem, boys, is I'm getting some financing to buy up to six hundred cows to put down here on the forest that we're not using now."

Buck said. "Man, that's great, Phil, but you don't need to be losing all of us right now."

"I know, Buck, but as you know, once we get cows settled in, they require a lot of work until calving time. And by then, we'll need to have a couple of good hands to replace you guys."

"Yeah, that's right. So, when are these cows coming?"

"As soon as I start finding them, and you can get corrals built."

Buck said, "Phil, maybe we should hold up on the house and barn and build some corrals up above the valley to bring them to."

"Yeah, you're right. Okay, let's change the plan. I'll go see Tomas tomorrow and ask him to bring as many as he can. Okay?"

The next day, Philip and I drove to Bear Valley, hoping to find Tomas. It had been about twenty years since he built the store in Ruby, so it was a long shot.

But Tomas was there—same place, same people, same everything—only everybody was much older. But he was so happy to see me. He had a big smile on his face and said everybody in the Yaqui villages remembered Felipe. He said most of the people who helped before might not be around, but he had lots of people who knew how to build mesquite fences. I told him what we wanted to do, and he said he would get his people together and come over in the next week or so.

Driving back to the ranch, I asked Philip what he was thinking. He said, "I barely remember when all those Indians came over to build the new store. But what I do remember is that they always laughed, and their kids always played with me while they were working."

As we begin to enter the little town of Ruby, Philip wasn't showing much enthusiasm for the place he spent most of his childhood. "Do you remember much about this place, Philip?" I asked.

"Sure, I do, Dad. I had lots of friends here, but when I think about what happened here, it takes away all the good memories I have. I think maybe that's why I haven't ever wanted to come back."

"I understand, Philip." At the same time, I thought to myself, *I wonder how much of this memory plays into his feelings about the ranch.*

"Well, Philip, just so you know, Mama and I both have very hard memories as well. It was a very bad time for all of us. We're just so glad we were able to get all of us out of here before that tragedy happened."

We went back to the ranch before we started for home. I wanted to tell Buck and Slim about Tomas and his plans for the next week or so. Also, I want them to know that now that the banking adventure was behind me, I planned to be a cowboy again, and we would be spending most of our time down here again. They could count on me to be around to help out.

They all seemed glad to hear that.

"By the way," Slim said as we were getting ready to leave, "I was over at the store in Arivaca yesterday, and I heard some people talking. I heard the name Placido Silvas, and I heard them say that the sheriff's deputy that covers the Altar valley was in, and somebody asked him if that guy was ever recaptured. He told them no; it was believed he disappeared into Mexico.

"Right after he escaped the prison in Florence, he was trailed south of Manuel King's ranch, and the searchers thought they were close to catching up to him. They had his trail and he must have gotten a horse from Manuel's place and wore him down because it looked like he was walking and leading the horse. Then the trail ended, out there just below the Baboquivari. They couldn't find any more footprints or signs of his trail and it looked like the horse returned to Manuel's."

"Well, I guess he's gone then," I said.

"Yeah, sure seems like it, doesn't it?"

"Just so you know, Bud and I are going to be moving our steers over to Marana from the Float soon. Our lease expires at the end of the year, and I found some feedlots at the Cortaro Farms, so we're going to operate out of there after the first. I sure would like to use you guys to help us move, but we need you here now."

As soon as fall was upon us, Bud and I, along with all the cowboys we could find, had gathered all our steers off the Baca Float and moved them into holding pens just north of Nogales and right next to the railroad tracks. One car at a time, with about forty head in each, we moved twenty-six cars of steers north through Tucson and on up to Marana, where we were able to offload them right into the Cortaro farms feedlots. We ended up with almost one thousand head in that move, and that's how many we started our Cortaro Farms feeding operation with.

While we were busy moving the steers, I was also locating cows to put down at the ranch. The boys, along with Tomas and his bunch, completed a huge corral set-up on the hill above where we're going to build the barn. We put in a large loading and unloading shoot, or ramp, which enabled us to easily offload and load cattle from trucks, so we no longer had to spot trucks up against an arroyo bank to unload the animals.

By the end of the year, Bud and I were already beginning to have inquiries from our old buyers and had found a new source for young steers in Mexico at good prices. We thought we had the capacity for as many as two thousand to twenty-five hundred head at a time there. And the better news was we had a good supply of feed. There was an abundance of hay throughout the Avra valley area as well as plenty of hay being grown down farther in the Altar valley.

Additionally, of great importance to a feeding operation, was the availability of feed supplements. We'd recently signed a supply contract with The Western Cotton Products Company in the Phoenix area to supply us with tons of prime cottonseed hulls and up to two hundred tons of prime quality cottonseed meal that was forty-three percent protein. The agreement provided us to be supplied with enough to feed approximately twelve hundred head of cattle. With our feeding agreements in place, we could begin to feed and fatten our steers and get them sold and moved out as quickly as possible. As long as we continued to have moisture and a strong market, we would do very well. We reminded each other of that every day.

CHAPTER 36

When the Depression finally hit, and we had to close the bank, I tried to continue my commitment to my role on the school board. In fact, during the midst of the recovery efforts, I was re-elected to the board and continued to serve. As 1933 was quickly coming to an end, I intended to leave so I could devote my full efforts to the cattle business. However, when I mentioned this to other members of the board, they exerted a strong desire for me to continue, at least through the end of the school year. Knowing that Gipsy would be disappointed, I agreed to do that.

When I got home that night, Gipsy told me she had received letters from her mama, Dora, and her aunt Minnie and sister Bert. She said, "I wrote them back and brought them up to date on our happenings around here. I told them we wanted to come down this summer, but with the bank closure and restarting our lives, we couldn't get away for that long. I told them we would try again next summer."

"Yeah, Gip. Let's plan to do that. By the way, did you tell them it's been so hot here that when we were in town, we slept out in the backyard?"

"Yeah, I did tell them that. I don't think it will make a big impression, though, because I think that's common down there," she said with a little laugh.

When spring of 1934 arrived, our cows began dropping calves. And boy, did it get busy. Luckily, Tony stayed with us, and Slim agreed to wait until after calving to leave for Texas. Bud came down for a couple of days and brought a couple of his cowboys to help, so with me and what help Dan could give, we managed to bring in about eight hundred new calves. We spent most of the spring and early summer doctoring, branding, cutting bull calves, and getting the cows bred for the next year.

After all the spring work was done, both Buck and Bud wanted me to know they had a couple of cowboys they knew of who would be interested in working for us. I ended up hiring both and was hopeful they could get started soon. I think they were going to be really good hands. I asked both to come back over to the ranch at the end of the week so we could talk about what we had going on.

The one Bud brought to us was a young Mexican cowboy from the Moiza Ranch north of here, near Sopori. His name was Francisco Leon, but he was called Pancho by some and Chico by others. He was about twenty-five years old and had a pretty wife named Angelita. He had been working at the Moiza for about six years, and according to Bud, they really liked him there. I asked Bud why he was leaving, and he said they had brought in a new boss from Texas who didn't speak much Spanish, and Chico doesn't speak any English so that didn't leave much of a chance for the young Mexican.

"Why the hell would they bring somebody in here who doesn't speak the language?"

"Phil, the people who own Moiza now are from Nebraska, and they haven't learned that Spanish is the language down here."

"Well, they sure will soon enough."

The guy Buck brought to me was from just over the valley, and his name was Bob Wells. He was from up around Winkelman but came down here with Eugene Shepherd and got hooked up with Jack McVey at Las Jarrillas. And when the big consolidation plan fell apart, Bob Wells didn't want any more to do with Shepherd and Las Jarrillas. When he heard I might be stepping down, he said he sure would like to talk to me. I liked him a lot, and I thought I could likely fit him right into Buck's job. He's fairly young, maybe thirty or so, and has a wife and one or two children. He's a gringo like Buck and me, but he's fluent in Spanish and knows the business. I'm really excited to get both guys on board as soon as we can, especially now during what slow time we have out here.

I brought Danny down with me because I thought this would be good for him to learn more about the ranch. Even though he's only sixteen years old, I think it's good for him to start learning what puts food on our tables.

The new cowboys came over Friday morning, and I got Buck and Slim together with them, got a pot of coffee going, and told Buck and Slim to jump in at any time to help me out. "I want them to know all about the herds and where they are," I said. "We've got cows some places, steers other places, weaned calves other places, and bulls in yet others. I want them to know where the pastures are and where all the Forest allotments are and everything else about this ranch."

After a few hours of that, I told them a little of the history of the place and how we came to be. I thought both of their eyes were going to pop out. When I was finished, Bob said, "I've heard lots about you, Phil, but I've never heard this story."

"Well, it's a bit different, I admit, but that's how we got this thing going, and it's what we have to do now to keep it going."

I went on to explain, "We're going to move the bunkhouse we currently have at Oro Blanco up here and put it down by where we're going to build the barn. And I'm going to build a new house over there below the new corrals. When Buck and Slim leave, we'll put you and your families over here."

Not long after that, we had Tomas back with his bunch, making adobes and building a home for our two cowboys. At the same time, we moved what we could of the old barn and bunkhouse. I told Bob and Chico they could share the bunkhouse or stay where they were until Buck and Slim are gone.

By early 1934, we were back to normal as far as being a cattle ranch again. Gipsy and I still called Tyndall our home, but we both had been spending a lot of time at the ranch, me more than her since the kids were still in school. She started painting a little more again, and she was very busy writing.

One day, I asked her how she managed to put so much time into her writing.

"Phil, this is the time of my life when I need to be writing because these are the busy years. It's the time of our lives when so many things are happening. I must take advantage of it because now is when the stories come to me. So, while the stew simmers in the kitchen, I sit at the dining room table, typing my short stories and poetry and the magazine articles I write.

"I've sent many of them to publishers and agents, and I've received many very favorable and positive comments and feedback, but unfortunately, all have been accompanied by rejection letters. But I still have the large novel I've been working on for the past year."

"Yeah," I said, "I know you've been working on that novel for quite some time." I asked, "What's it about?"

And that day is when I began to understand the magnitude of what her writing was all about. She told me to sit down, and she would tell me about it.

"Phil, it's a story about two young Mexicans in south Texas beginning during the Mexican Revolution that took place way back in the 1830s and 1840s. It's kind of a love story and historical fiction together. It's a story of a young girl, Marta, but she is called Sinsonte, the Mockingbird. In the story, she sings like a bird, almost nonstop. When she was young, the villagers gave her that name. But the story actually covers three or four generations of her family and her love for Elishio. It covers life all the way through south Texas during that time of war. It's a love story, Phil, but it's filled with sadness, war, death, family, and some happiness. I haven't gotten far enough along yet to know how it's going to end, though."

"Wow, Gipsy, that is really good. When do you think you'll have it done?"

"I don't know, but I'm hoping before the end of the year."

GIPSY

Philip is now twenty-two and at in his third year at the university. He plays football and baseball. He thinks he's good enough at baseball to be able to play pro ball, maybe next year. He has a good job working at the gas company, but I think he only works enough to allow him to play baseball.

Ginny is nineteen now and just finishing high school at Tucson High. She turned out to be a pretty good student. Her first couple of years made Phil and me wonder if she would even get through. But in her junior and senior years, she worked on the school newspaper, sold all the advertising for it, and actually managed its publication last year. I don't think she will go to the University this fall, but she wants to work on the newspaper. I've told her she'll have to be a student to work on their paper, so she might enroll for a semester and see how she likes it.

Dan was still only sixteen but is just two years behind her. Like Philip, he liked sports. He didn't play football, but he really liked baseball and loved basketball. While he did all that, he worked a part-time job at the grocery store up on Speedway and still managed to keep up with his studies. He seemed to have a more inquisitive mind than Philip and Ginny did at his age. He also seemed to enjoy academics more than the two older ones. Phil spends a lot of his free time with Dan, too. I think it's because Dan liked to go to the ranch with Phil, and Phil said he really likes to be on the horses and around the cattle and he believed he would be a big help when he got a little older.

The younger three were still trying to find their way. Patsy showed a lot of interest in my painting and watching me play the piano that Phil got us all for Christmas last year. I told her that I would start teaching her how to play right after I finished my big novel. In the meantime, I reminded her to keep practicing her violin at school. I didn't want to wait too long, though; both she and Ginny enjoyed music and instruments.

Mike and Nancy were still in grade school. Mike already showed interest in the same sports as the two older boys. However, he also enjoyed trips to the ranch with his daddy.

Around Thanksgiving, the big novel, *Sinsonte*, that I had been working on for so long began to be more of a burden than a joy, so I decided to set it aside with plans to get back to it the first of the year. But, for a reason I didn't understand, a new book idea came to my mind. It had been swirling around up there for a couple of weeks, so I decided to get the typewriter out again and see where it took me.

Phil and I have experienced so much over the past twenty-five years or so that it seemed my mind too often wandered around the idea of two people out West, maybe not really knowing what they wanted or what they were doing or even where they were going. I decided to only think about it until after the holidays.

Christmas season arrived, and it was a busy time in our house. All the kids had friends around most of the time, and Phil and I were running all over going to school plays and Boy Scout stuff with Dan and Mike and music recitals with Patsy and her violin. But there were also parties. We went to four during Christmas week and two in one night. It had been so much fun for both of us. I got out my beautiful tangerine floral gown, and Phil got the cobwebs out of his tuxedo, and we went partying. We thought about how different things were year compared to where we were last year. Why, we didn't know if we would even still have this house.

On the night of our anniversary and my birthday, December 28, we had a party at our house. We had fourteen people for dinner and then we played cards until the wee hours of the morning. They gave us a set of twelve black and crystal cut glasses. Even though it is our china anniversary, they knew I already have nice china, so they gave me crystal instead.

On New Year's Eve, we went to one place and stayed put until midnight and then went to a dinner house and finished the night at the Pauli's house. What a wonderful holiday season for all of us!

Spring arrived, and I had been planting vegetables, getting a garden started, and trying to get my head back on the story of the couple out West. I had belonged to two writers' clubs at the university for a number of years and decided to attend some of the meetings and see if something or somebody might make an idea come to mind.

At one meeting, one of the members, Peggy Germain, suggested I write the story of Phil and I. I had considered that idea months ago, and told her so.

"But Peggy, that's not the story that's in my mind. What's in my mind is fictional. Two people we don't know today, but two who we might next year."

"Gip, I think maybe you just got started."

And she was right. Within three months, I had completed the manuscript of the first draft. When I told Phil I had finished, he asked me what it was about. I said, "It's a story of a young woman from out East on a trip to visit school friends out West, and by happenstance, she meets a young rodeo cowboy at a rodeo in New Mexico. He tells her he has a big cattle ranch in Arizona and convinces her to come see it."

"Do you have names for these two people?"

"Well, Phil, yes, I do. They are Dink and Annalee."

He looked at me as though I had lost my mind. "How did you ever come up with that idea, Gipsy?"

"Phil, I didn't know it when I started, but early on, I knew it was them. The whole story is about them. It just kind of evolved as I went along."

"Do you have a name for it yet?"

"Yes. I'm planning to call it *Out Yonder.*"

"Well, damn, Gip, that's a darn pretty name. How did you come up with that?"

"Well, Phil, I remember way back in Arivaca, about 1910, you took me for a ride out to the boys' place. On the way back, I asked you why you left New York, and you told me you left to go out yonder to become a rancher. Ever since that night, I've heard you call this country your 'out yonder' a dozen times."

"Wow, Gip, you have a heck of a memory. Can I read it?"

"Of course, but I would rather you wait until I hear what the publisher says."

I never asked anybody in my family to critique any of my writing before, but I felt good about this one, so I asked Ginny to read it and tell me what she thought. After sitting across from me at the dining room table day after day for what seemed to be weeks, she finished. She said, "Mama, this is good! It probably needs to be cleaned up a little, but I think you should send it."

So, I did. A few weeks passed, but one day in the early spring, I received a letter from the T. J. Cromley Publishing Company in New York. They wanted to buy the book, but they wanted it edited and to make a few changes. I told Ginny this, and she quickly volunteered to do the edit and rewrite. After many back-and-forth mailings, Cromley was satisfied, and when they had received the artist's design for the cover, a colorful painting of the Baboquivari and the surrounding desert in all of its beautiful blue and pink colors, they sent a telegram telling me it was beautiful.

There soon was lots of excitement around our house. Phil was so proud. I'm not sure that he has been all that excited about all my time at the typewriter lately, but he immediately called our attorney to ask him to look over the contract. He said it looked all right to him. After I had signed it and sent it off to Cromleys, I began preparing for the first copy to arrive. When it did, it was beautiful.

Suddenly, I was a celebrity. News of the publication, along with my picture and articles of interviews with me, were soon showing up in both local papers, the *Arizona Daily Star* and *Tucson Citizen*. One article included a brief synopsis of the story:

Instead of the usual Western story dealing with desperados and gunplay, Mrs. Clarke has developed this story to be one of character development, way out in the painted lands of Arizona. It's a story of a young cowboy who knows nothing but rodeos, horses, and cattle in a harsh, rough country—out yonder—and a young, innocent, tenderfoot woman who knows nothing of this kind of life.

From the day he took her as his wife to live in his old one room shack that he called his house, miles from the nearest neighbors, she tried so painfully to adjust to this difficult, new life. In the end, after much doubt and very little understanding, the cowboy finds in her a bravery and toughness he couldn't see before. And after many misunderstandings and a lengthy separation during the World War, they come together and create a new life out in this wild country.

All of this makes for a gallant saga of making a home and life together backed by the magic of the colorful mountains and magnificent desert. The book is being prominently displayed in the windows of the university's bookstore and Steinfeld's stores around town.

I decided that with my first check I would buy myself new dresses and gowns for all the parties and some new clothes for the kids and a new suit for Phil. And for the family, I'm buying a nice new glider for the front porch.

The Arizona Daily Star

PRESS RELEASES FROM GIPSY'S SCRAPBOOK

Home in the Desert

OUT YONDER. By Gipsy Clarke.
317 pp. New York.

INSTEAD of the usual type of Western story dealing with gunplay, the depredations of desperadoes, the doings of fighting or frolicking cowboys, this is a novel of character development in the painted lands of Arizona. It is the story of Dink Dale, the rancher who knows nothing but cattle raising and the rough country out yonder, and his tenderfoot wife Annalee, from the day he took her as a bride to his one-room shack twenty miles from the nearest neighbor; a story of honest effort at homemaking amid great hardships, but with the lure of the colorful desert and majestic mountains. The elements themselves were hard to cope with—great winds, sandstorms, cloudbursts, the burning sun, droughts—and there were other fights, with marauding Mexicans, hazardous border episodes, and the herculean work of cattle drives.

How Annalee painfully adjusts herself to the strange, new and harsh conditions; how Dink in turn, after much doubt and little understanding, finds in her that essential bravery that he designates as guts; and how these two, after many misunderstandings and despite a temporary separation and his devastating experiences in the World War, finally fare forth anew to wrest a living from a new wild country—all this makes up a tale of lively interest. This is Mrs. Clarke's first novel, and it is a good one. Her own experience has given her abundant material for its setting and its episodes. Her imaginary characters are realistically drawn, and her account of their life, surroundings, environment and contacts is both vivid and salty.

General John J. Pershing, it has been known for some time, has been working on his autobiography for years and is continuing that activity while in Tucson. If his book is as thrilling as his life has been and as varied in content as the scenes of his activities, the memoirs should make a best-seller.

Two resident Tucsonans will shortly appear in the featured books for Arizona. Gipsy Clark's first novel, "Out Yonder," has been announced by Thomas Y. Crowell for early spring and she is already at work on a second one for which the publishers have contracted. Charles Finney's first published book, "The Circus of Dr. Lao," is the second one scheduled for early spring, the Viking Press already carrying blurb announcements on it.

IN SUCCEEDING WEEKS

A reader writes in to ask when a review of Gipsy Clarke's "Out Yonder" is to appear in this column. The answer is that the book is in the hands of Bernice Cosulich, owner, conductor, originator and patenter of the Lantern. She will do the review. When last heard from by The Star's special shortwave radio, she was camped in a lonely mountain range, eating beans and writing a special feature for the paper.

If the Indians and bandits spare her, no doubt she'll come through with the review.

But in the meantime, the book already has a nice notice from no less a journal of enlightenment than the New York Times.

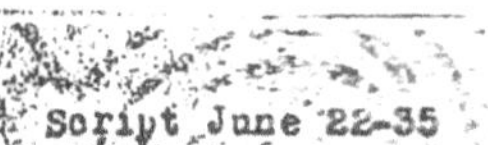

MOST WESTERN stories bore me, so it was with no enthusiasm that I started to read "Out Yonder" by Gypsy Clarke. This is a story of the painted lands of Arizona and the attempt on the part of an Eastern girl to adapt herself to the wide open spaces, the loneliness, and to a husband who knows nothing but cattle and who sees nothing menacing in the surroundings in which he has always lived. I found to my surprise that a western yarn can be enthralling, that descriptions of desert storms can make you hold your breath, and saving a herd of cattle just about the most dramatic thing yet.

'OUT YONDER' TO APPEAR APRIL 5

Gipsy Clarke's Novel of Southwest Published

The publication date for Gipsy Clarke's novel, "Out Yonder" has been announced as April 5 by the publishers, Thomas Y. Crowell company of New York City. Mrs. Clarke is known in Tucson, except to intimate friends, as Mrs. Philip M. Clarke of North Tyndall avenue.

The jacket cover for the new book, which is the author's first published work, will show a desert scene, mountains in the background and a rancher and his eastern bride in the foreground. The ranchman is the type who knows nothing beyond cattle life and its rough surroundings, according to the publishers, and his eastern bride has been reared in totally different surroundings. How they adjust themselves to the harsh conditions of the desert forms the story. While it is a western book, it is not one of gun play and bad men as the enemies of the rancher and his wife are those of sandstorms, droughts, winds and sun.

"It is a gallant saga of home making and back of it all the lure of the colorful desert and magic mountains," state the publishers. "Not the least charm of this realistic novel is its scene painting."

Mrs. Clarke is a native of Texas, a graduate of the North Texas Teachers' college and has taken work at the University of Arizona. She has taught in the southwest, lived in a mining camp and on a cattle ranch. At one period of two years, Mrs. Clarke was so isolated that she never saw a white woman. At another time her husband's store was twice raided by Mexican bandits. The family has lived in Tucson for many years now.

The book will be dedicated to "Philip, Dan and Mike", her husband and sons.

As time went on, accolades from the book continued and fans asked for more. I think the newfound success mostly served to motivate me more. I spent more time writing than before and seemed to enjoy it more as well. I even pulled the *Sinsonte* manuscript out of the closet and started on that again.

CHAPTER 37

Time moved along for us, much more rapidly than we would have liked. I continued to write, but I painted much more than before. I enjoyed getting in the big Studebaker and driving out to the mountains, setting up my easel, picking a tree or a mountain or a stream, putting some oil on the canvas, and seeing what happened. I usually ended up with a nice landscape.

Over the last couple of years, we enjoyed good times with the cattle operations. Phil and Bud have done very well out at Cortaro. I don't know how they do it, but they have probably bought and sold 100,000 head of steers out there over the last four to five years. Even though we have experienced a number of droughts, they have been able to continue.

It seems there is no end to the availability of cattle in Mexico. They're able to buy them in poor condition at really good prices then get them up here, fatten them, and make a decent profit. He continued to be a busy and active member of the Cattlemen's Association. We went to many of their meetings and different functions. He recently told me he was likely going to be voted into one of the officer positions at the next convention.

Just a year or so ago, he got introduced to a group called For America. It was an ultra-conservative association that represented numerous past and current political issues. The group's main objective, which Phil seemed to be almost totally immersed in, was the repeal of the 16th amendment of the Constitution. This amendment is what created the Federal Income Tax in 1913. Phil aggressively admonished the Taft Administration for introducing it. After becoming active in the group and getting elected chairman of the Pima County chapter, he gave talks and speeches all over the state to many groups, such as the Rotary Clubs, the Kiwanis club, the Elks, and many others.

In a recent presentation before the Tucson Kiwanis club, he said the income tax law was conceived by those who advocated the redistribution of wealth. However, instead of it being a relief for the poor, it worked out to be a major burden on the poor. Would you believe that 80 to 85 percent of the tax comes from people who earn less than $6,000 per year?

This income tax has destroyed American initiative and encouraging dishonesty by forcing people to testify against themselves. It says, essentially, that you are guilty until you prove yourself innocent. It gave the power of controlling our income into the hands of a single government agency. His ongoing message was that during the first 150 years of this country's existence, a man was able to work or start a business and keep what he earned. He contended that those men would spend on goods and services being provided by others doing the very same thing. And the country prospered.

Then Roosevelt and Hoover started the New Deal and introduced the concept of "the rich should give to the poor." This philosophy is exactly what has existed ever since and has angered him ever since he was a young man.

TUCSON DAILY CITIZ

Income Tax Raked By Phil Clarke

An attack on the federal income tax and an appeal to join in a move to repeal the 16th Amendment to the Constitution that made the tax law were voiced yesterday by Phil M. Clarke, chairman in Pima County for the For America organization.

Clarke, a semi-retired rancher and pioneer Arizonan, was the principal speaker before the Tucson Kiwanis Club in the Pioneer Hotel.

"We feel that this is the only provision of the Constitution that grants unlimited powers to an agency of government," Clarke said.

Under federal income tax provisions, the government can require any person to produce all his business records.

Under federal tax law operation, every person is assumed guilty until proven innocent and a person accused is often made to testify against himself, Clarke said.

The federal income tax amendment was originally proposed by those who wanted "destruction of great fortunes," Clarke said. However, 80 to 85 per cent of the tax collected comes from those who earn $6,000 a year or less, he said.

"It turned out to be a detriment to the poor man—and there are still as many great fortunes as there every was," Clarke said.

Passage of the 16th amendment "sold the American people down the river . . . and it's taken the very heart out of the Constitution . . . with an all-powerful central government," Clarke said.

Elimination of the tax and its loss of revenue to the government could be compensated by economies in the federal government, he said.

He called for elimination of all subsidies; a $10-billion "safe" cut in defense spending; removing government from all private enterprise competition; enforcement of all of the suggested economies of the Hoover report and backing a program by Sen. Harry Byrd of Virginia, "the watchdog of the government spending."

If the $35 billion now collected in income tax were left in the hands of the citizens "can you imagine the boom, the fundamental boom this would cause?" Clarke said.

Other threats to the Constitution, seen by the For America group, are the United Nations, the foreign aid program of the United States and socialism, he said.

It was very sad back in 1935 when Albert died unexpectedly. He had been everything to Phil for so many years, from the time of our start down in Ruby to the Consolidated Bank to the acquisition of the United and on through the Depression. He and Phil were great golf partners and actually won some tournaments together. He had been ill for a while, but his passing was still unexpected.

And, when we lost my brother Bruce—my Buddy as he was to me—it was very hard for me. He had walked down to the grocery to pick up some things and on his way back home was run down by a reckless driver right in front of Mama's house. I immediately caught a train down to be at his funeral. I'm glad I went, but the trip wasn't as enjoyable as I would have liked. I stayed for nearly a month. The Harper family seemed to be everywhere down in that part of Texas. It made it difficult to go and not stay for a month or so.

But as sad as I was over his loss, we have to accept that life moves on. Our children grew up so fast. Philip and Ginny were adults now and moved away. Philip went to Washington State with some friends and worked as a miner and logger for a while.

Ginny also went to California to attend the Armstrong College of Education and Secretarial Science. I think she still had an interest in the advertising business and thought this college would help her. I received a letter from the chancellor of the school telling me what a good student she was.

He said, "No doubt she has written to tell you, but she is studying a new system of shorthand. The fact that she is making such remarkable progress with this system is helping me greatly in introducing it into other schools, as well as our other business schools." He went on to say that he considered himself fortunate to have such an enthusiastic and industrious student.

Shortly after finishing her schooling at Armstrong, she went to work for Standard Oil Company in San Francisco. Without any expectations, soon after starting her new job, she met a young man who she said she liked very much. His name was Stoner Beard, and in just a short time, she called to tell us that she and Stoner were getting married in May. "Damn," Phil said. "That was pretty quick." Phil and I rushed around and got everything in order and made the trip over to Carmel, where Ginny and Stoner were married.

Dan had been at the university for three years, and he continued to be as busy as he was in high school. He still played on both the baseball team and the basketball team. In fact, he recently told us he was going to be the captain of the team next year, and he was in the agriculture college studying farming and animal husbandry.

Phil was really glad that he enjoyed that and that he liked to go to the ranch. He's become a big help to Phil down there and often goes down to help Bob and Chico with the cattle and horses. When he was first starting out at the university, he got interested in trapping, and for the past couple of years, he went down about every week to set and run his traplines. He trapped coyotes and foxes and sometimes raccoons and otters. He usually has a few pelts when he comes back that he sells to a leather guy near the foothills. In fact, his friends at school started calling him "Trapper" Dan. We chuckle when he calls himself that. In the fall, he never misses deer hunting season at the ranch. I don't think he's missed getting a deer for many years.

The other day, he was home for a while and told us he and his friend Bill Bishop were planning to take a trip up to Idaho and Washington in the summer as soon as school got out. And sure enough, as soon as school was out, he left for Idaho, but Bill wasn't with him. Instead, Philip came home from California and said he wanted to go, too.

It turned out that Bill had gone on ahead. Dan said that they worked all kinds of jobs along the way and experienced numerous problems with their car. But when they got to McCall, Idaho, they got jobs as extras in a Western movie that was being filmed near where they were camping. The movie was called *The Northwest Passage* and starred Spencer Tracy, Robert Young, and Walter Brennan. All the boys played the part of trappers, had a great time, and even made some good money.

Philip wrote to us and said they all had a chance to meet all three stars and got to visit one day while they were on lunch break. They were gone about a month but got back safe and sound. Dan actually brought a leather jacket back that looks just like a trapper's coat and was part of his costume. He spent the rest of his summer at the ranch with Phil, helping with the cattle.

When he started school in September, he got right back to his studies and getting ready for basketball season. He was really excited since he was chosen last year to be the team captain for that year's team. After basketball, it was baseball, and soon, school was out.

He came to the house shortly after that, and one night after supper, we were sitting and talking about how the past year had gone by so fast.

"And guess what?" he said. "I have a job lined up with the county extension office up in Casa Grande, but I told them I didn't want to start until September."

I asked him if he was still going to go to New York in August to meet Patsy there, and he said, "Yes, that's still my plan. My friend Bill has family in Cleveland, Ohio, so we're planning to go there in early August and meet Patsy somewhere in New York. I'll get with you soon to make specific plans beforehand. I want to see as much of daddy's family as I can."

"That's wonderful to hear, Dan." Phil spoke up and said, "You know, Mama and I have been married nearly thirty years, and neither she nor any of you kids have met any of my family in New York, so this is really going to be exciting for both of us that you two are going back there, and at the same time, too. Patsy will go ahead of you because she is going back to Interlochen, Michigan, to that national music camp. But part of her curriculum includes going to New York for a week of performances at the World's Fair in August."

"That will work well for both of us," Dan said. "I'm planning to ride the train to Cleveland and meet Bill there, and we'll take the train over to New York and meet up with Patsy there."

"When are you going down to the ranch again?"

"I've been planning to go next week. I've had some traps set for a while, and I need to check them"

"Well, I'm planning to go down too. Why don't we just go together? I'd like to ride along with you when you go to check them."

"Yeah, that would be swell, Daddy I'd like that a lot. And I can tell you about my new job and other things."

"What kind of other things?"

"Oh, just ranch stuff."

PHIL

Tuesday, Dan and I drove down together in my old coupe. When we drove through the Arivaca Ranch headquarters, we saw Charlie Boice and his young nephew, Freddie, out at the corrals, so we stopped and visited for a while before driving on through to our place. Charlie asked me how Bud and I were doing with our steer business out at the Cortaro Feedlots.

I said, "Well, Charlie, Bud and I have enjoyed some very good years out there. We probably moved over 100,000 steers back and forth from Mexico over the past dozen years. As a matter of fact, that little business probably saved my butt after the depression years and bankruptcy afterward. But we ran into a little disagreement with Ormande, the farm manager out there. A little misunderstanding of feed cost and some other issues. It actually ended up in court, but the judge ruled in our favor. But as a result, our relationship ended this past summer, and both Bud and I are now back at our full-time jobs. It was good, though, Charlie. More than a dozen years, even through some of those tough droughts and down markets.

"Say, Charlie, Dan and I have been talking about some things that you have been doing down here with that bulldozer you got from that guy over in the Ruby area. I think his name is Rucker or something like that?"

"Yeah, what are you thinking?"

"Oh, maybe we should think about doing some of that ourselves. You know, a lot of water comes out of those mountains."

"It sure does," he said. "Let me know if that's something you want to do, and I'll try to give you some help."

The next day, we got the horses saddled up and started off toward Chimney Canyon where Dan had set some traps. On the way, I said, "Dan, let's take a look at what all this rain is doing up where the water comes out of the mountains."

"Okay, Dad, I've got a couple of traps up there, anyway."

We rode along up through the cienega, along where all the rainwater runs down through on its way to Arivaca and on out toward the Altar valley. We came to a narrow draw where the water gathered into a fairly strong stream before it opened up into the cienega, and Dan stopped and said, "Dad, I want to show you something. A week or so back, Freddie Boice was riding along with me, and we were talking about some of the watering holes his dad has been building around their ranch the past year.

"He said he's doing that to catch enough rainwater to hold the cattle when it doesn't rain for a while. I thought that was interesting, so we talked more about it. He has a guy he hires to come into places around the ranch and push dirt up into dikes, so when it rains, the runoff fills up those holes so the cattle don't have to go so far for water.

"Dad, I have this idea I've wanted to tell you about. See, we're stopped right here between these two rock cliffs, right where all that water coming out of Chimney and Bartolo Canyons comes together and makes almost a river right here. Then it just runs on down past Arivaca.

"This might sound silly, but think of what we could have here if we built a huge dam right across here between these two cliffs. Why, we could back up enough water to have a big enough tank to water all the cattle on the ranch. You know, it's about halfway between our north fence and the border."

"Dan, I think that's a darn good idea! Let me give that more thought. But Dan, let's not talk too much about this idea just yet. You know, we're about the only ranch in the district that has these two big canyons feeding this water down below. I don't think it would be good to get folks excited about something like this until we know what we're going to do."

We rode along a way to where the water was coming out of the two canyons, and I stopped and said, "Dan, you see over there? That's what's left of Bartolo Caviglia's homestead. When Mama and I were still at Ruby, he had his headquarters right along the creek there. He's been gone a long time now, though. He sold his place to my good old friend Billie Marteney way back when, and then Billie sold it all to me."

I continued, "Dan, let's ride over to that little clump of oak trees there."

"Where we sit right now is where I proposed to your mama way back in 1910. I had written to her pa to ask for his permission to marry his daughter, and I had just got his reply a couple of days earlier telling me I had his blessing. So, I didn't want to waste any time. After we had been down to Ruby that day, I brought her back this way, just so I could sit her down under these trees in this beautiful little meadow by the creek. And it worked!

"One day, Dan, this whole ranch will probably belong to you and Mike. The girls don't have any interest, and Philip is up in California doing his accounting work."

"Well, Daddy, I never really thought about that. You know, I've kind of had my sights on getting a little farm down in Tucson someday."

"I know that, son, but this applies wherever you are and in whatever you're doing. My old friend Billie Marteney once told me about a story that old Bartolo Caviglia told him. He said, 'The eye of the master is what fattens the ox.'"

"What does that mean?"

"Son, it means that whether you own cattle or horses or your farm in Tucson, you are the master of what you own. You have to take good care of it to be successful. These cattle are your oxen. When you put that Bar-V-Bar on their shoulder, they're your responsibility."

"Thanks for telling me that. Speaking of proposals, I've been wanting to tell you and Mama about this girl named Virginia Leake I've been dating since last spring. I like her a lot and think you two should meet her. I'm not sure just yet how serious it is yet, but you never know. We've been to some socials together over the past few months, and I decided I would like to bring her over to meet you before I leave for New York. Would that be okay?"

START DAN

Leake, as all my friends and I called her, came over to the folks' place the next week. I introduced them all, and after Mama served a great supper, we sat around and talked about Leake and her family.

As it turns out, Leake was going to be leaving soon to visit her family in Nashville, so I would probably come through there on my way home from New York so I could meet them.

Mama said, "Well, Dan, this sounds somewhat serious."

"Maybe, Mama. We don't know for sure, but we've talked about things. And, since I can come back that way without too much trouble, I said I would like to meet some of her family if she wants me to."

Leake spoke up then and said she really does, so that's what I'm going to plan.

I left for Cleveland in early August, I met up with Bill, and we both went to Jamaica, New York. Bill and I separated there. He went to Long Island to see family, and I met the first of Daddy's sisters, Lizzie, there. After a few days and a wonderful visit, I went on down to Manhattan and met Kittie and Daddy's younger brother Matthew and his family. While I was there, they took me to meet my Grandmother Elizabeth. She had been very ill for a long time, and Daddy was especially hopeful that I would be able to see her.

I was in New York for over three weeks and met all the family. It was a great time, and when I caught the train home, I thought about how I hoped to be able to see them again soon.

I returned from my long trip on the 13th of September and learned that I was still being considered for the assistant county agriculture agent job in Casa Grande. I accepted the job when the position was offered a week later, so now, all three of us oldest kids have moved and are on our own.

CHAPTER 38

GIPSY

The war in Europe seems to be intensifying, and Phil and I paid close attention to what was going on. Both Philip and Dan were eligible to be drafted, but we hoped they wouldn't be. We learned recently that Germany broke their promise to Poland and invaded Warsaw. The radio broadcast called the situation critical. When we got up the next morning, we learned that Great Britain and France had declared war on Germany.

Hitler invaded Poland, and Great Britain signed a pact to aid Poland. Right now, it looks as though a second and probably much greater war is imminent. The United States has indicated that we will stay out of it for the time being, but if Great Britain gets in trouble, the US will go to her aid. And Japan has declared that it will remain out while the world watches to see what Russia and Italy decide to do. It's hard for either of the boys to make any plans for the future.

On November 24, Dan and Virginia Leake were married here in Tucson. Philip was Dan's best man, and Ruth McKale was Virginia's maid of honor. It was an exciting event with lots of friends and family. But Dan and Virginia had to get back to Casa Grande, so the festivities were short-lived. Soon after, they moved into the apartment they rented in Casa Grande. Dan worked his job at the extension office during the week, but on weekends, he and Virginia, along with his good friend Gene "Mac" McGuire, would head for the ranch to help Bob and Chico and deer hunt.

Patsy was in her senior year at Tucson High, and Mike and Nancy were in the same class as sophomores, also at Tucson High. Mike was an excellent athlete and did very well on the junior varsity football team. I always chuckled when Phil would get home in the evening and tell me he had stopped to watch the football team's practice.

One day in early spring, Phil had just returned from the ranch, and Dan had come down from Casa Grande and stopped in on his way to the ranch. Phil said, "Hey Dan, I've got something to tell you. I've been visiting with Charlie Boice about the idea of getting that bulldozer over to those cliffs and pushing some dirt up out of Caviglia's meadow and building a little dam for a water hole. He thinks it's a smart idea. I told him I'd talk to you some more about it. So, why don't you start working on a plan that might work?"

"I will, Daddy."

"I think sometime this summer, if you can get off for a while when Mike is out of school, we might try getting that dozer over to do something there."

"Great, Dad. I'll get some ideas from some of the people in the extension office."

Then, on Mother's Day, I got a call from Doctor Kibler. He and Phil and their good friend Fred Pauli had been playing golf out at the El Rio Golf Club. He said, "Gipsy, I don't want to alarm you too much, but I'm at St. Mary's Hospital. We were on the seventh hole at El Rio, and Phil sat down. He said he wasn't feeling too good, and then he just fell over. I thought he had died, but he was breathing okay. We hurried as fast as we could to get him here. He's out of emergency and in a room right now. He seems to be doing better."

When I arrived, I asked Dr. Kibler what they knew. He said he had a heart attack, a coronary occlusion caused by arteries being enlarged to the point where the blood flow is restricted or blocked. "We have him on medication now that will help to open these restricted arteries."

"What caused this?"

"It's a diet issue, Gipsy. It's from eating more red meat than he should and the same with salt and dairy products. I want to keep him here for a couple of days, then we'll get him home and into his own bed. I'm going to try to keep him down for maybe six weeks or so. Getting these arteries unclogged requires lots of rest and a very serious change in his diet and eating habits."

We brought him home three days later and got him situated comfortably in his own room. Dr. Kibler lined up a group of nurses to come in and help me with his care and to help keep him quiet as much as we could.

His recovery was very slow. Dan came down as often as he could get away and always made a trip to the ranch to help Bob and Chico and a new cowboy by the name of Chui. After about four weeks, he began to get up and move around the house a little. But knowing that his activities were going to be limited for some time, he began to think about the future of the ranch. When he got to a point where he could discuss the operations of the ranch with all of us, we decided that, when Phil got older, Dan and Mike would try to fill in and do what he had done all these years.

Dan and Virginia had their first baby, Dan Junior, the first of March, and as we moved into summer, we asked Dan and Virginia to move down to the ranch. Mike was still in high school, and Philip joined the Army last month and was getting ready to ship out to North Africa. Dan resigned his job with the extension service, and he and Virginia moved down to the ranch.

In August, Phil and I went over to the coast so he could spend a week in a special cardiac clinic in La Jolla. Doctors there determined that his condition was, in fact, not any clots or blockages but partial closing or shutting of arteries, and he could make close to a full recovery if he continued to get his rest.

Patsy had joined the WASP program and became a pilot. She learned to fly at the old Gilpin Field airport in Tucson and later trained at the Spartan School of Aeronautics in Tulsa, Oklahoma, where she was trained to ferry planes. She was actually getting ready to report for duty when Congress canceled her program at the last minute. She returned to Tucson and worked at Davis-Monthan Air Force Base as flight controller for the latter part of the war.

In the spring of 1942, Phil recovered to the point where he could help at the ranch. About that time, both Dan and Mike were called by the draft board to come take their physicals. After writing numerous letters to the draft board declaring that both were essential producers of agricultural products, Phil was able to get both deferred because agricultural production was critical to the war effort.

Because of that, Phil had to pull Mike out of his freshman year at the university and had him live and work full-time on the ranch. Having Mike there full-time meant Dan and Virginia would not be able to stay there. Dan and Phil had some serious words over that decision. Dan thought he should be able to stay there and do what he'd been doing for the previous couple of years, but Phil convinced him and Virginia that the only way to get Mike deferred was for him to be working full-time in agriculture.

Dan wasn't sure he agreed with that, but soon after, they moved back to Tucson, where he went to work at Consolidated Airplane in south Tucson, working on one of the plane assembly lines. And though he wasn't full-time at the ranch anymore, he continued to be active with the operation, helping with calving, branding, the round-ups, and whatever else he could do to help.

Phil's heart attack three years prior had pretty much put a hold on the idea of the dam that he and Dan had come up with, but when 1943 arrived, Phil and Dan started putting their thoughts and plans together again and decided to move forward with the idea. Throughout the cattle country of the Arivaca district, drought has been an annual concern. When the monsoons don't come in the summer and rain doesn't fall throughout the year, the grasses don't come back, and the cattle don't get the water or feed they need. The entire cattle economy comes to a standstill. In cattle country, we needed water and grass to survive, and that's why all the water holes that Charlie has been building over the years made it easier for his herds to survive the hard times.

Prior to Phil's heart attack, Dan had gone back to the extension service and enlisted the expertise of a couple of the engineers to help him with his idea. What he showed Phil and Mike was a drawing of not just a little dike to hold back a small pond of water, but a dam that would reach all the way across the opening between the two cliffs, approximately 180 feet. It would be about 30 feet high and would capture all the water that came out of the confluence of Chimney Canyon and Cedar Creek (or Bartolo Canyon).

I thought Phil was going to have another heart attack, but Dan said the engineers who helped him with this convinced him that this was one of the brightest ideas they had ever seen. A dam of this size could hold back enough water to satisfy all the needs of the cienega and the town of Arivaca for more than three years, even if it didn't rain at all. The only hitch was that it would have to allow the water from the mountains to continue to flow through while we built the dam.

Soon, with Charlie's help and the use of his big concrete mixing machine and the bulldozer from Rucker, construction began in early 1944. A road had to be excavated up and out of the cienega just to get to the site, and we needed teams of mules to pull Charlie's concrete mixer up there.

What a project! We soon had folks from all over the district hiking up to the site to watch. We hauled rocks and boulders out of the cliffs on the ends and gathered sand out of the bottom of the cienega just to mix concrete for the base and the discharge pipe that would release water in a constant flow downstream.

Before long, up it went. It happened in small steps in the beginning because the base was about fifty feet wide, and as it rose, a tower to accommodate the opening and closing of the valve was built at the same time. As it rose higher, the dirt and gravel required grew less, and when it reached a height of thirty-six feet, it was topped off with a spillway about six feet high, which was built on the east side. This allowed water to release over the top in the event we should have more water flowing than the dam was designed to hold back.

When it was completed in 1945, Phil looked up at it and said, "This is a monument! When this thing gets full, we will have more water than the cienega will ever need."

It took only two years for the lake behind the dam to fill. And when it was full, it created a lake about ¾ of a mile long and ½ mile wide and approximately 18 feet deep in the center, where Bartolo Caviglia's ranch headquarters once stood. It covered about 110 acres at the surface and held approximately 1,000 acre-feet of water.

In the beginning, folks called it Bartolo Lake, likely because it covered what was once Caviglia's place, but then somebody pointed out that Bartolo sold his place to Billie Marteney before the Clarkes. In a short time, it became known as Clarke Lake to almost everybody around the district, but Phil didn't like that.

Sometime around late 1947, Phil and I were on our way to the ranch, and as we passed through the Arivaca headquarters, we stopped to visit with Charlie. Charlie asked Phil if the fish were doing okay at the lake.

"Well, we stocked it with a whole bunch of bass and perch right after it filled, and the boys have been catching some nice-sized fish. You know Charlie, I want to get that Clarke Lake name changed. We need to call it Arivaca Lake."

"Why do you think that, Phil?"

"Because that thing never would have been built without your help and your equipment and Arthur and Fred Noon's help. You know Fred gave us all some good direction about things we could and couldn't do. And lots of other people from around here helped out a lot. The boys and I never could have got that done without all that help."

"Yeah, well, it's on your ranch Phil, and hell, Phil, you don't even have a road up to it. The only way to get to it is by hiking ¼ of a mile up through those rocky bluffs. Because of all that, it just seems right."

One day, Dan came up with an idea, "You know, Daddy, with this lake, we could put discharge gates down along the creek and irrigate pasture along the cienega and have a good place to bring cows during calving season. Or we could just plant barley or wheat and harvest a grain crop every summer."

"Lots of good ideas, Dan. Let's see how this all works out down below. We need to make sure there is always water for the entire cienega and the village. If it looks like that works, then yeah, let's put in some pasture."

As the years moved along, we used the water for some recreation but primarily for ranch water and to always have water for irrigating the farmland below on the cienega. It also provided water for all the needs downstream during drought years.

Arivaca Lake

CHAPTER 39

The war in Germany ended in May 1945 when Germany surrendered to the Allies. On August 10, shortly after we had dropped atomic bombs on Hiroshima and Nagasaki, Japan surrendered onboard the battleship USS *Missouri* in Tokyo Harbor. The four long years of war were finally behind us, and soldiers and sailors returned home, looking for the jobs they had left behind years ago.

The plane factory out at Consolidated closed soon after, and Dan was looking, too. He and Virginia were out driving around the San Xavier Mission one afternoon and came across a big farm near there. He later told us there were green tractors and other farm machines everywhere.

He stopped and talked to one of the foremen and asked about the place. He learned that it was a farm owned by the grandson of John Deere. Dan asked for his name and if he was around the farm. The guy told him that his name was Charles Deere Wyman, but he went by Colonel and he was over at the shop.

Dan went over and introduced himself and asked if he had any work. Wyman asked if he was related to Phil, and he said he was one of his sons. "Are you the one who went to the university and majored in agriculture? Well, son, we could use you here. We'll have you work with our crop people for a while and see what happens."

Within six months, Colonel moved Dan's family into the manager's home and made Dan the farm manager of Midvale Farms.

Phil spent much of his time at the ranch, helping Mike and the cowboys. He stayed very active in the many organizations he'd belonged to over the years. On one occasion at a Cattlemen's Association meeting in 1948, he was approached by a few other cattlemen, Harold Thurber, John Goodman, Rukin Jelks, and some others, who said they had been talking about organizing a group of livestock people to meet in a central location and have constructive business conversations about the conditions in their industry along with social gatherings. They thought that Tucson was a good central location for many ranchers, some coming from considerable distances like Sonoita, Patagonia, Sasabe, Willcox, and even Arivaca.

"You live here, Phil. You know the area. Do you have some ideas about where we might have a meeting place?"

"I sure do. Right down the street at the Santa Rita Hotel."

During the war, with many servicemen looking for entertainment, a nightclub had opened in the basement of the hotel. When the war ended a couple of years ago, the passion pit, as it was called, was vacated, and the hotel hadn't been able to find a tenant for it yet.

The group of organizers got together to decide on a name for their new group. Someone suggested calling it The Mountain Oyster Club, which is cowboy lingo for the vital organs of a bull calf that when removed, make him a steer. And so it proudly became The Mountain Oyster Club.

In the beginning, the community shied away from using the club's specific name and chose to simply call it, The Cattleman's Club or The M.O. Club. In time, the city, name, and club became a proud reference to all those involved in the business of raising beef. In time, this group became one of the more powerful and influential livestock organizations in the state.

During this time of Phil's ongoing civic involvement, we continued to enjoy a very busy and active social life. Wives of the M.O. members soon got together and created a women's version. We called ourselves The Cowbelles. We functioned in a similar manner as the men, though our activities were more of a social nature.

After the excitement of building the dam had settled down somewhat and our lives began to get back to normal, I began to realize I missed my painting and writing and determined to get started again. One day while playing the piano, a verse of a short song I had written years ago came to mind. It was called "Love's Hope." I had written this love song when we lived at Ruby at the time of the murders of the Pearson family. It was a song of lost love and pining for it to return, and I could have published by the Letgers Music Company in Chicago.

Out Yonder was certainly successful. I thought about getting the Marta and Elisia manuscripts out again to finish, or my favorite *Sinsonte*, the Mockingbird, the story of the young Mexican girl who had the voice the village people believed was that of the bird. That manuscript was over six hundred pages. *Why did I not finish this one?*

I went back into the closet and pulled out the many boxes of manuscripts of novels and short stories I had written over the years, stories I was unable to get published. I was amazed at the number of them, and it would be good to go back through them.

I had written many short stories, such as "I Left my Home and Children," "Foretelling the Future," "The Girl in Yellow," "The Roomer," "The Home Under the Cliff," "Prairie Lightfoot," and "All Quiet on the Western Front."

Additionally, there were the many novels. *A Life to Live* was approximately five hundred pages, *The Liberation of Eva Selms* was also almost five hundred pages, and *Wives to Benjamin* was almost four hundred pages.

My gosh. I can't believe that I have done all this writing over these many years. I think I want to finish the Sinsonte *story.*

Then I remembered all the paintings I had done as well. At that point, I had only done twelve. Setting up the easel on the back porch or putting my stuff in the car and going to the country was easy to do. Getting set up with the typewriter at the table and being able to focus on writing was a different matter. I decided I would only focus on painting for now. There were so many places that would make such pretty paintings.

Over the past four or five years, I managed to paint fourteen more pictures, most of them landscapes in or around the city. One of my favorites was of the San Xavier Mission, and I decided to keep it for the house or at the ranch.

Phil was staying busy with his organizations, but recently, he developed an interest in racing horses. One of the members of The M.O. Club, Rukin Jelks, was very involved in that and helped develop that interest in Phil, as well. It didn't surprise me when he came home one evening and told me he thought we should think about turning the ranch over to the boys.

He said, "You know, Gip, we're in our sixties now. Going back and forth to the ranch all the time is still enjoyable, but the boys are doing a good job, and I'm not real sure they still need me."

"Or are you just wanting to be closer to your horses and your friends in town?" I asked.

"Maybe a little of that, too," he said and chuckled, "but I think you and I should start going over to the coast more often. What do you think of that?"

"Well, I always like that too, but I'm really enjoying my painting again."

"Sure, but we can do both. When summer comes around again, let's see. Since Dan bought that farm of Roger's out on Mission Road and he doesn't work for the John Deere farm anymore, he might be in a better position to not only help at the ranch more but also use his pens and corral set-up at the farm. That could be good for us moving cattle in and out from the ranch."

It was around 1955 when Phil and I decided to sell the ranch to Mike and Dan. Even though Phil remained actively involved in the ranch operation, he developed more of an interest in racing horses. He soon began to raise quarter horses in Tucson and got involved in running them at the Rillito Race Track out in North Tucson.

Soon after, he began to run his horses in other locations across the United States, including entering many of the horses at the Louisville Fairgrounds, which later became Churchill Downs, and in Ohio, and especially in Southern California. He spent many of his last summers at the Del Mar and Los Alamitos racetracks.

Phil Clarke and Henry Boice at the horse races.

For the next four or five years, we continued to live very active lives. We traveled back and forth to the coast frequently. For many trips, it was the both of us, but often, he would go by himself and spend nearly two months between the two tracks. While he was gone, I would be back at my paintings. And when he was home, we would make numerous trips to the ranch. On many of those trips, we would take one or two of the grandkids along.

Many evenings, I would look out on the front porch at the ranch, and Phil would be telling one of the kids his many wild stories of life on the ranch. I remember one in particular. I heard him ask Jimmy, "If a mountain lion comes charging at you, would you know how to keep him from eating you?"

Jimmy looked up, scared, and said, "No, Papa, what should I do?"

"Well, son, when he gets right in front of you, with his mouth wide open like he's just about ready to bite your head off, you just shove your arm in his mouth, all the way down to the end of his tale. Then you just grab his tale on the inside and pull it as fast as you can."

"Then what happens, Papa?"

"Well, Jimmy, now you've got him turned inside out, and he's running the other way, and you're safe."

Jimmy looked startled for a minute and then his Papa started laughing, and pretty soon, so was Jimmy.

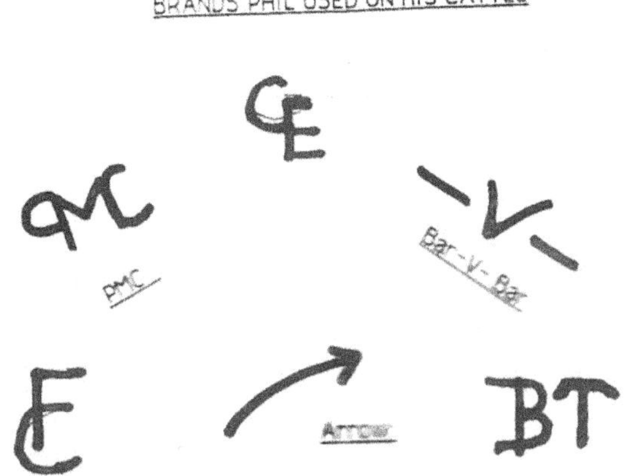

CHAPTER 40

Early in 1958, I began to see signs from Phil that he wasn't feeling well. He always shrugged it off as just old age. He continued to be very active, but he didn't go to the race track as often as he used to, and he wasn't nearly as active and vocal with the For America group. However, he loved to go out to Dan's farm and help. He and the boys would brand and cut on Saturday afternoons or Sunday mornings after Dan had been to the sale barn and bought a few head of calves.

Four of his older racehorses lived on the farm, and some of the boys used them when moving calves from pasture to pasture around the farm, all of them with their new Bar-V-Bar brand on their left shoulder. One Saturday evening, he had just come from the farm, and when we sat down, he had a slight smile. I asked him what it was about. He just smiled some more and said, "It sure didn't take those boys long to figure out that old thoroughbred racehorses aren't worth a hoot as cow horses. All those horses understand is, 'Run, run, run as fast as you can!' And that's about all they do when those boys are up on them."

Those were days and times when Phil smiled and laughed a lot. I knew he was hurting, and I didn't learn entirely why until late 1959. He finally agreed to go see his doctor, and that's when we learned he had cancer throughout much of his mid-torso.

For the next four years, we stayed pretty close to home, but on one occasion in the early 1960s, when his health was failing more severely, we were able to get all the members of the family together out at Dan's farm. What a day! We took a picture of all our children, except Philip and Lillith, and all the grandchildren except little Gipsy. It would be the last time we would have the three generations of the Phil and Gipsy family together.

On the evening of March 24, 1963, Phil was resting peacefully at home. He looked up at me and said, "You know, Gip, our journey out yonder has given us quite a life."

"Yes, it has, Phil. And along the way, we have seen all the colors of this beautiful land."

"It was our destiny, Gipsy!"

That night, Felipe, the little Irish gringo, passed peacefully in his sleep.

POSTSCRIPT

After Phil's death, Gipsy continued to paint and entertain her many friends. She especially loved having her grandkids come stay with her, even those attending the university. However, as the years passed, she seemed to fade slowly into a quiet, reclusive life, living alone in the big, empty house. Eventually, she moved to a care home in 1970. She died there on March 30, 1984.

Dan and Mike continued to operate the ranch until 1964. Numerous reasons can be found for their decision to sell the ranch, some understandable, some not so much. But in 1964, a large portion of the ranch was sold to the Maynard Gaylor Cattle Company. The sale excluded the Bar-V-Bar brand and a small portion of the ranch. Mike held back that small portion for his children.

His second son, Chris, remained on the ranch and continued to run a few head of cattle as the Bar-V-Bar ranch near Oro Blanco and the old Tonkin Well until he passed away in 1994. Though Chris has passed on, the small ranch remains in the hands of Mike's three remaining children…

The Clarkes used the lake for recreation but primarily for ranch water and to always have water for irrigating the farmland below on the cienega as well as to provide availability of water needs downstream during drought years. Unfortunately, when constructed, the dam wasn't sealed to the bedrock, and it seeped water continuously, to the great benefit of the groundwater supply downstream along the cienega. During the winter of 1965–66, it was very wet in the district, softening the dam, and it collapsed in December after approximately eight inches of rain had fallen. The resulting flood, four to six feet deep and about six miles long, caused many homes to be evacuated along with many pasture fences being damaged or washed out down through the cienega.

A few years later, the Arizona Game and Fish Commission approached the Gaylors with a proposal to purchase the dam site and the land surrounding it. When the land was acquired, plans were put in place to rebuild the dam in 1969.

For many years prior, Fred Noon, a long-time local rancher, had been observing and monitoring water conditions and rainfall throughout the district and pointed out to Game and Fish that even though the old dam had only spilled over six or seven times in its eighteen-year life, safety measures should be taken to assure water would flow continuously and be allowed to be released when drought conditions existed. As a result, it was determined that a safety discharge system would be installed. Construction on the new dam started in late 1969, sealed firmly in the bedrock.

It was dedicated in 1970 as Arivaca Lake and holds a capacity of approximately 1,100 acre-feet of water when full and covers close to 130 acres on the surface. A small road was built to the south end of the lake off of Ruby road about six miles south of Arivaca. A ramp to accommodate small fishing boats was installed as well. Today, the lake serves as one of southern Arizona's premier bass fisheries, popular with many locals and visitors as well.

Though the story of the Bar-V-Bar Ranch's history is legendary, the story hasn't ended. The Bar-V-Bar Brand, established in 1913 and now over 100 years old, remains a registered brand in Arizona and Idaho.

Phil's and Gipsy's children all led lives very differently from their parents. Virginia, who married Stoner, divorced, and later married Melvin Cooper, an Air Force officer. They had two children, Gipsy and Clarke, and unfortunately, were struck by tragedy when little Gipsy died at age twelve.

Philip, who had married Lilith in Houston shortly after he had enlisted in the Army, moved back to Richmond, California, when the war ended. He worked as an accountant in San Francisco. In

January 1957, he died of a heart attack. He and Lillith did not have any children.

Dan and Virginia raised their four children—Dan Junior, Jim, Rick, and Peggy—on their farm near Tucson. They later divorced, and in 1963, he married Eileen. Virginia remained unmarried until she passed in 2009.

Mike, who married Carol in 1947, had five children: Mike Junior, Chris, Scott, David, and Laura. When the ranch was sold in 1964, Mike retained a quarter of a section of the ranch, near the Tonkin Well and the corrals for his children. Chris remained on the ranch and ran a few head of cows until he passed in 1994. Mike and Carol lived on the ranch until it sold. Shortly after the sale in 1964, they moved to Tucson, where the children would have better educational opportunities, and built a beautiful home on the east side. In 1968, with an old friend, Mike found an opportunity for another ranch in Colorado, and the family sold the Tucson home and moved near Gunnison, Colorado where Mike and his friend started their new ranching operation. Unfortunately, just a short time later, Mike died suddenly of a heart attack.

Nancy and Art Rice married in 1948, and they had two daughters, Diane and Bonnie, and continued to live in Tucson. They were divorced in 1973, and he died of a heart attack in 1975.

Patsy married George Grove in 1946 and had three children: Andy, Phoebe, and Susan. They moved all over the country during George's career in the construction industry, finally settling in central Oregon to enjoy their retirement years.

The story of Phil and Gipsy's life journey "out yonder" is a marvel to us all. They remained connected and committed to each other, to family, and to friends while being far away and apart from each other for long periods. However, they remained side by side in heart and soul throughout the entire journey. We find their letters and photos convey great love, care, devotion, and decency to all who shared their journey. Through both difficult and joyous times, their spirit is an inspiration for all.

Phil and Gipsy Clarke

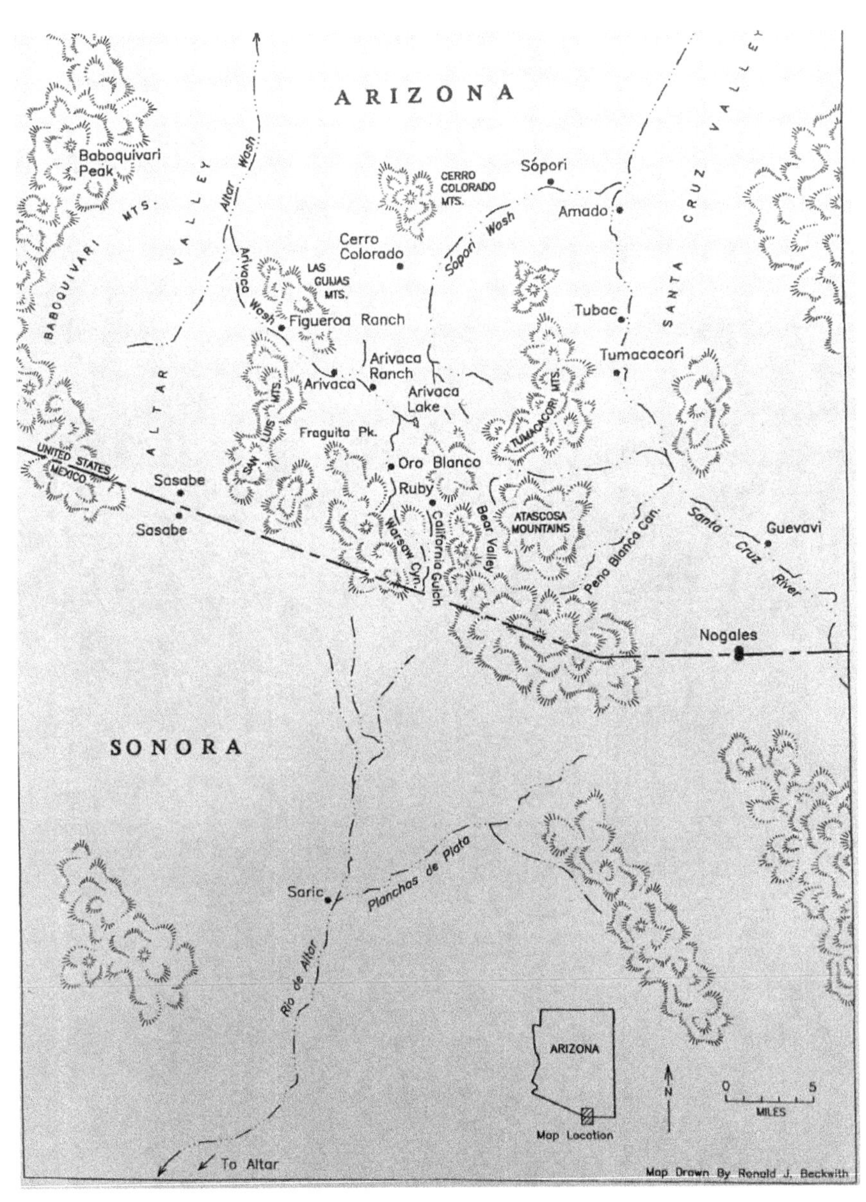

Map of the Arivaca and Ruby area

About the Author

Jim Clarke is a native of southern Arizona. He was born in Tucson in 1942 and spent his early years between the Bar-V-Bar Ranch in Arivaca and the family farm near the San Xavier Mission south of Tucson. After graduating from high school, he joined the US Navy and served on the flight deck of the aircraft carrier USS *Yorktown* during two tours of duty in the Far East and the south China sea just as the United States was entering the Vietnam War. After his service in the Navy he attended the University of Arizona where he majored in Marketing and agricultural economics.

After college he pursued a career in the agricultural equipment business, starting his career with Arizona Machinery Company, the John Deere dealer in the Phoenix and Salt River Valley area. After a number of years in Phoenix, he accepted an opportunity to become a partner in a multi-store dealership in the Boise Valley of Idaho.

After many years with the dealership, he started an agricultural consulting company and continued in that venture as it evolved into an agricultural equipment sales and marketing company. In this endeavor, he consulted and assisted in the sales and marketing of new farm equipment for numerous manufacturers of farm equipment from throughout the US, Canada, Europe, and the Far East. Over the next twenty-five years, his company, Sunshine Agri-Product Sales and Marketing, enjoyed many highs, and a few lows, and after a four-decade career in the agriculture equipment industry, Mr. Clarke retired in 2016 to enjoy a retirement of golf, leisure, and the joy of reading historical western novels.

It was after reading a great trilogy, a story of four generations of a cattle family's journey through west Texas to southern New Mexico from the 1880s to present time, by one of his favorite authors, Michael McGarrity, that caused him to realize that he has a similar story that should be shared. As a result, he has written his own historical fiction story, inspired by the life journey of his grandparents, Phil and Gipsy Clarke

Many grandchildren and great-grandchildren reside in southern Arizona, but Mr. Clarke still calls Caldwell, Idaho, home.